The Stepmother

Also by Carrie Adams

The Godmother

The Stepmother

Carrie Adams

HARPER

An Imprint of HarperCollins*Publishers*
www.harpercollins.com

THE STEPMOTHER. Copyright © 2009 by Carrie Adams. All rights reserved. Printed in the United States of America. No part of this book may be used or reproduced in any manner whatsoever without written permission except in the case of brief quotations embodied in critical articles and reviews. For information, address HarperCollins Publishers, 10 East 53rd Street, New York, NY 10022.

HarperCollins books may be purchased for educational, business, or sales promotional use. For information, please write: Special Markets Department, HarperCollins Publishers, 10 East 53rd Street, New York, NY 10022.

FIRST EDITION

Designed by Jessica Shatan Heslin/Studio Shatan, Inc.

Library of Congress Cataloging-in-Publication Data is available upon request.

ISBN: 978-0-06-123265-7

09 10 11 12 13   ID/RRD   10 9 8 7 6 5 4 3 2 1

For Roxana, Ruby Ann, and Reva.
Light, love, and strength regained.

Contents

The Stepmother

One

Crunchy Nut

I WAS SURROUNDED BY LAUGHTER BUT, FOR ONCE, COULDN'T EVEN pretend to join in. I wanted to place one of my daughters on my lap and hug her tightly, but I had taught myself not to do that. At eight, even my youngest considered herself too old for such public displays of affection. On our own at home was fine, but that wasn't when I needed her protection. I felt a hand land on my shoulder, and I automatically formed a smile as I turned.

"Thank you so much for everything you've done," said the woman looking down at me.

"I'm happy to help," I replied.

"Everyone tells me you've been amazing."

My eight-year-old beamed. If her headmistress said I was amazing, I must be doing something right.

"I am so looking forward to this," the imposing woman said as she took her seat. The nerves tightened. My nine-year-old, sitting on the other side of me, had not noticed the giant presence of her principal, because she was too busy craning her neck to search the back of the room. Ever since we'd sat down, she'd been keeping a vigilant eye on the entrance. I eased her shoulders round to face the stage. "He'll be here," I said, glancing at the empty seat. "Don't worry."

"I'm not worried," she said, immediately turning back.

The lights dimmed and an awed murmur rose up from the assorted parents, siblings, and extras, and dissolved into a hush. Four worried chestnut-colored eyes sought mine in the gloom of the darkened assembly hall.

"He'll be here," I said again, taking their hands, and, as the first note drifted up from the piano, he was.

"Daddy!" squeaked the girls, bouncing off their chairs.

Jimmy eased his way along the narrow aisle with such charm that no one other than me seemed to mind. He even stopped to kiss a particularly good friend of ours, and shook some of the other dads' hands. "Sit down," I mouthed at him.

He leaned over and kissed me, then both of the girls. "Sorry," he said. "Meeting went on."

I put my fingers to my lips and pointed toward the stage. The thick green velvet curtains were being drawn back to expose the mean streets of Hell's Kitchen, New York, where girls dressed as boys clicked and hissed and spat at one another, marking out the infamous territories between the Jets and the Sharks.

Then the aggression left the stage and there was our eldest daughter. She peered out at us through an invisible mirror, examining her reflection as intensely as everyone else was now examining her. Was it my imagination or did a collective gasp ripple through the audience? She looked phenomenally beautiful. Older and more self-possessed than her fourteen years—how was it possible that we had a fourteen-year-old child? I stared at Amber, moving around the stage as easily as liquid, my brain leaping ahead to her next line before she'd finished delivering the one she was on. I was impressed, mesmerized, and terrified in equal measures. As for Amber, I could tell by the hem of her dress that she was as steady as a rock.

She looked beautiful. Did I say that already? Her dark red hair was pulled off her face with a white ribbon, her long, slender body still startling inside the neat, sensible dress of a good Catholic. She had skin the color of milk, but when she opened her mouth to sing, the London girls' school faded away and we fell into the world of a Puerto Rican on the eve of her first dance.

Jimmy reached over our nine-year-old and gazed into my eyes. He squeezed my hand hard, but then our middle daughter took ownership of her father and placed his hand firmly in her lap. I looked down at mine and watched as the warmth slowly left my skin and my fingers returned to their perpetual cold.

At the interval, Jimmy and I were thickly showered with compliments by our parental alumni—some genuine, some tinged with green, and some downright barbed. Why is it that I always remember the barbed ones?

"You must be so proud. When Talullah won her scholarship I made sure she stayed grounded by insisting she make her bed every day. It worked a treat, you should do it with Amber so it doesn't all go to her head."

"She already makes her bed," I replied, confused.

"Oh," said the woman, equally confused.

We stood awkwardly until another "compliment" cut through the air like a missile.

"Wonderful, isn't she? You'll have a job on your hands keeping Amber's feet on the ground now," said a starched woman, whom I had tried hard to avoid. "It was quite a big decision to pick a girl from year nine. She's quite brilliant, absolutely the right choice, but I think there were some rather put-out mothers in the year above."

I opened my mouth to respond, but Jimmy got there first. "Thanks for the tips, ladies. We'll watch our backs." They tittered. Jimmy grabbed my elbow. "Let's go to the bar," he said.

"You'd better check for poison."

"Why me?" he asked.

"Do you want to sew on the name tags?"

"Can't you get iron-on ones, these days?"

"Yes. But answer me one question. What is an iron?"

The lines on Jimmy's face deepened in mock concentration. "You win. I drink first."

There were more "helpful" comments as we pushed our way through the crowd, but fortunately, since I have amassed a staggering eighteen daughter-years at this school, I know who and where my friends are. Manning the bar. Womanning the bar, I should say, because women dominate my life.

I left Jimmy happily surrounded by some, walked to the sheeted trestle table, and picked up a handful of crisps. "Hey, Carmen," I said to one of my favorite fellow maternal inmates.

She was pouring cheap red wine into disposable cups. As she refilled one, she mouthed, "My God, Bea, she's fucking brilliant."

This, I knew, was a genuine compliment. "One mother told me no one liked a show-off."

Carmen's jaw dropped. She reached below the table and handed me a bottle of decent white. "You'll need this, then."

I poured generously into a plastic cup, and handed it back. "She went on to reassure me that of course Amber wasn't like that."

"And so screamed a silent yet," said Carmen.

"Exactly."

"Shark-infested waters."

"And that's the ones who like me."

"Sweetheart, you sewed eight hundred school scrunchies by hand. No one likes you."

I raised my plastic cup to her. "Ah, but Lulu got a star on her reading test, so it was worth the bleeding fingers."

"Why do you think I'm behind the bar?"

We smiled conspiratorially at one another.

"Enjoy," she said. "It's Sancerre."

"In which case you're forgiven your evil tongue."

Carmen emptied a party-size bag of ready-salted crisps into the bowl in front of me with a wink, then rushed to the other end of the bar to open several more long-life orange-juice cartons.

I helped myself to some more crisps and studied the field. The cheap wine and the accomplished show were working their magic on the throng. These were paying punters and they wanted their money's worth. Laughter moved through the air like ripples on a pond in the rain. I stood at the end of the bar and watched it. Occasionally I saw my younger two dart between adults, followed by a growing crowd of children. Amber's star status was trickling down to them. Be careful, I thought, experiencing the familiar knot of anxiety I feel for all of my daughters. Star status can vanish just as quickly.

An arm slipped around my shoulders. Jimmy stood, as usual, nine inches above me. He smiled at me and his arm dropped away. He took a quick sip of my wine. "That's unusually good for this sort of thing," he said, and took another.

"Carmen's behind the bar."

His forehead creased as he tried to remember who she was. "Sarah's mother?"

"Daniella and Sophia's mother."

"Oh, yes, of course." He had no idea who Daniella and Sophia were. He bluffs well, though. Suddenly he smiled widely. "Isn't she doing an amazing job? I mean, we all knew she could sing, but sing and act and—my God, I feel disgustingly proud. I'm trying to be modest, but it's no use. When anyone tells me how great she is, I grin like an idiot and agree with them."

"That's no way to get yourself invited onto the playground committee."

Jimmy laughed at my joke. I was grateful. All too often I say things like that and the person I'm talking to starts grilling me about how important the playground committee is to their daughter's chance of becoming leader of the free world. Or, at least, marrying well.

"You're thinking evil thoughts again, aren't you?" said Jimmy.

"No."

"Yes, you are."

"How do you know?" I challenged, though, damn it, he was right.

"Because I know you."

He studied me with an intimacy that I no longer knew what to do with, so I covered my discomfort by grabbing another handful of crisps. "Okay, yes. I spend too much time inside this building. I've become institutionalized and, though I loathe my captors, I'm afraid to leave."

"Well, stop volunteering to make the sets, organize the fair, redecorate the school, and take netball practice. Though why anyone has to practice hopping about on one leg is beyond me."

I elbowed him. "Would you rather your daughters played rugby?"

"Yes."

"Bullshit."

"I would. Great sport."

"And you'd go to watch on the sidelines every Saturday afternoon, would you?"

Jimmy hesitated for a fraction of a second.

"Didn't think so."

"You're right, I wouldn't want to see any of our girls facedown in a ruck." He shuddered.

The silence thickened between us. I reached for more crisps, but the bowl was empty. Jimmy pretended to scan the room for familiar faces. I knew what we were both thinking. That it would be different if we'd had a boy. Everything would be different if we'd had a boy. Where were some of those "helpful" comments when you needed them?

"You've been mouthing all the words," said Jimmy, with a smile that I knew was forced.

That's the trouble with having spent the better part of your life with another person. You do know them. Sometimes, I think, too well. But I took the baton gladly. Tonight was a night to enjoy. "I wasn't, was I?"

"All the way through the first half you mouthed the words—and not just Amber's, everyone's." Now he was genuinely laughing at me.

"Oh, God," I moaned.

"Complete with intonation and expression."

"Why didn't you tell me?"

"You looked too sweet. But don't worry. Any sign you're about to stand up and prompt her, I'll bind and gag you." He then proceeded to take the piss about all the other times that binding and gagging me might have been an appropriate course of action, until I was laughing, despite my attempts not to. That's the problem with Jimmy. He's always made me laugh. Except for the times when he's made me cry.

The bell rang and everyone filtered back to their seats in a neat, orderly fashion. What is it about being back on school premises, even though it's more than a quarter of a century since you last wore a uniform, that makes you feel like a schoolgirl all over again? I walk through the corridors of my daughters' school consumed by irrational thoughts of popularity and bad hair. Outside the gates I feel competent, capable, efficient, and together. Inside, I feel small, fat, and unworthy. And it's not that I'm reliving my own terrible schooldays, because I loved school. It's that I'm reliving my future . . . without the potential. And it scares the bejesus out of me.

I shook my head as I took my seat. This was Amber's night. Not mine. And certainly not a night for my maudlin thoughts. I may not have a great deal of potential these days, but my daughters had it by the bucketload and that was enough. It had to be.

The second half was even better than the first. Amber's performance seemed to grow with the story. I watched as my slip of a girl went from naive to womanly to worldly as the songs spilled out of her. All of the girls performed with a gravitas that reminded me how easy it was to underestimate them. Amber wept over the bleeding body of her beloved Tony—a big-boned girl called Sammy—then stood back and sang as if her heart were breaking, while we watched Tony's limp body carried out of the assembly hall by Jets and Sharks alike. Jimmy and I cried. But we cried separately. We did not hold hands.

The applause was thunderous. Everyone stood. I clapped and cried and laughed simultaneously as the cast took their bows. The girls in the audience stamped their feet, and with a surplus of energy, I did the same, which made me laugh and cry again, because I'd forgotten how much fun stamping your feet could be.

Amber stood, holding Sammy's hand, and smiled. Everyone had been impressive, but our eldest daughter had stolen the show. I don't know why that should have surprised me. She always had.

Jimmy grabbed me and the girls into a huge bear hug, and my ugly thoughts were forced aside.

CARMEN TRACKED ME DOWN AND passed me a white plastic cup with another fabulous long wink. I sipped and was startled to feel the sting of tiny bubbles bursting on my lips. I pointed at her. "You're a bloody marvel," I said, as she raised her own cup in a toast.

Suddenly a burst of applause rippled through the crowd, and people parted to let Amber and Sammy parade through like royalty. Careful, honey, I thought, careful. I scanned the room like a secret agent for the subversive enemy fire I knew was out there.

Jimmy squeezed my hand, leaned down, and spoke softly into my neck. "Give her tonight. We'll recalibrate tomorrow . . ." Then he did something he doesn't often do anymore. He kissed my head. As I felt the hairs on my scalp settle back into place, my single thought was this: Me, Jimmy. It'll be me. I'll be the one doing the recalibrating. On my own.

Amber saw us and let go of her costar's hand, smiling at every compliment—"wonderful," "brilliant," "stunning"—and shaking every outstretched hand. She floated over to us.

Jimmy lifted her clean off the ground, threw her up, and caught her. All eyes were on them, the women's on Jimmy, the men's, I'm ashamed to say, on Amber. No one looked at me like that anymore.

Eventually Amber saw me, grinned, and put a wet kiss on my cheek. "I did it!" she shrieked.

"You did more than that, sweetheart. You were brilliant. I'm so proud of you."

"Thanks, Mum," she said, and glanced around for the next compliment. She didn't have to wait long. She blew me a wide-eyed, got-to-go kiss and allowed herself to be dragged away by a friend, whose father put his hand around her waist—slightly lower than her waist, actually.

With every compliment I imagined her puffing up like a hot-air balloon. Rather than happily watching her sail up, up, and away, I found myself clinging to imaginary anchor ropes, fighting to keep her feet on the ground. "Exceptional," "phenomenal," "genius." Genius? Too much hot air was dangerous. Explosive. My knuckles were white. I stretched my fingers, half-expecting to see rope burns crossing my palm.

I RETREATED TO MY SAFETY zone. The women at the bar. Women I would be friends with irrespective of the accident of birth. Don't misunderstand me, I like most of the women at this school—that's three classes of thirty mothers—but there's a big difference between like and like-minded.

Angie slapped me on the back.

"What are you all laughing about?" I asked.

"Don't. It's too painful," she said. She had one girl at the school and three boys elsewhere.

"What?"

"Last week's Save the Animal Day." She grimaced. "I forgot. Poor Ella was the only one in uniform. She screamed blue murder when she realized she wasn't an endangered animal."

"I don't know. Regent's Gate School girls are a pretty rare breed," I said, "especially the non-Russian-speaking ones."

Carmen had left her post behind the bar. She prodded me.

"Careful," I said, pulling my jumper down. "You'll lose your hand."

"Don't be silly," said Angie.

"I not only took mine to school the day after the term finished," said Theresa, a GP who ran her own practice, "I brought them back a day early. My therapist would say I'm subconsciously afraid of being left alone with my children. He'd be right." Everyone laughed.

I racked my brain for a story of my own hopelessness, but couldn't come up with one. You know what? It embarrassed me. Angie and Theresa worked full-time, as I used to, and Carmen still worked part-time. Sometimes it ran smoothly, sometimes it didn't. But now I had nothing other than my children to think about, so they went to school with their ballet kit clean and ironed; their homework done; a fresh, healthy snack in their bags every day without fail.

"Therapist?" I asked, wanting to change the subject.

"Fantasy therapist, along with the fantasy Pilates classes, fantasy diet, and fantasy lie-ins. He's quite dishy, puts his hand on my fevered brow and tells me I'm doing brilliantly."

"You *are* doing brilliantly," I said.

She shrugged. "I know, but sometimes it would be nice to be told."

"I'll drink to that," said Carmen. The women raised their plastic cups.

Then Carmen gave her perfect, sexy smile, and a second later I felt hands on my shoulders. I know that Jimmy is one of everyone's favorite dads, boasting a near-full head of hair, a sense of humor, and an innate ability to talk to women. In a popularity contest with me, he'd win hands down. Years ago I trained myself not to mind.

"Ready to go?" he said.

"You've got the girls?" I asked, surprised.

"No."

I imagine only the other women heard my short sigh while I silently listed the irritations Jimmy's "no" had created. But female subtext to men's ears is like a dog whistle to any human's: they simply don't hear it. "I'll get them," I said. I'll be the bad guy. Years ago I would have sent Jimmy, but experience had taught me that he would come back empty-handed. He couldn't force his will on his eldest daughter, because, where she was concerned, his only will was hers. I left him with my friends and sought out my shining star first.

AMBER WAS HOLDING COURT BUT I could tell she was tired. Overtired, in fact, and that meant dangerous. Highs like that come at a hefty cost. I held back, forming a quick strategy. Finally I came up with something I thought had a chance of success. "Amber, darling, Dad's offering to take us to Nando's on the way home and pick something up."

"Nando's! Yum, I'm starving," said her friend Emily.

"Lucky you! We're never allowed to go there," said a girl I didn't know.

"What I wouldn't do for a plate of chips now," said a third.

I smiled. I get a big kick out of the ravenous appetite of the prepubescent girl. I savor it, actually. I have friends with older daughters, and I know it won't be long before the Special K diet worms its way into my child's consciousness.

Amber stood up. "Sorry, guys, gotta go."

"You coming tomorrow night?" Emily asked me.

"I'm coming every night. We've got the grannies and the aunts tomorrow, too."

"Mayhem," said Amber dramatically.

Here we go, I thought, taking her arm gently.

I managed to scoop up the other two on the way, and the person it was the hardest to prize out of the assembly hall was Jimmy. He left behind a horseshoe of crestfallen women when Maddy pulled him away from his adoring audience. Amber and Jimmy are more alike than I ever realized. Charmers. It makes them attractive to be around, but the trouble with charmers is that they need an audience. Always.

I climbed into the driver's seat, Jimmy next to me, and the girls in the back. It was a cold night, and I put on the heater. Winter was stubbornly refusing to move aside for spring. I knew people were desperate for the clocks to go forward, for the season to change, but the cold early evenings suited my life. It was easier to be a hermit in the dark. I had whispered the plan and, having slipped Jimmy thirty quid because he'd spent his last cash getting a cab to the school, drove us to the fast-food place. "Anything for you?" he asked, leaning back through the open door.

"No, thanks. I'm not hungry."

A little later I let us into our small house in Kentish Town and the girls ran ahead to fight over the bucket of cholesterol now sitting in the middle of the pine kitchen table. Jimmy went to the fridge, got himself a beer, found an open bottle of wine, and poured me a generous glass. The five of us sat around dissecting the performance again, as we had in the car, while the kids dipped chips into an assortment of glutinous sauces. As usual, Jimmy had ordered too much, and after a ten-minute eating frenzy, the girls pushed themselves away from the table and groaned.

"Bedtime, you lot," I said.

For once no one protested. Even Amber stood up without a fuss. "I need to rest for tomorrow. Do you mind if I don't help clear up?" she said.

Cunning . . . I thought. I'd happily throw the rest of the congealing food and the paper plates away if it meant no bedtime tantrums. "Go on up. I'll put this away."

"I'm too tired to walk upstairs," said Maddy, knowing full well how her father would respond. Dutifully, he picked her up, and then Lulu was begging to be carried too. But Jimmy wasn't as young as he once was—they'd have to take it in turn. It seemed like yesterday he could carry all three.

"Daddy will carry you to bed tomorrow," I said, sensing a storm brewing.

Jimmy gave me a look. I had to concentrate on stopping my jaw clamping. I knew what that look meant: he wouldn't be around to-morrow night to put them to bed. He was going to be "busy" again. I implored him not to say anything. They were too tired, and news that Daddy wouldn't be home again guaranteed a meltdown. Instead I picked up Lulu and carried her up to the room she and Maddy shared, then went downstairs to throw away the leftovers. Well, tidy up, anyway. I found it difficult to throw food away. It seemed such a waste.

"Mum! Can you bring some loo paper?" yelled Lulu.

I swallowed a cold chip. "Coming," I mumbled.

I could hear Amber singing in the bathroom as she reluctantly took off her stage makeup. I was relieved to see her emerge barefaced and swamped by Snoopy pajamas. I hugged my eldest child. "I'm so proud of you, Amber. You put so much work into that show and it paid off. I don't think even you thought you were going to be *that* good. Did you?"

"But Mummy, when the lights came up I forgot about me and became her. It was like I'd gone through the looking-glass. It wasn't until I saw you guys that I remembered who I was. It was weird."

"You were Maria absolutely. Even I forgot it was you at times," I said, stroking her hair. "But as brilliant as she was, I'm very glad I have my beautiful Amber back."

"I'm pooped," she said, flopping into her bed and reaching for a tendril of hair, which she curled around a finger and held to her face. She's been using her hair as a security blanket since the first tufts appeared behind an ear. So much easier than Lulu's rabbit, which I've lived in fear of losing for nearly a decade now. I didn't make that mistake a third time. Maddy had a muslin cloth to cuddle up to and I used to buy them by the sackload.

"Love you, Mum."

"I love you, my amazing girl. I'll come and give you a kiss after I've settled the other two." She waved her hair-ringed fingers at me. It was these gestures, not her perfect pitch, that made me love my daughter.

JIMMY SAT ON THE FLOOR cross-legged between the two single beds and read from a book he'd picked off the shelf. It didn't matter that it was babyish, it didn't matter that they didn't like the story, it didn't matter that they were virtually asleep: their eyes and ears were on their father, drinking him in. My heart constricted and I retreated to the corridor. By the time I'd picked up the discarded clothes, screwed the cap onto the toothpaste, flushed the loo, put out clean uniforms for the following day, checked all three book bags, hung up the wet laundry, disposed of the empty Nando's bucket, and sorted out breakfast, the house was quiet. I went back upstairs to kiss my sleeping children, then joined Jimmy at the kitchen table. He opened the box of Crunchy Nut Corn Flakes and grabbed a handful. A few spilled out, and more dropped from his hand as he threw them into his mouth.

"Sorry about tomorrow night. It'll be a late one," he said, crunching. I stared at the cereal scattered over my recently cleaned table. "I had to juggle some things to get to the play, and they've been moved to tomorrow." He put the packet back in its place but without folding down the plastic innards or the top of the box.

"It's okay," I said, itching to close it but resisting, because I knew it would be seen as an act of aggression.

"God, she was brilliant, wasn't she?" said Jimmy.

I tore my eyes away from the bloody cereal and forced myself to remember the show. The smile returned to my lips. "Yes, she was."

"I hope they're making a movie. Lucy's coming tomorrow, right? She's got one of those digital recorders. Shall I ask her?"

I had already called Jimmy's wonderfully left-field sister and asked her. "She's bringing it."

"Perfect. That's the sort of thing we need to save up for Amber's twenty-first."

"Or her wedding," I replied. We caught one another's eye, then looked away.

"Right," said Jimmy, standing up. "I'd better be going."

I glanced at my watch. "Gosh," I said, faking a yawn, "how did it get so late?"

"Bea, I'm sorry I can't collect Lulu and Maddy tomorrow."

"It's all right. I'll sort something out. Maybe they'd like to come and see the show again."

"I would."

"Really? Do you want me to get you an extra ticket? The last night is Friday."

"Friday, Friday . . . Yes. I can come on Friday. I could take the girls afterward for the night. Make it up to them for missing my night tomorrow, give you a break."

"Well . . ."

"Have a think, let me know. I won't make any plans."

Nor would I, since it was never going to happen. "Okay. Thanks."

He gave me a brief hug. "Night, Bea."

"Night."

I heard the front door close, and as the latch clicked into place, my spine collapsed and I folded with exhaustion over the kitchen table. For a moment everything went blank. When my eyes opened again, my vision was filled with the Kellogg's rooster. I reached for the packet, picked it up, and scanned the enticing health figures. "Fortified, my arse," I said to the rooster. "If you were fortified, I should have the strength of ten men by now." Then, as if the spirit of that damn bird had possessed me, I emptied a small hill into Lulu's bowl. By leaning back in my chair, I could open the fridge, yank out the milk, pour, and replace it so quickly that it was almost as if it hadn't happened.

I walked through to the front room and switched on the telly, put my feet on the table, and spooned sweet, crunchy mouthfuls of honey-coated happiness into my mouth. Hell, everyone needs a love interest. I placed the empty bowl on my chest and gazed, weary-eyed, at the telly.

"I really should go to bed," I said to myself, picking up the remote and flicking through a couple of channels. I had stopped paying for cable as part of my new economy drive, and didn't miss it. The kids had incredible ways of downloading all the latest series from America, and knowing I did a lot of "babysitting," my friends and family were generous with their boxed sets. Anyway, there was always a *CSI* on Channel Five at about this time of night.

Sure enough, there was Grissom, his head in a jar of cockroaches, and some fancy film-work to ease my whirring brain.

"Five minutes," I said to myself. "Then bed."

I woke with a start and stared at the luminous green numbers on the video recorder: 12:56. I lumbered up from the gap between the sofa cushions and rubbed my eyes. I ran my dry tongue over my dry lips and knew, as clearly as if I were my old granddad, that I'd been snoring open-mouthed for a while now.

I stood up, stepped on something hard, and heard the clatter of cutlery on china. I'd upturned my cereal bowl. For once I was grateful that I had the bad habit of drinking every last drop of sweet milk at the end.

Sliding the bowl with my foot under the sofa, I reached for the light switch and forced my way up to bed. I put my clothes on the small armchair in the corner of my room, in reverse order to how I would be putting them back on in an unbearably short time.

Less than three minutes later, I was in bed with the lights off, perched precariously close to sleep but not quite stepping over the precipice. Why was I always so cold?

I curled up into a ball and tried to get warm, but all I managed to do was surround myself with a sea of cold. It was too cold to stretch my legs out, and too uncomfortable to stay trussed up like a chicken. Thinking about chickens made me think about my archenemy, the rooster, which made me think about my stomach, which made me fling myself into another position with such forceful loathing that I sat up and turned on the light. I picked up the novel lying by my bed and started to read. I read and read and read until the words swarmed before my eyes and it was dawn.

Two

No Model Lady

THE PLAY'S RUN ENDED AND AMBER FELL INTO POSTPRODUCTION BLUES. I was sympathetic at first, adoration is hard to replace, but one more rendition of "Somewhere" and I was ready to shove a scouring pad down her gullet. "One Hand, One Heart" made me want to take up arms, which, I was fairly sure, had been neither Bernstein's nor Sondheim's intention. Add to this artistic misery the natural ability of the teenager to self-indulge and, for once, I was happy to see her walk through the school gates the following Friday with her weekend bags to go to her father's. Sadly, my daughters were a job lot, which meant I lost the little ones too.

However, this Friday was different. This Friday I was going out. By some miracle, Faith, who is married to Jimmy's younger brother Luke, had remained one of my closest friends. Jimmy's family is huge and varied, and somehow I'd got so lost in the crowd that they'd forgotten to ask me to leave. I wondered whether they were the reason Jimmy and I had stayed friends. Even with the best intentions to part amicably, divorce is unimaginably hard. Whatever knots two people may

have wound themselves into, the unraveling is worse. We had our moments, of course—what couple, divorced or otherwise, doesn't?—but
considering the circumstances, I would have said we separated well.
And, most of the time, I was pretty happy. Well, if not happy, then certainly busy. And weren't they the same? As Dory in *Finding Nemo* sings,
"Just keep swimming, swimming, swimming . . ."

I saw Faith through the frosted-glass window of the bar and pulled
at my jacket self-consciously. I watched her push open the door as I
stuffed the empty packet of nuts into the empty half-pint glass and slid
it away from me.

Faith raised her arms in a celebratory salute. "Friday!" she exclaimed.

I pointed to the bottle of wine and the two glasses. "What's it doing
still in the bottle?" she asked, giving me a hug. "Get pouring."

For a second, I leaned into her shoulder, but bodily contact is not
something Faith misses, with an adoring husband, a marsupial five-
year-old, and an office team of fifteen. Her personal space is anything
but personal.

She plonked herself on the stool next to mine. "So. How are you,
Bea?"

"Good," I replied. If Faith had heard my voice rise a decibel or two,
she didn't mention it. "Really good."

"I'm so sorry I had to blow you off the other week—bloody work
dinner."

"I totally understand," I said. "I had some crocheting I really wanted
to get on with."

"Stop it. You should start going to a class or something on Wednesdays."

"I would if Jimmy was reliable. But one Wednesday out of three,
something comes up."

"Because you make it too easy for him," said Faith.

"This is my night out. We're not talking about Jimmy."

"Sorry. Has Amber come down from on high yet?"

"No. And she's got all weekend being worshipped and adored," I said.

"I thought we weren't talking about Jimmy," said Faith.

"You're right. Fine me."

"A shot."

"Shit! On an empty stomach?"

"Best place for it. Come on, it's Friday, I'm jangling and, to be honest, I can't be bothered to wade through half a bottle of wine before I level out."

"Tequila?" I suggested.

Faith giggled like a naughty schoolgirl. "Brilliant," she said, then hollered for the barman.

"Hey, I'm the one getting fined," I protested.

"Did I tell you I saw Jimmy the other day with a young woman?"

"Ha, ha." The barman reached us. "Two shots of tequila, please, and make hers a double."

I sucked the lemon until I felt the enamel on my teeth creak.

"Aaah," said Faith, closing her eyes. "That's better."

"Bad week?"

"Well, Friday's always better than Monday."

"Not in my life."

"What I wouldn't do to have a couple of free days to myself. There are so many things I never have time to get done."

"Faith, you overestimate my life, as usual. All I have is time to get things done. And you know what? The list never gets any shorter."

"Then stop adding to it."

"I can't. It's a terrible compulsion. Sometimes I add things just to cross them off. Talking of which, I have a lovely list for you." I reached down and pulled a plastic folder out of my handbag. "Eats," I said.

Faith bounced excitedly on her stool. "I take it all back, List Lady, Queen of the Lists, Mother List. What are we having?"

Luke, my ex-brother-in-law, was turning forty in a few weeks' time. Faith had passed that milestone a couple of years earlier with a twelve-hour lunch and a cake iced with the Mae West quote "I'm no model lady. A model is just an imitation of the real thing." It had been brilliant, but this time Faith wanted dancing. It was costing them a fortune, so I had offered to make the hors d'oeuvres. I pushed the file her way.

"Roast beef in mini Yorkshire puddings?"

I nodded. "With horseradish mousse."

"Luke's favorite."

I nodded again.

"Smoked mackerel pâté?"

"On rye," I added. "Cut into little stars."

"Oh, my God, Bea, this is amazing . . . Are you sure you want to do it all?"

"Nothing makes me happier than producing a hundred lobster profiteroles."

"It's too much."

"You're right, I'll use crabsticks." Faith started to protest again. I stopped her. "You know I love doing it and, anyway, it's my present to Luke. Time is cheap. Time, I have."

"Luke'll get so excited when he sees this."

I grabbed the file playfully and hugged it. "This is my master list. I have a copy for you."

"It's going to be such fun—the band is phenomenal. Are you bringing someone? You know you can."

I shook my head.

"What about that date you went on?"

"Please don't remind me." I'd been strong-armed into a blind date by Angie. The guy was a friend of her brother, who had D-I-V-O-R-C-E'd a year previously. On paper, it looked possible: architect, father of two daughters, forty-six, accomplished cook and gardener. He sounded nice, I thought. The split, I was told, had been amicable, all things considered. It was the "all things considered" that should have rung the warning bells. But since I stand in a glass house of my own, I owed it to myself to give the man the benefit of the doubt. Maybe one day someone would return the favor. I should have turned on my heels the moment I saw his entirely tucked-in self. When he ordered a green salad with the dressing on the side, I should have run. I was on my best behavior the whole day long, but even I couldn't keep it up indefinitely.

"He was a mad anorexic," I said to Faith, refilling our glasses. "The man wouldn't eat. He watched every mouthful I took. It was unnerving. He was obviously starving, so I kept offering him some, which gave him the excuse to launch into a lecture about heart disease being the number-one killer. I made some joke about it being cheaper than divorce and that was basically that. So, no, Mr. Dressing-on-the-side will not be escorting me to Luke's fortieth. The girls are. They're very excited about it. My mother's taking them shopping for new outfits."

"That's nice of her," said Faith, in a way that let me know "nice" was exactly what it wasn't.

"Can't wait for that little outing," I said.

"Don't go, then. Let her have the girls on her own."

That conjured up such a horrendous sequence of disasters that I shuddered. "They'd come back looking like little czarinas." I drank from my glass.

"She is something of a relic, your mother."

My mother was born old. But old did not mean wise in this case. She claimed she was "traditional," and though I tried to convince myself that she was not a bad person, she had turned "traditional" into an ugly word. I loved my mother, of course. But I didn't often like her. I'm pretty sure the feeling was mutual.

"I'm always amazed by how normal you turned out," said Faith.

"Don't be fooled," I said, but allowed myself to enjoy the compliment.

Faith laughed. "Did you know Maddy and Lulu asked me if they can be in charge of Charlie on the night of the party? Since I plan to be inebriated by eight, I said yes. I'm pretty sure they'd adopt him if they could."

Amazing how quickly a good feeling can be replaced.

"When Jimmy brings them over to play, I can hear them in the garden, pretending he's their brother," she went on. "It's the sweetest thing. Charlie calls them his sisters when he talks about them, which is all the time." Faith watched me drain my glass. "I know what you're thinking, but you don't have to worry about me anymore. I'm completely happy with what I have. Really, Bea, one makes sense to me."

I couldn't look at her. She didn't know what I was thinking. I waved to the bar staff, ordered a packet of posh crisps, tore it open, and seized a handful.

"So," said Faith, picking out one, "this guy, he was telling you off about what you ate?"

"He had antiseptic gel in his pocket, Faith. It was nothing to do with me."

She nodded, but said no more on my failure to date. I used to tell everyone about future dates. But these days I kept my own counsel. Too many hopeful faces to disappoint when it flopped. Which it always did. I had no idea what I was doing wrong. That was a lie. I knew where I went wrong. I talked about my children too much. My children and Jimmy. It always came back to Jimmy.

"So how are you going to serve all the food?" asked Faith.

"I kept hold of the disposable party trays from the school picnic. One of the perks of organizing it was being able to pilfer some useful catering equipment."

"Genius."

"And I'll make sure there's enough so that all Honor has to do is a main dish."

A wicked smile crossed Faith's face. "Just so long as she isn't it."

My ex-mother-in-law was an increasingly full-time naturist. The urge to get naked had come to her late in life. Her husband, Peter, had tried it out, but he didn't like his "bits and pieces" swinging about in the wind and had returned to the land of the fully clothed, where he had remained. After all, he had his fishing, and some people found that harder to live with than the occasional game of naked boules. They were a bit old for volleyball now. Having checked out the competition and come to the conclusion that the need to bare all had nothing to do with sex, he had agreed to support Honor in her latest craze. "More interesting than cross-stitch," he had said to anyone who dared show disapproval. Peter and Honor had been married for nearly fifty years. He had fallen in love with her beauty, she with his promise of escape from the terraces of Leeds and a puritanical existence.

"It was just luck," she said to me when I quizzed her on the success of her marriage, "that we survived as well as we have. Frankly, even with the best intentions, it could have gone either way."

I don't think luck had anything to do with it. Unified in their commitment to their family, they were also fiercely independent. And when they discussed their plans, I got the sense they were asking each other out of courtesy, never for permission.

Peter, I suspect, is the true romantic in their union. On the eve of my marriage to his eldest son, he said, "The thing about marriage is it makes the good things twice as good and the bad things only half as bad." Like a fool, I believed him. I believed them both.

I DON'T KNOW WHY I agreed to this, and I deliberately hadn't said anything to Faith about it, but the following evening I was off to a singles night for the over-forties. Can you imagine anything more depressing? What the hell was I thinking? Hadn't the mad anorexic been enough punishment for one year? My trouble was that beneath the excess flesh lies a basically enthusiastic person. She may be buried deeper than I'd like her to be, but she's still down there. Occasionally she makes her way to the surface, and I start accepting invitations with impunity. Needless to say, these moments coincide with a little lost poundage. But the pounds are back on and now all I want to do is dive, dive, dive. Damn that rooster and all who are packaged in him.

I would have canceled, except in this instance I couldn't. My friend Cathy had lost her husband to cancer. She wasn't looking for a date. She just wanted a night out when she could pretend she wasn't a widow and didn't have to talk white-blood-cell count. Her husband took a long time to die. She was bored with cancer. She was bored with death. Infidelity, gay husbands, physical abuse, and good old-fashioned itches were light relief in comparison. And that was why I had to go. If laughing meant laughing at me, I would accept that, because Cathy needed a laugh. I promised I wouldn't welsh on the night. But that was before I had to stand in my bedroom, staring at my wardrobe, trying to find something other than sweatpants and fake Ugg boots to wear. My sartorial mainstay.

"Okay, Bea," I said to the clothes. "You can do this. Things haven't got that bad." I flicked through a couple of hangers. There were dresses I hadn't worn since before Lulu was born. I'd always thought I'd get back to that slim person I used to be. Without mirrors, I managed to believe I'd never left. There were no mirrors in my house except the small ones above the basin in the bathroom and the downstairs privy. There is one attached to the inside door of Amber's wardrobe, but it's covered with cut-out photographs of Zac Efron, so even when I open the doors to put away clean clothes, I'm saved from myself by Blu-Tack.

Tonight I wanted to make an effort. The ever-hopeful idiot at the core of me had allowed herself to imagine, miracle of miracles, that there was going to be a decent bloke at this over-forties, left-on-the-shit-pile-of-life get-together. I was going. My friend was going. We were both all right. Was it so wrong to hope?

I pulled out a black skirt, got it halfway up my thighs, then kicked it off. During the long postpartum years I had built in a pretty good early-warning system for clothes that would not do up. I took a couple of shirts off their hangers and held them up, then spotted some black trousers I'd forgotten. I grabbed them and pulled them on. They fitted. I was suddenly enthused. High boots, nice shirt, bit of cleavage, the fabulous necklace Jimmy had given me on our tenth wedding anniversary, and I'd be okay.

I reached behind me to check what trousers they were that had been hiding from me all this time. Then I read the label. "Mimi Maternity." I straightened up and stood stock-still. That couldn't be right. I'd given all my maternity stuff to Faith when she was pregnant with Charlie. Surely I'd read it wrong. I forced myself to peel back the waistband again. "Mimi Maternity NYC." I sat down on the bed. If only those trousers could talk.

Jimmy had gone to New York when I was pregnant with Amber. He was about to hit the big time. Universal wanted to make him executive producer on a show he'd put together. The money was going to be brilliant. He came home with all these wonderful clothes, even though I had only a couple of months left of my pregnancy.

I pulled off the maternity trousers and threw them across the room. They had been a bad omen. The deal had fallen through. As deals do. Not that we cared. We had a beautiful baby girl. Our happiness was secure. Other deals would happen. I had a good job. We were young. What mattered was our little unit. Jesus, I was so fucking naive.

I put my jeans back on, knowing they were past the washing stage and well into the running-about-on-their-own stage. But they fitted and I felt comfortable in them. Especially with my long black jacket and the cripplingly high boots that put me at a willowy, ha-ha, five foot six. Eyedrops and concealer covered most of the damage the Mimi Maternity trousers had caused; makeup did the rest.

When the doorbell went, I was ready. As ready as I'd ever be. Okay, over-forty single males, here I come . . .

"You look great," said Cathy as I opened the door.

"So do you," I replied.

We were both lying.

We had decided not to drive and I followed Cathy to the minicab. The "event" was taking place in a private room in a bar on the wrong side of Camden High Street. I was nervous as hell when I walked in. Naturally, the women outnumbered the men by three to one, but I was pleased to see that a lot of the women smiled semi-conspiratorially at me. Well, hey, at least I might make a friend, I thought.

"Bar," said Cathy.

"You bet."

It was a moneymaking racket, that was for sure. First, we'd had to pay to join this illustrious gang. Second, we'd had to cough up for the event, and third, they'd jacked up the bar prices. I peered over the bar menu at Cathy. "Can I tempt you with a gin-based Take a Chance for the reasonable sum of twelve pounds fifty?"

"You're kidding, right?" she said, trying to grab the menu. I held firm and pretended to study it again.

"Or a very refreshing The One. A fruity mix of juice and white rum served with a little false hope."

"Bea!"

"No, hang on, found it. A very large Will You Please Shag Me I'm Desperate!" I looked up at Cathy. "That one comes with a cherry."

Cathy was still chuckling when she ordered the wine. White for me. Red for her. Bottles. No point doing things by halves.

We watched for a while as the more experienced participators worked the room, handing out cards to all the men before the competition had a chance to stake claim.

Because I was with Cathy, I didn't find it intimidating. Instead I found it funny. Not *Blackadder* funny, more *Mr. Bean* funny, which, on reflection, isn't very funny at all. Cathy and I stayed by the bar, having a quick catch-up. It lasted so long that, after a while, the men started to sidle up to us. A relatively decent-looking one made a beeline for Cathy, so I made my excuses and went to the loo to give her some space. When I returned, she was in full swing about her evil ex-husband who had got the babysitter pregnant. Only I knew it was an act. A bit of sport. A break from the mourning. I chatted to the young Polish girl behind the bar, who had been in England a few months and was finding life difficult. She missed her family. So did I. Water always finds its own level. But then something strange happened.

A young-looking man—might have been forty, might have been younger—came and leaned up at the bar next to me. He introduced himself as Robert. He seemed a bit too good for an outfit like this, and I wondered if he was lying about his age to get in to where the pickings didn't need picking up. I made a silent vow to myself not to seem grateful for his attention. I'd be friendly, but that wasn't the same thing. He asked me about myself. So I told him.

"I'm forty-two, I have three daughters and got divorced two years ago." If I were a product, my label would read "No Frills."

"Do you work?"

I felt the shame creep into my cheeks. "No. Well, I look after three kids."

"That must be tough," he said kindly. "On your own."

"Sometimes I think it's easier," I replied honestly. "The parenting bit. You get to do it your way. Total autonomy. Except every other weekend and Wednesdays." Except those Wednesdays when something came up.

"Who decides these things? Why is it every other weekend and Wednesdays? I think it should be split equally."

"Why? Nothing else about parenting is equal."

He took a step back and raised his hands in mock surrender.

"Sorry," I said. "Didn't mean to sound so defensive."

"No, no, fair point, I'm sure."

I was crap at this. I searched my stagnant brain for a cheery opening. Reopening. Nothing came to mind.

"So, how old are your children?" he asked.

"Fourteen, nine, and eight."

"Ouch," he said, squirming as if he'd bitten into a bad skate.

Now what had I done?

"Two pregnancies in under two years, brave woman." I thought he was being nice, but I could have sworn he glanced at my stomach. I shifted in my seat.

"So they're at school now?"

"Shit!" I slapped my forehead. "I knew I'd forgotten to pick something up."

He laughed unnecessarily loudly. I couldn't decide which of us was regretting the conversation more.

"So, you have a bit of time to yourself, then."

"Not really," I replied, wanting to end this stilted, fruitless exchange.

"But you can find an hour here or there, can't you? If you're honest with yourself."

I frowned in confusion. What on earth was he going to suggest? That I cancel all my coffee mornings, ha-ha, and meet up for a quickie?

He pointed a finger at me. "Good," he said. "You should be easy."

"Excuse me?"

"Settle down." He leaned closer to the name tag still plastered onto the lapel of my obviously-doesn't-quite-hide-everything jacket. Then he reached inside his pocket and pulled out a card. He handed it to me. "Bea," he said, "my name is Robert Duke. I'm a personal trainer. Use me, and you won't ever have to come to one of these tragic functions again."

I opened my mouth to reply, but was so stunned I couldn't find any words.

"Listen, I know I've shocked you, but, Bea, you more than anyone in this place needs to be shocked. Remember the beautiful woman you were before pregnancy, breast-feeding, and exhaustion ripped you apart? She's still there. Underneath all this shit." He shook me slightly. I felt things wobble but was incapable of resisting. "I understand how hard it is, how frightening, but you can change. And I will help you every painful step of the way. But, my God, it'll be worth it. Think of it—you could be in a bikini by the summer." All I could do was stare at him. My resistance, my voice, my spine . . . gone. Who was this guy— the divorcée whisperer? "I know you've been through hell, Bea, but I can help you. This I know. You're a great lady in bad shape."

Again I opened my mouth. Again nothing came out.

Then he touched my shoulder, so gently that I almost fell off the stool. "Wouldn't it be nice to be a bad lady in great shape?"

With that, he squeezed my shoulder and was gone. The spell, or whatever it was, shattered. A strange sob came out of my mouth as I found myself sitting in a shitty bar on the wrong side of a bad bottle of wine at a soul-shatteringly sad event for leftovers like me. I stared at the card. "Bastard!" I hissed. It felt good. "Motherfucking-bastard-shit!" I threw back the rest of my wine, ripped up the card, and ran.

WHAT FOLLOWED AT HOME WAS nothing short of disgusting. What saddened me most was that it wasn't the first time it had happened. Worse than that, I knew I had sworn over the heads of my sleeping children that it wouldn't happen again, but there I was, cramming food into my mouth without the slightest idea of how to stop. The first to go were, of course, the bloody Crunchy Nut Corn Flakes. I didn't bother with the bowl. Four stale Wagon Wheels biscuits that had been sitting in the cupboard since Christmas chased the cereal. My kids don't like Wagon Wheels. They're right. Foul things. Didn't stop me scoffing the lot.

Robert Duke. I spat out chunks of marshmallow and biscuit as I regurgitated his name. "I'll show you a bad lady!" Cheese next. Cheddar. The cheap, waxy kind that has a suspicious buoyancy. I bit into the slab and squeezed it between my teeth and gums until my tongue stuck to the roof of my mouth; then washed it down with a carton of apple juice. I saved myself a few calories by spilling a lot.

I was halfway through a chicken breast—cooked, at least—when I felt the first swell of my stomach juices. I heaved, swallowed the bile, and, squirting mayonnaise out of the squeezy bottle straight into my mouth, managed to get the rest of the chicken down my throat. Feeling bloated, strange, and angry, I paced the kitchen floor, panting, throwing open cupboards, searching for more, a couple of crackers here, some nuts there, a handful of raisins—but then the spirits left me as quickly as they had possessed me, and I was suddenly empty and bereft. I mean empty of energy, chi, power, self. My belly hurt like hell.

I slumped to the floor, undid my jeans, and let my bloated torso ooze out over the cold linoleum. I felt as if my stomach was tearing. I wanted to split it open and take it all out. I started clawing at my jacket, my shirt, my disgusting overweighted bra, but however hard I pinched my sorry fat pink flesh, it wouldn't let me get inside.

After what seemed like a nighttime, I heaved myself onto all fours, exhausted. I stopped, staring at my body as it hung down, loathing it with a hatred I didn't know what to do with. Eventually, I crawled down the corridor to the loo. I threw back the seat and stuck my fingers far enough down my throat to feel my larynx. I heaved a dry, tight, painful retch. But nothing, not one damn crunchy nut, came out. It never fucking does.

AT SIX O'CLOCK THE FOLLOWING evening the house was immaculate. The shelves were restocked. The bathroom shone. The air was fresh. The beds were made. The ironing was done. When I heard Amber's key in the lock, I jumped up from my listening post at the kitchen table, threw open a cupboard, and busied myself with rearranging perfectly arranged tins.

"Mum! We're home!"

I peered around the open cupboard door. "Hi, you guys, just coming." I gazed at the baked-bean tins, counted to ten, closed the cupboard, then returned to my rightful place in the world. I went into the hall, took the bags, the wet swimming things, the coats, hats, and scarves, the dirty school uniforms, and my exhausted children through to the kitchen. Like a machine, I sorted everything into piles. Jimmy followed us and, watching me, leaned up against the kitchen wall. I put a load of uniforms into the washing machine.

"I'm starving," said Amber.

I looked at Jimmy with comedy knowing eyes.

"Sorry," he said. "I didn't realize the time. We were swimming." I nearly kissed him. I had to use all my willpower to stop myself smiling and instead feign weary disapproval. I clicked the machine to quick-wash, and straightened up. My heart was leaping for joy inside its well-covered cage. "Sit down, all of you. How about a cheese-and-ham omelet, with beans on the side?"

I got unanimous approval from the girls.

"God, that sounds good," said Jimmy.

"Well, why don't you sit down too?" I said. "It'll only take ten minutes." Actually, it took five.

We sat down like a proper family. Even though the girls were tired, they helped set the table. It wasn't much—a knife, a fork, a plate, some glasses—but they all helped. It made me think that maybe they were happy to be home. Jimmy was all about big gestures: water parks, fairgrounds, toy shops, pizza, late-night telly, telly, a bit more telly . . . But sometimes the little gestures mean more. I sat and watched them eat. Me? I drank hot water with lemon. Involuntarily, I glanced at the kitchen floor and saw my bloated self, heaving about on all fours. Never again. This time I meant it.

I must have breathed a huge sigh, because Jimmy looked at me. "You okay?"

"Just thinking how nice this is."

"It is, isn't it?"

I held his gaze and the strangest thing happened. My stomach flipped. I looked away. Must be hunger. I had eaten a boiled egg for breakfast, a small chicken salad for lunch, and I was determined not to touch the children's food. I'd have some vegetable soup when they'd gone to bed. I was going to change, not because of Robert Duke or antiseptic dates, or even Faith's aborted attempts to talk to me about my weight. I was going to change for me. The time had come, the walrus said, and, my, what a walrus I had become.

"You look well, Bea," said Jimmy.

"I did some exercise for the first time in a decade. Nearly killed me."

"Hardly. You never sit down."

"I'm not sure washing-up counts."

"It does with this lot," said Jimmy, running his hands through his thick hair. "I've resorted to paper plates on weekends. Much easier."

"It's very wasteful," said Maddy, taking the words out of my mouth.

"Which is why Maddy washed them up, dried them on a washing line she built in the garden, then made monster masks with them."

I blew my youngest a kiss. "I'm very proud of you," I mouthed. She smiled and returned to chatting with her sisters about underwater handstands. Jimmy and I let their talk babble around us like water around two rocks, swirling, eddying, and doubling back on itself. We smiled at each other. Even though I knew what was coming next, I felt . . . I barely recognized the feeling—content?

As the girls scraped the last of the yogurt out of the cups, what I had been waiting for came to pass. The last-minute admission that there was some homework to do, Jimmy's protest that the girls had promised they didn't have any, and the surefire knowledge that I would be up for a couple of hours coloring in the map of Canada, or making a family tree, or sticking leaves in a scrapbook, or whatever parental torture the education system had concocted for the vicariously ambitious. Did I mind? Not a bit. I was happy to do it.

Jimmy came downstairs, having tucked the girls in and kissed them good night, then watched me spread out the contents of their book bags on the table.

"I'm sorry, Bea."

"I like coloring," I said. "I find it therapeutic."

"That's lucky. You've been doing it for years."

"Careful, or I'll make *you* color in the solar system."

Jimmy looked at his watch. "Is that the time?"

I continued going through the file and pointed to the door.

"I'm teasing. Come on, I'll give you a hand. Astronomy was one of my few strong subjects."

I was surprised. He opened the fridge door. "A glass of wine. It'll take half an hour if we both do it." He pulled out a bottle and held it up questioningly. Alcohol wasn't really on my diet plan, but I nodded.

It was just over four years since Jimmy and I separated. Four years I had been living alone, two years officially divorced, and here he was, standing in my single-parent kitchen, in my single-parent terraced house, seeming very much at home. We sat down opposite each other and started. We talked about the girls mostly, a bit of stuff about his work. I told him about the sports day coming up and the vegetable patch I'd started in the garden. It was the sort of Sunday night we would have had if we were still married. Which meant one of two things. I had either got this very right. Or very, very wrong.

Three

What Beast Is This?

THREE DAYS LATER, I MET UP WITH SOME OF THE MOTHERS AFTER drop-off. It was one of those rare February mornings when the pale opaque clouds lifted their low-lying lid on London, and we were reminded of the potential of the vast blue skyscape above. There was a clarity in the air, which felt good. Or perhaps I was beginning to see things clearly. Either way, I was more positive about my future than I had been in a long time. We were supposed to be planning the swimming gala, but I can safely say that we were all looking forward to a good old chat. We had elected Carmen's house. It was nearest to the school. She always provided an incredible array of mini croissants— plain, chocolate, and, my favorite, almond paste. She had a posh coffee machine that produced real foam. I loved going to her house. The keeper of the clipboard, I was poised to make more of the lists that made my life worth living.

"Darling," said Carmen, "latte?"

"Actually I'll take mine black, thanks."

Carmen didn't say anything, but I'm pretty sure I saw her exchange a rapid look with Lee, our resident fitness queen, who hails from the States and appears to have had her cycling shorts surgically attached. Then again, perhaps I was being paranoid. Hunger does that to me, and I had now been accompanied by hunger since Sunday. But I was doing so well that it was giving me a little buzz.

I sipped the hot black coffee and felt it swill around in my empty stomach. I was on a liquid diet. Slim-A-Soup. Coffee. Water. The occasional glass of V8 when the stomach juices went from choppy to storm force ten and needed quelling.

"Anyone do anything fun over the weekend?" asked Carmen, handing out the last custom-made coffee and sitting down.

Since no one had anything particularly interesting to say other than that they had performed the usual taxi and food service for our assorted children, I decided to tell my friends about Robert Duke. The Bea way. I built up the story with an exaggeration of pelmet-haired men with high waistbands and women with the hunting skills of a great white, and li'l ole me, sitting forlorn at the bar when Superman himself approached. I try to make my tales of tragic dating funny, though at the time they rarely are. I find a strange satisfaction in watching women I like walk away feeling that maybe their own monotony—sorry, monogamy—ain't such a bad thing, after all. I wouldn't want anyone to make the mistakes I did.

"So, after about five minutes, this dishy blond actually put his hand on my leg and leaned in close and personal and I was thinking, Wey hey, at last, I'm going to get some, when he slipped me his card and said . . . 'You're a great lady in bad shape. Wouldn't it be nice to be a bad lady in great shape!' Turned out he was a personal trainer fishing for business."

Chins dutifully dropped.

"Bastard," said Carmen.

"Poor thing," said Holly, my fellow nonworking mother of three.

"Good line, though," said Lee.

"What did you do?"

"I told him to get down and give me fifty to prove his mettle. For thirty quid an hour I wanted to know what I was getting," I said.

"What happened?"

"He only managed twenty-seven," I said, shrugging. "So I said, 'Honey, I may be desperate for an overhaul, but I don't think you're man enough for the job.' Next thing I knew he had his hand around some other lady's gluts, telling her how hard he could work them!"

"You should have reported him," said Lee, who, despite having lived in this country for years, still hadn't grasped the nation's sense of humor. Everyone laughed again.

Then Carmen said, "Is that why you're taking your coffee black?"

I sighed heavily. "He succeeded in sending me screaming to McDonald's. However, my mother's coming to town."

"Oh, no," said my friends.

I nodded sadly. "Oh, yes!"

ONE OF THE ONLY GOOD things about my divorce was that, due to serious financial constraints, I had moved into a tiny terraced house in Kentish Town. The drive to school wasn't too bad, but the best thing was that my mother couldn't come to stay. I would have taken the sofa, I often spend the night there accidentally, but she couldn't lower herself to our standards and preferred instead—oh, I shiver just thinking about the place—the Sloane Club. My world is so different from that of the Sloane Club that on the few occasions I find myself there, I'm startled all over again that such a place, such people, still exist. Apparently we're losing forty thousand species a year, a hundred and twenty a day. If there was ever a candidate for extinction, surely it was the Sloane Club member, with their coiffed hair, giant pearls, booming voices, and thick tweeds. But my mother loves it. She and I are chalk and cheese. I wonder whether I am only chalky because she isn't. I would have liked to ask my father, but he died before I realized I didn't have all the answers. I miss him now, though, and more than ever since I've been alone. I miss having a male in my life. I'd like to ask him whether Jimmy was a bad man or just a man. I'd like to ask him whether he'd been tempted to stray. I'd like to ask him whether sometimes he'd lie in bed and watch the outline of his sleeping spouse and hate her with a passion that scared him. I'd like to ask him whether my brother and I made a difference to his life. Whether we were worth the sacrifice.

My mother never remarried, more's the pity. She likes autonomy too much. I nearly didn't get divorced, because I couldn't face her inevitable "told you so." She never liked Jimmy. He didn't come from "good stock." What does that mean? His dad, Peter, began life climbing telegraph poles and ended regional manager at BT. Isn't that the sort of strong stock you want infusing your family soup? Isn't that a good base from which to start? My mother has never worked a day in her life.

Waiting in the car for the kids outside the school gate, early again, I put my fingertips to my forehead and felt the panes in my glass house creak. I had to get back to work. Thankfully, my moment of introspection was cut short by four fists hammering on the window.

"Mummy!" Maddy was always so delighted to see me that thoughts of work vanished. They piled into the car.

"I made these in cooking," said Lulu, holding forth a mass of twisted pastry in a wad of paper towels.

"Wow," I said. "What is it?"

"Cheese puffs for the party. Now you won't have to make everything." Lulu is a peach. Always thinking about others. She has many more traits of an eldest child than Amber. Amber is more like a typical youngest and Maddy, well, she's just cute.

"Brilliant. Thank you. Luke will be over the moon."

I handed around homemade hummus-and-pita-bread sandwiches, carrot sticks, and juice boxes. We always had to wait for Amber. The class times were staggered, so this corner of north London didn't come to a standstill, but she still managed to be the last. That girl sauntered through life to her own metronome.

Today, however, she surprised me by running out first. Amazing how the promise of Granny's cash could focus a clotheshorse's mind. Shopping trips to Harrods were quite the norm for some girls in Amber's class, but not for Amber. She was buzzing with excitement. We set off a happy foursome, and I allowed myself to banish the dread I'd been feeling all day.

My mother is a thin, statuesque woman. Where I get my stunted height from, I don't know. Another one for Dad, I guess. I think she wonders herself. I have often caught her looking at me with an expression that, as a child, I never understood. I do now. I sometimes find myself gazing at Amber with something like it. How could such a creature have come out of my womb? At fourteen she is taller than me. Her legs are longer than mine. Her hair is a deep dark red that reminds me of Rossetti's palette. That I created her mystifies me. It's almost the way my mother looks at me, but not quite. As I watch my offspring, I generally celebrate the miracle of the gene pool. My mother distrusts it. I do not do her justice. Whatever I do. So I gave up trying a long time ago.

"Mother," I said. Mother! Who says "Mother" these days, other than aged Hollywood types who still live with theirs? We kissed awkwardly.

"Hello, Belinda." She looked me up and down.

I would have liked to tell her about my diet, about my marches around the park while the girls were at school, that I'd already lost two pounds, but her expression silenced me. Instead, the sound of my name on her lips conjured up an image of a giant chocolate-chip cookie. I could have murdered for one now.

"Hello, girls. Are you ready to shop till you drop?"

They jumped up and down in grateful excitement. Make that two giant chocolate-chip cookies and a butterscotch malt to wash them down.

"I thought I'd take Amber first to the grown-up section. We'll come and meet you after a little browsing and see what you found in the young ladies' department. My dear friend Sally has a large changing room waiting for us on the fourth floor. Whatever you think you like, send it there to her. Any *decent* staff member will know her." At a little clap of her hands, we sprang into line. I brought up the rear. I'm sure my children were confused by my reticence. But they didn't understand the code. I knew what my mother meant by "decent"—she meant white. I had to physically hold back—otherwise I got dangerous.

Maddy and Lulu had a ball, and I forced myself to focus on that. I couldn't give them this memorable treat. Nor could Jimmy, though he tries. He'd never stopped trying. That was almost the worst thing. Maybe if he'd given up his dream and got a job, we wouldn't have ended up where we did. "If ifs and ands were pots and pans, there'd be no room for cheesecake." Stop it, Bea! I was on day five and doing well. No cheesecake, chocolate-chip cookie, or malted shake was going to pass my lips—I'd done too damn well.

Maddy passed me yet another bustling creation. I put it over my arm with the rest and we set off to find the others on the fourth floor. One of the price tags fell out on the way. I winced. I fed my family for a whole week on half of that. My mother, I suspected, wasn't parting with her long-sat-upon money just for the sake of my ex-brother-in-law's fortieth birthday party, to which she was most definitely not invited, but because it was her seventieth that year and she was taking us to some fancy night at the English National Opera. The dresses would suffice for both events. But, really, she liked the idea of the girls turning up at the dreadful "common" ex-in-laws looking like girls, in her mind, should. Velvet and ribbons and netting and petticoats and a thin string of freshwater pearls to finish the look.

Trying on the dresses, my girls did as I had never done. They squealed in excitement at every increasingly frou-frou creation. They twirled and skipped and danced, to Sally's and my mother's delight, and for a moment I was happy that, unlike me at their age, they weren't tugging self-consciously at the hem or the bodice, standing pigeon-toed and uncomfortable, longing to be skinned.

"And now it's Amber's turn," said my mother. She pulled back the curtain, and presented me with—

My jaw fell. Soft midnight blue satin clung to my daughter's alabaster skin and fell in a puddle on the floor. I had a sudden flashback to a happy family holiday in Wales when Amber was Maddy's age, maybe a little younger. We'd found a pool with a waterfall. Entirely free of inhibition, Amber had stood naked under the water and pretended she was a mermaid. Now, as she held her arms over her head, the dress created the same effect, though the cascading water had revealed less of her body than the satin did now. I swallowed hard. She spun around to the applause of her sisters, her hair fanning out, then falling about her neck like a scarf. The dress was practically backless.

"Oh, my," said Sally.

"Stunning," said my mother.

Over my dead body, thought I.

Amber could not take her eyes off her reflection. I knew what she was thinking. I'd always known what my eldest child was thinking, even when, like a psychic, I'd wanted to block out the noise. *West Side Story* had been one thing, but this—this Amber person who needed no stage or costume, was real power. We stared at each other in the mirror. She knew me too. That was why she looked away and, with a glint in her eye, beamed at my mother.

I relaxed. There was no way my mother would allow it. But the moment we could at last stand like comrades, she failed me again. "There's no doubt about it," she said, "you look magnificent. We'll need a stole, of course."

What? No!

Amber hugged her. "Oh, Granny, thank you."

Hey, I wanted to remonstrate, I wasn't saying, "No." I was saying, "Not yet." I was saying, "Wait a bit, it will all happen in due course and the sooner you start the sooner it will end and the rest of your life is a very long time." I had to think fast. "It's beautiful, darling, but at least give us the fun of trying on a few more. Like the scene in *Pretty Woman*." I hummed the opening bars. *Pretty Woman* was one of Amber's favorites.

"I do have some other wonderful gowns," said Sally. "Let's see what we can find."

Dresses came and went. Amber paraded around the room like a peacock in the kitten-heel shoes Sally had provided. She's like a young Kate Moss, I thought, in her childish briefs and white cotton bra. All leg and pout.

"And what about Mama?" said Sally, pulling another dress over Amber's head. "What is she going to wear to the ball?"

I waved my hands in protest, heat rising to my cheeks. "Today isn't about me. It's about my daughters."

"Well, you have to wear something," said my mother. She obviously didn't want my ex-in-laws thinking they'd got rid of bad rubbish, even if *she* thought that.

"I'll find something," I said. "Hey, Amber, what about trying this red velvet one on again? The black isn't so interesting."

"Your mother's right," said Sally. "I like the red best, too. Brings out the flames in your hair."

"Come on, Belinda, let me buy you something too. It'll be my treat."

"It's okay, Mother, you're doing more than enough."

"Don't be ridiculous. Sally, see what you can find for my daughter."

"Yes, madam." Sally retreated through the thick beige curtain that separated the large changing area from the fitting-room lobby.

"Honestly, it's far too late for this. It's way past their suppertime already."

"Darling, you can't always hide behind your children. You need something to wear, we're at a dress shop, Sally is the best, and if she can't find something for you no one can. End of discussion."

I bit my lip and savored the taste of blood.

"Come on, Mummy. We had a picnic in the car. It'll be fun," said Lulu. "She'll make you look like a princess too."

I smiled at my middle daughter and was thankful that my children, at least, did not see what I could no longer deny. Their mother had let herself go. Sally might be the best but even the best wasn't going to be good enough.

"Have you all chosen?" I said to the girls. Maddy and Lulu held on to their dresses like life rafts. Amber was wearing the red dress, but kept looking longingly at the blue. Not the blue, please, not the blue. Suddenly, Sally appeared through the curtain carrying four dresses of different lengths, color, and fabric. My chest constricted. "Why don't we take yours to the counter to wrap them up and give your mama a little space?" she said to the girls.

"Will you do a parade, Mummy?" asked Maddy. "We'll sit on the sofa outside and give you marks out of ten."

My heart thudded. I knew she meant the dresses, but it didn't feel that way. I could see three solemn faces holding up placards. Fat. Fatter. Fattest.

"When we've packed everything up," said Sally.

"Which one are you taking, Amber?" asked my mother, as if she were talking to an equal, not an impressionable, malleable, easily wounded fourteen-year-old.

Amber looked at Sally. "Well, you look wonderful in the blue, there's no doubt of that." My heart sank as Amber beamed. "But," Sally continued, "I think you should choose the red and I shall tell you why. You cannot wear underwear with the blue. That's fine in here. It's warm and you're standing still. But what about dancing, jumping up and down?" Amber didn't understand what Sally was implying. So Sally glanced down at her chest.

Amber reddened. The thought of unwanted attention to her not-yet-womanly womanly bits made her feel self-conscious. Not a bad thing right now. Vanity lost. For today. Amber chose the red.

As they filed out, I almost went with them, but Sally turned, stopped me, and drew the curtain in my face. I was left to face my demons alone. I had been avoiding my own reflection in the mirrors. Hard, since they were on three walls and angled at the corner to give you a perfect surround-sound view—but I had been good for five days, I was feeling a million times better, maybe I would be pleasantly surprised.

Feeling brave, I peeled off my awful stretchy black trousers and polo-neck. I threw my Gap T-shirt onto the pile and stared at the beige carpet. I took a deep breath and raised my head to see the new me. Immediately, I knew it was a mistake. I grabbed a dress from the rack and held it in front of me, but it was too late. I had seen myself, a mass army of myselves, waiting for battle. I was outnumbered by infinity to one. I was surrounded.

I held up the dress in surrender and let it fall to the floor. What beast is this? What sad, fat, ugly cow stared back at me? Five days hadn't made a dent. Nor would fifty. I didn't think five hundred could . . . I rapidly fell from whatever false peak I had been standing on as the first tremor of panic hit me like a breaker, winding me. I let out short, staccato breaths. I had no idea what invisible force had hit me so hard, and I looked around, frightened, searching the cubicle for my assailant. Turned out the assailant was me. Daring to look back at myself from the angle-poised mirror, I saw with every rutted pocket of fat how my bottom had bled into the back of my thighs. *Who are you? What are you doing here?* Boom. The air left me again. Scared, I pinched my sagging flesh hard until the pain made me inhale again. I held on to the wall. Something strange was erupting inside me, but I could not look away. A mottled sack of skin hung over my knickers and pulled a grotesque smile from above each buried hip. I flicked it. Then I blew out my stomach even more, hunched over, and flicked it again. "Blubber" was the word that came to mind. How could I have lived with myself, yet avoided myself for so long?

I faced myself again and saw the panic of a drowning person staring wide-eyed back at me. My heart was pounding. I couldn't breathe. The air had left me. Oxygen had deserted me. All I needed to do was inhale. I stared at myself. Inhale, you stupid fat cow! But I could no more fly. My heart screamed. My chest knotted like a gnarled tree, solid. Breathe! I yelled at myself. Please! *No.* I was going to die. *Good.* I was dying. My reflection shook its head at me, mouthing, "I can't breathe." BREATHE! *Pathetic.* I yelled at myself from deep inside. BREATHE! *Why?* "I can't." My face crumbled, my grotesque body folded, I stretched my jaw wider than it wanted to go and felt the skin tear at the side of my mouth. I screamed, as tears poured down my cheeks, I screamed and screamed and screamed. But not a sound came out.

"Mummy!" It was Maddy.

I straightened up. I could hear soft footsteps on the carpet and the rustle of her uniform. No, no, no, no, no . . .

"Which one are you in? Are you ready?"

As if someone had punctured a hole through my solar plexus, air refilled me. I held on to it. Terrified it might leave me again.

"Mummy?"

"Coming," I croaked, furiously rubbing away the tears, the fear. "In a minute," I said.

"Okay."

I staggered back and, in my graying bra, pants, and socks, slid down the mirrored wall and wrapped a bit of curtain around me. I put my head on my knees. I couldn't stop the tears. They kept slipping out of me. What was happening? The panic had only lessened its grip on me. Sporadically, it would give me a squeeze, just to let me know I wasn't alone. I couldn't get up. I gathered up the clothes and held on to them, as if they were one of Maddy's blankets. Soothed by the feel of satin lining on my cheek.

"Let's see you, then."

It was Mother. As soon as I heard her voice, I slammed my leg across the entrance to the changing room and clasped the curtain to the wall. I wasn't ready to let anyone in and I wasn't ready to leave. My mother must have sensed something, because she stopped just outside the curtain.

"Found anything you like?" she asked tentatively.

"Mother, could you do me a favor . . ."

"Are you all right, darling?"

Just keep breathing, I told myself, feeling my chin wobble. Just keep breathing. "I . . . need a few minutes."

"Well, okay, we'll be outside."

"No," I said, more emphatically than I meant to. "Could you take them to get something to eat? I think there's, um, a diner, isn't there? A café?"

"I'll take them to the restaurant upstairs next to where I get my hair done."

I closed my eyes. "Thank you."

"How long will you be?"

I don't know. I could feel my breath shortening again.

"Belinda?"

I felt my face scrunch up as I fought tears.

"Please let me buy you something nice."

From some deep memory of childbirth, I found a spot on the curtain rail to focus on and blew out long exhalations of air. I watched the curtain move. "God, Mum, just give me a moment."

"Honestly, Belinda, that's no way to speak to me. I've just spent a fortune on your children. And don't call me Mum!"

I curled up into a tighter ball and let the tears fall. It wasn't supposed to be like this. Who the fuck was the fat woman huddled on the floor, unable to stop crying? How had this happened? Where had I gone? Who had I become? Once upon a time, a long time ago in a land far, far away, I had been a catch . . .

I was bright, small, *slim,* and fit. I had black hair and weird pale-blue eyes. I was striking. Not a pinup in my teens—only eclectic boys like small, shapeless girls with dark hair—but by the end of university I had grown into myself. I possessed a certain force, an energy that attracted others, and I learned how to change other people's perception of me from weird to unusual to unique to special. I was so determined not to be the incapable woman my mother was that I threw myself at everything. Languages, cooking, sport, partying—I could stay out all night and still get up for lectures in the morning. I was the indefatigable Bea Frazier. When I graduated, people told me I could do anything and I believed them. I had blind faith that I would make it as a journalist, then an editor, and perhaps one day run a newspaper. The printed word, one subjective view versus another, life processed on the page . . . These were the things that consumed me.

I got a job working in the business sector of publishing. It might sound dull, but during the heady eighties it was far from it. I know Thatcher's Britain was reviled by many, but when tattooed market-traders with more street smarts than any public-school boy (and I met a lot in the City) were hitting the big time, I reveled in seeing the grout crumble on these thick class barriers I had always believed kept me locked in. Not protected, as my mother thought. While I wasn't doing it for the money, I soon realized it helped. Jimmy's projects were always in "development" and someone needed to pay the rent. Then the mortgage. Then the child care.

I heard movement outside my safety curtain. And tensed.

"Mum?" It was Amber.

I let out a silent sob. "Just coming, honey."

"You okay? Granny said you were having a fit."

I clenched my jaw and balled my fists, willing myself to pull it together. I stood up. "I just got a bit hot, that's all. I'm going to get dressed and I'll come and find you."

"Did you faint?"

"No, honey."

"Camilla didn't eat for five days and she fainted. Xanthe had called her fat, which she isn't. It was just stupid of her."

I should have reached out, grabbed my daughter, and hugged her to me, but I didn't. I was too busy concentrating on breathing.

"I told Granny you hated shopping. That's why you never go with the other mothers. But she said I was being silly."

The other mothers went shopping at Prada, but that wasn't the reason I didn't go. I didn't go because I wasn't asked.

"I'm sorry, Amber, I'll be out in a minute."

"You sure you don't want my help?"

I tried to sound light. "I'd prefer it if you protected your sisters from Granny."

"Okay." Amber didn't sound convinced.

I gathered every ounce of strength to leave the changing room. I got my T-shirt over my head, but while I was bending down to put on my trousers, the blood rushed to my feet. I held on to the wall, staring at my reflection, unsure who stared back. I couldn't go out there. I couldn't. Seconds later I was crouched on the floor again, hugging the curtain. That's the problem with indefatigable. There's no such thing. Somewhere, somehow, you pay.

I'd sworn I would never accept handouts from my mother, since I knew the interest repayments would be crippling. But things change when you have children. I put their needs ahead of my pride. When my mother offered to pay for Amber's education, which we could not afford, I accepted. I couldn't, however hard I ruminated, dissected, and kneaded my desire to decline, turn her down. It would not have been fair. Isn't that what being a parent is all about? Doing the best for your children? Even if it isn't the best for you?

I'd thought I'd always work. I'd thought Jimmy would earn a bit more eventually. I'd thought the couple of thousand pounds a term weren't unreachable, the debt didn't seem too deep. But what you do for one, you have to do for the others. I guess my mother won in the end. I am totally and utterly beholden to her now. What kind of job would I have to get to clear the thirty-three thousand pounds a year required for school fees and still find enough to feed, clothe, and house my children? Not one I'm qualified for, that's for certain.

"Bea?"

I lifted my head off my knees.

"Bea?"

You've got to be kidding. How long had I been sitting there? "Jimmy?"

"Can I come in? I don't think loitering outside women's changing rooms is a good idea."

I was so shocked to hear his voice that I forgot I couldn't move and scrambled around on all fours, gathering up my clothes.

"Bea?"

"No, you can't come in."

"Please. I'm worried about you."

"I'm not dressed," I said, clutching my clothes to me for protection.

"Nothing I haven't seen before."

"Not this much," I replied.

"That's enough of this nonsense. I'm coming in."

I couldn't have stopped him. It would have meant dropping my clothes. All I could do was look up at him from the floor. He drew the curtain behind him, crouched in front of me, and brushed aside a strand of my hair.

"Hello," he said.

I smiled weakly and let a tear plop over my eyelid. Jimmy removed his coat and placed it over me, like a blanket.

"What are you doing here?" I asked.

"It's not that chivalrous. I only work around the corner."

"I mean why."

"Amber called me. She said you wouldn't come out."

I frowned.

"Your mother was being a little less cautious with her words than she should have been. Amber was upset."

I sighed.

"What happened, Bea? Amber thinks you fainted."

I put my hand up to my heart. The pounding hadn't lessened much. "I think I had a panic attack." I couldn't recall the sensation of being unable to breathe, but I could still see myself in the mirror, screaming in silent panic because I couldn't. I shuddered.

My ex-husband put his arm around me and I let myself lean into him. "What did she do this time?"

"Amber's been lovely."

"Your mother."

"Nothing. It wasn't that."

"Bea, it's always that."

My mother. The convenient excuse we both used. "I'm just like her. I don't do anything of value."

"You couldn't be more different."

"I don't work."

"You're doing the most valuable job in the world."

I scoffed. "Hardly."

"You're developing the next generation. Somebody needs to. And you do it effortlessly, generously, imaginatively. Brilliantly, in fact."

"I don't feel very brilliant. In fact, right now I feel pretty repugnant. The three-way mirror didn't help."

"Ssh, you're beautiful."

"No, Jimmy. I'm not."

"You are. To us."

"I'm a fat cow."

"Stop it. God, Bea, okay, so you've a few extra pounds—"

I laughed harshly.

"It's because you take on so much. If you didn't eat, you wouldn't be able to stand, let alone look after our children, help everybody all the time, and pick up my slack."

I nearly protested, but changed my mind.

"Which I know you do, so don't protest."

I exhaled shakily.

"It's not important enough for this," said Jimmy. "Pounds you can lose—"

"But not my sanity?"

"It's not worth it."

My rational self knew that, of course it did, but the monster would rear up, roar, and awaken all my insecurities. And I would feed it. It was the most demanding of all my babies and the one I had never been able to get into a routine.

"You know, Bea, you can get fit again, if you want to. It's bloody boring but you could." I must have looked pained, because he added, "You don't have to. You look great as you are."

I raised an eyebrow.

"Okay, maybe not right now."

I laughed weakly.

"But when you smile you do."

I tried to remember what it felt like to smile. Really smile, I mean, rather than out of politeness. I couldn't.

"I, for one, would like to see more of that smile."

What was he saying? "I've become so dull, haven't I?"

"We can change that. There was a time when you were up for anything."

"A long time ago." I paused. To hell with it, what did I have to lose? "When I had you."

Jimmy tightened his grip around me. "No, Bea, you never needed me for support. It was always the other way around."

Here I was, seminaked on a changing-room floor, confessing things I didn't realize I felt to the man I had divorced. "I do now."

"That's why I'm here. And I always will be."

Desire threw a grenade into my gut and the vice around my chest lessened its grip. "I wish we'd had chats like this when we were married," I said.

Jimmy was quiet for a while and I was afraid I'd overstepped the mark. "We did. In the beginning."

I exhaled a long breath, and was grateful when the inhalation followed. Breathing. What a strange thing to be so conscious of. What a foolish thing to take for granted.

"Do you think you can manage to get up?" he asked.

I nodded, though I was reluctant to leave his hold.

"All right. Well, let's stick your mother in a cab and I'll drive you guys home."

"Thanks, sweet pea," I said. It was only when he looked at the floor that I realized I'd called him by the old term of endearment, the one I reserved for my children, the one that wasn't appropriate anymore . . . maybe it could become appropriate again.

HE PUT HIS ARM AROUND my shoulder defensively, manhandled my mother into a cab—that was enough reason to love the man—then got into the driver's seat of my car and drove us home. At a red light, I looked at my ex-husband, then back at our three girls, and took my first easy breath since I'd been left with my reflection in the changing room. That was when it hit me. What had been very bad had seemed only half as bad the moment Jimmy had arrived. And the shitty drive back through rush-hour traffic with Amber playing the latest inappropriate girl-band CD at full volume, teaching Maddy and Lulu inappropriate words, didn't seem bad at all. Usually it got me baring my teeth.

"'Waving me tush smack at ya!'" chorused the little ones. Jimmy and I laughed.

* * *

INSTEAD OF LEAVING JUST BEFORE the girls reared up at the homework-reading-teeth-cleaning triple jump, which I alone had to coax them over every night, Jimmy stayed. Again. More than that, he put me in front of the telly with a glass of wine and took over. So this was what it felt like to be supported. When all was quiet on the western front, he made me a delicious, nutritious Slim-A-Soup with extra crudités.

"Promise me you won't skip meals again."

I nodded.

"You scared me," he said.

"I scared myself."

"How are you feeling now?"

"This is helping." I was pretty certain he knew I didn't mean the soup. "Thank you."

He smiled at me. "You seem to have got some color in your cheeks at least."

We were definitely not talking about food.

Four

You Do Something to Me

I COULDN'T GET HIM OUT OF MY HEAD. EVERY MORNING I WOKE UP and knew I'd been thinking about him in my sleep. I stared at the place where he used to lie and wondered where on earth he'd gone. I tried to tell myself the diet was making me feel so light on my toes, but I knew it was something else. I denied it was happening at first, because it was (a) so ridiculous and (b) so quick. But the fact of the matter was that Jimmy consumed my every waking thought. I took mundane chores in my stride, since they were perfect opportunities to daydream. He called me every few days to see how I was doing, and we'd have lovely friendly conversations. I had to remind myself not to get too flirty.

A couple of days before Luke's party, I was making and freezing a zillion cheese straws when the doorbell rang. It was 11:32 a.m. I nearly didn't open it, because 11:32 meant carpetbaggers, chuggers, Hari Krishnas, or bailiffs. But I was finding it easier to look on the bright side of life, so I went to the door.

A courier in a big black helmet stood squeaking in leathers on my doorstep. I would have been alarmed, except he seemed to be offering me a large Harrods bag. Stapled to it was a white envelope with my name on it. I signed. I had recognized the handwriting immediately. Was one of my increasingly erotic fantasies going to play out? The one with the evening dress and the invite to dinner and me playing the dish? Didn't matter how my fantasies began, they ended the same. Me shuddering with the feel of a man entering me. I'm sorry if it sounds perverse but, my God, this was something I needed. And not just any man. My man. Jimmy. My stomach lurched with wanton desire. No wonder the pounds were falling off me. How could I eat when I had a swarm of butterflies in my belly?

I took the bag through to the sitting room and pulled off the envelope. With a shaking hand, I drew out the note.

Darling Bea,

I know how much you hate shopping. So I've done it for you. You shall go to the ball.

All I ask is save one dance for me.

Love, Jimmy.

P.S. I am so proud of you. We all are.

I held up the Diane von Furstenberg dress. It was a midnight blue silk jersey knee-length wrap dress with a swirling ivory pattern. It looked tiny. I sighed. It would have to stretch some to cover me. I returned to my cheese straws, reluctant to ruin my happy mood with another disastrous trying-on session.

But eventually curiosity got the better of me and I took the dress upstairs. I put my best bra on, took off my knickers—nothing like seeing elastic cut a ravine through flesh to get a girl running to the fridge—and slipped it on. I couldn't believe how well it suited me. The wrap hid a multitude of sins, the cleavage distracted from the rest, and the material floated over my bottom in a way that made me think more of "Jell-O on springs" Marilyn Monroe and less of Harvey Fierstein. I ran to the loo. The top half looked okay. I jumped up and down to get a better look. It was no good. I needed full-length satisfaction.

Scraping back a mound of dirty clothes, I prized open Amber's bedroom door and, having slipped on some very high heels, opened her wardrobe. The color was perfect. It made my hair look blacker and my eyes more blue. But it was more than the color. It was the cut. The shape. The fit. Actually, it was even more than that. It was me. I looked . . . I caught my reflection in the mirror and smiled. I looked . . . okay. I looked okay! I turned to look at my bum. The swirling pattern confused the eye so much even that didn't look too bad. I turned back grinning and did a celebratory jump. Oh, my God . . . I really looked okay!

I tried to ring Jimmy, but he was in a meeting, so I sent him a text. "Thank you. Thank you. Thank you. Thank you. Thank you. Thank you. Thank you. Thank you. X." A couple of hours later I got one back. "You're welcome. Glad you like it. See you Saturday. XX." Two kisses. Two kisses! What was happening here?

After that it was easy not to eat, and by Saturday night the dress looked even better than okay.

When I came down the stairs, I was greeted by shocked silence. It saddened me that I'd allowed myself to look so shitty for so long that my daughters were rendered speechless by my improved appearance, and made me happy that I was finding my way back. I had the fire of a recent convert in my belly, and knew that, as sure as sugar lows follow chocolate highs, trans-animal fats would never pass my lips again. Finally Amber spoke: "Wow, Mum, you look *superlative!*"

"And you look stunning yourself," I replied. "All three of you do. I simply don't know how I made three such brilliant, clever, wonderful daughters. Now, let's show them how to party!"

One of the best bits of the evening was sitting in the black cab heading back to Bush Hall. Amber took out of her handbag an old compact of mine and we all checked our reflections, then touched up our lipstick. Even Maddy had been allowed to wear a little clear lip gloss, and I thought, again, how lucky I was to have daughters with whom I could share the wonders of womanhood. I know girls are tricky and complex, conniving and multifaceted, but, hey, I wouldn't have it any other way. It's why we're the interesting, contradictory creatures we are. And I, for one, felt like celebrating that. Neurotic? Damn right we're neurotic! It means we're thinking.

I skipped up the steps to the hall with my daughters behind me and knew, for the first time in a long time, that the appraising, admiring glances were not reserved entirely for them. As a group, we looked good, my redheaded daughters and I. There was only one thing missing, and we'd have looked perfect.

Almost half of the guests were already there, and we were bang on time. A nod to Luke and Faith. They're a lovely couple who, despite having had their fair share of troubles, work like machines, raise a child, and always have time for everyone else. They make it seem easy. And I know it ain't. Faith rocked in a white-leather skintight trouser suit that made me think of Pattie Boyd. Charlie, their five-year-old son, was in jeans and a baseball jacket with "Daddy" and "40" sewn on the back. As soon as the girls saw him, they were off, ushering him around like a miniature prizefighter.

Forty minutes later and two glasses of champagne down, Jimmy hadn't arrived. My youngest ex-sister-in-law, Lucy—the woman who allegedly sees auras and spends her life puncturing the depressed with needles—touched my arm. "Don't worry, he's coming. I was going to pick him up, but he said a meeting had overrun."

"On Saturday?" I asked.

She shrugged. "You look the best I've seen you look in ages," she said.

"It was about time."

"I wasn't saying that. Have you met someone?"

"Lucy!"

"What? It's been four years since you separated. You are allowed, you know."

"I haven't."

"Well, you're going to soon, looking like that. Mark my words." Lucy laughed. Hope so, I thought, scanning the room again. "Oh, look, there's Mum and Dad," she said. "And, hey, Jimmy's with them."

My heart did a little cha cha cha, then went off like a Catherine wheel. He was here. He walked up the stairs behind his parents, patting down some tufts of wet hair that weren't behaving. He was untucked, disheveled, and pink in the face. He'd been running. Hopeless creature. Did I care? No. I loved him more because he hadn't changed a bit and that was the way I wanted him to be. My Jimmy. The man I'd been with for nearly twenty years. Minus the last four. But what was that? A drop in the ocean. The blink of an eye. A second in time. But how did it feel to him?

Honor and Peter embraced me warmly and told me how well I looked and that the girls were stunning. I smiled, but I wanted to get past them to Jimmy. He grabbed a couple of drinks for his parents, then passed one to me. An electric shock went through my hand as he touched it. I was sure he'd felt it too. We smiled coyly at each other. I knew I should eat something before having another drink. After three weeks' abstinence, the champagne had gone straight to my head, but it tasted so good I couldn't resist.

"You're beautiful, Bea," he said.

"Thanks to you. I don't know how you did it."

"Did what?" asked Honor. She may have been dressed for polite society, but her ears remained naked, always.

"Jimmy chose this dress for me," I said.

Honor looked from me to her son. "Did he?"

"Well, Bea kind of had her hands full, and I work right next to the shop." I knew he was covering up, protecting his mother from worry. But she didn't have to worry. Not this time.

"Why are you so out of breath?" said Honor.

"Squash," said Jimmy.

I frowned. "Lucy said you were in a meeting."

"Then squash. That's why I'm so late. More drinks, anyone?" We shook our heads. Our glasses were full.

As Jimmy went off in search of a drinks tray, I heard silver on glass.

Faith had climbed onto a chair and was persistently tapping her glass with a spoon, pleading for hush. A ripple of applause and quiet cheers went through the room. "I was going to do this later, when everyone was sitting down and eating, but I can feel myself getting too pissed too quickly, and no one wants a drunk woman rambling on about how blessed she feels to have the man she does, the son she does, and the life she does. It would just get embarrassing as I howled about how much Luke means to me, all the tiny things he does for me that make me love him more every day. And who would believe it, coming from an inebriated mess? So I stand before you now, semi-sober, to raise a glass, which will be followed by many more, to Luke—my beloved husband. Happy birthday, my darling. I hope you know as you look around this room how very loved you are, and how very loved you deserve to be. You are a great, great guy and, not to dis the weaker sex, there aren't many of you out there."

There was a moan of disapproval from the gentlemen in the room, but it was lighthearted: everyone knew Faith.

She held up her hand. "Present company excepted." She laughed, then put her hand on her heart. "I love you, and not just for taking an old lady off the shelf."

Luke stepped up to her, lifted her down, and kissed her. It wasn't very passionate, because they were both laughing, but it was wonderful to see. Charlie ran up and squeezed between their legs, wanting in on the action, but he was kept waiting. Sometimes you had to put your other half before your offspring. Faith and Luke were good at that. I looked at Jimmy, who was watching his brother with a beatific smile.

As if sensing my stare, he turned to me. The smile fell away. It's okay, I wanted to shout. I'm going to make it all better. I promise. You'll see.

I WAS DELIGHTED TO SEE my food disappearing within minutes of being brought out by the serving staff. And when dinner was announced, no one rushed off in search of sustenance. Which meant the bar area remained packed with nicely pissed happy people. It was only when the champagne ran out that people trickled downstairs to where food and wine were being served.

Honor stood resplendent behind the table—she had covered her beautiful purple velvet trouser suit with an apron of a busty naked wench in garters. "What—this old thing?" she kept saying, with a wicked smile, to anyone who mentioned it.

Peter's apron depicted a buttoned-up member of the Household Cavalry. He winked at me as he handed me a plate of food. Later they swapped aprons. Another clue, I thought. The ability to laugh at each other without causing offense. A very tricky thing to do.

Dinner was a relaxed, sit-where-you-like affair. The girls and I had been at the hall in the afternoon, decorating the table with twists of ivy from Honor and Peter's garden and tea lights bought en masse from IKEA. Maddy and Lulu had suggested hurling glitter over the waxy green leaves, and now, in the candlelight, the tables looked as if fairies had danced on them. But the best was yet to come.

Emboldened by weight loss and alcohol, I put my plate next to Jimmy's and sat down. I was about to ask him if he wanted to join us some time over the weekend and do something as a family, when Faith appeared. She'd been working the room and sticking to her promise to consume nothing but champagne (she obviously had a secret stash, which I made a mental note to raid) and was in flying form. She was followed by Lucy.

"Hey, Jimbean, do you know what a superstar Bea's been? The food, the tables, keeping me sane . . . I tell you, the woman could be an MP the number of plates she spins. And you turn up late, looking like you've been dragged through a hedge, without so much as a gift!"

"But clean at least," he said. "And the gift is a surprise."

"I'll bet. Where have you been recently? We haven't seen you for months."

"Working," he replied. "Loved your speech."

"Whatever you do, don't let me near the mic, even if you have to rip it out of my hands. I feel a terrible gush coming on. Isn't he amazing, though?" Faith was grinning inanely.

"Amazing," mimicked Lucy. "We've always congratulated ourselves on how lucky we are to have such an amazing brother."

Luke joined us. "Quite right too." He kissed Jimmy. "All right, mate?"

"Couldn't be better. A great party."

"A great party? You guys are all huddled up with family. Shouldn't you be circulating?"

"With a family as good as this one, why go anywhere else?" I said.

"Hear, hear," said Faith.

"Except you did," said Lucy.

"Lucy!" exclaimed Jimmy.

"Didn't get very far, though, did I?" I said, laughing it off. Lucy had always been the most ardent defender of the clan. I didn't see Jimmy give her a stern look, but I guessed he had, because Lucy didn't say any more. Not that it usually put her off. Spoke her mind, did our Lucy, regardless of consequence. It was admirable directed at others, and extremely uncomfortable directed at me. But tonight was not a night for discomfort. Tonight was a night to dance.

About half an hour after Charlie had pushed into the room a trolley with a huge cake with forty burning candles, the grown-ups at last had a chance to dance off their sugar high. As the band came on, Jimmy sought me out.

"Ladies and gentlemen," said the dishy lead singer, "we would like to ask a very special lady onto the stage. Faith and Luke, if you wouldn't mind taking your place on the dance floor . . ."

They seemed confused. I could tell this wasn't part of the program, not Faith's anyway, and it certainly wasn't something I'd known about, but Jimmy was smiling. The siblings were up to something. I heard the first bars of "You Do Something to Me" by Paul Weller, and the entire room let out a communal "Aaah." It was the song Luke had played to Faith when he proposed. It was the song that summed up everything about them. But it wasn't sung by the lead singer. He had stood back and a woman's voice filled the room.

At first I was confused. Who was singing so beautifully? Moments before the spotlight picked her out, I knew. Amber.

Faith and Luke stopped dancing and clapped madly, then everyone crammed onto the dance floor, joined by Honor and Peter. Jimmy held out his hand to me and, without taking my eyes off my daughter, I allowed myself to be guided to the floor. I was nervous. We'd stopped dancing a long time ago.

We fell quickly into our routine. He spun me toward him, then turned me away. He put his hand on my waist and I encircled him. We wove in and out of each other's arms without a bump. It was as if we'd danced only the day before, and every day before that. I only realized that Amber had stopped singing when everyone else started whooping, clapping, and yelling for more. Jimmy and I clapped and whooped louder than all of them. Amber stood on the stage, the mic in her hand, beaming. I had a million questions.

"How did you know she was going to do that?"

"We've been rehearsing. It was a surprise."

"Why didn't you tell me?"

"It was a surprise," Jimmy said again.

"But she didn't say a word."

"She thought she might lose her nerve and didn't want to let you down."

The clapping was not abating. "I hope you rehearsed an encore," I said, laughing over the din.

"We did," said Jimmy.

The band started playing again. "Sorry, Luke," said Amber. "But this one is for my mum and dad."

"It's for you, really," said Jimmy. "I wanted you to know what a great lady we all think you are." Amber started singing "Son of a Preacher Man," one of my all-time favorite songs—well, at least in the top fifty. I looked at Jimmy, the only boy who ever did reach me. I took a step toward him, but we were surrounded by Lulu and Maddy, clamoring to join us. Jimmy and I split and took a daughter each as our eldest sang like a pro to a crowd of a hundred.

That was what I meant when I said the best was yet to come. I couldn't remember ever being so happy. I couldn't remember ever feeling so complete. I couldn't remember ever feeling so loved.

When she finished, Amber took several more bows. Then, slipping back into her fourteen-year-old skin, she jumped off the stage and ran to us. The lead singer launched into a rowdy rendition of "Carwash." I stepped back a bit to catch my breath and watched Jimmy and his girls dance together, my heart bursting with love.

Eventually I had to sit down. The trouble with killer heels is that they kill. Blood had ceased to circulate in my toes, and the balls of my feet seemed to have been stripped of cushioning. Every step hit bone. I was happy to watch my family cavort around the dance floor.

"What's going on, Bea?" asked Lucy, pulling up a chair beside me.

"What do you mean?"

"Come on, Doe Eyes, you can't fool me. What's going on?"

"Lucy, can you turn your witching eye on someone else for once?"

"No. Not when my brother's sanity is at stake."

I decided to assume that this conversation was lighthearted banter, though the sudden rise in my blood pressure warned me otherwise. "That's a bit dramatic."

"Is it?"

"We were just dancing."

"You weren't *just* doing anything."

I pulled a you're-not-being-serious face, which she returned deadpan. We both turned to the dance floor. Jimmy was laughing with the girls. When they saw we were watching, they blew kisses in our direction. All four of them.

"You'd better be sure about this, Bea."

"Look, Lucy, Jimmy and I are big enough and ugly enough to work out our own shit. All right?"

"Not all right, because that's a bloody lie and you know it."

I exhaled dramatically.

"Don't do that, Bea. We all know what happened," she said.

No. No, you don't.

"Shall I refresh your memory—"

I put up my hand to stop her, but Lucy is Lucy.

"You broke his heart, you took his kids, you decided life with no one was better than life with him. Now you turn up looking like this, dance with him like that . . . Just because what? You've changed your mind? You're bored? Well, get a job. It's not fair, Bea. It's not fair to him."

Outraged, I opened my mouth to retaliate. "I . . . How . . . If you . . ."

When I was lying on my own in bed, imagining a new future, it had seemed so clear. I could defend the indefensible, I could justify my actions—hell, I could spin them better than any Labour Party flunky and make them seem like salvation rather than the destruction they had been. But under the cool, knowing eyes of my ex-sister-in-law, I faltered. I lost my nerve. I was back in the dock. Guilty as charged. "Lucy, things happened that you don't—"

Jimmy joined us, red in the face from being outdanced by much younger partners. "What are you two gassing about?"

I stood up. "Take my seat," I said. "I need to pee." I shot Lucy an imploring look and escaped to the sanctuary of the ladies' loo.

That was where Faith found me, twenty minutes later.

"You okay, honey?"

I was sitting on the loo with my head in my hands.

"Too much booze?" she asked knowingly.

I looked up at her through my fingers and immediately all mockery left her voice. She crouched next to me. "Jesus, what's wrong?"

I shook my head slowly.

"What? What is it?"

"I don't want to do this here. You should be dancing."

"Shut up, you arse. A party isn't a party without some drama in the ladies' loo. What happened?"

"It's Jimmy . . ."

Faith waited for me to elaborate. I wasn't sure I could. Something that had seemed so easy to reverse in my mind was impossible to say out loud. "I think . . . I think I might . . ."

"Like him again?" said Faith, finishing my sentence.

I clutched my head. "Oh, my God, that sounds mad, doesn't it, after everything that happened?"

"Not really. He's a great guy who happens to be the father of your children and was the love of your life."

"Lucy all but warned me off the notion."

"Well, she would. She had to pick up the pieces the first time. We all did."

I could hear the cogs in my brain grind. "But you were all so nice to me."

I guess Faith was pissed, her tongue loosened by alcohol.

"We were ready to lynch you, honey. Pitchforks at dawn."

"What?"

"You can't be that surprised."

"No one said a word to me!"

"Oh Jimbean, we weren't allowed to."

"Huh?"

"It was Jimmy! *He* insisted we didn't take sides. *He* made us swear we wouldn't freeze you out."

Freeze me out? They were going to freeze me out? My best friends? "Literally, on pain of fucking death. He said it was for the sake of the girls, but we guessed why he wanted us to keep it sweet."

I continued to stare at her with my mouth open. You have to understand that the support of my ex-in-laws had given me the courage of my convictions. They saw my side. They must have, or there would have been revolution. To think they wanted to freeze me out, take sides, *his* side . . .

"He hoped you'd change your mind and everything would go back to how it was," said Faith. I got off the loo. "I thought you knew that."

I shook my head again. "Oh, my God, Faith, I've made a terrible mistake."

Faith broke into such a huge smile it nearly knocked me over. "At last! So put it right!"

I laughed, wary that someone as loved-up as Faith might have a skewed view of the capacity of other people's hearts. Surely it wasn't as easy as that. "You think he still loves me?"

"Sweetie, he's never stopped. Bea, it's only ever been you."

The air left me again, but this time in a good way.

"Oh, Faith, when we danced, I just . . . and I think about him all the time. God, I want to rip his clothes off." I was laughing now. "When did he get so handsome?"

"He's always been handsome—not quite as dishy as mine, of course, but not bad."

"I feel like a teenager. God, Faith, I want him all the time."

Faith eased up on the joviality stick. "There was a time when you couldn't stand him touching you."

"I wasn't myself," I replied, not wanting to think of such things.

"And now?"

"How do I look to you?"

She didn't answer, because one of her godchildren had come in.

"You be careful," she said, as we walked out. "And I don't just mean for your sake. I haven't seen him so happy for years. He's only just got his shit together, so you'd better be sure. And I mean fucking sure." No problem. I was. Absolutely fucking sure.

So the plan was this. Monday night, Jolen. Tuesday night, hair tint. Wednesday night, tell my ex-husband I still loved him and wanted him back. Easy. What could possibly go wrong?

I laid out my beauty products before me. Jolen. Tweezers. Face scrub and pack. Dye to cover the gray. I was going to be up all night. I stared at my reflection. The lines didn't bother me so much. There weren't that many. I didn't need to inject fat into my crow's-feet; cream puffs worked just as well. Lines I would welcome once I'd climbed out of this fat suit. I listened carefully to the silence of the house, and when I was sure it was deep enough, I opened the jar of hair bleach. I didn't want to have to explain myself to the kids, especially not Amber. Not yet, anyway. I was sure they'd be happy to see Jimmy and me back together again. Well, almost sure. Almost nearly sure.

I had just finished plucking my right eyebrow when the doorbell made me jump. "Ow!" I rubbed the tender skin near my temple. There was no way I was answering it. I had a thick smear of bleach cream over my upper lip, one bushy eyebrow to tame and a plastic bag over my head. The doorbell rang again.

Shit. I went to the intercom.

"Hello?"

"Bea, it's—"

"Jimmy! What are you doing here?"

"I was just passing."

"It's ten o'clock."

"I really wanted to speak to—" I held my breath—"you."

My mind raced. I could buzz him in, do the other eyebrow, take off the bleach . . . but what about the red mark it left? Makeup! Of course, but I hadn't worn makeup for— God, my hair!

"Bea?"

"Yes?"

"Is this a bad time?"

I was desperate to let him in. "I'm sorry," I said truthfully.

"No, no. I should have called."

"Wednesday would be better." How could I wait that long? Bloody Jolen. Bloody aging process. Bloody hell.

"Okay. Wednesday, then. I'll see you Wednesday."

"Great. I look forward to it."

"Me too. 'Night, Bea."

"'Night, Jimmy." I love you. Soon, I thought, replacing the door-phone. Soon.

I WAS A JITTERBUG BY Wednesday. Another two pounds had fallen away in two days, spent on nothing but emotional energy. I was whizzing. Couldn't sit down. I had the energy of a twenty-year-old. My mood was effervescent. My libido was off the scale. Jim and Bean were to be reunited and my girls would have their father back. It would be the happy ending I'd always planned. The happy ending I'd ruined.

Finally I heard Amber's key in the lock. I bounded up from the kitchen table and raced down the hallway. Who cared if I seemed desperate? I was desperate. Desperate to have my family back together again.

I kissed and hugged the girls, then, full of gay abandon, kissed and hugged Jimmy. He looked really happy to see me, if a little nervous. So to put his mind at rest, I was as easy and relaxed with him as I'd been long ago. There's nothing to worry about, I whispered silently in my head. If you can forgive me, I can forgive myself, and all this will be behind us.

I let Lulu off the dreaded reading and did Maddy's homework for her while they ate supper, then practically frog-marched the children to bed. There were no complaints, because they knew Daddy was stay-ing for a while, not running off at meltdown point. So there was no meltdown. I wondered happily, as I watched the younger two brush their teeth, whether with Jimmy back at home meltdowns would be a thing of the past. Not completely, but vastly reduced. The girls missed their father. That was why they got upset when he left. It was my fault and I would rectify it.

I looked at my watch. Almost lights-off time. As we pulled the younger girls' bedroom door nearly closed and kissed Amber good-night—she was allowed her light on for another hour but had to stay in her room—my heart was playing Pac-Man in my chest.

Downstairs in the kitchen I allowed myself to open a bottle of wine. Since I reckoned I'd expended those calories in just the last few min-utes, I wasn't worried. And I needed something to settle my nerves. I poured out two glasses and handed one to Jimmy. He raised it to me and drank—quite a lot, I noticed. We were both nervous.

"Thanks for sticking around. It does make life easier and I've got something to tell you," I said.

"So have I, Bea. I've got something to tell *you*." Suddenly he seemed so excited, so keen, that I relaxed. I had read the signs right. Those last slow dances we'd had as the party ended had meant to him what they'd meant to me. We should be together. Starting now.

"Well, you first," I said, relishing this newly discovered bliss.

"I've met someone."

"I know. Me too . . . Um, what? Sorry." I swallowed hard.

"That's great. Who?"

"Wait. What? Start again. You've met . . ." I willed something different to come out of Jimmy's mouth.

"Oh, Bea, she's fantastic. I know you two will be friends."

I doubted that.

"I didn't think it was possible, you know how I . . . Anyway, she's just wonderful and I feel blessed. She fell into my life. I'd thought, Never again, right? You don't get it twice! But, Bea, she's so funny and strong, and intelligent."

"How old is she?"

Jimmy laughed. "That's your first question? She's twenty-two and she comes from Latvia."

"You've got to be kidding!"

"Yes, Bea, I'm kidding. I wouldn't do that to you."

I don't care if she's fifty-six and comes from Bournemouth—you bloody are!

"She's thirty-eight and, Bea . . ." He paused. My stomach lurched. "I want to marry her."

The muscles in my jaw collapsed.

"I know, I know, a man of my age but, my God—"

"Is she pregnant?"

"Bea!"

"Sorry . . . This is all a bit sudden." That's a fucking understatement! Marriage! Be civil, Bea, be civil. Your only way out of this is civility. It won't last and you'll be there to pick up the pieces.

"What does she do?"

"She works for a record company."

Oh, Christ. She's cool.

"The girls adore her."

Record company. All skinny jeans and pumps. "What?" This time I couldn't disguise the frown. "The girls have met her?"

"Not really, I mean, no, I mean—"

"Jimmy, either the girls have met her or they haven't."

"Not knowingly, is what I mean."

I heard my voice harden. It brought back a million miserable memories. "How many times have they not knowingly met her?" The charade. The fucking bullshit charade! The deals, the scripts, the long nights entertaining those ever-thirsty creative types. All bullshit. Years of it.

"Twice, a few times, hardly at all . . ."

"They've hardly met her but they adore her?" Cold. Hard. Steel gripped my heart and stole my voice. Rein it in, I pleaded with myself, but I couldn't. Mess with me, don't mess with my children. They are mine.

"You've been telling me to get out there," said Jimmy.

I lied.

"I'm really . . . Obviously I'm a bit shocked but, er, but, um, I'm pleased for you." Every word stuck in my throat. I wanted to lean over the table and grab him by the collar and scream in his face, "Don't fuck this up! We have a chance of making this right!"

"Thanks, Bea. You'll love her. A real girl's girl."

I very much doubted that. On both counts. The wine bottle was emptying faster than I could recall drinking it. I swallowed a mouthful. "You should have told me before the girls met her."

"It wasn't planned, I promise."

I didn't care. I wanted something to hang him on, them on. Her on. "How much have the children been exposed to her?"

Jimmy laughed. "You make her sound like a disease."

You said it!

"Sorry." What was I apologizing for?

"They've never been alone together. We just bump into each other in the park sometimes."

"She has kids?"

"No. Never been married."

Oh, pure . . . How sweet. Untainted. No fucking stretch marks. Bitch. I swallowed back the hate-filled words with more wine.

"But she's great with kids."

I smiled with gritted teeth. Until the ring is on her finger. Haven't you read the stories? Cinderella! Snow White! I must remember to dig those old books out. Late thirties. Still time to breed. She'll present you with a shiny new baby. God, a boy! Next thing, she'll have our girls packed off to boarding school and sleeping in the kitchen during the holidays!

"Thank you for being so pleased for me."

Was I still smiling? Inconceivable! The dog whistle was blasting an alarm to wake the dead, yet he believed my smile. Had ignored my tone, more like. He was always good at that.

"I thought it might be odd telling you, but we've been getting on so well lately, the mates I always hoped we'd become once, well, you know. I've felt so close to you. We've been having such great, honest chats . . ."

That was enough. I couldn't take any more. All those things I'd been saying, which I'd thought so obvious, had passed him by. I'd been having a one-sided romance in my head. I feigned a wide yawn and stretched out my arms for good measure. Seemed he could read that message.

"You're tired. I'd better go." Jimmy stood up. So I stood up. He walked around the table to hug me. It broke my heart.

"Hey, you haven't told me about your new—"

"Another time," I said.

"There are no secrets between us." The temperature dropped a couple of degrees. I had to get him out of the house now. Before I did something really awful and made his statement true. "At least tell me his name?"

"It's not serious, Jimmy."

"Okay." Jimmy smiled at me, the same beatific smile I'd seen at Luke's fortieth. I knew then, as sure as I would eat a packet of Hobnobs the moment the front door shut, that when Jimmy had been listening to Faith's speech about Luke, his mind had been on a thirtysomething record producer with no stretch marks and a skinny arse. Not, as I had thought, on me. Stands to reason. Why would he have been thinking about me? Who the hell was I kidding? Look at me!

"You didn't ask her name." He had turned back, halfway down the path.

Because I don't want her to have one, I thought. "I forgot in all the excitement."

He seemed to be waiting for something.

"Um, what's her name?"

He broke into another smile. "Tessa King," he said.

So? What was he smiling about? That wasn't such a great name. "How lovely."

"She is. I can't wait for you to meet her."

I waved him off with a smile that tore my cheeks, then shut the door and drifted into the kitchen. I opened the cupboard door like a robot and removed the packet of chocolate Hobnobs my children adored. In turmoil, I sat at the kitchen table while my family drifted into deep, peaceful sleep. I was too late to make it up to them. Too damn late.

I stared at the packet, turning it round and round in my hand. A tear splashed onto the cheap pine; I wiped away its successor angrily. I couldn't fool myself anymore. The biscuits weren't going to help me. If I ate them, I was beaten . . . And I wasn't ready to be beaten yet. I had three children to think of. Our DNA was intertwined in them. I had twenty years in the bag. I was the Bean in Jimbean. Another tear fell, then another. Tessa King? Tessa King? I poured myself more wine and let the tears spill out of me. Who the hell was this Superwoman, Tessa King?

Five

Enter the Dragon

MY FINGERS WERE TAPPING MY THIGH, AND WHEN I SLAPPED MY HAND down hard to make them stop, my foot took over. Nervous energy ran through me like acid on sheet metal. My insides fizzed. James was somewhere in Kentish Town, telling his ex-wife about me and thereby making me "official." I didn't know if I was excited or petrified.

A passing waiter refilled my glass. I looked at my watch. He was half an hour late. I drank. Half an hour . . . Was that good? Or bad? Would I be welcomed into the fold? Or banished to Siberia? James had never said much about the failure of his marriage, except that Bea had left him. More than that I hadn't wanted to know. As far as I could tell, it was a pretty good separation, and I knew he saw his beloved girls as often as he could. All he'd said was that he'd never expected to fall in love like this again, and he felt blessed. What was the point in raking over old ground once a man had said that to you? What had been had been. What would be was ours to discover. It hadn't been my intention to fall in love with a divorced man who was pushing fifty, had salt-and-pepper hair and three children. One a teenager, for God's sake. But I had. He'd made it impossible not to. Once he'd relented, of course, and finally taken my calls.

I sensed him moments before I felt the blast of fresh air around my feet. James removed his coat, handed it to a waiter, and, beaming, joined me at the table. It was good news, I could tell from his face.

"Hello, gorgeous," he said, leaning down and kissing my collarbone.

The touch of his lips sent a shockwave to my rude bits. I shuddered, grabbed him around the neck, and pulled him down for another kiss. He fell forward and sank into a crouch. "How did it go?"

"Great," he said, eyes locked on mine.

"Really?" I was shocked by how relieved I was to hear the words.

"I told you," he said, running his hand over my head, through my hair, over my cheek.

I leaned into it. "I thought she'd want you back." This was true. But I hadn't realized it until he'd walked into the restaurant with a smile.

James laughed. "No."

"I would."

"I'd prefer it if you simply never let me go."

I took his face in my hands. "Never."

"I love you, Tessa King." He was shaking his head, as if flabbergasted by his own good fortune. "I really, really do."

I'd spent my life reading crappy novels about people falling in love, and hurling them across my bathroom (preferred reading location) in fury as another grateful maiden's heart skipped a beat. But when James looked at me like that, and spoke to me like that, my heart—dear God, they'd been right all along—skipped a beat. I leaned forward and kissed him gently on the lips. "Good," I said. "That makes it even."

He groaned, getting up. I decided to take it as a sign of intense longing rather than an aging arthritic knee. He sat down opposite, and immediately cleared a path through the glasses and carnations to hold my hands. For a moment we sat there looking at each other. It felt like the most normal thing in the world, to stare at someone's face and get lost in it. But I knew it wasn't normal. I knew I was very, very lucky. And to think I'd come within a whisper of ruining the whole thing.

It will go down in *Schott's Almanac* as one of the most disastrous dates. Ever. It had started well. Dinner. Cocktails. Nonstop chat.

Kissing . . . Oh, the kissing. A hotel (my idea). A bath (his). A lot more kissing. Some soap. Quite a long time being dried. And finally, at dawn, sex that felt as natural as skinny-dipping. And later the next day waiting for him to return to the cocoon of excitement, desire, and a freshly made bed. Then the dreaded phone call from a "friend" to warn me that the man I felt I'd just shown my soul to was married with kids. I had been played. Life was a bit of a trial back then, and to me James was the honest judge my case had been missing. When I heard he was just another adulterous womanizer, I surrendered. Beaten. It wasn't as if I was a novice.

I knew life wasn't fair, because if it were, my mother wouldn't have MS. I knew life wasn't fair, because my friend Claudia, the most maternal woman I knew, couldn't have children. I knew. What I didn't know was that the devil played with loaded dice. He threw bad news onto bad luck onto bad timing, which usually resulted in some seriously bad judgment. That sort of onslaught leaves a person feeling they're being singled out, self-pity turns to anger, and anger causes mayhem. Well, hearing James was married was one bit of bad news too many. A switch tripped in my psyche. I left the hotel and any hope of a happy ending behind me.

Apart from a couple of disastrous dates while he and Bea were separated, James later told me, he hadn't slept with anyone since the divorce had come through. He'd been as bowled over by the night as I'd been and had rushed back to the hotel after his last meeting, thinking about nothing other than the feel of my skin on his. Anxious to discover whether what had happened had been a one-off or, as he hoped, that something extraordinary was taking place, he had let himself into our room only to find it empty. He said he told himself I'd popped out for coffee, but he knew I hadn't, because there wasn't a note. And if I was the girl he'd thought I was, I would have left one. And he was right. He called and called until he had to face the fact that I had bolted.

Then he saw all my extras on the hotel bill. And the last vestiges of concern for my safety (he could only assume that something must have happened to me or someone in my family) were annihilated. I was a nutter. Pure and simple. A nasty little money-grabbing one at that. He vowed I would be wiped from his memory. But the trouble was, over the following weeks, I kept creeping back into his thoughts. There were days, he had told me, when he had wanted to read about a body being discovered, or an exposé that the hotel was drugging its guests and selling them to the sex-slave market. Anything to excuse my behavior. But eventually he discovered I was alive and well. Well, alive, anyway.

"What are you thinking about?" asked James now.

"How terrifyingly close I came to losing you." That was the weird thing about my relationship with him. When we finally did see each other again and everything was explained, some silent pact was forged between us. Honesty was essential. Lives had been ruined because of misunderstandings. Mine would have been. I was never going to feel like this about anyone else. That I knew. I wouldn't have known what I was missing out on. I hoped I would've made the best of it, but now that I'd felt it . . . A hot tear prickled my eyelid. Stupid girl, I thought, wiping it away. The only terrible thing about loving someone so much was how scared you felt at the thought of losing them. I was as vulnerable as a newborn, yet safer than I ever had been.

"You okay?" he asked.

I nodded. "I love you."

He smiled.

"So, tell me what happened," I said, pulling myself together. "I want every detail."

"Let's order first." James let go of my hand and picked up the menu. Now that he was here, and my nerves had relinquished their octopus hold on my stomach, I was ravenous. I went for two courses with every intention of tucking into some cheesecake for dessert. When the waiter left to fetch another bottle of wine, I leaned in for the blow-by-blow.

"How was your day?" he asked. "Didn't you have a big signing?"

"Don't change the subject. Come on, I want to know."

"Nothing to tell."

"James!"

"Okay, okay. We put the kids to bed. It was all very nice. Then we went downstairs, had a glass of wine, chatted a bit. Bea told me she'd met someone, which I thought had happened, because—"

"She wouldn't let you in on Monday."

"Yeah. I figured she didn't want to tell me over the intercom."

"Who is it?"

"We didn't get that far, because I started blathering on about you and how wonderful you are."

I sat back in my chair. "And she really didn't mind?"

"Of course not."

"You said she was in a bad way, though, when you couldn't meet me at the theater because you had to go to Harrods." I'd been pissed off at the time. I'd booked the tickets ages ago.

James shifted uncomfortably.

"That was different. I didn't want to tell you, because, I don't know, it feels . . . well, Amber asked me not to tell anyone. But Bea hadn't been eating. She's trying to lose a bit of weight, not that she needs to—well, maybe she does a bit, but she beats herself up about it and I wish she wouldn't, because it makes it worse. Anyway, she looks great now. Really great. Amazing willpower she has." Okay, that was probably enough of the amazing Bea. "She was meeting her mother, who she doesn't have the best relationship with—"

"That's sad."

"She never liked me."

"Stupid dragon."

"And they'd been shopping for hours for Luke's fortieth . . ."

Luke's birthday party had been the event that had precipitated my "coming out." James had wanted to take me, and if I were honest, my categorical refusal to entertain the idea hadn't even been skin-deep. I was desperate to go. But even I knew that turning up unannounced at a family party was a bad idea. He needed to do this right for the girls, and that meant doing it right by their mother. My decency was entirely Machiavellian. My future was at stake.

". . . It was probably about money. Apparently, she wouldn't come out. Basically, Bea fainted or something like that and it scared her. Scared me too."

"Why do they argue about money?" I asked, trying to fill in the bits where I hadn't been listening.

James grimaced. "It's complicated."

"Okay." I waited a second, but he didn't elaborate. So I changed the subject. To me. "Did she want to know anything about me?"

"'Course. She asked masses of questions. What you do, whether you'd met the girls, how old you were."

"Sounds more like an interrogation."

"Now you're being ridiculous."

"Sorry. You didn't tell her I'd met the girls?"

"Only in passing."

"Good. It would have freaked her out if she knew we'd been to the zoo and things."

James tore open a packet of breadsticks. "I didn't go into details."

"She'd think we'd been cavorting behind her back."

"Tessa, she's not like that." He was laughing at me. "Honestly, she's a straight-up lady. Funny, kind, and the best mother in the world—though, of course, she's too modest to accept a compliment. She grows her own vegetables, for God's sake. You'll like her," he said.

He sounded so sure. Why did I feel that pinch of doubt?

WE WENT TO BED AND for once my mind didn't turn to sex. I had eaten far too much, so my belly was distended and uncomfortable. All I could do was lie next to him and groan. That crap about women wasting away with love was a big fat myth. Along with all the others peddled during our lifetime about handsome princes and happily ever afters. I'd done nothing but eat since I'd got together with James, and it was wreaking havoc on my waistline. Luckily, the amount of horizontal jogging I was doing was just about keeping the scales in check.

In the beginning, I feared I was confusing lust with love, but because James had the kids a lot, there were long weekends and half-terms when I didn't see him at all. After they went to bed, he'd call me and we'd talk long into the night. There had been some nights when I just lay with the phone next to my ear and listened to him breathe. On others, I'd writhe around with longing as he told me the things he would have done had he been there. And one night I got into my Mini, drove over to Hampstead, sneaked up to his room, made mad, silent, passionate love, then left again. But the thought of his kids waking up scared the shit out of me, so we never did it again. Now I wouldn't have to. James was going to tell the girls about me and then, well ... we'd see what happened next. But I had a fairly good idea.

"James?" I whispered in the dark, an hour or so later. There was no reply. "James?" I said, a little louder. Nothing. I prodded him.

"Huh?"

"You awake?"

"No."

"Did she break your heart?"

I felt him deflate and regretted the question. But I had been lying awake, thinking. He had never pretended he hadn't felt like this before. I was glad. I was glad that he was the sort of man to marry a woman he truly loved. And I knew she'd left him. What worried me suddenly was not the thought of Bea wanting James back now that I was on the scene, but James wanting Bea back because someone else was.

"Tessa, do you remember I told you when we first had lunch that we wouldn't go over old relationships?"

"Yes. I thought it was because you were hiding a wife and two kids."

"Three."

"I only knew about the younger two."

"I remember. Lainy and Martha and a wife called Barbara."

"I was misinformed," I said.

"Horribly, as it turned out."

I reached over, found his hand, and squeezed it. Neither of us enjoyed going over that ground. The stench of my bad behavior could have polluted the most fragrant moment.

"My wife left me and took my kids. I wouldn't say I was jumping for joy." I felt him prop himself up and could see his faint outline in the dark. His hair was all over the place, like it was in the morning. He looked like Shaggy from *Scooby-Doo* before he'd showered. Maybe I didn't want this conversation, after all.

"The truth is, I'm ashamed to say I didn't realize things had got as bad as they had," said James. "I certainly never thought we'd split up. I suppose I naively thought that three children were enough to keep us together. But when she took the girls to her mother's house, I knew things were critical. She'd rather starve than accept charity from her mother. She wouldn't go there because she wanted to. She'd only go there because she had no alternative. Apparently, I was no alternative."

"But why?" I asked, sitting up too.

"I don't know."

"You didn't ask?"

"'Course I bloody asked."

"Sorry."

We slipped into silence. I watched the room's furniture slowly take shape as my eyes got accustomed to the dark.

"This is why I hate talking about these things," said James tensely. "People are always banging on about needing to understand the past so you can create a better future. Bollocks. The past just gets in the way. Yes she broke my heart. For a while I thought I'd been decapitated, widowed. I looked after Amber every day until she went to school. Suddenly she wasn't there. None of them were. It was hell."

"I didn't know that," I said, liking the thought of him and his toddler at playgroups.

"That's why we're so phenomenally close."

I didn't know you were, I thought, as the warm image cooled. "What about your work?"

"I could work around her. Bea had a fantastic job in the City. It would have been madness for her to leave, since I was around."

So Bea had a fantastic job, was the best mother in the world, and grew her own vegetables. I realized, suddenly, that James was right. Talking about these things was dangerous. Between knowing your enemy and blissful ignorance, I think I'd prefer to remain ignorant. Except . . . No. Stop it now. "I'm sorry I asked. 'Night, my love."

I thought James would be grateful for the out, throw the duvet back over himself, and drift off, but he didn't. I felt the first rumbles of fear in my belly as he started to speak. "I've heard my friends talk about their ex-wives and I find it really offensive," said James quietly. "I don't want to have to say, 'Bea was this, or that, or the other,' to justify why our marriage failed. Bea is actually an extraordinary person and I loved her. I loved the woman I was married to, but, Tessa," he turned to face me, "you have to understand this. I'm no longer married. I can't give you an easy answer to your question about why our marriage failed, except that Bea had two children very close together at a time when I was away a lot, doing a job I didn't like. Marriage doesn't survive on tidbits."

"What do you mean?" I asked.

He sighed. "I've thought about this a lot. You need to feed a marriage, Tessa."

"What, three-course meals?"

"Exactly. Day in, day out, and five courses on the days you feel like takeout."

I had married friends who'd been kind enough to take the sheen off the illusion. "I know it isn't easy."

"Sounds like a drag, doesn't it?"

"Sounds like a challenge," I replied challengingly. "I like challenges."

He put up his hand and found my cheek. "I should have known you'd be great about this. I was afraid you'd go off me if we ever had this chat."

"Go off you for loving your wife?" I shook my head. "No. It just confirms that you're the man I think you are. Cheating on your wife, stumbling into marriage by accident, simply existing on automatic pilot, going through the motions while more and more children were born . . ." I sighed. "If you'd said that, I might have gone off you."

The words were worthy enough but, hell, I wasn't so naive that I couldn't see the detestable-ex-wife had some merits.

"You are my life now, Tessa. You and the girls. All I want is to make you happy. Seeing that smile on your face, I don't need anything else. When I make you laugh, I feel ten feet tall. Just being able to reach out and touch your leg makes me feel complete. I love you and you never, ever have to doubt that."

That helped . . . and I watched the green-eyed monster slink back into the shadows. James slipped down the headboard and lay in my lap. I stroked his hair.

"I know I keep saying this, Tessa, but I feel blessed. I can't believe you exist. I think you were made for me." He kissed the top of my thigh.

"James?" I said.

"Hmm?"

"I'm not feeling quite so full anymore."

He turned to look up at me.

"Other way," I said.

"Yes, ma'am."

I WAS LATE TO WORK. Cycling from my flat in Victoria to Fulham Palace Road is one thing, a fabulous ride along the river, but from the deepest, darkest burbs of Hampstead is another, and I always underestimate how long it'll take. I bolted my bike to a spare bit of steel and knew I was going to get into trouble for caging in two other bikes. People thought I had such a glamorous job, record-company lawyer, first-name terms with all the artists, but mostly I sat around and read very, very small print with very, very long words, and the more I knew about our yard of celebrities, the less impressed I was.

They come in so keen and grateful. A couple of hits, and it's amazing how quickly the gratitude wears off. The older acts are the best to hang out with. They're the pros. They're the people who still say thank-you to the sandwich guy, and the makeup girl, and the lawyer. They're the ones who realize it's a game of luck. And they got bloody lucky.

I pushed open the door to the meeting room and took my seat with the bigwigs. I was backup in this case, otherwise I would never have been late. I made a quick apology and opened my enormous file. One of the side effects of a legal career was good biceps. I carried half the rain forest everywhere I went.

I was partially concentrating on what was being said, but the better part of my brain was trying to envisage the best way for James to tell his girls there was a new woman in his life. I had "bumped into" Lulu and Maddy a couple of times in Regent's Park, with Cora, my eight-year-old goddaughter. The perfect foil. I didn't want the girls going home talking about Tessa this and Tessa that before we were sure we were going to last.

They didn't even know my name. It hadn't been an important enough fact for them to "save," and it was discarded from their memory at the end of any of our meetings. There were many more interesting facts for my name to compete with. Like the fact that frozen boogers were crunchy, and Mia Turner was going to be ten even though she was in year whatever, and all the other gobbledygook I overheard in the playground. I thought the zoo was a risky decision, but the animals won hands down and, once again, out of sight, out of mind. Cora was their focus. Not me. But that was going to change. James wanted me to move in.

"What did you say?" asked Matt, my wonderful assistant, over soup and a roll.

I shrugged. "That I was flattered."

He rolled his eyes.

"I am. It's just . . ."

"Your apartment is so much nicer."

"That's not it."

"You're not ready for suburbia?"

I was about to answer when Linda, the doyenne of the company, approached. She'd broken more acts onto the market than any other producer, partied with the hardest, and had a couple of marriages under her belt before changing tack and moving in with Sylvia, her assistant. The very first case I'd had to fight for the company was against a band Linda had brought up from nothing to superstar status: they ran off with another record company. Not uncommon. But Linda owned the backlist and they'd gone ahead with a new version of their greatest hits, arguing that the revised sound was different enough not to belong to the backlist. We won. It was worth a stack of cash, and Linda had taken me under her wing. Every other word of hers was an expletive. "You're not going sodding anywhere, sweet pea, until there's a fucking ring on your finger. I don't give a fuck about the vows, but you wanna protect your sodding rights. You hear me, girl?"

Loud and clear, Linda. "It's not really about the—"

"'Course it fucking is. Don't be naive, darling. You want to be his children's lackey, on best behavior for eternity because you don't have the right to lay down any rules? And trust me, one weekend in, you'll be washing the dirty pans, cooking the fish fingers, and picking the peas out of your hair that they've thrown at you when your back's turned." It was sweet of her to share her thoughts with the rest of the cafeteria. "And, whatever you do, keep your fucking finances separate."

"I honestly don't think we're going to have a problem," I said. "They're friends, him and his ex. It's not like he walked out on them after some torrid affair that went wrong. In fact, she left him."

"Why? What did he do?"

"Nothing."

Linda raised an eyebrow.

I wanted to end the conversation. "You don't understand. This is a good divorce. There isn't any acrimony. I'm not going to be a problem," I said, more emphatically than I felt.

"Like hell you're not! She hasn't seen you yet. Presumably, you're younger?"

"Yes, but—"

"And he has daughters?"

"So?"

She leaned over the table. "Darling, you're going to wish she was dead."

"Linda!"

"I take it back. Sod the ring. Find someone with no kids. I've often caught Sue in Accounts checking you out."

"Thanks, but—"

"Hey, don't knock it till you've tried it. Take my advice, darling. Run for the fucking hills."

I smiled as though I was grateful for her wisdom and watched as she flung herself out of the room, but inside I was seething. Why was everyone so negative all the time?

"Let me guess? Linda's ex-stepchildren don't send Christmas cards," said Matt, grinning over his sandwich.

"My God, that's depressing," I said.

"Linda a stepmother? I feel more sorry for the children."

"I meant her attitude. Does everybody hate their stepmother?"

"I do," said Matt helpfully. "She told my father that my *homosexuality*—just the way she says it makes me shiver—was purely a rebellion against his naval past."

I was relieved at the change of subject. "Silly woman. Of course it isn't."

Matt gave me a cheeky smile. "Of course it is. But it isn't her place to go saying such things."

I frowned.

"Stepmothers," said Matt, shrugging, "they can't win."

"Thank you so very much."

"Best to go in with your eyes open."

"God! He only asked me to move in, not marry him. I don't think I have to worry about becoming a wicked stepmother just yet."

"Wrong again. It's all you should be thinking about. Plan now. Plot, scheme, bribe, suck up, buy off, undermine the parent. That's essential. Divide and conquer. Basically, do whatever you have to do . . . but get the brats on-side."

"They're not brats," I said, trying to claw my way back to the funny side of this conversation.

Matt took a large bite of bread and chewed. "Not yet, they aren't."

"No, really. The girls are great."

"One's fourteen, right?"

I nodded.

"Batten down the hatches. You're in for one hell of a storm."

That was enough. Sod Matt and Linda, with their shitty, negative, polluting thoughts. James Kent was the best thing that had ever happened to me, especially because he hadn't come at a high price. I hadn't broken up a marriage. He hadn't left his wife and children for me. He'd been single for *four years*. This had nothing to do with me. Maddy and Lulu were great kids. He was great with them. I had seen it with my own eyes. I didn't know Amber, because I hadn't met her. But I would. And she couldn't be so different from her sisters. James had nothing but good to say about her. I couldn't wait to meet her. I took a mouthful of soup, but it had gone cold. Suddenly I had no appetite for the bawdy cafeteria and took myself back to the sanctity of corporate law.

A WEEK LATER, THE CHOSEN Saturday arrived, and we were blessed with a prematurely spring day. James had taken his daughters out to breakfast and explained that he had a special friend he wanted to introduce to them. We had decided to meet in the park again. That way it wouldn't feel like an interview; the younger ones could play and Amber and I could chat while James went and got hot chocolate for everyone. Something like that, anyway. We tried not to overplan it.

I had changed seven times before I left my flat, and felt physically sick when the text came through and I had to leave the café I was waiting in. I checked my bag again. Everything was there. I wasn't going to sink to Matt's level of bribery and corruption, but it didn't hurt to have a few essentials, just in case. As well as the contents of my handbag, I had brought along my secret weapon.

"You're very quiet, Godmummy T," said Cora.

"Sorry."

"Normally you never stop talking."

"Coming from you, chatterbox."

"Mrs. Bloom calls me that."

"Mrs. Bloom?"

"My new form teacher. I'm in year four now, remember?"

"'Course you are. How did you get so big?"

"Green beans," she said seriously, then broke into a smile. "Hey, there's Maddy and Lulu." She slipped her hand out of mine. Cora's extraordinary. She can meet someone in the park once, then see them again a year later and tell me exactly what happened at their previous meeting, what was discussed, where they lived, and what they were wearing.

"Hi, everyone," I said, a smile scorched onto my face—do not show them you are afraid, do not show them you are afraid. "I'm Tessa."

"They know that," said Cora. "Silly."

Maddy and Lulu hovered beside each other and, for a moment, they looked like twins. I felt a fleeting sympathy for Bea. Amber stood next to her father. I put out my hand. "How do you do, Amber? You look just like your dad. Except far more beautiful." That sounded rehearsed, but it wasn't. Amber really was staggering to look at. A combination of Kate Moss and Lily Cole. I couldn't believe she was fourteen.

"Oi," said James, doing a jaunty model turn, "I'm not that bad."

"Daddy!" said Amber, embarrassed, but she giggled when he put his arm around her. For a terrible moment, I wanted to rip them apart, but it was so fleeting I thought I must have imagined it. Right. It was time to deal.

"I'm not sure you'd look as good as she does in those leggings. They're great, by the way. Where did you get them?"

"Top Shop."

Straight in with three of a kind! "Top Shop? You're kidding. I've just been given a gift certificate from there. I'm never going to use it." I reached inside my bag, flicked past the Monsoon envelope, the Jigsaw,

Gap, and Next (I'd thought the latter unlikely, but I'd wanted to cover all bases), and brought out the Top Shop one.

Amber opened it. "Wow, fifty quid!"

"Is it? It was free. I never looked. Have it. I insist."

"Are you sure?" asked James. "I thought you liked Top Shop."

"I do. I love it. But I'm too busy to go in the week and too old to go on the weekend. Anyway, nothing I'd find there would look as good on me as it would on your daughter."

Amber beamed. And, rather annoyingly, so did James. Divide and conquer. Divide and conquer. I dealt again. "We used their clothes for a photo shoot with the Bonne Belles—"

"The Bonne Belles! I love them!" Amber squealed, and I thought, Yes, she is fourteen, after all.

"You like the Bonne Belles?"

"Love, love, love them," she said, then burst into song. "'Smack ya tush back at ya!'"

"That's not bad, better than the Bonne Belles themselves."

She shrugged shyly.

"Didn't I tell you Amber had an amazing voice?" said James.

"Oh, Daddy."

Yes, several times, I thought coolly.

"Tessa works with those girls all the time," said James.

"Wow! What do you do?"

"I'm a lawyer for a record company."

"Cool."

A straight flush fanned out before my eyes. "Would you like their new album?"

Amber looked at her father.

"As long as I don't have to listen to that rubbish."

"It's not rubbish," I said, rolling my eyes at him.

"Yeah, Dad, it's not rubbish. Anyway, it hasn't even come out yet."

"I can get you a copy next week."

"Really? That's fab!"

"I could probably get my hands on a few more, if you wanted some for your mates."

"Yes, please!"

Make that a royal flush. Always important to leave them wanting more. I noticed from the corner of my eye that Maddy and Lulu had crept forward during this discussion and were now running in and out of our legs with Cora, playing some odd game where they pretended to be puppies. Plot, scheme, bribe, suck up, buy off, undermine the parent. I didn't know what Matt was talking about. I folded the cards. The table was mine.

Six

Enter the Beast

I'D HAD A MULTITUDE OF WEEKENDS WITH JAMES, AND AN EQUAL AMOUNT without. What I'd never done before was share him. Two weeks after meeting Amber in the park, I faced the prospect of our first official sleepover. I'd grossly underestimated how hard that was going to be. I had naively assumed it would be much the same as our weekends together, but with the addition of the kids. Delusional is the word.

Like all good horror films, the weekend started normally enough. I'd had a busy time at work and it was after ten on Friday night when I finally arrived at James's flat. All was quiet. We shared a bottle of wine, ate a salad, and went to bed. Within seconds, James was asleep and I willed myself to follow suit. But I couldn't. I kept thinking about the three other bodies asleep nearby and found it unnerving. James had gone in to kiss his sleeping children good night, but I hadn't. It felt as if I was intruding. It reminded me of the night I had driven over there with a crazy lust in my pants, desperate for the feeling of James on top of me, in me, attacking him with an urgency that was really quite unbecoming.

I looked at him. Asleep. I knew that with one kiss my desire for him would flare up again, but that crazy lust? I couldn't imagine taking such a foolhardy risk now. The damage we would have caused if we'd been caught didn't bear thinking about. I turned to face the wall, my back to James. But that didn't feel very comfortable either. I molded myself to his body, put my arm over his waist, and waited for sleep.

Several long minutes later, I heard a door open and some feet pad along the corridor. The handle on our bedroom door slowly started to turn. I hid under the covers. This was when the film turned scary.

"Daddy," came a whisper through the dark and duck down of the duvet.

James lay still, undisturbed.

"Daddy."

I prodded his back.

"Herumph."

"Can I have a glass of water?"

I was beginning to overheat. For God's sake, get the girl some water. I prodded James again. Actually, it was more like a stab.

"What?" He sat up.

"Can I have a glass of water?"

"Oh, Maddy, there's one by your bed."

"No, there isn't. You always forget."

I heard an irritable sigh escape James's lips. "No, I didn't. You just didn't look. As usual." James threw back the cover. I withdrew into a tighter ball. He seemed to have forgotten I was there and padded out after his daughter. Next I saw a light go on, heard a tap being turned and a glass being filled. Maddy was right. He had forgotten the water. A few minutes later, he was back in bed and I was safely out in the open air.

"Everything all right?" I whispered.

"Fine," James grunted, and fell straight back to sleep.

I WORK HARD AND PLAY hard. On weekends, I rest. I thought that was pretty normal. Respect the Sabbath and all that. So why was the light on when it was still dark outside? I squeezed my eyes shut and burrowed into the duvet. Where were my eye masks? Then I remembered. Eye masks had been surrendered in pursuit of sexiness. James didn't know about my vast collection under the bed at my curtainless home. I was still missing a few of the Baltic republics, but I had most of the world's airlines covered. Anyone who traveled far afield would bring me back eye masks and ear plugs, and I revered them as if they'd picked up a pot of duty-free Crème de la Mer. James emerged from the bathroom—a shower behind a stud wall—in his dressing gown, looking, for once, his age. I peered at him through one eye.

"Ugh."

"Morning, beautiful girl."

"Ugh," I said again.

James kissed my head, then walked out of the room. "Morning, girls!" he shouted.

"Morning, Daddy!" came the chorus.

"Are you coming in?"

Shit. Shit. I looked around in a panic and spotted an old T-shirt lying by the laundry basket. "James," I hissed.

He put his head back around the door. I pointed at the T-shirt.

"That's filthy."

"I don't care. Chuck it to me."

"You look lovely as you are," he said, laughing.

I gave him the finger.

"Charming."

"Petrified!"

"They love you."

"Not naked."

"I love you naked."

"You're a dirty old man," I said, and flashed him.

James laughed. "Hard not to be, with you around."

I had just pulled the T-shirt over my head when Maddy, the youngest and—not that I'm allowed to think such things—my favorite so far, came bounding into the room with Lulu. They leaped onto the bed.

"Okay," said James. "What's it to be?"

"Marmite," said Lulu.

"Jam," said Maddy.

"Chocolate spread," said Amber, from the doorway. She sauntered into the room and the hairs on the back of my neck stood up. Enter the beast. In every scary movie a lurking presence taunts you from the shadows. You haven't seen it, but you know from the rustle in the fallen leaves and the snap of branches that it's never very far away. It is the beast that has you peering through your fingers, wanting it to come yet dreading its arrival. Amber was wearing one of her father's T-shirts too. And she looked good. Better than me. Please, I prayed silently, please, don't let me be jealous of a fourteen-year-old girl. My father had told me—along with things like life isn't fair—that there was no more wasted emotion than jealousy. I had carried that with me my entire life but, my God, I couldn't take my eyes off her legs. Grrrr.

"Right. And for you, my darling?"

The only person who didn't look toward James was me.

"Tessa?" asked James.

I noticed Amber's chin lift and I was reminded of Grace Kelly in *High Society*. She would be that beautiful. Lord, give me strength. "Sorry?"

"What do you want on your toast?" asked Maddy, climbing over the bed to sit next to me.

"Toast?"

"Daddy lets us have breakfast in bed at his house. He says he doesn't mind sleeping in our crumbs."

"Maybe Tessa feels differently," said Amber, sounding like my old headmistress.

"You sweet girl," said James. "Always thinking about others." Hmmm, thought I. Grrrrrr.

"Maybe she's like the princess and the pea, and the smallest crumb will make her black-and-blue," said Maddy.

"Maybe she shouldn't sleep in Daddy's bed, then," said Lulu.

Isn't it about time I was going?

"Nonsense. Tessa is staying right there. In fact"—Oh, no. He paused, looking at each of them in turn—"I've asked her to move in with us. What do you think, girls?"

Maddy and Lulu were smiling, but I realized they had no idea what they were smiling about or why.

James turned to Amber. As did her sisters.

"Have you told Mummy?" she asked.

"Yes," said James.

"Hey, James," I said, interrupting, "I was wondering whether I could take the girls to Cora's ninth birthday party."

"You'd have to check with Mummy," said Amber.

Mummy, Mummy, Mummy. I hadn't expected the fourteen-year-old to be the Mummy's girl. "Of course," I said.

"How many godchildren do you have?" she asked.

"Four," I said proudly.

"Do people feel sorry for you because you've got no children?" said Lulu.

"Lulu!" said James.

"That's what Mum says," explained Amber.

Okay. "Who are your godparents? Your mum and dad's greatest friends, I'm sure."

The girls looked to James. Oh dear. Did godparents get divided up too? "We didn't pick very well," said James. "We don't see them much."

Right. Okay. "Why don't I go and make that toast?" I said, moving to the edge of the bed, then realized I couldn't. The T-shirt wasn't that long and it was bunched up around my waist. "James, could you pass me a dressing gown?" I asked, trying to sound calm and nonchalant and not as if a boa constrictor had me around the gullet. He peeled off his and threw it to me. I did the best I could at putting it on and pulling it down as I stood up, but I was pretty sure the girls got a flash of buttock cheeks, because Lulu sniggered.

Feeling more aware of myself than I had at my first disco, I walked out of the bedroom. Marmite, jam, and chocolate spread. Marmite, jam, and chocolate spread. If I kept thinking about condiments, I might be able to block out the small voice that was singing to me, in the evil whisper of Rumpelstiltskin, "Banish Cinders to the Hearth" from behind a large oval mirror. What was it with all these fairy-tale metaphors? One hour with the children and I was turning into the Brothers Grimm, hardly the kings of happy endings. Marmite, jam, and chocolate spread.

THE MORNING WAS SALVAGED BY devotion to a James and the Giant Peach coloring book and endless rounds of Guess Who?—the game in which, by process of elimination, you work out what character the other person has. This seemed to be Lulu's favorite thing to do, but I soon learned that her brain processed information differently from others. So when I said "No" to "Do they wear glasses?" she would put down all the characters who boasted twenty-twenty vision. This meant I kept winning, though I tried valiantly to lose. The sweet thing was that she didn't seem to mind. She just wanted to play again, and again, and again. I heard the door slam and was thankful that my replacement had returned from a rather long newsagent run with Amber.

"Sorry," shouted James. "We stopped for coffee." I assumed he meant he'd stopped to pick some up, and happily awaited mine.

"Again?" asked Lulu.

"Why don't we ask your daddy to play?"

Lulu didn't seem hopeful. James put his head around the door. "Everyone happy?"

"Great," I said, trying to convey otherwise and desperate for caffeine. "It's your turn to play Guess Who?"

"Hang on," said James. "Let me put the shopping away." And he disappeared into the kitchen. Ten minutes later, no large latte with an extra shot and sugar had appeared and I could hear them still chatting. Which meant he'd stopped for coffee with Amber. Grrrrrrrrrr.

"Claire?" said Lulu.

I didn't have the heart to tell her I was looking at a boy. "Nearly," I said. "Sally."

"Oh, Sally. I like her. Again?"

Shoot me.

"James!"

No answer.

"What about something we can all play?" I said brightly.

Lulu looked at Maddy, then shook her head.

"Amber always cheats," said Maddy, by way of explanation, returning to her coloring.

"What do you normally do on weekends?"

"With Mummy we do arts and crafts, or make cakes—"

"Or build time machines," said Maddy, interrupting.

I was sorry I asked. "What about with Daddy?"

"We watch telly," they said in unison.

Don't panic, I told myself. I had saved a few tricks up my sleeve. Unfortunately, I didn't get a chance to bring a canary out of my arse, because I heard the front door slam again. "James?" I called, panic rising.

There was no answer. I got up and went to the kitchen. The "shopping" was on the kitchen table. There was no sign of Amber or her father.

"James!" I called again, and peered into the downstairs loo. The girls stared at me from the sitting room as I walked back down the corridor. Maddy held up her coloring. I gave her a thumbs-up. Delighted, she started another. God bless the child . . .

I walked up the stairs and pushed open the bedroom door. He wasn't there. The other two were empty. What had I expected? To find James cross-legged in front of the dollhouse? I could feel myself getting disproportionately furious. He'd obviously forgotten something and nipped out. Again. But halfway down the stairs, I heard a grunt.

"James?"

"Up here," called a voice.

He was in the loo? "I've been calling you."

"Sorry. Didn't hear."

Beyond comprehension. Impossible. This was a small flat. I could hear the next-door neighbor fart. "I think Amber went out," I said.

"She's meeting some friends at Starbucks. I hope you don't mind but I had to raid your wallet. I gave my last cash to the pizza-delivery guy."

"Oh."

"It was only a tenner. I'll pay you back."

"Doesn't matter," I said. Though I was pretty sure I'd only had a twenty left in my wallet . . . "You ever coming out?"

"Sorry." I heard the loo flush, then the door opened. He was holding a Lee Child novel. "Hi. Having fun down there?"

A Rolodex of pithy answers flicked through my mind, but I couldn't voice a single one without causing mortal offense. "Hi," I said instead.

"Hi. So, what shall we do for the rest of the day?"

Another Rolodex appeared, but pithy answers were dangerous, and I knew it. "I guess we should think about lunch."

"Already?"

Yes, already. Time flies when you're having fun.

"Great. I bought stuff for spag Bol. The girls love it."

"This I'd like to see." I'd never seen James cook. We went out. Or I cooked in my flat when he came over.

"My pièce de résistance," said James.

"Meaning it's your only dish."

"Does cheese on toast count?"

"No."

"Then yes. But I boil a fine egg."

"Anyone can put an egg into boiling water for four minutes."

James walked up to me and put his arms around my waist. I felt the itch of anger fade.

"Ah, but mine are perfect. Not too hard, not too soft."

"I should hope not too soft."

"Never that."

"No," I said, lowering my hand to between his legs, "that doesn't seem to be your problem." But your children are. I looked around. Who'd said that? James kissed my lips. "Let's go downstairs, see what the monkeys are up to, and I'll start cooking."

Actually, I cooked. James's phone rang as the first layer of onion came away, and he didn't end the call until I'd sprinkled the finishing touch of Lea and Perrins into the pot. Pièce de résistance, my arse.

The spaghetti was perfect. But we were missing one, so it sat, congealing, on the side, while we waited for Amber to return.

"Why don't we start?" I suggested. Lulu and Maddy had been so good and I could tell they were hungry. I'd been godmothering long enough to know what happened if you didn't feed children.

"I told her to be back at one," said James, ignoring that it was now a quarter past.

Finally, we heard the key in the lock.

"Great! I'm starving," said Amber, plonking herself onto a chair.

I waited for James to say something. He did: "Okay, then, let's dish up."

I bit down on a carrot stick I had cut to stave off meltdown, and crunched it noisily.

"Mummy says it's rude if people can hear you eat," said Amber, giving a death stare.

I stopped crunching. James put the plates of food on the table, then brought the bowl of cheese that the younger girls had helped me grate. Amber grabbed a huge handful, half the bowl. Again, I looked at James. Again, I waited for him to say something. Again, he did. "Okay, girls, tuck in."

"We might need some more cheese," I said, and passed the bowl to Lulu.

"Great idea," said James, sitting down. I didn't say much else through the rest of lunch.

"That was delicious, Daddy," said Amber, carrying plates to the dishwasher.

"Don't thank me, thank Tessa. She made it."

I was too late to retract the it's-my-pleasure-you're-welcome expression that had started to eke across my face, and therefore returned Amber's frankly ungracious pout with a grateful smile.

"What about pudding?" asked Maddy.

I looked at James.

"We'll get ice cream later," he said.

"There are some apples," I said.

"Mummy always makes a pudding on weekends," said Maddy.

Again I looked to James for help.

"I can't cook like Mummy can," said James.

"But Tessa's here. Can't she cook? I like banana soufflé best."

"That sounds impressive."

"Mummy makes up her own recipes," said Lulu.

Of course she does.

"She can give you a lesson. Then you'll know how to make it." Maddy seemed pleased with herself. Problem solved.

"And strawberry cheesecake," said Lulu. "I like doing the biscuit bits."

"Obviously Tessa can't cook," said Amber. I was astounded by how hurtful her words were. I tried to smile at Amber, but she put her earphones in and turned away. I made a mental note: book a course at Prue Leith immediately. I'd show her.

Finally, they drifted out of the kitchen and I sat down with a cup of instant coffee. Okay, I thought, okay . . . So we were going to have to up the ante. I was a trained negotiator and an able-bodied woman. I could get myself out of this, and what I didn't know I would learn. I raised the cup to my lips—

"Aaahh!" The scream came from the living room. I was on my feet in less than a second. Lulu was crouched in the corner, holding her head in her hands. Maddy stood against the wall. Amber was trying hard to look nonchalant, and failing.

"What happened?" I asked, running to Lulu.

"Mummy!" she sobbed.

"Let's have a look," I said.

"Ow!"

"What happened?" I asked again, watching a red patch develop on Lulu's pale skin just above the temple.

Amber put her hands on her hips. "Why are you looking at me?"

"I was only asking if you saw what happened."

"She hit her head on the coffee table."

I'd kind of figured that out on my own. Where the hell was James? Surely he didn't need another poo. "Let's get you up. There's some ice in the kitchen. We'll put it on your head."

Lulu was still crying, but quietly. "Brave girl," I said, leading her out of the room.

I pulled out the ice tray, but there was only one cube in it. I slammed it hard on the work surface. The cube shot across the Formica and spun into the aluminum sink. James was pacing about in the jungle out back. On the phone.

I put the solitary ice cube into some paper towels and passed it to Lulu, then refilled the tray. As I replaced it, I spotted a bag of frozen peas. Much better. I tipped a few into a clean cloth and gave that to Lulu instead.

Amber was watching from the doorway. "Arnica," she said.

"Sorry?"

"Arnica." She suddenly seemed very interested in her feet. "Mum always puts it on Lulu when she takes one of her tumbles."

"Does she fall a lot?"

Amber nodded. "She never looks where she's going. Dad keeps it in the cutlery drawer."

"Thanks, Amber." I tried a smile again and this time received a dismissive shrug. I opened the drawer, found a near-empty tube of arnica, squeezed some out, and rubbed it on Lulu's head.

"Thanks, Tessa. That feels nice."

I put my arm around her. "You're going to have a big bruise."

"Will you kiss it better?" asked Lulu, which was how I discovered the thick, sweet taste of arnica.

James came to the window. He saw Lulu leaning into my chest and, smiling, gave me a thumbs-up. I reassured him with a smile of my own. But it was an empty gesture. I was afraid I wouldn't last the afternoon. I didn't.

The day was already darkening as I locked the car door, yet it was still hours from bedtime. I walked up to Billie's flat in West Acton and pressed the bell long and hard. She opened the door. "What are you doing here? Isn't this your first weekend playing mom?"

I pushed past her. "I sincerely hope you have wine."

"It's been open a couple of days."

"I don't care."

"Oh dear. That bad."

Billie and I used to share a flat, and I mean *share*. There were no demarcation zones between what was hers and mine. Nearly twenty years on, I still felt I could use her toothbrush and drink her wine.

"What's happened?" asked Billie, following me down the hall. I reached into the fridge, opened a cupboard, pulled out a glass, and poured. I was slurping at it as I offered some to Billie.

"It's three in the afternoon," she said, shaking her head.

"This day is never ending," I moaned. "I've been up for hours. Where's Cora?"

"At a party. She has about three a week. Sit down. Breathe."

"I can't. I've only got an hour. I said I had to go to the bank."

"The banks are shut, Tessa."

"Shit!"

"What happened?"

"Well, it was weird being there with them in the bedroom and then

James buggered off with Amber, I made lunch—no one said thank you . . ."

Billie was suppressing a smile.

"What?"

"Nothing. Go on. It sounds terrible."

Her sarcasm took the wind out of my sails. I sat down. "It wasn't really that. I don't mind a bit of housework, but . . . Oh, I don't know. They talk about Bea all the time. Amber brought out the photo album, which was sweet."

My old flatmate sat down opposite. "Go on."

"She's Superwoman. Beautiful too."

"All mothers are superwomen. And you will be too. But we learn on the hoof. It just doesn't look that way to the uninitiated."

"No, but she's Super-superwoman."

Billie opened her mouth to protest.

"I mean it. Vegetable patch, bakes banana soufflés, makes life-size leatherback turtles for class projects. She can probably tap dance while singing the national anthem backward."

"Did you ever see my papier-mâché head of Nelson Mandela?"

I frowned.

"Never mind. Go on . . ."

"And then I was putting on some washing for the week and James just dumped a whole load of uniforms on me." I waited for her shock and awe.

"And?"

"I'd been cooking, cleaning up, and entertaining them all day. Washing too? Is that my job?"

"You were doing some anyway," she said, dismissing my complaint with a shrug. "And yes, frankly, it is your job. If you're really intending to do this."

"James never usually does it."

"Any of it?"

"Don't get me wrong, he's brilliant with them but, well, he got stuck on the phone. There was nothing he could do." I couldn't hold Billie's gaze. "We're still at the sniffing-bottoms stage. I needed him."

"Did you tell him that?"

"I would have thought it was obvious."

Billie pulled a face.

"I had to come up for air. I told him I had to go to the bank and came here."

I watched Billie scrape back her ridiculously long black hair and knot it. It was shot through with gray now, and I was struck by how quickly the last decades had passed. Here I was, though, still sitting on her sofa discussing men. "It might be nice for Bea not to have a bag of laundry dumped on her on Sunday night," she said.

"But—"

"If Bea is Superwoman, then you need to be Superwoman. Get her on-side. Do the ironing. If she likes you, they'll like you."

"But she isn't in the picture anymore. She left James."

"Tessa, don't be thick. You have her children. The only difference about the picture now is you're in it."

I sat back against the sofa. Maybe Billie had been the wrong person to come to. With a failed marriage and an estranged ex, she carried too much of her own baggage to be impartial.

"I'm not being unsympathetic, Tessa, really, but with all due respect, you're the least important person in this equation. If you want to be with James you have to make the girls your priority. They didn't ask you to date their father. This has been foisted upon them. If Bea can see you're putting their interests before your own, she might be okay about some other woman tucking her children in at night."

"But you said I have to get her on-side first."

"That's how. Send the girls back happy."

"That's not going to be easy. I compare unfavorably. I can only make chocolate crispies and the girls told me they'd moved on from those in year one."

Billie bit her lip.

"What?" I asked again.

Billie held up a hand. "You know, that's probably no bad thing. Don't emulate her. Worse, whatever you do don't try to beat her. Be Tessa. Find your own thing."

"Share with them my encyclopedic knowledge of tort?"

"Music, Tessa. Freebies. Spoil them. Hannah Montana tickets and the like."

"Doesn't that look a bit desperate?"

"You do it for Cora."

"I love her. It's easy."

"Then fake it," said Billie, "till you feel it."

I stared at her. What if I can't feel it? But I was too scared of the answer to ask the question, so I nodded.

When I got back, James and his girls were ensconced on the sofa watching *Strictly Come Dancing*. I didn't want to sit on the floor or boot James out and take his place. Anyway, I had some washing, cooking, and ironing to do. A fine fairy-tale role reversal. The wicked stepmother banished to the hearth. I stopped myself. I wasn't a stepmother yet. I wondered if I would ever become one and realized, as I thought this, that I wanted to. Desperately. I wanted to get this right. I didn't want to be sitting on Billie's sofa in another twenty years' time having the same conversation. I put the first load of shirts in and started preparing the supper I had bought on the way back.

When everything was ready, I called James and the girls into the warm kitchen and watched happily as they tucked into the sizzling chicken fajitas with red peppers and sour cream. I could say one thing for those girls: they ate. At least I didn't have to worry about any bird appetites pecking around me. I rolled myself a fajita. This was just a period of adjustment. It was bound to be a bit bumpy. All would be well. I was feeling more rational about the whole thing. Billie was right: put the girls first and the rest would fall into place.

They got into their pajamas and I started to look forward to an evening alone with James, but then came the grim realization that on weekends Amber was not banished to her room to read but allowed to stay up and watch telly. I didn't want to watch cheap reality television, but I was unable to complain, afraid I might say something that could later be used against me by a precocious fourteen-year-old in a crooked court of her imagination. I retreated to the kitchen again and took up my place at the ironing board. Maybe rational was a fraction premature.

James walked in. "You don't have to do that," he said, but didn't stop me.

"It's almost done."

James put his arm around me and kissed the top of my head. "Thank you for being such a trouper. Why don't we go around the corner and I'll buy you a drink?"

My eyes lit up. But it was a flash in the pan. "What about the girls?"

"Amber's here. She wants to watch some crappy girly film anyway. We'd only be an hour or so. She has my number."

"Is that allowed?"

James laughed. "This isn't boarding school."

"I mean, is it okay with Bea?"

"We do it all the time. I usually have to pop out for something—collect pizza, pick up some beer. It's fine."

Alarm bells were ringing. But my thirst was ever thus . . .

Being out of the house, arm in arm with him and him alone, eased the tension that had built up in me over the day. It was only a four-minute walk to the pub on the corner, but I felt relief wash over me as we pushed open the door. James brought me a large vodka and tonic and sat down. I drank a sizable amount before I remembered to thank him. "Sorry. Thank you and cheers."

He raised his pint. "You okay?"

I stared at him. Yes, I believed in honesty, but we had wandered into new territory and I wasn't sure how to continue.

"It's okay to find this difficult, you know, Tessa. I find it hard spending the day with my nephew, and I have children."

"I could certainly survive life without another game of Guess Who?"

"Lulu can sniff out fresh blood like a great white shark," he said, taking a swig of his beer.

"You could have given me a heads-up."

He shook his head. "Are you mad? I got to read the whole of the sports section."

I opened my mouth to respond.

"Tessa, I'm joking. I didn't even buy a paper."

"Not funny."

"The therapeutic effects of ironing didn't help, then?"

I swallowed my response with vodka.

"I find it works better if I smack it against my head," said James.

"I'd happily do that for you."

He was watching me with a wry smile. "That isn't your sense of humor returning?"

"No chance. It's been eroded by Guess Who?"

"I'd better get you another drink. I'll hope by the fourth round you'll forget all about my demanding children and love me again."

I drained my glass. "You're in luck. I'm a sucker for punishment." I handed it back to him empty. "It only took one."

He held up four fingers. "It was a quadruple."

So that was the sudden warmth spreading through my solar plexus. "You know me well."

"I know my children." He started toward the bar. I called his name and he turned. "I'll get better at this," I said. "I promise."

"You don't have to get better at anything. The girls adore you already."

I shook my head.

"They do, Tessa."

I couldn't hide the fear in my eyes.

"What?" he asked, watching me.

I swallowed. "They talk about their mum a lot."

James returned to the table, put his hands on it, and bent down. "Oh, sweetheart, that's *my* fault. I never wanted them to think they couldn't, that it was taboo, that our divorce was their fault. I engineered it that way. I'm sorry. Please try not to take it personally."

I tried to appear reassured but inside I was wondering, Is that possible? Everything I said, did, ate, wore, how I drove, when I slept, was going to be judged by children who belonged, in essence, to my boyfriend's ex-wife. It couldn't get more personal than this. "I'll try," I said.

He straightened. "And, Tessa, I don't blame you for needing to go to the bank at three-thirty on a Saturday afternoon, and it's okay with me if you have to go to the bank every Saturday afternoon." He paused. "Or Sunday. Just while you acclimate."

I took his hand and kissed it. "How long will that take?"

He held on to my hand. "Forever, I hope."

* * *

When we got home, all the lights were on, and I knew immediately that something was wrong. We'd stayed longer than we'd intended, because we were having such a lovely time. James refused to admit his anxiety, but his jaw was tight as he strode up the garden path, kicking up gravel. I trotted behind him, nervous and unsure. We found the girls huddled in our room. James's room. Rapid-fire questions told us that Lulu had been sick and Bea was on her way to collect them.

James was devastated and distraught. He scooped Lulu into his lap. "How are you feeling now?" he asked.

"If you've bumped your head and you're sick, it's very dangerous," said Amber.

"Why didn't you call me?" James asked.

"I did. Seven times. You didn't answer."

The phone had been on the table in front of us the whole time. I had insisted. "It never rang," I said.

She shot me a look. "I must have misdialed," she retorted.

"Seven times?"

"I pressed redial. I'm sorry, Daddy."

Daddy. Daddy. Daddy.

"When were you sick? Have you been sick again?" asked James, placing his hand on Lulu's forehead.

"I was sick in my tummy."

"How do you feel now?" he asked.

"Hang on, Lulu, have you been sick?" I asked.

"I thought I was going to be," she said. Apologetically.

"If you bump your head—"

"Yes, Amber, we heard you the first time. Pass me the phone, please."

James dialed Bea's mobile number. "Hi, Bea—"

I don't know what she said but she cut him off.

"Hang on, hang on," he pleaded. "She didn't throw up. She just feels a bit sick—" She cut him off again. "She couldn't have choked, we were only around the cor—" Bea was shouting. Very loudly now. "You're right, it won't happen again. Sorry." I watched Amber intently. She was staring at her father.

Maddy was yawning, so I took her hand and escorted her back to bed. "Is Mummy coming?" she asked.

"I don't think so. Lulu's fine."

"I told her not to eat the rice pudding."

"What rice pudding?"

"The tin Amber gave us. It's very sweet. I don't like it. Lulu does, though. I think she ate the whole lot." Maddy pointed to an upturned tin under the bed opposite, the discarded spoon welded to the carpet.

I picked it up. "You shouldn't leave food under the bed."

"Mummy does," said Maddy.

"I very much doubt it." I lifted the sticky tin off the floor.

"Don't say I told. Midnight feasts are supposed to be secret."

"Don't worry. Your secret is safe with me. Now cuddle in, little one."

"Nigh'-nigh', Tessa." She curled up, stuck her thumb into her mouth, gathered the sheet in her fist, and fell asleep.

As I shut the door, James walked down the corridor, his arm around Amber. I put the tin behind my back. "Bea's not coming," he said. "False alarm."

False, certainly. I walked past them without saying anything. I didn't dare. The effects of the vodka had passed the rosy stage and moved into the black. In our bed, Lulu had fallen asleep. I turned off the light and went to the window to draw the curtains. Outside on the pavement, I watched a couple weave up the street laughing and kissing. That had been us a few moments ago. Opposite, a lone woman was standing by a nondescript car. She appeared to be staring straight up at me. I could tell from the way her large, round shoulders were shuddering that she was crying. Was that Bea? Perhaps she saw me move closer for a better look, because suddenly she lunged for the car door and climbed inside. Briefly, the interior light illuminated her face. I sighed with relief. The sad fat lady was nothing like Bea.

On Sunday morning, I'm ashamed to say, I woke up in my studio on the river, with a man beating hard on his warning drums in my head. But I wasn't taking heed. I couldn't go around to Billie's again, so I turned up at Al and Claudia's house. Claudia, Al, and I have been friends since secondary school, and they therefore had no choice but to let me in. I'm sure they'd have preferred to remain in bed with each other and the papers, but it was an emergency. Because they had no children, I knew I'd get their undivided attention as well as the unconditional sympathy I was looking for. I kept forgetting we were a bit long in the tooth for that.

"So, then what happened?"

"Let's put it like this. It didn't end well," I said.

"That is self-evident, Tessa, since you're sitting in our flat bitching about James and the girls when you should be with them," said Al.

"I'm not bitching."

Claudia picked at a croissant. "Maybe she really was scared. Amber's only fourteen. You left her with quite a big responsibility." Claudia was genetically programmed to see the best in people.

"The girls were asleep. We were at the end of the road."

"But they weren't asleep."

"Because Amber woke them up!"

"You don't know that."

"Claudia, whose side are you on?"

"Yours, of course. Which is why I don't think you should blow this out of proportion. She panicked when her sister felt ill and called her mum. It's what kids do. She probably didn't even try James's number."

"It was plastered all over the fridge."

"Exactly. She was embarrassed because she'd forgotten what she was supposed to do. Then it was too late to back out, so she exaggerated Lulu's illness and, to give credence to her story, mentioned how Lulu had banged her head. Otherwise she'd look foolish—worse, childish. And no fourteen-year-old wants that."

I opened and closed my mouth, like a goldfish. I could just about see the logic in it. Then I recalled Amber's beautiful face huddled in the crook of my boyfriend's arm and shook my head. "She's out to get me."

"Don't be ridiculous. She's fourteen."

"Going on . . . well, fifteen, which is bad enough, these days."

"Now who's being childish?" said Al.

Claudia put a restraining hand on her husband's leg. "Tessa has a right to be upset."

"No, she hasn't. They went to the pub. Why couldn't they have stayed at home and had a drink? She drank too much, then when it all calmed down she decided to have more to drink and tell James everything that was wrong with his parenting skills."

"He spent nearly an hour 'settling' her." I mimed the quotation marks, still furious a fourteen-year-old required so much "settling." "It wasn't like that."

"I'm sure he didn't feel as if you were lecturing him when you told him he indulged his daughter."

"All I said was he couldn't see what was in front of his eyes." To be honest, I couldn't remember exactly what I'd said. Al was right. The half-bottle of wine had not improved my mood or my memory.

"You spent a few hours with him and his children, then decided in your arrogance that you could do it better. No wonder he let you leave."

"Al!"

"Personally, I think you've both been stupid about this," he said, unabashed. "You were a secret until a couple of weeks ago and now, suddenly, you're moving in! Amber may have it in for you and she'd be entitled to, frankly, but she probably doesn't even know she's doing it. Who are you? She doesn't know you. You should have given her a lot longer than this to get to know you. How would you feel if you walked into your father's room and there was some random bird in it, wearing his T-shirt, being called 'darling'?"

"I'm not a random bird," I said.

"You are to her. Ask Ben how it feels. It happened to him enough times."

Our other oldest friend Ben had a mother who had taken women's liberation to new heights and hidden none of her conquests from her young son. "Al, that's enough," said Claudia.

"James is nothing like Ben's mother," I said, offended. "I'm the first person since his divorce he's taken home."

Al's face said it all.

"I am," I insisted.

"Either way, it makes no difference. You're the adult here. Act like one. Go back and sort it out. And apologize, too, for leaving at the first hint of trouble." He left the room.

I expected Claudia to apologize for her husband's mood, but she didn't. "He's right, you know. You left James having to explain to the girls why this morning you're not there. What does that tell him and them? If the girls make a mistake, willful or otherwise, you're gone. Every parent knows that children need consistency. If I were him, the alarm bells would be ringing. So, be careful. If he's the man you think he is, he'll protect those kids even if it means he doesn't get the girl of his dreams."

The winds of anger dropped and my momentum trickled away.

"And that would be a shame, Tessa, because I've seen you together. I think you are the girl of his dreams and he's absolutely perfect for you."

My phone rang. Salt-and-pepper Man. I was afraid to answer. Claudia pressed receive and passed it to me. "No games," she whispered firmly, and left me alone on the sofa.

"So?" SHE ASKED, WHEN I walked into the kitchen ten minutes later.

"I apologized profusely and promised it would never happen again."

"Well done. Not easy."

"Easier than I'd thought it would be. You're both right. Leaving was stupid. It's the sort of thing you do in your teens. He was characteristically gracious about it."

"Of course. He's a decent bloke," said Al. Which meant a lot to me, because they don't come better than Al.

I nodded.

"So what are you going to do?"

"He's taking the girls swimming."

"You'd better get going."

"I think it's best if I leave them alone for the day."

"Bollocks," said Claudia, "and you know it. Where's your spine, girl? You've got to face the music."

"I haven't got a swimsuit."

"Borrow mine."

"Honey, you're half my height."

"Cow." She narrowed her eyes. "I never liked you."

I laughed. "Ditto."

"Go on, bugger off," said Claudia.

I found I was rooted to the spot. "I'm nervous," I said.

"Good," said Al, looking up from the paper. "Nerves mean you're not sure about what you're doing, which means you might tread a little more cautiously from now on."

"I apologized, Al. Everything you said was right. Please lay off me a bit?"

"No."

"Why not?"

"Because I happen to agree with my wife. You and James are great together and I want to see this work for all of you. But there's no point in pretending it'll be easy."

I ran my hands through my hair. "Bloody hell, is it always this complicated?"

Al and Claudia looked at each other. "Yes," they said in unison, and smiled sadly but with love. Al and Claudia knew all about complications. They couldn't have children. "Now, stop procrastinating and get thee to a swimming pool."

I turned back at the door. "I suppose I could always wow them with my synchronized swimming," I said.

"That's my girl," said Claudia.

I wasn't joking.

THAT EVENING, AFTER AN AFTERNOON of James making things easier for me than I deserved, he joined me on the sofa with a bottle of wine and two glasses. The girls had been safely returned to their mother. And, yes, I had indeed wowed them with my synchronized swimming. Even Amber had been impressed.

"I'm sorry—"

"Enough, Tessa. It's all forgotten. Please, no more sorries."

I nodded.

"Okay. So go on, tell me?"

"Tell you what?" I asked.

"In what scary part of your previous life did you learn to synchronize-swim? Do you have a collection of plastic caps with flowers on? Should I be afraid?"

"Very," I said. He poured generously. I drank gratefully. "Well, it wasn't quite summer camp."

"What was it?"

"The Queen Elizabeth Rehabilitation Centre in St. John's Wood."

James looked at me seriously.

"Not me," I said quickly. "Mum."

"Oh."

I had taken James to stay with Mum and Dad a few times. The weekends had been easy and I could tell they liked him. I didn't blame him for forgetting about the ticking time-bomb. MS was a bastard of a disease, you never knew when or where it was going to strike. It was nearly twenty years ago that Mum had woken up and not been able to move her legs. Dad thought it was a stroke, but they diagnosed MS. James saw a reasonably fit woman, but that's because he hadn't known the whirlwind my mother had been before. Her legs were her weak point. I watch her step with caution. She's walking through life on a tightrope, with no harness and no safety net.

"Dad and I took turns accompanying Mum to the pool for physical therapy. The therapist, Bess, was an ex-Olympic Canadian synchronized swimmer. She was incredible. She made it fun, and some time during the fourth month or so, I realized we'd all stopped dreading it. The worst bit was helping her dress and undress. Dad can still do a mean dolphin flip." I'd never know whether those repetitive pool exercises got Mum on her feet again or whether it was Bess's magic, the amazing generosity of her care. "She and Mum are still in touch."

James pulled me toward him. We didn't speak for a while. I felt comforted by the silence. Usually I filled moments of fear with noise. TV, radio, long phone calls, the pub, mischief . . . But with James the bad things didn't feel so bad. My mother had MS. Yes. She had weak days and bad days and days when her medicine committed her to bed, which she hated, but I no longer had to be brave during those times. Or the times when there was nothing wrong with Mum and I was more scared than ever. It was a huge, unbelievable relief. Teenage pouting I could deal with. What I didn't think I could deal with ever again was being alone. Al, Claudia, and Billie were right. I had to make this work. For all of us. James kissed me.

"I love you so much," he said. "Sometimes it scares me. I don't know what great thing I've done to deserve you and I'm afraid someone up there will realize you've been sent to the wrong man and someone else should have the right to call you his."

I blinked at him, stunned. "You don't really think that, do you? I behaved like a prat last night."

"I told you, it's forgotten. And, yes, I do. I wasn't expecting a second chance. When Bea left and I realized she wasn't coming back, I sort of put myself into neutral. I have friends who've lost their wives to some god-awful disease, then met and married other people, and it's always amazed me. The new wives were great, lovely, but they weren't the same. I always saw them as slightly inferior models to the original. That's a terrible thing to say, isn't it? But you? You're perfect."

I wanted to disagree. Convince him otherwise. But he kissed me again, soft, gentle kisses on and around my mouth, until I groaned and my insides flipped, and all thoughts of protest left me. We had the flat to ourselves. And we made good use of it.

I MADE A PROMISE TO myself. I would do whatever it took to make this easy on the girls. Billie, Claudia, and Al had given me sound advice and I'd be a fool not to listen. James loved me. And he loved his girls. Nothing else mattered. So I adopted a form of self-imposed schizophrenia. Monday to Friday, I was a working girl. The legal kind. Though sometimes I wondered. On the weekends I had James to myself, I was selfishly in love. Nothing else existed apart from him and me. And I appreciated it all the more because every other weekend and Wednesday night I put on my invisibility cloak, spoke only when spoken to, made food, washed clothes, and spent money. A lot of money.

Seven

Eau Sauvage

INTERESTING, ISN'T IT, HOW LIFE PLAYS TRICKS ON YOU? FOR A LONG time I had assumed without query or question that I would marry. There might have been playful nights out in the past with Helen, Claudia, Francesca, and Billie, my girlfriends of old, when we imagined our perfect proposal. But if there were, I couldn't remember them. But I'd assumed one would come. Then there was a long period when I believed I was well past my sell-by date and that I'd be taken off the shelf only to be thrown away.

Then, in a sort of premature-midlife-crisis-cum-meltdown-cum-moment-of-madness, I'd imagined that the person to whom I should be married was Ben, my best friend. That would probably have been fine, except he'd married his perfect woman eight years earlier. Al and I were their best men. Great speech, if I say so myself . . .

Eighteen months ago, I learned the hard way that I would never know what lay ahead.

My beautiful friend Helen was killed in a tragic car crash.

Tragic doesn't come close, actually. I decided then that I wasn't going to waste the rest of my thirties imagining the worst or the best, since whatever I came up with was not how it would play out. That's the trick life plays. It has a library the size of Getty Images, full of unforeseeable events. And the one it had pulled for me today was about as unforeseeable as it got.

James and I were pressed together in the aisle of an overcrowded train, clutching the pole like toddlers on a carousel. It was raining outside, and the windows had fogged up with the steam from wet coats. I didn't mind.

Nose to nose, we grinned inanely at each other. I was aware I'd become everything I'd ever hated, but I didn't care. Our lips would rest against each other's between sentences. I was blissfully unaware of my surroundings. I loved this man. This was it. He was the one and I wanted to be with him forever.

"Tessa?"

"Hmm?" I smiled dreamily.

"Will you marry me?"

"What?"

"I said, will you marry me?"

The rest of the world returned and I became acutely aware of where I was. On the tube, during rush hour. Someone's umbrella was wedged between my buttock cheeks. I could see the blackheads in the crease around the nostrils of the man sitting below me. Somebody was wearing way, way too much Eau Sauvage and somebody else had farted. This was it? This was the moment I'd pretended I hadn't been imagining? Where was the sunset, the champagne, the privacy? Where was my answer? Well, proposals weren't as easy as they looked. Imagining being asked and being asked were two completely different things.

I noticed that people were listening to my now lengthy pause. Someone even pulled out their iPod earplugs. I had to say something. "Are you asking me seriously?" I was stalling for time. I seemed to have left my heart and stomach in the tunnel, where he'd first asked.

"Categorically. Will you marry me?"

Stop saying that! We're on the goddamn tube! But James had this intent look on his face, and I knew he was back where I'd been, cocooned. He'd lost track of the seven hundred and fifty-nine people we were sharing the carriage with. I, however, could feel fifteen hundred and eighteen eyes on me—fifteen hundred and seventeen if you counted the one-eyed bandit lurking out of sight. Focus, girl! Hadn't I just been wallowing in contentedness?

Good grief, this was harder than it looked in the movies. If I loved him as much as I thought I did, why didn't I leap into his arms and yell "Yes!" and why, oh why, was my gut telling me there was way too much Eau Sauvage in the air? If I said what was on my mind, would I ruin it forever?

"Yes," I said. But before his ears had relayed the message to his brain, I said, "No." Quite loudly.

"No?"

"Sorry. God, James, I want to, I do, I love you so much. But I don't think the girls are ready for this. It's too soon. It's not fair on them."

I saw a woman nod. Get off my set!

"We don't have to get married immediately. We could have a long engagement," he said.

"I don't want a long engagement. I'd marry you today, but I haven't even met Bea yet, or your family."

"They'll all love you."

"Have you asked the girls how they feel about me? Amber particularly." Things had been better with the younger two girls but Amber was impenetrable. I felt I couldn't do more, but it wasn't enough. They were pulling away. If I mentioned it to James, he'd say I was imagining it. So I hadn't. I took his face in my hands. "She's more protective of you than you know." I wanted to say "territorial," but I was trying to be honest and diplomatic at the same time. Not easy. "James, I'm an only child. I worry that I might not be very good at sharing."

"You're saying no?"

"I'm saying I need to learn how to do this."

"So you're saying yes?" He grinned. Seeing him happy made my heart pound.

"It's complicated."

"Don't make it complicated. It isn't complicated. I love you. You love me."

"You have three daughters who don't know me."

"Marry me, and they will. They're my children. Please trust me. I know them. They'll be over the moon. Lonely dad is much, much worse."

"They love you no matter what. What's not to love?"

He smiled at me. "So that *is* a yes."

"James—"

"Come on, Tessa. What are we waiting for?"

Oh, to hell with it. Sometimes you've just got to jump. We'd iron out the details later.

"Ask me again."

"When?"

"Now."

"Tessa King. Will you marry me?"

"Yes," I said.

James kissed me then, and I was enveloped by so much love that my heart took over and all I could see was rose petals, white dresses, and happy endings forever and ever and ever. Amen. The fairy tale was ingrained in me, more than thirty-five years deep. It would take more than three stepchildren and the Northern Line to get out that stain.

I WALKED TOWARD MY OFFICE, oblivious to the Monday-morning pandemonium. Had I been operating normally, I would have noticed the increased level of gossipy activity in the corridors. But I was not operating normally.

"Oh, my God," said Matt, reaching for my coat. I let him remove it from my shoulders. "Have you heard?"

I stared at him blankly.

"Sulky Jo has been caught by the *News of the World* shagging Danny Treadfoot."

"What?"

"Carmel's betrothed."

Matt shook his head in frustration. "Jo and Carmel. The Bonne Belles." Still nothing. "Danny Treadfoot, her fiancé, the number-one striker at Man U?" I frowned at him. "What the hell's wrong with you? Are you sick?"

"James proposed," I said.

"What?"

"James. He asked me to marry him."

"Oh, my God!"

"On the tube!"

"What?" He sounded horrified. "What line?"

"Matt!"

"Was it at least a nice line? The Central or the Piccadilly? Or was it the depressing Hammersmith and City?" He shuddered. "Oh, God," he said. "It was the Northern, wasn't it?"

"Packed is what it was."

My office door opened. "Carmel's trying to sue Sulky Jo for future loss of earnings because she won't be able to promote the new album now that being in the same room as her former bandmate apparently makes her physically sick. She has a doctor's note to prove it. Legal wants you to get an injunction. I want you to sit on it." Linda cackled like a forty-a-day witch. "Bless the stupid little twat, we won't need any promotional shit after this. Fucking genius! If I hadn't known Sulky Jo was screwing Danny, I'd think I'd made it up." Linda looked at Matt and me. "Cheer up, troops. Crap like this sends records platinum."

"It's not that," said Matt.

"Somebody die?"

Since I had no inclination to talk, Matt answered for me. "James proposed."

"No shit!"

"On the tube," he said.

"You can't take it seriously," said Linda emphatically. "It was obviously impromptu and therefore null and void."

"Knee-jerk," said Matt. "She's right. Ignore it."

"Absolutely. Forget about it," said Linda, then they both looked at me. I wasn't sure what they were waiting for. "All right about the Sulky Jo crap?"

I nodded.

"Great. I want this in the press for days. Where they did it, how many times a night. Man U won't mind as long as he's made out to be the stud. That's imperative. I'll promise them five times a night, minimum.

We do not get an injunction on this story. By the way," said Linda, backing out of the office, "what did you say?"

"I said yes."

"Oh, fuck." Linda came back into the room. She sat down heavily on the chair opposite my desk. "What the hell possessed you to do that?"

By lunchtime everyone knew. The company seemed split. Half thought he should have waited the few days until Valentine's, the other half thought a proposal on Valentine's was worse than a proposal on the tube. I'd lost ownership of the subject by five past one, so, in desperate need of headspace, I left the office, walked through the churchyard opposite and onto the towpath along the Thames. I always feel better next to water. My phone rang. It was a private number. Desperate to ignore it, but too conscientious to do so, I answered, "Tessa King."

"Hello, Tessa King," said a voice I knew better than my own.

The smile returned to my face. The knot between my eyebrows vanished. We hadn't spoken for so long and he called me now. "Oh, my God, Ben, your timing's perfect."

"You okay?"

"Can you get out of work?"

"What's happened, Tess?" He was the only person in the world who called me Tess. I'd missed it.

"James proposed."

There was a pause. "Tell me where to meet you and I'll be there."

Twenty minutes later he walked into the pub I had hidden myself in. I hadn't seen him for over a year. He looked good.

"Oh, my God, Tess, you're getting married?"

"Seems that way."

"It's a bit quick."

Might appear so to Ben, since not very long ago I had declared myself to be in love with him. But then it was Ben who'd told me, wrongly, that James was married with kids, so neither of us had behaved impeccably. "Well, I don't really have time for the perfect two-year courtship at my age."

"What about kids? Are you going to try?"

"Good grief, man! Get a girl a drink before you start asking questions like that!"

"Sorry. Pint?"

"Better make it half."

"You've changed."

"You bet your bottom dollar I have," I replied.

He smiled. "It's good to see you, my friend. It's been too long."

It had been as long as it had to be to allow things to settle between us. But now, more than anything, I needed my old friend back. "Thank you," I said.

"For what?"

For giving me an out. For forgiving my moment of madness. For not leaving your wife. For welcoming me back. "For coming," I replied.

"That's what friends are for," he replied.

With two halves in front of us, we'd both clearly changed. We sat and discussed marriage.

"This is what I've learned," said Ben, opening a bag of crisps. "Marriage gives you invisible protection against the world. You have a punching bag when you need it. You have a partner in crime when you want one. You have a lover on tap. You have support. The tricky bit is remaining aware that the person is providing all those things all the time. You start to think you're doing it alone. That you provide those things for yourself. As a result you get a bit pissed off with all the demands, with the cost of those services. Loyalty. Respect. Faithfulness. Changing lightbulbs when you'd happily live in the dark. Hardest of all, maintaining a sense of humor . . . Resentment creeps in. Boredom. A feeling that you're missing out when actually you've got everything. You just can't see it."

I tried to digest what he'd said. But I couldn't. "Bloody hell" was all I managed. "When did you get so wise?"

"I've been reading. It's incredible, really. We all think we're unique but we're just a bunch of wankers." He laughed. "Seven-year itch. You know what that is? A statistical fact. Around nine years, divorce rates spike, relationships hit a whiteout. Lost, no sense of direction, sick to death of one another, tired because you keep hitting moguls you didn't see coming." He noticed I was frowning. "Keep up. Skiing analogy."

I was confused. "I got the bumpy bits, but you said *nine*."

"Well, how long are most courtships and engagements?" He answered himself: "Two years. Makes nine. It's no coincidence that you and I nearly got ourselves into trouble at just that moment. Don't take this the wrong way. If it hadn't been you, I'd probably have made a complete cock of myself with some intern. I was a statistic waiting to happen. I love my wife. Sometimes I don't like her very much, because she's a bossy old trout who knows too much about too many things. But that's also why I love her. Following me?"

"I think I need another drink."

It was my round. I came back with two more halves.

"How's everything with his kids?" asked Ben.

I made a so-so gesture. "I fear I'll become the wicked stepmother whatever I do."

"Don't try to be a stepmother. Do what you do best."

"Get drunk and fall over?"

He ignored me. "Just add three more godchildren to your list."

"My godchildren want to like me."

"The girls don't like you?"

"I thought I was beginning to wear them down with trendy designer clothes and CDs and sparkly cherry-flavored lip gloss, but I think they're beginning to see through my cunning ruse."

"Subtle."

"As a beginners' violin class." I frowned, remembering the strangely solemn children we'd had staying with us the previous Wednesday. "I'm doing something wrong."

"Give them time," said Ben. "It's impossible not to love you." I squeezed his hand and was reminded how much strength my friends gave me. And how much I'd missed him.

"James asked me to marry him. They're not going to get any time."

"You think it's a bit premature?"

"Oh, I don't know. The rest of my life might not be enough time. But if that's the case, should I do it at all? Does anyone like their stepmother?"

"Of course they do."

"Who?"

"You want a name?"

"Yes."

"Well, not Cinde-fucking-rella."

"No," I said, laughing in despair. "Not her."

"So what was it? Cloud-writing, hot-air balloon, Jamie Theakston asking you live on air on James's behalf while you had tea in bed in the morning?"

My shoulders dropped.

"Oh, no," said Ben, with a grand smile. "He messed up."

"You could say that."

"Thank God. Couldn't have been worse than mine."

"You asked Sasha in Paris, Eiffel Tower. You're going to tell me now she had vertigo?"

He pulled a face. "That was the second time."

You think you know a person . . . "What was the first?"

"Not my finest hour."

"Please tell me. You'll make me feel so much better."

"You ever tell Sasha I told, and we're finished."

"I hear you. Now, spill."

"Six o'clock in the morning, off my tits on E—"

"What?"

"I had a brief purple patch. Anyway, stripped down to jeans, all sweaty and jittery, I shouted my proposal outside her bedroom window, then slipped into some semiconscious state and had to be taken to a hospital to have my stomach pumped."

"Nice."

"She swore me to secrecy."

"Not a hard one to keep."

"No. Absolutely humiliating. But I meant what I'd said."

"I always thought the Eiffel Tower was a bit over the top. Now I understand you had some ground to make up."

"And did you note the size of the diamond?"

"Often."

"Okay. Your turn."

"Northern Line. Eight fifty-three a.m."

"Late!"

"Exactly."

* * *

THAT NIGHT I WENT BACK to my flat happy, thanks to Ben. What did the tube matter? What did surly kids matter? Kids *were* surly, they answered back, had tantrums, sulked. I shouldn't take it personally. All that mattered was the question and who had asked it. My James Kent. Salt-and-pepper Man was going to marry me. I heard his familiar rat-a-tat-tat on my door and ran to open it. I threw myself around his neck and clung to him like a monkey. We struggled toward the sofa, with him holding me, an enormous bouquet of flowers, and a bottle of vintage champagne. I realized I wasn't making his life easy, but now he was here I didn't want to let go.

"I'm sorry I didn't say yes immediately," I said.

"You did. I've forgotten the rest."

"I couldn't be happier," I said, kissing him all over his face.

"Good. Because you make me very happy."

"I'm getting married!"

He smiled. "I know."

"Exciting, isn't it?"

"Very. Have you spoken to your parents?"

"They rang a couple of times today, but I'd like to tell them in person. Maybe this weekend?"

"They might not be able to wait till then."

My eyebrows rose.

"I met your dad for a drink last Thursday."

"He didn't tell me he was coming to town."

"I went to Oxford."

"Why?" I was being slow. "Oh!"

James smiled.

"You asked my eighty-four-year-old dad for permission to marry me? I'm pushing forty, for heaven's sake."

"Well, I did it for—" James stopped. Coughed. "Tradition's sake. I thought he might like it."

That wasn't what he'd been going to say, but I buried that knowledge far behind boxes of tulle, silk, and choices of bouquets. "What did he say?"

"He said it was up to you, of course. But I wanted to ask him anyway."

"No wonder they've been calling!"

James squeezed out from under me. "So, Mrs. Kent, how about a drink?"

I stood up. "Ms. King would love one."

James crossed his arms. I uncrossed them.

I grabbed his hand. "I don't want to be the Second Mrs. Kent."

"There are a few others, you know. My sister-in-law, Faith, my mother . . ."

I pulled him toward me, rose on tiptoe, and kissed the end of his nose. "You know what I mean."

"I fell in love with Tessa King. You'll always be Tessa King to me."

"I'll drink to that," I said and opened the bottle.

After that we foolishly let the champagne get warm.

LATER WE LAY HEAD-TO-TOE IN a deep bubble bath and toasted our happy future.

"How will you tell the girls?"

"I thought we should do it together on Wednesday night."

"Don't you think it would be better to tell them by yourself in case they don't like the idea? They won't be able to say anything if I'm there."

"Tessa, when are you going to understand that those children think you're great?"

I didn't want to tell him he was wrong. "It's quite quick."

"Too quick?"

"Not for me. But it's a lot for them to take in."

"Children adjust better than adults."

"At least tell them on your own. I can materialize when they've asked you all the questions they'll want to ask you and might not if I'm there. It's important they don't feel I'm taking you away from them."

"They need to know we're a united front. I've made that mistake before."

"We will be. But let them have this last thing with you on their own. And until then we don't tell anyone."

"Okay, wise girl, though that'll be hard. I want to tell people on the street." He kissed my foot.

"What about Bea?"

"Well, that's a bit tricky."

I sat up. "I thought you said she—"

"Tricky because she already knows."

"What?"

I could tell James knew he'd made a mistake, because he reached out of the bath for the bottle and refilled my glass. Diversionary tactic. It didn't work so well on adult women.

"Well, I mean, I told her I was going to ask you, so it won't come as a surprise."

It surprised me! I'm sure that in my logical right brain, or wherever logic is supposed to reside, I was thinking, break it to her gently, in stages, warn her of what lay ahead. Bring the ex on-side. Very sensible. But all I could think about was that James had told his beloved Bea, his confidante, the woman he had stayed talking with long into the night before he'd told me.

"Tessa, she feels bad about what happened. She just wants me to be happy. And I am. And that makes it better for her, don't you see?"

"I guess," I said, though it sounded a bit cockeyed to me.

"Then, of course, you'll have to meet the rest of the Kent clan. They'll love you, I know it. Mum's offered to host an informal gathering on a Saturday when we have the girls."

"Your mother." I grimaced. "What's she like?"

"Well, she has a particular way of doing things."

"Okay," I said, none the wiser. "Do I bring my parents?"

"'Course. The more the merrier. That's our motto."

"What about some mates for backup?"

"Why don't we leave that for the engagement party?"

"Engagement party?"

"Well, you don't want to be meeting all the cousins for the first time on your wedding day."

"How many do you have?"

"Twenty-seven."

I swallowed hard and felt fear for my little three. "Big wedding," I said.

"Great wedding."

I felt myself being drawn in. "We could cover the orchard at Mum and Dad's with a marquee, keep the dwarf pear trees on the inside, and cover them with fairy lights."

"You've thought about it, then?" James seemed pleased. I didn't realize I had to alter my response accordingly. I was a novice. Learning on the trot.

"It's what I wanted to do for their ruby wedding anniversary. But Mum wasn't very well that year so we shelved the idea. I calculated we could seat about eighty."

"After family, that doesn't leave much space for mates," said James, a little tense.

"Well, since all those cousins went to your first wedding, perhaps they wouldn't mind missing out this time."

Too late, I saw I'd made a mistake. James put his glass on the side of the bath. "It's got cold," he said.

"I'll put some more hot in."

"Actually I forgot to phone someone back. They're waiting for an answer." He stood up. "Won't be a second." The water disappeared. I felt exposed. He wrapped a towel around his narrow hips and, leaving watery footprints behind him, went to find his phone. I sat in the shallow, cold bath. I hadn't meant it to sound so barbed. I just wasn't thinking. If anything, it was supposed to be funny. Ha-ha. But what did I know of the conflicts involved in facing an aisle for a second time?

WE PUT THE INCIDENT BEHIND us, or rather brushed it under the carpet. Then, a few days later, on a crisp, cold night, James wowed everyone by collecting me from work on a Virgin taxi bike. It spoke volumes to me that I hadn't shared a Valentine's night with anyone since I was eighteen and a hippie on a beach in Vietnam had presented me with a dreadlock as a sign of undying love. I had spent a long time loving a man I couldn't have, because it was safer that way. It had taken me more time again to work out that living in a precarious world was better than no life at all.

I didn't know where the bike was taking us, but as we passed the Brompton Cemetery, I had my first inkling. "A bit of making out behind a tomb?" I shouted through the helmet when we stopped at traffic lights. "Or a certain sexy hotel nearby?" He gave me a thumbs-up. I blew him a kiss. The location of our first date. Hopefully, it would end better this time.

IT WAS A SET PIECE. I assumed a room was booked, but didn't ask. Pink champagne at the bar. Everyone else a couple. The first thing I noticed was that there wasn't a lot of noise among my fellow lovebirds. In fact, the whole place felt a little tense. Well, we weren't going to be like that. Except it's quite hard to be normal when twelve other couples are listening to your every word. After a few hideous false starts about our day, which sounded so trite in the echoing silence, we, too, fell quiet. The music was atrocious. Every cheesy love song ever written on Pan pipes. Why didn't I know this when I was single? Why didn't someone tell me that Valentine's dinners were awful and cheesy and I was better off with a DVD and a takeout?

Pink crab pâté arrived in the shape of a heart. I laughed. A couple of women looked daggers at me. We did our valiant best, but the oppressive mood of the place swallowed any joy. It was simply impossible to be romantic to order. One couple was arguing. Thank God. At least it gave us something to talk about. But even that lost its amusement value when I realized that the poor girl was being dumped and not, as she'd hoped, proposed to. She left in tears.

"James," I whispered.

He looked like a fish out of water. This was his Eiffel Tower. And all I wanted to do was jump.

"I don't care how much this costs, but I'm paying the bill and we are getting out of here."

"What?"

I mimed slicing my neck. "I'm sorry. I did this to you, and thank you for trying, but let's get the fuck out of here before it kills us." I said all this in a throaty whisper.

"You can't pay," said James.

"Watch me."

I stood up. Walked to the maître d', told him I wanted to settle the bill and leave. Then I returned to the table, punched in a PIN number, and that was that. We were free to go. "Sorry," I said to the manager. "It's just too—"

"Don't worry. Worst night of the year. Chef's just won the pot."

"Pot?"

"How long before someone leaves in tears. Chef had thirty-six minutes. He was bang on. Have fun."

I took James's arm and we walked out into the night. We found a kebab house on the Fulham Road, ordered chicken kebabs with extra chili sauce, and walked, leaving behind a trail of spotted sauce on the pavement. It was bliss. It was fun. It was us. And I was happy. I couldn't wait to show him his Valentine's present.

THE LIGHTS WERE ON IN the front room. I looked at James.

"It's okay. My sister Lucy's there."

I saw my slow striptease vanish before my eyes and immediately a lump settled in my throat. I hadn't met any of James's siblings.

Lucy was James's younger sister. I stopped walking. "You didn't tell me."

"Well, Bea needed bailing out, so the kids are at mine. I didn't want to cancel and, luckily, Lucy had no plans."

"Why didn't you tell me?"

"Well, you've been so brilliant about making time for the girls recently that I knew you'd want to come home and see them, and I was determined to have our night."

"Want" was one interpretation. James walked up the path and put the key into the lock. I felt sick.

"Jimbean!" said a pretty, blond girl in the hall.

"Lucy, this is Tessa."

She walked toward me and I put out my hand. She brushed it away and gave me a kiss. "Great to meet you, he doesn't stop talking about you." She smelled of patchouli oil. "I'd love to stop and chat but I've got a date."

"I'm sorry," I said. "We could have come back earlier."

"Not that kind of date. I'm going with a bunch of mates to smash plates at a brilliant Greek restaurant in Soho, spend some pent-up sexual tension, a lot of money, drink too much, and flirt with handsome waiters. Then we're going clubbing."

"Can I come?" I asked.

"No. You have to stay here and shag my brother." She grimaced. "Rather you than me!"

"Pleased to hear it," I said.

"So long, see you at Mum and Dad's for the baptism by fire and, Tessa, it was great to meet you. Thank you for putting a smile back on the miserable git's face." She threw her patchwork bag over her shoulder and waved good-bye.

"I like her," I said.

"You'll like all of them." He frowned. "Now, what was she saying you had to do next?"

"Get upstairs, 'Jimbean,' you handsome beast. I'll be up in a minute with your Valentine's present."

"Can't I unwrap it here?" he asked, reaching for my coat belt.

I pulled away. "No. I unwrap it. You get to watch."

His eyes lit up and he headed for the stairs. "I'm gone."

I HAD NEVER DONE A striptease before. But, hell, I'd never got married and become a stepmother before either. Neither had I loved anyone so much that I couldn't even remember what it felt like to be inhibited, let alone shy. All the lights in our room were off, James lay on the bed, and I stood in a bright shaft of light that fell through the open bathroom door. It was all quite Jack Vettriano. I'd even prepared music and set my iPod to play quietly in the background. It was fun. Articles dropped to the floor and I could hear James moan occasionally but I couldn't see him. I stood in black lacy knickers, a bra, thigh-highs, and very high heels.

"Come here," said James.

"No."

The bra came off next, followed by each stocking, but the shoes and knickers stayed on.

"And now for *my* pièce de résistance," I said. I peeled off the knickers, threw them over my head, then struck a very wicked pose.

"AAAAH!"

A high-pitched scream wasn't the reaction I'd expected. The room was suddenly awash with bright light and girls in nighties screaming.

James scrambled over the bed and dived into the jeans he'd only recently cast aside, and I stood frozen to the spot, back arched, a wet finger pointing stupidly to the heart between my legs. I say stupidly, because my pubic-hair art needed no more attention than it was already receiving.

"AAAAH!" Lulu screamed again.

Too late, my legs whisked me to the sanctity of the shower cubicle. There, I wrapped myself in a towel, crouched behind a rapidly bolted door, and vowed never to come out. Well, I thought, at least I have water. What on earth possessed me to trim my pubic hair into a heart?

Eight

No-man's-land

THE HEART WAS NEVER MENTIONED. JAMES MUST HAVE HAD A WORD with the girls, but he neither confirmed nor denied it when I asked him. I would have preferred a snigger to the stone wall I was faced with. At least I could have been part of the joke. I alone felt the uncomfortable itch in my pants. I alone experienced the night sweats. But I don't think I was alone in pretending to forget about it. James kept a respectable distance from me in the presence of the girls, but when I tried to talk to him about it, he brushed it aside. In fact, whenever I tried to talk to him about anything to do with his daughters and me, he said what he'd always said: they adored me and everything was fine. I didn't share his confidence and became clumsy with them, knowing I was trying too hard.

Regardless of my inner fears, James insisted on telling them we were getting married. He took the afternoon off, picked them up from school, and took them for ice cream. Then he told them we wanted, with their blessing, to get married. I wasn't there, so I have only his word that they were delighted. Maddy and Lulu were excited about being bridesmaids, maybe even Amber, too, when she allowed herself to be. Or so it felt to me. One day she'd be quite enthusiastic, but then she'd become silent and sullen. I never knew which Amber I was going to get.

I would have loved to put it down to erratic hormones, but James told me Amber didn't have her period yet, so, despite my best intentions, I took it personally.

I had wanted to take things slowly, for her sake, but once news of our engagement was out, the momentum picked up and I had to face what I could no longer avoid. James's family.

"Come on, Tessa! I said we'd be there early." James had now called up the stairs three times. But I was no closer to being ready. My Jimmy Choo shoes, which turned my outfit from elegant but reserved to elegant with a whiff of fox, had vanished. I heard him galumphing up the stairs.

"What about those?" he said, pointing at the floor.

"My court shoes? They look like a prison warden's."

"You could wear wellies and still look great," he said. "Let's go."

Defeated by my own determination not to be "that kind of girl," I slipped my stockinged feet into what felt like moon boots and left. What I really wanted to do was throw a major tantrum and refuse to go anywhere until my glass slippers were back where they should rightfully have been.

Tearing my eyes from the depressing sight in the foot well, I faced the girls in the back of the car. "Oh, Amber, I nearly forgot. I've managed to get an extra ticket to the private gig for the Belles, and there's a party afterward, too."

"I hate them. Jo's a scheming cow for stealing her mate's boyfriend," said Amber, looking at me, then at her father.

"You know I didn't—" I stopped.

"Yes?" asked Amber.

What was I going to say? Didn't steal James from your mother, or didn't steal James from you? But I had, hadn't I, Amber? And therein lay the rub.

"Didn't realize you felt so strongly about it."

"Worst kind of girls, those. Real cows." She spat the word so venomously that it left me in no doubt that the animal she was referring to was in fact canine, not bovine. But Amber couldn't call me a bitch yet. Not to my face, anyway. She turned away and stared out of the window. I thought I saw pained confusion reflected in the glass, but I was mistaken. It was just another sulky pout.

When we arrived at James's parents' house, just outside Hatfield, the front door was flung wide, and a white-haired man, who could only have been his father, beckoned us in. He was James with more laughter lines and no pepper left. He was handsome like his son, had pale blue eyes and a Don Johnson smile. Behind him stood a striking woman in a black cocktail dress. The children ran to their grandparents. I hovered in the background, like the outsider I was.

"Mum, Dad," said James, bringing me forward, "this is Tessa."

Peter kissed my cheek. "Wonderful to meet you. I should think you need a strong drink. Martini?"

I grimaced. "Is that wise this early in the day?"

I got a big squeeze from Honor. "Imperative, I should think." She smiled. "Don't worry, it's going to be fine."

"I've got special fruit cocktails for you lot. Come and give me a hand in the kitchen. What about you, Jimmy? Martini?"

We followed them in. "Better make it a beer, Dad. I'm driving."

"Won't be a minute, make yourselves comfortable. Tessa, it's lovely to have you here. We're so happy about your news."

"Thank you."

The girls disappeared after Honor and Peter, leaving us standing alone in the hall.

"Jimmy?"

"'Fraid so."

I pulled a face. "Jimmy," I said again. "That sounds weird. I think I prefer Jimbean."

He thrust his hands into his pockets. "Don't worry, you can still call me Mr. Kent."

We stood a little awkwardly.

"Two down," I said.

"Three million to go."

He took me through to a perfectly orchestrated shabby-chic sitting room. Soft white sofas, a lit fire, myriad colorful cushions, scented candles, and big books on art and architecture—everything to make you feel at home—but we fell into an uncomfortable silence. Desperate that we should give the impression of a relaxed, happy couple, I filled the silence. I should have settled for quiet contemplation of my galoshes.

"What do you think of what Amber said in the car?"

"Impressive, I thought. Those sorts of girls are horrid, but in my day they were the popular ones. Never understood that."

A lengthy pause. "You don't think the comment was a little"—I sought a less inflammatory word than "barbed"—"barbed?" I failed.

He put his head to one side, confused. "In what way?"

You know what "barbed" means. "Well . . . directed at me?"

"Don't be ridiculous, Tessa. She was talking about girls in a band."

"You really don't see—"

"Jimbean!"

"Hey, Lucy."

Thank God. The one I knew.

She turned to me. "You ready?"

I shook my head.

"Well, it's too late now, they've come en masse."

A wave of noise erupted outside the door.

"Everyone was in the kitchen as usual," said Lucy. "They can't wait to get their eyes on you." The noise got louder. "Brace for impact."

I felt a strong urge to put my hands over my face, but luckily I couldn't move. The doors opened, and there in front of me stood a family montage that would have made the Victorians proud. Mater, pater, Faith and Luke, and, in front of them, the children. They stared at me. Or, rather, at my shoes.

"Hi," I said, "I'm Tessa." They moved forward like a multiheaded amoeba, and the force of their presence knocked me back into the sofa. I was kissed a lot, someone gave me a drink, then another, Peter made a toast to the happy couple, everyone clapped, and I was kissed again.

"So, you're a lawyer?" asked Luke, my brother-in-law-to-be. God, that was weird.

"Entertainment lawyer, right?" answered Faith.

"Copyright, libel, that sort of thing?" asked Luke.

"That's the fun stuff. Mostly it's contracts," I replied before his wife could answer for me.

"Got any brothers? I'm single at the moment," said Lucy.

"Lucy!"

"What? No point being complacent about these things. It's good to share."

"Sorry, Lucy. Only child. Got a couple of single mates I could hook you up with, though," I said.

"Not that civil servant," said James crossly.

"Is he dishy?" asked Lucy.

"Very."

A little boy appeared and climbed onto Faith's lap. "Are your parents coming?" she asked.

"Sadly, not. Dad hurt his foot dancing. They couldn't get here."

"Dancing?" said Luke. "I thought he was . . ." His voice trailed off.

"Luke! Honestly!"

"He is old," I said, coming to Luke's rescue.

"But not infirm, by the sounds of it," said Faith. She ran her hands through her husband's hair.

I felt Faith was trying to be my friend, but she was also protecting her patch. I also knew from Amber that she and Bea saw a lot of each other, so I wasn't sure.

"Tessa's father's amazing. At eighty-four, he could give me a run for my money," said James, taking my hand.

"So could most people, old man," said Lucy.

"What about your mother?" asked Honor.

My head was bouncing about, trying to keep up. I felt like I was at a doubles tennis match. "Unfortunately, she isn't well enough to drive at the moment either." Ever.

"Oh, she hasn't got that horrible sick bug that's going around? Charlie puked for days. Everyone's been off school," said Faith.

I'd assumed they'd know about the MS. I readied myself for the story I hated telling, but was always asked. When, how, what, where, poor you, I have a friend . . . But it didn't happen. There was a sudden shift in direction.

"Bea told me they'd closed the whole school down," said James.

"Not only that. Health inspectors found traces of salmonella. We are forming a cleaning committee. They've been outsourcing it to some company..."

This was followed by a semi-discussion on underage illegal workers. Someone mentioned a fourteen-year-old Vietnamese girl found working at a supermarket, which led to a brief debate about whether Vietnam would be a fun destination for a Kent family Christmas.

Then Faith turned to me. "So, Tessa," she said, "back to what we were talking about ..." I was poised for my rehearsed speech about my mother's health. "Where's the ring?"

"The ring?"

"The ring! Yes, where's the ring?" Faith waggled her rock at me.

"Haven't got one yet," I said, staring stupidly at my empty fingers.

"Couldn't prize Nona's ring off Jimbean's dead fingers," said Charlie, the five-year-old sitting on Faith's knee.

I laughed, but no one else did.

"Charlie!" said Luke, his father.

"What, Dad? That's what you said in the car."

"Luke?" It was James. I could see he was hurt. And it wasn't because this situation was awkward for me.

"Sorry, mate. Sometimes I forget we live with a human parrot."

"Not really the point."

Luke nodded, chastised.

"That ring is going to Amber," said James. "We've discussed this. Bea's keeping it till then."

Hang on. Bea? I thought we were talking about ... Oh God. It felt like the room suddenly expanded then contracted. Jim Bean. Bea. He wasn't Jimbean. They were. Together.

"She was wearing it at Luke's fortieth, Jimmy."

"So?" asked James, defending his ex-wife.

"Granny thinks she should have it," said Amber, coming over and sitting on James's knee. "To pay her back for some of the school fees." What? Pay *who* back? The ground beneath my feet shifted.

"Amber, darling, that ring wouldn't cover a single term these days," said Honor. "It has sentimental value. That's all."

"Which is why it's yours, my angel," said James. "For when you get married yourself."

"I'm never getting married," said Amber, looking sideways at me.

I wanted to jump up and shout, "Barbed! Barbed!" but the fight had left me.

" 'Course you will," said Faith.

"Never."

"Right," said Honor, standing up. "Lunch is ready. Let's go through."

Everyone started filing out. James put his arm around Amber. "So, will you look after your dad in his old age, then?"

" 'Course I will," said Amber.

"What a perfect daughter. Dedicated to her father and no boyfriends."

"Who said anything about no boyfriends?"

James's jaw dropped. Amber laughed. "Cheeky monkey," said James. They walked out together.

I hung back. Could this day get any worse?

Faith loitered at the door. "Don't worry," she said. "It gets easier."

"Does it?"

Her five-year-old came up and took my hand. He grinned at me. At last, a friend.

"Will you show me your bottom?"

I laughed.

"Charlie!"

"What? I want to see the heart."

Was that Amber sniggering in the corridor?

"What nonsense are you warbling about now?" said Faith.

Charlie opened his mouth to reply.

"Not now, Charlie, go and wash your hands."

"But, Mummy—"

"Now, Charlie."

He scuttled off. Was I being paranoid or did I catch a suppressed smile as Faith turned away from me? I shut my eyes tight and breathed out. And I'd thought the shoes would be the sticking point. It took every ounce of strength I possessed to follow her into the dining room. But I did, a smile stapled to my face, despite everyone's eyes on my crotch.

* * *

I HAD A LOT OF time to digest what I had learned at lunch. My first reaction was to shout at James, but that was what Amber wanted, so I kept my fury, my fear to myself. I realized that if our marriage was going to work, I needed her on-side. She had the ear of the king, the eyes of her mother, and my neck on the line. Defensive was never going to work. It was time to go offensive. Cora had worked brilliantly on Maddy and Lulu, so why shouldn't Caspar, my seventeen-year-old godson, do the same on Amber? He could show her that I might be a cool addition to her life, not the feared man-eating, mole-ridden monster from the fairy tales. By the time we had the kids next, I was ready.

Naturally, it didn't go quite to plan. When I introduced Caspar to Amber, he fell in love.

I ARRIVED AT THE FLAT with Caspar and called up to Amber's room. I wasn't hopeful—that morning she'd been particularly monosyllabic and had retreated to her room with her cereal. However, she immediately came skipping down the stairs, her long hair flowing behind her. The Snoopy pajamas had been replaced with an off-the-shoulder, *Flashdance*-esque sweatshirt, her pert, braless breasts bouncing through the cotton, micro-shorts, and Ugg boots. Her thighs did the concave thing that Kate Moss's do. She was wearing lip gloss too, and her hair stuck to it. I shouldn't have told her Caspar was coming. I shouldn't have told her he was seventeen. I shouldn't have told her he was male. She jumped the last few steps and landed in front of him, smiling like Miss World.

"Hi," she said.

One word was all it took. The invisible punch hit him hard. His jaw went slack, a million wet dreams were posted for future use in his mind, and the boy was down. My mute stepdaughter-to-be then decided to reclaim her voice from the evil underwater witch Ursula (I've been watching too many children's DVDs) and charm the pants off my moonstruck godson. Literally, as it turned out. Didn't take her long, either.

I retreated to the kitchen to put on another load of washing not my own, and watch them through the kitchen window while they sat and chatted on the swing in the garden. Caspar had grown a lot in the previous year. He no longer had the pasty skin of a cave dweller, his spots had cleared up, and he'd found some miracle product to tame his unruly curls. With his low-slung jeans and Quiksilver T-shirt (which I had bought him as a bribe to persuade him to come today), he looked cool. If I carried on hemorrhaging money like this, I was going to have to get a second job.

Amber kept throwing back her flaming mane and laughing loudly. All I could think was that she'd catch her death of cold. It wasn't an altogether unpleasant thought. I thrust yet more school kit into the washing machine and tried to banish it. But then Amber put her hand on his leg, so I threw in the rest of the washing, turned it on, and crawled along the kitchen floor to get a better look. They got off the swing and went to the back of the garden, where the undergrowth had taken over and borage ruled king. Somewhere in the weeds a hydrangea was fighting a losing battle. I saw Amber grab Caspar and pull him behind the garden shed. Fags, was my first thought. If only, my last.

I heard James's key in the door, and as the voices of the younger two carried through the Victorian colored glass, I had no choice but to get up.

"Hello, we're home!" called James. Lulu ran toward me to show me her stickers, then told me in great detail about the grazing habits of a steliosaurus. Maddy gave me a hug. James strode in carrying an overflowing box of groceries.

"Who's that boy I saw dart behind the shed?"

"That boy is my godson, Caspar."

"He isn't getting stoned, is he?"

"I told you, he doesn't do that anymore." But I heard the fear in my voice and went to the window. I saw no roach, but what I did see was a pair of Jimmy Choo shoes tangled with Caspar's Converse sneakers.

My shoes! was my first thought. My second was, What the hell is Amber doing with Caspar? My third blanked out all others. A firework of expletives exploded inside my head. I swung around to see James lowering the box onto the kitchen table. Calculating that I had about two seconds before James saw them, I yanked up the window and yelled, "Amber! Your dad's home!"

I saw her feet in my shoes retreat; Caspar stumbled forward, with swollen lips, and turned to the house.

"Is he stepping on the hydrangea?" James had spotted them.

I turned him away from the window. I knew who would be blamed for this. Me. For having a godson. "'Course not. Why don't you sit down? I'll make you a cup of tea."

Obediently, James sat. "Thanks, I'm exhausted." What had exhausted him was picking up two children from two separate parties and one box of preordered fruit and veg from the local shop. "Have you had a nice quiet couple of hours?" he asked. Yes, very, I thought, because, just like in fairy tales, the washing-up does itself and teenagers don't have sex.

Amber and Caspar walked in through the kitchen door. She was wearing Ugg boots again. What had she done with my shoes? I folded my arms, narrowed my eyes, and stared at Caspar.

"Dad, can Caspar and me go to Starbucks?" asked Amber. "Keira and Freddy are meeting us there."

"Sure, sweetheart. Do you need some money?"

"Thanks, Dad." She kissed his cheek. Daring, I thought, given where that mouth had been.

He handed her a twenty. No wonder James doesn't pay the school fees, I thought. He's single-handedly keeping Mr. Starbucks afloat. Caspar drifted out after her, dreamily.

You fool, I thought, you poor, deluded fool. Out of the corner of my eye I saw that James was wearing a similar expression. The bloody pair of you. Amber gave me one of her dazzling smiles. "'Bye, Tessa."

I was speechless. Now who was brazen?

"Have fun," James called after them.

I didn't trust myself to speak.

James turned to me. "See?" he said. "I told you, you were imagining things. Amber adores you."

God, give me strength.

THE FOLLOWING DAY, JAMES PROPOSED a walk in the park. I would have legged it, but I had nowhere to run, so I submitted to the tedious inevitability of tired legs, cold hands, spilled drinks, and moaning. It all came to pass. Family walks. What fun. However, I did manage to engineer time alone with Amber. We left the other three in the playground and walked up the hill to the coffee shop.

"So, what did you think of Caspar?"

She didn't bother to look at me. "He's a bit of a creep."

"What?"

"A drip, then. Couldn't get rid of him."

I was momentarily struck dumb. I tried to read her expression, but she was hiding behind her hair. "Looked to me like you quite liked him."

"What gave you that impression?" she snarled.

Well, I don't know! What about the make-out session five seconds after you'd met him? She shouldn't be that loose at any age, let alone fourteen. "I saw you, Amber," I said softly.

"Saw what?"

"You, Caspar, my shoes, the hydrangea bed?"

"What's a hydrangea?"

"Okay, the weeds your dad calls a back garden."

"Dad loves that garden. I'll tell him you don't like it."

Tough words, but she looked scared. I tried to reach out to her. "I'm not going to tell him, Amber."

"I don't know what you're talking about."

"I saw my shoes," I said sternly.

She shrugged, but I detected a waver as she lowered her eyes.

"Once you've got a reputation, it's hard to shake. Mud sticks, Amber."

That was a mistake. She glared at me. "You can talk!" Her face seemed about to crumple. "I saw what you were doing! If that's what Dad likes, well, he's welcome to you."

She ran back to the playground. I felt terrible and walked on alone to the coffee shop. I didn't care about the shoes anymore, and my delight in having ammunition to aim at Amber seemed infantile. I kept seeing her beautiful face crumple and hearing those angry words.

Back at the flat, I remembered the washing still festering in the machine from the day before and returned to the kitchen to finish my stepmother duties. Thankfully, I was alone when I pulled out the tangled mat of underclothes. Everything was mauve.

"Shit," I whispered furiously to myself, hoping I wasn't seeing what I clearly was. Everything had been dyed purple. I separated tights from leotards, tank tops from pants and my new dark blue Seven jeans. How had they got in there?

"Bollocks." The ballet kit was ruined. Think, girl, think. It was okay. One call to my friend Francesca, mother of Caspar and two younger girls, and I would know where to go. Ballet was . . . I racked my brain— well, it wasn't Monday, so that was fine. I heard voices, shoved everything into the laundry basket, and covered it. Then, like a Stepford wife, I set up the ironing board and got to work on the wash I hadn't ruined. In a quiet moment, I stashed the wet ballet kit into a plastic bag and threw it into the boot of my car. Guilt-ridden, I went through Maddy and Lulu's satchels, helped them do their homework, then got them into the car to be returned, in full working order, to their magnificent mother. I bet she'd never tie-dyed a leotard.

"Come on, Tessa, we're going for pizza on the way."

"I'm fine, thanks. I need to get stuff ready for work."

"Oh, come on, it won't be fun without you." James was being lovely but, my God, he hadn't seen Amber's face. And how could I say no after Maddy took my hand and said please? I couldn't.

So, to the dreaded Pizza Express we went with the rest of the world's offspring. One good thing: my body clock seemed to have ground to a halt. I operated on automatic pilot through supper, slicing pizza, mopping up drinks, avoiding Amber's sharp elbows, and got back into the car relieved. I must have been in a daze, because I didn't realize that instead of heading home, we turned east toward Holloway. I was lulling in neutral and missed the cinema, the high street, the superstore, and the railway bridge.

Suddenly we stopped and I came around. "Where are we?"

"Just dropping the girls off," said James.

"What?"

"Bea's house," he said, pointing.

"But—"

"Don't worry, I put all the school uniforms you'd ironed into their bags. We've got everything."

I didn't care. I had tomato sauce on the T-shirt I'd been wearing for two days because I hadn't had time to do any washing of my own, and my hair was filthy. I mouthed the next few words: "I. Don't. Think. This. Is. A. Good. Idea."

"Nonsense. You're part of the family now."

Ssh! You'll wake the beast. I turned to the girls. My future stepdaughters. Bea's daughters. Amber glared at me. I forced myself to smile. "Thanks for a great weekend, girls. See you Wednesday."

Lulu and Maddy smiled back. Amber got out of the car and said, "Come on, you two. Hurry up. Daddy has to go now."

Lulu and Maddy stopped smiling.

"Say good-bye to Tessa," said James. If he had been speaking to Amber, which I doubted, she ignored him and he let it pass. Lulu gave me a quick hug.

Maddy was fussing with her seat belt. I leaned into the back to give her a hand. "Let me help you, honey," I said, unclicking it.

As the seat belt sprang back, Maddy threw herself forward between the seats. She took my face in her small hands. "Can I tell you a secret?" she said quietly, nose to nose.

"Of course you can."

"I love you."

I wanted to weep. "That doesn't have to be a secret," I said, stroking her cheek.

But Maddy knew better than me. "Yes, it does."

"Why?"

Just as she was about to tell me what I suspected I already knew, that Amber forbade it, James leaned back into the car. "Mum's here," he said, and the moment was broken. Maddy was out of the car like a shot, running down the narrow path to the front door, where she threw herself into her mother's arms. In the moment before she was enveloped by her loving daughter, I saw her. The woman who had stood outside James's flat in tears the night Lulu was sick. I felt a gigantic invisible piece of the jigsaw puzzle land on my head. James was wrong. His ex-wife was nowhere near fine about this, and that explained everything. I looked again. At last. I'd found the solution. And the solution was Bea. Everyone was talking to her at once. She was smiling, managing to answer and listen at the same time. It was time to face this. It was time for her to face me.

"You not coming in?" said a voice that had to be Bea's.

"I think we're going to get off."

I could taste the silence. We? *We?* She hadn't seen me in the passenger seat, because she wasn't expecting me to be there. Now I didn't know what to do. The car door was already open. I put a foot out and stood. The girls moved aside. Bea took a step back. My heart sank. I'd got it wrong. She wasn't the fat lady in tears. In fact, she looked lovely. Dressed up. Better than me. I knew I should be polite. But I couldn't do it. I couldn't even say hello. We stared at each other.

"Mum! Phone!"

"What?"

"Phone!" yelled Amber, pointing into the house.

Bea looked back at James. "Sorry, hon. Another time."

Hon? By the time I'd straightened out, the front door had closed. Bea and the girls were gone. James shrugged, walked around the car, and got back in. I sat down. *Hon?* I wondered what term of endearment he called her when I wasn't about. Jimbean?

When I thought we were safely out of earshot and several more turns after that, I spoke.

"That was a bloody stupid thing to do," I spat.

"What?"

"You can't throw us at each other like that!"

"I wasn't. I was dropping the girls home."

"Not with me! It's not fair to them."

James signaled and turned the wheel methodically through his fingers. Foolishly, I believed he was registering what I was saying. "Why not?" he asked. "It's what I do every other Sunday night I have them."

"Not with me!"

"Why not with you? We're getting married, Tessa."

I gulped. "They're not ready. Amber, none of them."

"Really?" said James coldly.

"Yes, really."

"They're not ready, or *you're* not ready?"

"All of us, James . . ." I faltered. "Maybe even Bea."

"She looked fine to me."

"Did she, now?"

"Don't be ridiculous, Tessa."

"Christ, James, she's not your old mate from school who I just didn't quite meet. She's your ex-wife, who broke your heart, who dresses up on a Sunday night, who calls you honey—"

"Stop it." James pulled in behind a parked car and stopped the car abruptly. "Stop it. Now. I'm just trying to make this all as normal as possible. For everybody. Why are you making it into a big deal?"

"You know what? Sometimes things are a big deal, James, whether you like it or not."

He sighed heavily. As if he'd heard it all before. One justifiable complaint, and I was made to feel like a nag. "I'm sorry, am I boring you?" I asked.

James closed his eyes. "We just dropped off the kids. Bea seemed fine with it."

And I'm not? Stupid, silly, overemotional me? Well, you haven't been used as a punching bag by a deceptively strong fourteen-year-old all weekend. You haven't dyed a ballet kit purple. Your family can't list pubic topiary as one of your hobbies. You're not a secret love. A second-bride-to-be. You're *hon*. I'm nobody.

"You refuse to see what's at the end of your nose," I said.

"And you refuse not to."

"What does that mean?"

"That everything is fine. Why are you looking for drama? The expression 'mountains out of molehills' springs to mind."

"Well, maybe if you stopped thinking of your children's emotional welfare as molehills, we'd be able to talk about this rationally. They're not happy about this and you don't want to see it."

"Don't tell me my children aren't happy."

"Selective hearing. I didn't say they weren't happy."

"What did you say, then?"

"Oh, forget it. I'm going home." I opened the car door.

"Very good, Tessa. Run away. Seems to work wonders for you."

I turned to him, but he stared straight ahead, so I had no option but to get out. Well, maybe I did, but it didn't feel like that at the time. James pulled out of the parking space before I'd had a chance to let go of the handle, and it shot out of my hand, pulling my little finger painfully.

"Ow," I said, staring after the taillights. "Ow," I said again. Because I hurt.

WHEN I FINALLY WALKED INTO my apartment, I was exhausted. I retrieved a bottle of wine from the rack, opened it, and poured a huge glass of red wine. The whole flat was cold. Unlived-in. Dusty. This was my home and it felt as empty as I did. But the home I wanted did not want me.

I threw the thermostat up and curled into a ball on my sofa. A tear fell onto my lap. I wiped away its successor angrily. At thirty-eight, with no children of my own, I found myself in no-man's-land. Worse, it wasn't no-man's-land. It was Bea's. I was the unwelcome trespasser. She was their mother. They were her children. She held the one card the dealer could never pass to me. DNA. The winning card. So where did that leave me? The underdog. What sort of life was that? Another tear fell, then another. Bea Kent? Bea Kent? I poured myself more wine and let the tears spill out of me. Who the hell was this superwoman, Bea Kent?

Nine

Liquid Diet

"They've gone, Mum," said Amber.

"Hm?"

She folded her arms in front of her chest, reminding me of myself. "I said they've gone."

I restacked the vertebrae in my spine. "Sorry. Who's on the phone?"

"It was a wrong number," said Amber, not quite looking at me.

"Right, you lot, coats off. I expect you're starving."

"We went to Pizza Express," said Lulu.

"All of you?"

"Tessa likes the ones with raisins," said Lulu. "She said I could have an orange dress."

"No, she didn't," said Amber.

I herded my daughters out of the hallway. "That's nice. So, how was the weekend?"

"Great," said Lulu. "Tessa and I have invented a new game."

"That's nice. Maddy, stop scuffing your shoes. What's wrong with you?"

"I want a pink one."

"A pink what?"

"And she's taking us to a concert!" said Lulu, interrupting.

"A what?"

"A pink bridesmaid's dress. I don't like orange and Daddy said we had to match. Is that all right, Mummy? If I have a pink one. With lots of skirts like a fairy. Daddy says Tessa will look like an angel, so can I be a fairy? A pink one?"

"What are you going to wear, Mummy?"

I looked at my daughters. "Um . . . Um . . ."

"Any messages, Mum?" Amber asked brightly.

I sought her out like a rescue beacon. "Yes. Keira called, and a boy. He didn't leave his name."

"Keira. Can I call her now? We're planning the end-of-term show together. We've got lots of ideas."

"Great, okay, good. Right. Let's look at this." I unzipped the bag that took my children away from me in one order and brought them back in another. But for once the uniforms were not bundled in but folded neatly in piles. I inhaled the sweet, thick smell of detergent. "Wow, Dad's done the washing again."

Lulu opened her mouth to answer, but Amber, I noticed, gave her a little push. "You farted!" said Amber.

Lulu looked hurt. "Didn't."

"What's that smell, then?"

"Mum, I didn't."

"It doesn't matter," I said to Lulu.

"But I didn't!" she shouted.

I could see where this was going.

"Mummy, she didn't," said Maddy. "Amber just made that up."

"Why would I do that?" yelled Amber, and stormed off.

I didn't get her back to apologize, because I knew exactly why she would do that. "I think everyone's a bit tired. Shall we all go upstairs? Is there any homework to do?"

My sweet younger daughters shook their heads. God, it was great to have them home. "Lulu, what about reading?"

"Done it."

"Really?"

Lulu nodded. Maddy did, too, so I knew it was true. Maddy hasn't learned how to lie yet. She isn't anything like a typical youngest—I took a sharp breath.

"You okay, Mummy?" asked Lulu.

I rubbed my chest where the pain had been. "Just a little indigestion. So, no homework to do, no reading. Let's go upstairs, have a big bath, and we'll have lots of time for stories in my bed."

The girls shouted gleefully and tore up the stairs. No frantic supper to prepare, no homework to rush, no simple yet mystifying words to extract from Lulu ... so why didn't I feel relieved? Any normal person would. It meant the last hour of the day with my children would be fun and not the battleground it had historically been after an overstimulated, oversugared, underdisciplined weekend with their father.

I stared down at the pristinely ironed shirts and gave the bag a stupid little kick. I knew, of course, that Jimmy hadn't done any of it. That sort of thing just wasn't his forte. Which left only one person. Tessa King. I bet she'd done the bloody reading, too. Tough. I wasn't ready to be grateful yet. So Jimmy had found himself a nice au pair to do the dirty work. Stupid man! I would have done it. I would have done it all. I looked back at the door, half-expecting her still to be standing there, a patronizing smile on her face, her arms around my children. "Hey, Bea, just bringing the kids home. Yes, we had a *great* time! They're fabulous children ..."

Yes, they are fabulous! I wanted to shout. Fabulous, because I have given them my life! My soul! My energy! My wisdom! My whole! And in return I get you! The image of her was fuzzy around the edges. I'd only caught her profile coming out of the car. Big nose, I thought. Then Amber had called me in and it had seemed easier to retreat.

I hurled the bag over my shoulder and followed my children upstairs. Amber's door was closed. I knew better than to open it. I could hear the bloody Dumbbells playing, some ghastly song about getting felt up. The younger ones were already running around naked when I got to their room. Delighting in being back among their belongings. I had been to James's flat and it always felt like what it was to me and the girls. A temporary solution. Transient. A place where roots were tubbed, ready for easy removal. They had things there—but old things they no longer played with. Or things they would come to in the future, but the future was as unimaginable as a sky with no end and, like all things we don't understand, they were cast aside.

This was home. I had worked hard to make it so. And I could tell by the scrabble of bare feet on bare boards that they were happy to be here. And I was happy to have them home. And yet, and yet . . .

I used to dream of peace and quiet when I was married. I hated it now. I guess I had lived in the asylum too long. Open spaces and days that didn't move at the pace of a machine gun freaked me out. On my weekends without the kids I would walk around in circles waiting to be asked to fetch something, mend something, stick something, hold something, wipe something, be something. Then stop. And realize nobody was asking anything of me and I was nobody without them. I didn't need less time with them, I needed more. I needed them constantly. What would happen to me when Maddy reached Amber's age? Would she close the door on me, too?

A small hole opened in my stomach. It stayed with me through bath time and the constant chatter about bridesmaids' dresses. Through three stories. Through the chat I tried to have with my unresponsive eldest. It stayed with me as I walked along the corridor of a hushed household and down the creaking stairs. It stayed with me while I searched the house for things to pick up and put away and it stayed with me when I realized there were none. There was a hole. And I would have to dam it or risk losing what little there was left of me. I opened the fridge.

"THANK GOD YOU'RE THERE!" I said to Faith. "I've been calling and calling."

"Sorry, what's wrong?"

"Where've you been?"

"The cinema."

"What about Charlie?"

"He's asleep."

"Who was looking after him?"

"Bea, did you call late on Sunday night to discuss my child-care arrangements?"

"No. Sorry."

"The babysitter doesn't answer the landline."

"Oh. Okay."

"Happy now?"

I paused.

"Bea, what is it?"

I put my throbbing head into my hands. Maybe this call wasn't such a good idea after all.

"I'm sorry I didn't call you about the lunch."

I looked up through my fingers. "Lunch?"

"The official introduction."

"Introduction?"

"Bea, are you drunk?"

"I wish." I flustered and forced myself to sit up straight. "I'm on this ridiculous diet, couldn't risk the calories. What official introduction?"

"Tessa came to Peter and Honor's for lunch. The whole family was there."

If Faith realized her mistake, she didn't comment on it. Whole family but me, I wanted to say. Whole family but me! "I didn't know about it," I said faintly, picking up my glass.

"The girls must have told you."

"No. They didn't."

"That's weird," said Faith. "Are you sure you're okay, Bea? You sound a little—"

"Weary. Went out last night with some friends. Got a bit late."

"Bea! That's great."

Yeah. It was also a lie. I needed another drink.

"Meet anyone?"

"No one I'd see again," I replied. That would have been hard, since I was on the sofa alone for the duration of the night. "So how did it go, the grand lunch?"

"She did okay," said Faith.

Trying to be diplomatic but not nearly hard enough, in my opinion. My idea of diplomatic was trashing Tessa to the hilt. Anything else would incur my wrath and border skirmishes were bound to follow. I finished my glass of wine and poured again. But not yet. I needed Faith for information. "Okay, you say?"

"She was nervous, poor thing. Wearing these terrible shoes, which made her look like a matron. But she's bright, I'll give her that."

Intelligent. Interesting. Diverting, I bet. Full of witty anecdotes and up to date with the news. It's okay for some. I don't have time for newspapers.

"You still there?"

"Yes."

"There was the excruciating moment when Charlie asked to see her heart," said Faith, giggling despite herself.

"Her what?"

"Oh. Um. Nothing."

"What are you talking about?"

"The girls didn't tell you?"

No, they didn't tell me about that either. "Oh . . . yes . . . the heart. Of course. How could I forget?" I forced a laugh, wondering what I was supposed to be laughing about. "Excruciating is the word."

"I mean honestly! Heart-shaped pubes . . . doing a striptease. It's a bit over the top, isn't it?"

I retched, then swallowed hard.

"At least she had the decency to be embarrassed," Faith continued.

Decency! Heart-shaped pubes. Striptease. I retched again. Didn't sound decent. Nothing the woman did sounded decent. Bribing my children with fairy dresses. Concert tickets. Lip gloss! Did she think I was stupid?

"You okay, Bea?"

"Trying not to laugh," I managed.

"I actually felt a bit sorry for her."

"Well, don't. She just turned up here!"

"What? Why? Did you talk to her?"

"No."

"You didn't let her in?"

"No. She was in the car with Jimmy."

"Sorry. I don't follow. Why did they come over so late?"

"This was earlier," I said, my temper rising. Why was Faith being so obtuse? So slow?

"Oh," said my ex-sister-in-law. "So she didn't come alone to see you just now?"

"No. She was in the car with Jimmy."

"Yes, you said that . . . but . . . Oh, okay. You mean when he dropped the girls home?"

Obviously that was what I'd meant. Wasn't that bad enough? And what did "Oh, okay" mean? She had come to my house, with no warning, brazen as you like, as if it were perfectly normal for my husband and another woman to be dropping my children home! And another thing. She hadn't even bothered to say hello or anything . . .

"Bea, you still there?"

"Hm?"

"Bea. Are you okay? You sound really pissed off."

"I'm not pissed off, I'm just . . ." I stared at the near-empty bottle in front of me. "I'm tired."

"It's just, well, at Luke's fortieth you said—"

I sat up. Alert. Tuned to the danger. "A moment of madness," I said emphatically. "That's all."

"Really?"

"Absolutely."

"Because Lucy noticed you were wearing your engagement ring."

"It's the only decent piece of jewelry I have." Annoying, irritating, meddling, know-it-all, hippie-shit Lucy. What did she know about responsibility? Duty to care? Guilt?

"That's what I said. But I'd understand, you know, if, well, if you'd thought you'd made a mistake. You don't have to go through this alone."

"Honestly. It was nothing. We'd been getting on so well recently that I allowed myself to forget everything that had happened. I absolutely don't feel like . . . No, no. The whole family night went to my head for a second. It's hard when I see him and the girls having such a great time together. Dancing together like a family. As it should be."

"Are you sure—"

"It's fine, Faith. I didn't mean it. You didn't tell anyone, did you?"

"No! I've been feeling terrible about it. I said those things to you about Jimmy always loving you. I had no idea about Tessa—'course, it makes sense now. That's why he's been so much more relaxed with you. So much happier. He's finally over you. We've got Jimmy back. Sorry, that sounds very harsh, but—"

"Harsh?" I laughed again. Daggers. Hideous, jagged, cold, hot daggers. Stabbing. Stabbing. Stabbing. Not deep enough to kill but, God almighty, it hurt and the blood—there wasn't supposed to be that much blood. They said they'd got it all out. They lied.

"No, not harsh. Fair," I said, forcing myself to speak. "I left him. I ..." Did so much worse than that. I fucked everything up. But I wasn't myself. Couldn't they see? Love is a strange thing. He had so much. It overwhelmed me. I'd never been loved like that. Not even by my mother. I had trained myself to become lovable. I had worked out how to make a man fall in love with me. It wasn't hard. Men were easy. Mothers were harder to crack. But I couldn't return it. I couldn't live up to it. I couldn't love him back. It wasn't my fault—

"Bea?"

"Hi."

"You using your bloody mobile again?"

"Sorry."

"You keep cutting out on me."

"Sorry."

"Call me from the landline. You'll give yourself a tumor."

"Chance would be a fine thing."

"What?"

"Can't find the damn thing."

"What thing? Bea, you're not making sense."

"The portable phone. Anyway, I've got to get on."

"It's half-past ten on Sunday night."

"Name tags," I said. "Are we still going out for a drink on Wednesday?"

"Actually, sorry, Bea, I double-booked."

"Don't worry. A friend of mine's going to the cinema that night, so . . ."

"Okay, great. Another time, then."

Yes. And another evening home alone.

"And, Bea, it's great about the diet. It'll really help."

"Thanks."

Patronizing cow. I put the portable phone I had supposedly lost on the table next to the bottle of wine I supposedly hadn't drunk and drained the glass. It was a ridiculous diet, since it seemed to be nine-tenths liquid. It was working, though. The pounds were falling away and I liked the constant feeling of hunger. It was a close companion. And I was in need of one of those.

I woke up to the alarm bleating in my brain. I swiped at it. It fell from the bedside table with a clatter and went on bleating. I peered at my watch to see whether I could lie in for a few minutes but the footfalls on the landing told me otherwise. So did the time. I must have put the alarm on wrong. It was already twenty past seven.

I leaped out of bed and immediately regretted it. I rubbed my throbbing forehead. I'd forgotten to open the window again. I always get a headache if I sleep without the window open. My clothes were piled neatly on the chair next to my dressing table. But I noticed my pajama buttons were done up wrong. Funny that. I must have been so tired by the time I went to bed. I don't even remember putting them on. I looked at my neatly folded clothes again. I had a thought, like a diminishing dream. Before it was fully formed, it had vanished, and I couldn't grasp what it might have been. Except that it was uncomfortable.

I put my clothes on quickly, no time to choose different ones, splashed a lot of cold water on my face, brushed my teeth, and left my room. I wondered whether I was coming down with something. The girls were dressed and already in the kitchen. Amber was pouring bowls of cereal when I got there. Special K. Thankfully, they liked it. The dreaded Crunchy Nut had not passed the threshold. I could be proud of that much. I went to kiss the girls good morning.

"You smell funny, Mummy," said Maddy. "Ow! Amber kicked me."

"Did not!"

"Did!"

"Enough! I've got a headache."

I put in a round of toast and mashed some banana. The toast burned. Bloody dial. I think there might be a poltergeist in my house. I put in another round.

"What about the honey and yogurt?" asked Lulu.

"Give me a chance!" I retorted.

"I'll do it," said Amber, reaching out to the fridge.

"Don't lean back like that, Amber. You'll fall."

She was trying to be nice, no doubt feeling guilty about her surly behavior the night before. Well, I'm sorry I can't be as cool as Tessa and give you free CDs and tickets to concerts, and I'm sorry I have to be the one who is continually telling you not to lean back in the chair but someone bloody has to.

"Mum! The toast!"

Black smoke billowed out of the old machine.

"Bloody hell!" I swore. "What's wrong with this thing?"

"You've turned it too high."

"I haven't," I replied petulantly. "I just turned it down."

"That's the wrong way," said Amber.

It's very annoying to be put in your place by your child. "I just turned it—" I glanced at the toaster. The red dot sat under max. "If this is your idea of a joke, it's not funny. It's a waste of food."

"You'd still eat it. Even if it had been on the floor."

"Amber Kent! That's a terrible thing to say."

She glared at me. Fury in her eyes. Or was it something else? My anger was replaced by fear. "What is it, Amber? What's going on?" The little ones stared wide-eyed at me, then at their sister. A muscle twitched in Amber's cheek. Her father's the same. They're so unbelievably similar, those two. She was about to say something, I know it, but then she looked at Lulu and Maddy, dug her spoon into her cereal, and jerked it into her mouth. She must have chewed that mouthful a hundred times. By thirty, I knew I wasn't going to get anything else out of her. Finally, I got the bread toasted, the banana mashed, the yogurt smeared on top, and a drizzle of honey in the shape of a heart. But it was too late for anyone to eat it. We'd run out of time. I scooped the soggy mess into a Tupperware box, grabbed a pile of book bags, and hustled them out of the house.

"Are you sure you should drive?" said Amber, helping the girls into the car.

"What are you talking about?"

"You said you had a headache."

I was wrong-footed. "I'll be fine. Thank you for your concern."

She shrugged and squeezed into the back with her sisters. Normally, she sits up front with me. I knew what this meant: Tessa was winning and I was losing. Well, I would, wouldn't I? She didn't have to lay down rules, get three kids up and dressed every morning, fed, watered, supervised, educated. She didn't have to force civility on beasts that would rather run wild. She got to swan about in fancy clothes with pink pubic hair and spoil my children with endless pizzas and presents. It was obscene. Skinny cow probably only picked at the raisins—

Amber screamed. "Stop!"

I braked hard.

"What?"

She pointed. A woman and two small children were halfway across the pedestrian crossing. The bonnet of the car was inches from the children's skulls. The woman glared at me, terrified. I raised my hand apologetically. Where the hell had they come from? Bloody Tessa King. Pervading my thoughts. Ruining my life. I edged forward slowly and drove the rest of the way like a milk float. We were late. Well, I thought, waiting for the secretary to come out of her office and open the already locked door, there's a first time for everything.

I SAT IN THE CAR for a long time before I started the engine, breathing slowly. The adrenaline that had been released into my system the moment Amber had shouted was like detergent through grease. It cut a clear line through my brain and I saw everything perfectly. I'd seen the empties in the bin and I knew I hadn't put them there. This had to stop. All of it. Right now. Before any damage was done. Before anyone got hurt. If I could put the fork down, I could put the glass down. It hadn't been long. Miso soup would do just as well. Nearly. I didn't need to drink. It just made the hunger go away. I could stop. A couple of glasses a night did not an alcoholic make. It wasn't as if I was pouring it on my cereal. I'd fallen asleep on the sofa before. But I could always remember putting myself to bed. That was the difference. And the mornings ... they were getting harder. I was grouchy, I knew it. It was because I was hungry. That was the problem. I wasn't eating enough, so, of course, the wine went to my head. Well, I wasn't going to start eating again. Everyone said I was looking better. Especially Jimmy. I'd just have to lay off the wine in the evenings. Have some extra salad. Easy. I knew I could do it.

I stuck to my resolve until teatime. But the fear of fish fingers and peas overwhelmed me. My stomach juices growled inside their tripy cage; I needed to tame them. One shot of vodka is only ninety calories, which is quite a lot. I could have two apples for that, but vodka's appetite-suppressing qualities are equal to none. It was just one, after all. I wouldn't have any wine later. Enough to kill the beast. Or quiet it until the plates were empty and the leftovers had been masticated by the metal teeth of the waste-disposal unit. I didn't trust myself to scrape them into the bin anymore. I had discovered that that was not enough to stop me returning to them later and stuffing them into my mouth when no one was looking. Strange that when I was standing up and eating alone, I could convince myself that the calories didn't count. "Waste not, want not," my mother used to say. Her steely words had the opposite effect on me. Waste not, want even more. Amber was right. I had eaten off the floor. Cramming crumbs into my mouth. Always, always trying to fill the hole.

I was cleaning the oven when the phone rang. I peeled off my gloves and answered it.

"Mrs. Kent, so sorry to bother you, it's Mrs. Hitchens."

The ballet teacher? "Hello, how's exhibition day going?"

"Good, thank you, so far, except Lulu doesn't seem to have her kit here."

"She's like her father. It's on her peg."

"Well, actually we sent them home with their uniforms on Friday and—"

So, perfect Tessa King wasn't so perfect, after all. "I know what's happened. She was at her father's this weekend. Let me see what I can do."

"Can I tell her it will be here by this afternoon? I'm afraid there have been some tears."

Well, life's tough, honey, get used to it.

"Of course."

"That's wonderful, Mrs. Kent, thank you. Lulu has worked so hard on this performance." Good grief, it was a nine-year-olds' ballet class, not fucking Covent Garden. By the way, that's the "First Mrs. Kent" to you. Didn't you know. There's a second coming. "Let me see what I can do," I said gaily.

"Thank you so much. I'm sure Lulu will appreciate it."

Well, I haven't been thanked for the thirty-two hundred and eighty-seven times they've gone to school with clean ballet clothes before but, sure as eggs is eggs, she'll remember this one life-shattering moment and dangle it in front of me accusingly every time something goes wrong in her world. Poor Lulu, she had a terrible mother, you know.

Well, damn it, I wasn't taking the rap alone. I hung up and called Jimmy. He was at work, but I caught him just before he went into a meeting. He promised he'd go home, get the kit, and drop it off at the school by two-thirty. I thanked him profusely and ignored the strong sensation that I knew it was never going to happen. I finished the housework and then went to the supermarket. I told myself I may as well stop at the bottle bank. I could have waited for the recycling collection, but since I was going. I averted my eyes until each bottle had shattered inside the giant urn and the boxes were empty. The phone was ringing as I carried through the last of the shopping bags.

"It's not here," said Jimmy.

"It must be," I said, placing the bags on the sideboard.

"Bea, it isn't. I've looked everywhere."

Through a locked jaw, I said, "With all due respect, you're not really very good at—"

"Bea, I'm telling you, it isn't here!"

"Please don't get cross with me. Your daughter didn't call you up in floods of tears. You haven't had the teacher on the phone. They sent her home with it on Friday to be washed."

"Then Tessa would have washed it, ironed it, and sent it back with the other stuff."

"Well, she didn't, because I unpacked everything that night. Sorry, Jimmy, it's still with you."

"It's not her fault, Bea. It's mine. I'm hopeless at keeping up with the girls' things. I'm sorry, it's just not one of—"

"Your fortes?" I said, forcing a laugh. "Jimmy, I think I know that by now." But if your little au pair isn't up to it, then someone has to take charge. "You'll have to call Tessa and ask her what she's done with it."

"Isn't there another way we—"

"If there was I wouldn't have called you. Please, it's so important to Lulu. I'll wait on the line."

"She has this huge meeting today."

Bully for her, Miss Big Potatoes . . . "Lulu's been practicing for weeks and you know how she needs all the confidence she can get at the moment."

I heard him swear under his breath. "You're right, of course. Hang on . . . Tessa King, please . . . Yes, I know she's in a meeting, but this is important. It's her fiancé . . ." I winced. "Yes, hi—James, that's right, yup, thank you so much . . . I know how important it is, but it's an emergency." *James,* was he?

I waited in silence as he waited in silence. Another, less acerbic, thought drifted through the bile . . . This is a really bad idea, my friend, a really, really bad call. Get that person back. Don't interrupt her if it really is important. You know what you should have done? Got your arse to a shop, thrown money at the problem like you do for yourself, bought Lulu new everything, sewn the elastic on yourself, however halfhearted, and delivered it all to school by two-thirty. But you didn't even think of it, did you? And now . . .

"Hi, Tessa."

Here we go.

"So sorry to get you out of your . . . Yes, everyone's fine . . . No, not your mum, God, no." I confess I felt a bit bad at this point. What was wrong with Tessa's mother? "It's just, well, it's Lulu's exhibition performance at school . . . Yes, ballet . . . I know, but she's very upset . . . In tears . . . I'm sorry you feel . . . I think you're being a little unreasonable . . . No, I can't just go and buy new . . ." 'Least she was thinking. "Well, this should be important to you . . . Tessa, just tell me where the fucking ballet kit is . . ." Oops. "Tessa? Tessa?"

"What?" I asked. There was no reply. "What? Jimmy, where is it?"

I heard him bring the house receiver up to his ear. "She put the phone down."

I bit my lip so I wouldn't laugh. "Did you explain it was for our daughter?"

Jimmy sighed heavily. "Yes."

"Lulu will be devastated," I said, tweaking the blade.

"I'm so sorry, Bea."

I had no choice but to fall on my sword. "I'll ring around the mothers, see what I can put together."

"You're a godsend. Thank you. Please apologize to Lulu for me."

"You can do that yourself."

"I will, I will, of course I will."

"I'll call you back to let you know it's all sorted."

"Thank you," said Jimmy. "And, Bea, I'm so sorry. I know you do so much already . . ." I put down the receiver.

It was about then that I remembered Amber's old ballet things were kept upstairs, waiting for her siblings to grow into it. I went upstairs to her room. In the top cupboard there were boxes labeled with all sorts of clothes waiting to be handed down. There was a jumper box, trousers, summer stuff, swimwear, sports, and, of course, in such a female household, a huge ballet box. Everything was in age order. It was all clean, and neatly folded. I pulled out the pile marked AGED 10. It might be a fraction too big, but it would do. I got into the car and drove to the school. I handed over the already named uniform to Lulu and was rewarded with her huge hug, and grateful smiles from the teachers. They understood how hard it was to oversee three children, and one big one who caused more havoc than all the rest. I waved a hand, casual, in control. The cross we bear.

"You're brilliant," said Mrs. Hitchens. "We're not really allowed, but would you like to stay and watch?" Nothing would be nicer, I thought. When Lulu saw me, her face made me fill up. She is totally crap at ballet, but her enthusiasm wins everyone over. I clapped hard when she had finished, and took her smile with me when I left.

Jimmy had left three anxious messages. I decided to call him later.

I got into the car and drove home, humming to the radio. I went up to Amber's room and replaced all the boxes in the order I'd found them. Closing the cupboard on the hand-me-downs, I wondered, still smiling to myself, why on earth I hadn't thought of them before.

Ten

Movie Night

THE FOLLOWING WEDNESDAY EVENING, THE BELL RANG. THEY WERE LATE. And Amber, as usual, would rather get me up to open the door than bother to look for her keys. But they were here. And that was good. I pulled at my new dress and adjusted the neckline in the hall mirror. With a quick smack of the lips, I opened the door.

"Honor!" I exclaimed. "Er . . . What—"

"Hello, Bea. Jimmy asked me to collect the girls."

"Oh?" I peered into the street. "He's not with you?"

"No."

"Hi, girls," I said.

"Hi, Mum," they chorused, and pushed past me.

"Sorry I'm a bit late. We've been at the Science Museum."

"I wish Jimmy would tell me when he changes plans like this."

"Sorry. They're all fed and watered, though." She turned to go.

"It's not your fault. Please come in. I haven't seen you since Luke's party. It would be nice to catch up."

"I'd love to." Honor came into my small house, closed the door, and threw her coat over the banister. "You look great, Bea. How much have you lost?"

"I don't know. A bit."

"Bea?"

I couldn't suppress a victorious smile. "Um, nearly fourteen pounds."

"That's unbelievable. So quickly?"

I laughed nervously. "Doesn't feel quick. I'm told by my guide at WeightWatchers that the beginning is the easiest bit. I can't believe that's true. It's been bloody hard. But the scales are moving in the right direction, which is an incentive to continue."

"So you're doing WeightWatchers?"

I escorted my former mother-in-law to the kitchen. "I couldn't do it on my own. It's all very controlled. I need that. Too many temptations in this house, too many chances to cheat, what with the biscuits and the children's supper. Fish fingers are my downfall." I laughed. "This way I have to stick to certain amounts of points a day, but if I accidentally inhale one of those evil orange rectangles, I can deduct the points and it doesn't send me racing for the cheddar with the excuse that all is lost. Veggies are free, so I'm perpetually munching a carrot or something." My God, it almost sounded healthy.

"Well, congratulations, Bea. I'm very impressed."

Don't be. I'm lying through my black-coffee-stained teeth. "I was going to wait until the girls were in bed before I have my two-point glass of wine, but since you're here, would you care to join me?"

"Love to. Your girls are delightful, but exhausting. Just one. I'm driving."

"That's all I'm allowed," I said, smiling broadly. Maybe I do know where Amber gets her acting skills from.

"Lovely. Thanks."

"So what happened to Jimmy this time? Some big deal about to go through?" I asked knowingly.

"Oh, this was more of a personal nature," said Honor.

"Really."

"Some tiff, apparently. They've gone away."

All right for some, I thought, and wondered who was paying. "A tiff?"

"Something about a missing ballet kit. The poor girl might be finding the prospect of becoming a stepmother harder than she expected. Have you met her yet?"

"Seen her through a car door, but I'm not sure that counts. I don't think Jimmy's quite ready for the full ménage à trois. We might start comparing notes."

Honor laughed. I laughed with her. Ha. Ha. Ha.

"She seems a very nice girl, actually. Lulu and Maddy are clearly besotted, but Amber might be giving her a run for her money."

"Besotted. Yes. Lovely. I thought Amber liked her too. She's always playing that Dumbbell record. I think Tessa works with them or something." Obviously by now I knew exactly what Tessa did, and had Googled her several times, but I had to feign total disinterest or Honor would clam up. And with my children failing to keep me abreast of the gossip, I needed her on-side. No one could suspect a thing.

"A useful perk," said Honor.

"You're telling me."

"I think Tessa might have slightly overdone that one, though."

"Really?" I said again.

"Well, Amber did mention feeling as if she was being bought off."

That's my girl. "I almost feel sorry for Tessa," I said, completely falsely.

"Well, she's quite a piece of work, that one."

I decided to assume Honor meant Tessa, though I knew she didn't. I poured two glasses of wine.

"And that's only two points?" asked Honor.

I winked at her. "Well, I may cheat a wee bit on that."

"Don't blame you." She raised her glass. "To you. I'm very impressed. As always." I remembered just in time not to drink as if I were alone, and sat down.

Honor and I sipped our wine and had a nice, normal conversation while my children got ready for bed. What I really wanted to do was talk about the wedding plans. I had managed to play it cool for a while, but even I couldn't hold out forever. "The girls are very excited about being bridesmaids. The promise of a new dress is the way to any girl's heart."

"It's not just them. Tessa has a lot of godchildren and wants them all to be involved. One of them already knows the girls. They've played a lot over the year. Funny name. Corky or something. Same age as Maddy, I think. So it'll be those three definitely. Then there are two little boys, very sweet, who'll toddle up behind. And a bigger boy who's going to be an usher."

"Luke going to be best man again?" I asked wryly.

"Oh, no," said Honor. "That's the best bit of their plan, I think."

"What?"

"Jimmy asked Amber to be his best girl."

"Bet Tessa loved that." I tried to sound lighthearted to hide my shock. How much was my darling daughter keeping from me?

"Jimmy told me it was Tessa's idea—she did it once, apparently. Don't tell Amber, we're not supposed to know. Tessa is refusing to take the credit. Nice girl. Sorry, is talking about the wedding plans getting a bit too much?"

I shook my head and fixed the smile back onto my face. It was beyond too much. It was just the excuse I needed. I took a large swig of wine. I'll give you nice girl.

"Amber's been chatting about it all afternoon. She's so excited about it. Her idea is not to do a speech about Jimmy but to rewrite the words of 'Can't Help Lovin' Dat Man' . . . Loving that Dad of mine . . . Sweet, isn't it? She'll bring the house down, as usual."

"Singing it, gosh." No, no, no. This I couldn't bear.

"Well, they've booked the band—you know them, they did Luke's fortieth. Amber's already been on to them about rehearsal time. She's incredibly tenacious when she wants something. It's impressive for someone her age. She has real ambition. Most teenagers I know are sloths."

"They've booked the band?"

Honor nodded.

"So they have a date already?" Could this get any worse?

Honor held up her hands. "I'm so sorry, Bea, I assumed you knew."

I brushed away her concern. Bluff now, fall to pieces later. "Jimmy can't remember to tell me when he isn't picking up his children, I don't know why I'm still surprised. So, when's it going to be?"

"June the twenty-first. Midsummer night."

"No guessing who plays Bottom."

Honor studied me.

"I'm kidding—so, a big summer wedding, then?"

"About a hundred and twenty, I think. Tessa has a small family but a ridiculous number of friends to make up for it. We're going to Oxford for lunch to meet her parents, see the house and the lie of the land. Tessa wants to tent over an orchard."

"Sounds very grand." Damn, was my glass nearly empty already?

"Not that grand. Dwarf pear trees. It'll be rather beautiful dining among trees, under a twinkly-light canopy, fairy lights up the tree trunks."

Sounded beautiful. "Sounds expensive," I said.

"Well, Mr. and Mrs. King only have one daughter so I imagine a little pot was put aside. They've been waiting long enough. Actually, I get the feeling that Tessa thinks it's a bit quick, but Jimmy's determined and, well, she isn't getting any younger."

From what I'd glimpsed, she looked like a child to me. Childbearing, certainly. The hole opened again. I swallowed the last slug of wine to close it. "A hundred and twenty guests," I said. "That's"— the same as we had—"quite a statement, isn't it, for a second marriage? I mean, don't you sort of slip it under the radar for appearances' sake?"

"It's not her second marriage."

"Of course not. Silly me. Big white dress, then, I guess?"

"Somehow I doubt Tessa King is the big-white-dress type."

"Second wives rarely are. More wine?"

"Are you allowed?"

"My ex-husband's getting married," I said. "Sod the points."

I refilled my glass and topped up Honor. She watched me. When my marriage had been failing, Honor was the person who had tried to talk to me about it. She was an astute woman and that rare breed of mother who could love her son and still see his faults. I should have confided in her then. But I couldn't. I still couldn't. "Are you finding this Tessa thing difficult?"

I sat back in the chair. A little bit of truth would make the lie sound convincing. "What I find difficult is that no one's telling me anything.

That makes me feel weird. I don't like being kept at arm's length and I don't need protecting."

"What makes you think you're the one being protected?"

I blinked at my ex-mother-in-law.

"Do you have any idea what a daunting prospect it must be to follow in your footsteps?"

"Me? Overweight, overwrought, over-the-hill me?" I laughed. "I don't think so."

Honor folded her arms in front of her chest. "Shall I tell you what we see?"

I wanted to say no. Sometimes it was easier to believe the bad things.

"I see a woman who is bringing up three children pretty much single-handed. Jimmy's wonderful with the girls, but he spoils them—"

"So would I if I only had them every other weekend."

"Maybe. But it means the nuts and bolts of it are down to you and you alone. The organizing, the arranging, the picking up and dropping off, every meal, the washing, and that's before any of the discipline stuff. You have three lovely girls, you must be doing something right."

I stood up and went to the sink. I brushed away a tear. "You're describing pretty much any mother I know. Married or not, the buck stops with us. I can't imagine you got much help from Peter."

"It was different then. The pace of life was much slower, expectations lower. Jimmy and Luke spent hours playing football in the street. Couldn't do that now, could you? I think you're under much more pressure than I ever was. Motherhood has become some sort of competitive profession. I've collected the girls. I've seen the club lists, chess, Mandarin, debating! All the women look immaculate. It's terrifying and I'm not easily terrified."

I leaned against the sink. "You know why we do it?"

Honor shrugged. "Why?"

"Because deep down we don't value what we do. If I really believed that being efficient, sewing hundreds of school scrunchies, helping out on school trips was an achievement, I wouldn't feel like such a waste of space. I'm just as educated as my children will be. And I do nothing."

"Weren't you listening to me? What you do is *amazing*. You have wonderful children."

"So do my friends who work. Trust me, I've been waiting for that not to be the case."

"I don't understand."

I finished my second glass of wine. "I'm not as altruistic as you think. Actually, I'm not as nice as you think."

"Bea—"

"It's true. All that worthy crap is peppered with a terrible hope that somehow my presence at the cake stall will make my children happier than those of the mothers who aren't there because they're still at the coal face. There's nothing scarier than discovering their kids aren't distressed and, in fact, the children who don't have any balance are yours."

"I had no idea you felt this way."

I bit my lip. "Neither did I." I went to the fridge. "Fancy another?"

"Better make it a small one. I've got to drive home."

"Well, I'm not going anywhere," I said, topping up Honor's glass and filling my own.

"Has all this been brought on by Jimmy getting married?"

I thought for a while. "Partly, I suppose. My daughters are going to have a stepmother who is a better role model than I am. That sticks in the throat a little."

"Single, childless, and nearly forty. You want that for your daughters?"

"Independent, working, old enough to know what she's letting herself in for. It won't be twenty years of unpaid servitude for Tessa King, I tell you that. And she isn't single, childless, and forty. She's soon to be married, will have three lovely stepdaughters, no war wounds, and a great relationship. I'll be the one who's single, childless, and, God damn it, nearly fifty."

"You are not."

"I will be. They'll grow up very soon and then Tessa and I will be equals. We'll share an adult relationship with each of them. Eventually childhood will be forgotten. What will all those scrunchies do for me then?"

"But the base, who they are—"

"Is who they were always going to be unless we did something terrible. Well, I've done one of the most terrible things you can do to children. I took them away from their father. Between her and me, she's the one who's looking pretty amazing. And the annoying thing is, it's no more than your lovely son deserves."

Honor reached over and took my hand. "You are the mother of my grandchildren, Tessa King or no Tessa King. Nothing will change that. I love you like a daughter and I thank you for them every day and I will continue to do so. I know this is hard. Maybe you're right and it will get harder. But, please, never, ever tell me that what you do is of no value. It is invaluable, Bea. Invaluable. Do you hear me?" I couldn't speak. So I drank instead.

I HEARD FOOTSTEPS ON THE stairs and dragged myself off the floor in a hurry. I was back on the sofa when Amber came in. "You okay, Mum?"

I smiled at her innocently. "Hmm?"

"I thought I heard a crash."

"Must have been next door. You should be in bed."

"I was," said Amber, watching me closely.

"I'll come and give you a kiss."

"What are you watching?"

"There's nothing on. I thought I'd watch a video."

She stood looking at me, then peered over the sofa to get a better view of the TV. I noticed too late that I'd left the cover open on the floor.

"Please, Mummy, don't watch that again."

"What do you mean 'again'? I thought you must have had it out. Getting some tips for your best-man speech."

"Did Gran tell you about that?"

"She shouldn't have needed to. You should have." She looked at her feet. "Amber?"

"I didn't want to upset you."

"I wouldn't be upset."

She looked at me. Hearing my words, believing them, because she knew I could be trusted, but sensing a trap regardless. The ground seemed safe, but . . . She hesitated.

I lured her in. "It's very exciting. A real privilege. And very grown-up."

"Daddy asked me," she said suddenly, beaming broadly, bursting to tell me her plans. "It's almost the most important role on the day, he said. I've got to carry the rings. Usually a boy does it, and they have pockets, but I want to wear that blue dress from Harrods. I've already asked Granny if she'd buy it. She said yes, but it's got no pockets and, um, so, I was thinking maybe a handbag to match, and shoes."

"Were you really?"

"To carry the rings."

"Daddy has already got a ring."

She didn't pick up the danger signs. Neither did I.

"And I'm going to sing my speech. I've got a friend helping me with it and he's brilliant. I think he's going to be a songwriter and I could sing his songs. He has all these big thoughts, you know, about the world and poverty. He's so refreshing."

Refreshing? You're fourteen! How refreshed did you need to be? "You're going to sing a song about poverty?" I said, through an aching jaw.

Amber laughed. She thought I was joking. "No, Mum. I'm going to sing about Daddy and what a brilliant guy he is. He's so kind and funny and he's just the best dad. All my friends say so. I tell you, Clara's dad barely speaks. He'd never play dress-up and sing."

"Daddy does that?"

"Well, he did. Until . . ." Amber's beautiful face frowned with confusion. I knew what she was thinking: Where did that happy feeling go? Alarm bells were ringing. She was learning to read the early-warning signals, but still wasn't sure what to do with them.

I jumped in. "Until Tessa came along. It's okay, Amber, you can not like her, you know. It's difficult to share sometimes."

"I do like her, Mum. That's okay too, isn't it? I'm allowed? Shouldn't we be glad that she makes Daddy happy? That's good, isn't it?"

My anger rose like lava. "Good?" I laughed meanly. I could see Amber feeling the cracks underfoot. She tried to leave. I wanted to let her, but the anger put a mallet in my hand, and all I wanted to do was smash those cracks until the house came down. "Jesus, you're naive.

Happy! Refreshing! Good! You have no idea what the real world is like." I laughed again.

If there was terror on her face, I couldn't see it. The red mist of alcohol had descended. I was in a Baskervillian fog and I couldn't see the beasts. Or the damage they could cause. It was the laugh that scared my daughter most. The mealy, mean laugh, that condescending, ugly sound that echoed my drunken, irrational thoughts about my beautiful child. I turned back to the television screen. "No, Amber," I said, "it's not good. It's not good at all." I picked up the remote control from where it had fallen. From where I had fallen.

"Please, Mummy, don't watch that again."

"Go to bed, little girl," I said.

Consumed with irrational anger, I rewound the tape and watched our pristine white invitation emerge on the screen. Mr. and Mrs. Harold Frazier request the pleasure of your company at the marriage of their daughter Belinda (Christ, how I'd fought that, fought and failed, as usual). No one knew me as Belinda, I lamented, but I didn't understand that my wedding had nothing to do with me and was, in fact, all about my mother showing the rest of us how it should be done.

I have to give it to him: Jimmy was a saint. We'd lie entwined at night, bitching about her ridiculous, snobby ways, and how we would stand up to every stupid request she was making. And then, the following day, we'd acquiesce again. Maybe it pushed us together. Whatever my mother did was irrelevant. Because as long as we were there and said "I will" at the right time, what else mattered? We were so young. We knew so little.

Now I was laughing at the camera. My hair in rollers. My nails drying. Wearing a green silk kimono, which had worn so thin now it was translucent in places. I was holding up my nails, my hands about fifteen inches apart. And I'm laughing because Suzie, another friend I no longer see, was asking me whether that was how "big" Jimmy was. We were using my dad's old eight-millimeter camera. It had long since been transferred lovingly to video by Jimmy but, thankfully, hadn't lost any of the slipping, skipping quality of the old home movies.

I fast-forwarded to the wedding. My dad. Alive again. Holding my hand. Holding me up. It was only when I'd got out of the car that it had hit me. I was getting married. Nine months of painstaking minutiae, of sugared almonds and placements, of hemlines and hors d'oeuvres, and only now did it register, one foot on the gravel, that I was going to a place from which I would not return.

I looked at my bare hand. Divorce or no divorce, I'd been right about that. I still had not returned. I looked at the girl I had been. Her tiny waist, her shiny black hair, her bright, bright blue eyes. Immaculate ivory shoes, a dress so pinched I could barely breathe, a dress that only Amber could wear now, a dress I kept hidden in a vacuum-packed bag because of the grotesque comparison it made when I held it up against my post-partum silhouette. It had two hundred silk-covered buttons from the neckline to the end of the train. And Jimmy had undone every single one. Slowly, methodically, each one accompanied by a kiss, stripping me down to what was finally, rightfully, his. And I had been laid bare.

What had that day done for me—to me? It had given me my children. My wonderful, beautiful children, whom I loved beyond comprehension, whom I loved beyond breath, for whom I would gladly die and die again. Whose sleeping bodies I stood over and cried because I was looking at perfection. Whose chubby baby fingers had gripped mine, who had depended on me for life, and a life it had cost me. I stared at the television screen—where had I gone? Where had that smile gone?

I watched my perfect form turn into the church doorway and be sucked into the darkness inside. The camera did not follow me in. That had been deemed inappropriate by my mother. The film cut and a second later I emerged a wife. I paused it, and stared at my shuddering form. Was there a difference already? A tiny atomic shift? Had I shrunk? Had Jimmy grown?

Who giveth this woman to be married to this man? I hadn't thought of the implication of the traditional words. My mother had wanted them. Said it was tacky to have anything else and, once again, we had acquiesced. If I had been thinking about the implication of the words, maybe I would have fought harder. But I wasn't thinking about anything beyond the day. Frankly, I wasn't thinking at all. I loved Jimmy. What did the words matter? So my father had stepped up and given me away.

What was the difference between the girl who had gone in and the one who had come out seconds later? I knew the answer. The one who came out had been given away. I wasn't even allowed to do that for myself. We think we are so in control of our futures. We think we are in the driving seat of our lives. We believe our decisions are our own. But it isn't true. We are molded, manipulated, forged, and formed by society and expectations and biology—especially biology. Our biggest strength is our womanhood. It is also a profound weakness. The species needs to feed off us to survive. We die so that they may *live*. Procreation falls to us. Men might give up part of themselves to their offspring, but we offer up our whole. We give everything we can and they owe us nothing. They didn't ask to be born. We did that. Jimmy and I thought we were making a decision to start a family, but that outcome had been put into motion before I was born. I had eggs before I had eyelashes. In my mother's womb I already carried my unborn children. All of them. The three I had given birth to and the one I had killed.

I threw the remote control at the television set. What did I know? What the hell had that stupid, naive girl known? Nothing. No wonder she had made mistakes. The anger slipped away, the hole reopened, and regret flooded in.

"I'm sorry," I sobbed. "I'm sorry ... I'm sorry ... I'm sorry ... I'm so, so sorry."

To MAKE IT UP TO the girls, Jimmy had called me and asked if they could stay with him on Friday night. I said no at first, it was too disruptive, but he told me Amber had rung and asked specifically if they could come to stay. It was fear that had made me change my mind. The fear of a dream you can't quite remember. The plan was that he'd take the kids to Faith and Luke's on Saturday morning and I would collect them from there at lunchtime.

I didn't quite stick to the plan. It wasn't yet eleven when I arrived at their lovely double-fronted house in East Acton. "Sorry," I said to Faith. "The house was too quiet."

Faith laughed loudly, which I didn't understand. "I bet. Come on in. You look amazing. I can't believe how much weight you've lost."

Funny how hearing that wasn't making me feel as good as I'd thought it would. I was winning the battle with food, but it was an empty victory. All my willpower went into denying myself solids. Which left me dangerously open to liquids. Once again I'd woken on the sofa with a throbbing head and the taste of death in my mouth. It always happened when I was alone. The emptiness consumed me. The bitter regret. The acrid self-loathing.

"The kids are in the garden. Coffee?"

"Love some." I followed Faith to her immaculate kitchen, where Charlie's artwork hung framed on the wall, alongside his week's itinerary and meal plan. "We've had a giant trampoline put in. Can't get them off it," said Faith, putting fresh coffee in the pot. "Lulu's pretty good."

"Maybe it's the circus for her. Her reading's still atrocious."

"I think Amber's more likely, isn't she? After her dramatic running-away performance."

"What?"

"Last night."

"I'm getting a bit fed up about not being told anything. What's happened now?"

"Haven't you seen Amber?"

"No, Faith. She's here."

Faith was beginning to look deeply concerned. "She's not. She went home."

"When?"

"Last night. I thought you were being sarcastic about it being quiet at home."

"She stayed with Jimmy. They're all here."

She grabbed the phone off the wall. "Call Amber now. She isn't with him. They had a fight."

"What are you doing?"

"Calling Jimmy."

Panic was swelling in my chest. I was racking my brains. Had she come home? Would I have known? "Bea, call her. Jimmy, hi, it's Faith. You said Amber didn't stay with you last night, right?"

I was frantically pressing buttons on my mobile and listening, trying to remember to breathe. I pressed the wrong button. "Shit!" I tried again. "It's ringing," I said.

"She left the flat at about nine last night," Faith said.

"They let her leave without calling me?"

Faith shrugged.

The ringing in my ear ceased. "Yeah?"

"Amber, is that you? Thank God . . . Where are you?"

"Home," she replied.

I ignored the surly tone and glanced at Faith. "She's at home."

"It's all right, Jimmy, she's at home. Yes, I'll tell her."

"What happened?" I asked.

Silence.

"Amber?"

I looked at Faith again, confused. "I'll tell you," she mouthed.

"Stay there. I need to talk to your father. I have absolutely no idea what's going on."

"You wouldn't," Amber said, and ended the call.

I was flustered. Faith thought she knew why. "What did she say?"

"Nothing," I replied.

"Sit down, have this."

"What on earth happened?"

"Amber took your wedding video to Jimmy's flat."

"What? When?"

"Last night."

I tried to swallow, but my mouth had gone dry. I sipped the scalding coffee.

"Tessa came home to find Jimmy and the girls curled up on the sofa eating takeout, which, I gather, she has some sort of bugbear about, watching the wedding video. Amber said she'd only taken it because she wanted to learn about best-man speeches."

I'd heard those words before. They'd been a lie then, too. My child was defending me. Protecting me. Lying for me.

"Trouble is, they were listening to Jimmy's speech about you. Do you remember it?" asked Faith.

Remember it? I knew it by heart. It played like a mantra in my lonely, sleepless hours.

I know everyone in this room knows this story, but I'm going to tell it to you again, because it amazes me every time. I met Bea at a dinner party. We sat at opposite ends of the table and I was having a ball with some great mates on my end, but every time I looked over, and I looked over a lot, all I could see was this laughing girl with the biggest blue eyes I'd ever seen. The evening went on, people swapped places, and finally I found myself next to her. We started chatting as a group but the only voice I heard was hers. At one point her leg touched mine and I felt as if something had been missing all my life but I hadn't realized it until then. Without even looking at her, I reached under the table and put my hand on her leg. For a split second she stopped talking, then she continued. She never moved my hand away. I became a double act that moment. And I will remain one as long as I live. Bea, the words "I love you" are not enough but I will spend the rest of my life making up for what words cannot do. Ladies and gentlemen, please raise a glass to the precious, hilarious, cautious, adventurous, caring, wicked, beautiful Bea. My wife. Forever.

I put my head into my hands.

"Tessa was very upset and Jimmy, as ever, wouldn't take sides, so . . . I'm not defending what Tessa did—"

"What did she do?"

"It was Friday night. She'd been at work all week—"

"Faith. What did Tessa do?"

"She said Amber was sabotaging the wedding, had somehow planned this Friday-night attack, accused her of being selfish and not wanting her father to be happy. Jimmy tried to be diplomatic. He failed. Amber walked out. Apparently, Tessa followed suit this morning."

I stared at her. "I'd better call Jimmy."

Eleven

You're Still Alive

I RANG THE BELL AND WAITED NERVOUSLY ON THE DOORSTEP. I HADN'T been alone with Jimmy for a long time. Too long. He opened the door. He looked terrible.

"Oh, Jimmy," I said, hugging him.

"Thanks for coming. I'm up a shit creek."

"Faith told me."

"I just don't know why she brought the bloody thing over."

"Hey, she didn't force you to sit down and watch it," I said, defending Amber. "I can't believe you let her walk out of here."

"Hardly. She made me call a taxi first. I gave the driver your address and he took her home."

"I might have been out."

"She told me she'd called you."

"She's fourteen!"

"I'm sorry. I had Tessa in tears . . ." He stopped. "You're right. I don't know what I was thinking. This is all my fault. As per usual." He sighed. "Do you want a drink? Glass of wine?"

"Yes." I followed him into the kitchen. I watched too closely as he poured out honey-colored liquid into a glass. Stop, think, and pour some more. He handed it to me.

"Why did you watch it, Jimmy? You must have known Tessa was coming."

"She was supposed to be working late. Instead she made a special effort to get back and see the girls. It couldn't have been worse."

"But why did you watch it?"

"Amber put it on. I came into the room," a fleeting smile crossed his lips, "and I hadn't seen it for so long. I daren't, to be honest. There was your dad, he looked so well, and you getting ready . . . You looked about four. Me and the boys at the pub—do you remember Talbot? What happened to him? He was so tall, how did we lose him? It was great watching it again after so long. I just got sucked into it."

"I felt the same when I saw Suzie. She was such a good friend," I said. "I can't believe I don't see her anymore."

"You've been watching it too?"

I stared at him, guilty, guilty, guilty. "All this wedding chat . . ." I said slowly. "The girls wanted to see my dress. Amber probably told you."

Jimmy shook his head. So Amber hadn't told on me. Yet. "You looked incredible, but what was Luke wearing?"

Looked incredible. *Looked.* "What about Mum?" I said, forcing a laugh. "Bloody peacock."

"God, she was a pain in the arse."

"You were always so patient with her."

"It was the only way to get you any peace. I hoped I could win her over with charm and then maybe she'd see what I saw."

"Never happened," I replied.

"Stupid bat's blind, that's why."

Jimmy had always managed to ease the wounds my mother inflicted on me. How had I forgotten that?

"You know that—right?"

I nodded. No. What I knew was that my mother had X-ray vision. She saw right through me. If I wasn't with her I was against her. Is that how Amber felt? Another layer of guilt settled on me.

"There were so many people in the video, and the girls just loved seeing Luke and Lucy. They were so young," he said.

"So were we."

Jimmy shrugged off our youth. "I didn't feel too young. I knew exactly what I was doing. Your dad's speech was brilliant. Then came mine and the girls really wanted to hear it. It was so nice all cuddled up on the sofa together. They were in hysterics about my hair. God, Bea, I didn't even hear the key in the door."

"Which bit did she see?"

"Cutting the cake . . ." He paused. I knew what came next better than anyone. "Me kissing you."

"It was quite a kiss," I said. "Did she see any of the speech?"

"Maddy caught her watching the whole thing in the middle of the night." We lulled into silence. There were so many things I wanted to say.

"Tessa was still so upset in the morning. Not because of what she saw, but because, I don't know, I think she felt plotted against."

I wasn't so sure about that. "She may have said that, Jimmy, but if I'd seen that, I'd worry if . . . I don't know, if it would ever compare," I said. Cautious. Adventurous. Me.

"I have never lied to her about how much I loved you. I couldn't. I don't bang on about it, but I've never denied it. Of course I loved you. I was marrying you. You were my wife."

Past tense. Always the past tense.

"I guess hearing about it and seeing it for yourself are two different things."

"What are you saying? You think she thinks I don't love her?"

"It's a question of degree, Jimmy."

For a while we stood looking at each other. I could hear my heart working overtime in my chest. You may think you love her, but how much? Really?

"If I were her," I said wickedly, "I'd be wondering if you'd ever love me as much as you loved your first wife or your children. Love at first sight doesn't happen to everyone, Jimmy, it just doesn't, and playing second fiddle isn't what the fairy tales are about."

I could see that muscle in his jaw and knew my words were working.

"Do you remember the last few lines of your speech?" I asked.

"Of course."

"You said you'd spend the rest of your life showing me what the words 'I love you' meant. Well, to quote Alanis Morissette, 'You're still alive.'"

"I tried. You wouldn't let me, Bea. Remember? You wouldn't let me anywhere near you."

I felt sick with nerves. I had to tread very carefully now. Very carefully indeed. "I'm sorry, Jimmy. I know we never really talked about that, but you must know I wasn't myself. I couldn't have done what I did if I had been. I needed help but I was too proud to ask. I see that now. I blocked you out and I shouldn't have. I'm so, so sorry."

"It doesn't matter."

"Maybe it does, Jimmy."

"I don't think now is the time."

Why not? Now was perfect. Before we made another mistake and stayed apart. "Perhaps we should try and understand it better."

"You think understanding it will make it easier for Tessa?" He was shaking his head.

It was a strange sort of logic, but I was prepared to go with anything just to keep him on track. "Well, think about it. If we never understood it, how could she?"

Jimmy was suddenly stern, hurt. "I think we understood it perfectly," he said. The ground shifted and opened up. And there it was. The impasse. The crevasse into which we habitually fell. The great divide. A rift valley of such daunting magnitude that we hadn't even attempted to traverse it. I had blown us apart. For a while, I had stood on one side. But he wasn't even standing on the other anymore. His camp had packed up and moved into the gentle, sloping hills, far away from danger.

"Bea, I just want to make this better. I love her. She makes me happy."

He was right, of course. We understood it perfectly. Words, any words, wouldn't change the facts. I'd had my turn and ruined it. I deserved the situation I was in. I had killed our love. It wasn't Jimmy's fault. He was owed a second chance. All he'd done was love me and it hadn't been enough. Maybe I could do something for him. It was a long time before I summoned the courage to answer. "Then what are you doing here?"

"Huh?"

"Go to her."

He stared at me, nonplussed.

"Jimmy, you're hopeless. Find her. Convince her you *do* love her more than you ever loved me." The words coming out of my mouth were not my own. I wasn't doing it for her. I was doing it for Jimmy. The man I loved. The man I had always loved. The man I'd lost.

"She said she didn't want to see me for a day or two until she'd sorted out her head."

"She's lying."

"How do you know?"

Men! "Trust me on this. Go!"

Jimmy grabbed his car keys off the kitchen table, then stopped. "Would it have made a difference if I'd come to your mother's house?"

I clamped my jaws shut.

"Is that what you wanted me to do? Bea? Is it?"

I put my hand on my heart. "You have to go now," I said painfully.

"God, Bea—"

"Go!"

"Okay. I'm going."

"Good," I said. No. Very, very bad.

He jogged down the hallway.

"Wait!" I shouted.

He turned.

"I . . ." I swallowed. "Oh, Jimmy, I'm . . . I want you to know . . ." Just tell him. Just tell him you still love him. Now, before it's too late.

"It's okay, Bea," he said softly. "I know."

You don't know. You don't know what I was going to say. I watched him walk to the front door. What sort of crazy upside-down nonsense was this? I didn't want it. I didn't want it at all. His hand was on the latch and, for a moment, I thought he wasn't going to go. But that was wishful thinking on my part. I stood behind him. I was way beyond too late. I was trapped in the past tense. Tessa was his future.

"Not 'more,' Bea," he said. "I don't love her more. Just differently. But thank you."

The tears came instantly. But by then he was out of the door.

I RETURNED TO FAITH'S HOUSE to pick up the children.

"Everything all right?" she asked.

I nodded.

"Christ, Bea, you've been crying."

My jaw was aching.

"What happened?"

"I told him to go and join her," I said quietly.

I could hear the children's voices. "Mummy!" All I wanted was to feel their arms around me, their breath on my neck, their inane chatter in my ears.

"Hang on, girls, we'll be out to see your show in one second—"

"I need to get back to Amber."

"You're not going anywhere. I'm worried about you."

"I'll be fine."

"Bea, please, let me help you." Faith ushered my children back outside. Lulu looked forlornly over her shoulder at me. I blew her a reassuring kiss.

"Have a drink," said Faith.

"No. Thank you."

"Go on, it'll make you feel better."

Actually, it wouldn't, but I didn't have the strength to refuse a second time.

"You know, if there's anything I can do—"

"Faith, there's nothing anyone can do. I'm fine. All this, it just kicks up a lot of dust. Our marriage didn't work but you know what's so stupid? I don't know why. We had all the right ingredients. I wish I'd thrown that bloody video away."

"Why?"

"Well, our wedding was genuinely amazing. I feel sorry for Tessa. I know exactly how she must be feeling. Jimmy loves her, but he loved me, too . . . We probably have more in common than we realize. I don't know how it all went so pear-shaped."

"Because it's tough. I find it tough with one child and enough money. It still amazes me how quickly we can go from laughing about something to bickering about something else. If you don't keep your eye on the ball . . . Sometimes I feel like I have three careers. Marriage, motherhood, and my job. I've finally worked out that working on the marriage is the most important, but it's the one we give the least amount of time to. It needs to come first, and that's not easy, especially when the times you have to work the hardest are the times you'd rather not be in the same room."

"But you and Luke always seem so—"

Faith brushed my words aside. "Trust me, we have ups and downs like anyone else."

"You never tell me."

"I feel disloyal. We're good at the moment but when we were trying for number two it was shit. If it hadn't been for you, I don't know that we'd have made it. You were brave enough to warn me of the pitfalls."

"Easy to recognize them when you're lying at the bottom of one."

After I'd watched the girls and Charlie nearly skull one another on the trampoline a few times, my nerves were shot and I was extremely conscious of Amber at home. I belted my two into the car and drove back to the Westway.

"So, what did you think of Mummy's wedding dress?" I asked, opening the floor.

I ran up against the wall of silence that was usually reserved for when Amber was about.

"It's all right," I coaxed. "I know about the video and Amber. You can tell me what you do with Daddy and Tessa, you know. Otherwise I feel a bit left out." They looked at each other. "I like knowing what you've been up to. Like at school, or what you did with Charlie today. Do you understand?"

They nodded. But tentatively. Which meant they didn't.

"Well, let me put it another way. Why didn't you want to tell me about lunch at Gran and Poppa's?"

The sisters regarded each other. Communicating silently, like twins. They were so close in age. Less than a year. They were twins, really.

"We're not allowed to," said Maddy finally.

"Not allowed to what?"

"Tell you," said Lulu.

"Says who? Daddy?"

They shook their heads.

"Amber?" I was guessing, but from the change in their expressions I knew I was right. "Girls, how many times have I told you that you don't have to do what Amber says? It's always worth checking with me first, because sometimes Amber is . . ." Careful now, keep the tribe a tribe, no matter what . . . "Well, she likes to joke and you shouldn't always take her seriously. That's all. You can tell me anything." They were plainly relieved. "Why didn't she want you to tell me?"

"Because she said it would upset you."

"I get upset if you don't tell me. And Amber is naughty, because she only said that so she wouldn't get into trouble, and then I get cross with her, not upset . . ." I said, misunderstanding her words.

But Maddy cleared up my mistake with the piercing clarity of youth. "No, Mummy. If we talk about Tessa and Daddy, you get sad and we can't wake you up."

I clutched the steering wheel.

"What?" Maddy whispered to Lulu. "Mummy said we can tell her anything."

I forced my eyes to concentrate on the road ahead and my voice to stay steady. "And you can. And I won't get cross or upset ever again."

"Even if we draw on the walls?" said Lulu, sensing an opening.

"No, you monkey, house rules still apply. And if you run across a road without looking, I will smack you. We're talking about Tessa and Daddy here, that's all. You can tell me whatever you like."

"Does that mean we're allowed to be excited about the wedding?" asked Maddy.

"Yes."

"And we're allowed to show you pictures of our dresses?" asked Lulu.

"Yes."

"And Amber won't have to put you to bed?"

My head shot around, then back again. "What?"

Maddy looked scared. Maddy, my light sleeper. My night vision.

"No," I said quickly, to soothe her. "No. She won't."

Lulu and Maddy smiled at each other. I moved the rearview mirror away so they couldn't see my face scrunch up to keep the bloody tears at bay. No, I swore silently to myself, she would never have to do that again. And this time I meant it.

"Mummy?"

"Hmm?"

"Does that mean we can love Tessa too?"

It was Maddy's voice. I sucked in beams of light through the windscreen and forced it into mine. I turned briefly to my daughters. "I think you should," I said, smiling.

Maddy seemed satisfied. "So do I," she said.

"Me too," said Lulu.

They were the children I wanted them to be, and more. Now I had to be the mother they deserved.

THUMPING MUSIC GREETED US, BUT I was determined to keep it friendly. I had been warned. I walked up the stairs and knocked on Amber's door. I got no answer, so I opened it.

"We're home— Oh! Sorry! I didn't know you had company."

The boy was on his feet. Which I liked. He looked terrified, too, which I didn't completely dislike.

"Hello? I'm Amber's mother."

He lurched forward and stuck out his hand. "Caspar," he said, then went to the stereo and pressed a button. Much better.

"You should have told me you had someone coming over," I said, trying to hold on to those feelings of peace and love.

"*You* should have knocked."

"I did."

"How do you do?" said Caspar. "It's very nice to meet you."

"And you. Amber, we need to talk."

"Nothing to talk about."

"But last night—"

"I didn't want to stay at Dad's." She couldn't quite look me in the eye, so I assumed she was lying, but then I wasn't so sure. "You were asleep on the sofa. I didn't want to wake you."

Caspar looked anywhere but at me. I felt the ground shift beneath my feet.

"No one was here when I woke up. I figured you'd gone to pick up Maddy and Lulu."

I had thought about putting the clean clothes away in the girls' rooms this morning but, to be honest, I'd been feeling too ropy and had drowned myself in tea instead. I'd gone to Faith's early to escape the temptation of toast. I had no idea whether Amber was telling the truth or not.

"Are you staying for lunch, Caspar?"

Amber glanced at her watch and pushed herself out of the beanbag she'd been partially filling. "We're going to the park to play football with some friends."

Since when had my fourteen-year-old started telling me what she was doing and not asking? Since she'd started putting me to bed. "Let me at least make you a sandwich."

Caspar looked keen. Oh, the bottomless appetite of the teenager.

Five minutes later, I called up to them. I heard the floorboards shift and knew I'd been heard. Amber and Caspar came thundering down the stairs. An oval plate stacked high with sandwiches sat in the middle of the table. Caspar placed a guitar case up against the wall and sat down. I called the girls in. "So, you play the guitar?" I asked.

"He's brilliant, and he's only been playing a year," said Amber, momentarily forgetting she was ignoring me. Caspar blushed.

"You must be the person helping Amber with her best-man song, then."

"She doesn't need any help."

She giggled and prodded him playfully. "Yes, I do."

"No, you don't."

"Yes, I do."

"By the sound of it, she'd like your help."

"Doesn't matter anyway," said Amber. "It's not going to happen."

"Of course it is, darling," I said. "Tessa and Daddy are going to be fine. Nothing happened last night that can't be resolved. You know what Friday nights are like, everyone tired and crotchety. You will be the very best man ever, and I think singing the speech is a brilliant idea."

"You do?"

"Yes."

Amber looked a bit unsure. A bit confused. I didn't blame her. Living with me recently must have been like living with Dr. Jekyll. When the nights came in, the unknown came out. But I was determined to reassure her that all that was behind us.

"Mrs. Kent—"

"Bea . . . please." Maybe it was time to revert to my maiden name. We didn't need too many Mrs. Kents on the block.

"Um, it's my mate's seventeenth tonight. I was wondering if I could take Amber to the party."

"Seventeenth?"

"It's not far, Mum. Tufnell Park. It's at a bowling alley. His mum and dad will be there."

"Um . . ." Was Caspar seventeen too? Wasn't that a bit old? Wasn't Amber a bit young? I wanted to say no, but my white flag was so fresh out of the box that putting it back would cause more damage.

"I'll have to come and pick you up at ten."

"Yes!" said Caspar. "Great!"

"Wouldn't it be easier if I got a minicab?" asked Amber. "At that time?"

"No. They're dangerous." But I knew what she was thinking.

"Who will watch Maddy and Lulu?"

Oh, yes. Hadn't thought of that. I was entering new territory. Again. That's the thing with kids: just when you've got a handle on them, they grow a year and start a whole new phase.

"I could bring her home, Mrs. Kent. There's a bus that goes direct to the high street."

"Bea," I repeated. "I'm not sure about that. Amber's only fourteen. Maybe Dad can pick you up. He's not far."

They exchanged a brief look.

"Honestly, Amber, everything's fine with Dad, I promise you. But he might be with Tessa, so let me think about it. Polly from next door might be able to watch the kids while I come and get you."

"Thanks, Mum." Amber beamed.

"It's a maybe."

"Maybe's better than no," she said. I would have agreed to anything just to see a smile replace the concern that had taken hold of my daughter's flawless face. Since I had put it there, it was up to me to take it away.

THE SOLUTION, IT TURNED OUT, was Caspar's dad. He rang and offered to pick the pair up from mine and drop Amber home again. He took my address and assured me Amber would be back by ten. Trying to sound like the rational woman I used to be, I told him ten-thirty would be fine. He sounded nice.

With the younger two in bed and Amber dressed for her first boy-girl party, I kissed her good-bye and waved them off. Amber asked if I'd prefer her to stay at home and keep me company. If I had needed any more telling, that would have been it. But I didn't. I had been told. This time I was going to listen. I tried to convey to my child that I would be fine, absolutely fine, but she had no reason to trust me and I knew that it wouldn't be my words that convinced her otherwise. I had a date, too, one I needed to be alone for.

I shut the door and went to the freezer. The first thing I was going to retrieve was the vodka. But it wasn't there. I opened the fridge. The wine was missing too. I went to the cupboard high above the fridge, which the kids couldn't reach, where I kept the spares, but the spirits had been spirited away.

Normally, I would wonder whether I had done a bit of a Winnie-the-Pooh and forgotten how much honey I'd consumed, but I'd gone to the supermarket and knew I replaced the empty bottles. Just in case I had guests. My first thought was amnesia. My second was thief. Turned out I was wrong on both counts.

I found the vodka bottle in a Jimmy Choo shoebox at the back of Amber's closet. It was the Jimmy Choo box that caught my eye, since I knew she couldn't possess such an item. I never found the open bottle of wine, but the six spares were under her bed. The Bailey's, gin, and whisky (left over from Jimmy days) were behind her oversize, old-fashioned stereo, which she had begged me to replace. I carried them downstairs and placed them, side by side, on the kitchen counter.

Neither amnesia nor a thief but the guardian angel who put me to bed on nights when I could no longer walk. She was not the enemy. Nor was Tessa. The enemy was me and the crap in those bottles. It was the hole I tried to fill. It was what had been before the hole.

I unscrewed the vodka first, took a long, hard sniff, and emptied it into the sink. Glug. Glug. Glug. It belched out of the big, cheap storebrand bottle. Glug. Glug. Glug. I didn't open my eyes until all I heard was a few intermittent drips. Alcohol filled the air. The whisky, Bailey's, and gin followed suit. They were easier to dispose of. By the time I drank those, I couldn't taste them and I wouldn't miss what I couldn't taste. The wine I couldn't throw away. I put the six bottles into a box and carried them next door.

Polly was a little surprised to see me.

"A gift," I said, holding out the box.

She smiled, bemused. "For what?"

"For watching the kids when I need to be somewhere else, signing for parcels—"

"Don't be ridiculous. You're the one who does that for me."

"Please take them. I'm on a strict diet and can't cope with the temptation."

"Now you're speaking my language. Tell you what, I'll keep them and when you're at your target weight we'll drink them together."

"They'll have corked by then," I said.

"Rubbish. Keep it up, girl, you're looking so much better."

I returned home and, feeling empowered, got out the cleaner and went at the kitchen like a surgical cleaning team. I ate a tangerine, an apple, and some celery. I drank peppermint tea a few degrees off boiling point, and cleaned and cleaned and cleaned while I sang to the radio. Amber wasn't the only one in the family with a voice. I had acted and sung at university. I had been a backing singer in some crappy college bands. I could hold a tune in a karaoke bar and loved nothing better than a good old sing-along. It was time to reclaim that person. It was time to let go. It was time to forgive myself, for my children's sake. It was time to dry out.

At ten twenty-five I heard the key in the lock. It was stealthy, tentative, nervous.

"No, it's okay, you don't have to wait," said Amber. Only I could hear the worry in her voice. Only I knew why it was there. Amber might have hidden the booze, but she still didn't know what she was going to find inside. She didn't want Caspar seeing what she had seen too many times.

I raced to the door to put her out of her misery.

"Mum!"

I was still wearing an apron. "Sorry, catching up on some housework. Hi." Caspar was on the path. A car was parked on the other side of our little gate. As soon as the man inside saw me, he got out and walked up the path toward me.

"Thank you so much for bringing Amber home," I said, with the diction of Dame Maggie Smith. I put my arm around Amber so that she could smell I was sober. I looked at her. "Did you have fun?" She nodded, too startled to talk.

"Hi, I'm Nick. Caspar's dad." We shook hands.

"Bea." He looked about twelve and just like Caspar. Handsome.

"It's very nice to meet you. Amber's been a delight, as usual."

"As has Caspar."

"In which case would you like to keep him?"

"Dad!"

"We could swap," I suggested.

"Mum!"

"Perfect," said Nick.

"Can I stay?" asked Caspar hopefully.

"No!" exclaimed Nick and I in unison, which made us laugh—at ourselves, though I don't think the kids realized that.

"Maybe another time," I said, squeezing Amber. "Thank you again. Good night." I turned to go.

"Mum," whispered Amber, turning out of my grip.

"What? It's cold."

She glared at me.

"Oh, sorry. 'Night, Caspar, see you soon, no doubt."

Amber rolled her eyes, which made Nick and me smile at each other again.

I went back into the house but left the door open a fraction, and Nick went to his car but kept the engine running. The message was clear. There would be no heavy petting tonight. I could hear the soft murmur of their voices from the other side of the door. I could see their distorted selves through the glass. They moved closer. The voices dropped to an inaudible whisper, then stopped altogether. Then, suddenly, Amber was inside, the door was shut, she was giving me a huge hug and belting up the stairs to bed. To be alone. With Caspar. In her head.

About twenty minutes later, I took up two cups of chamomile tea and knocked on her door. She was in bed in her Snoopy pajamas, her face illuminated by the phosphorescent light of her mobile phone. She was smiling. Texting. The modern-day love letter.

"Thanks, Mum," she said, finishing a lengthy reply.

"So, was the party good?"

She grinned.

"It wouldn't have mattered if you were in a traffic jam on the M25, right?"

She shook her head. "He's nice, isn't he?"

I sipped my tea. "Very nice. I liked his dad too."

"They were only twenty when Caspar was born."

That explained the cherubic face. Nick was a child himself.

"They've been together since the first day of university practically. They're always cuddling. It's sweet. Nick's a very romantic man."

"And I take it his son's just like him."

Amber pulled herself into a little huddle, partly embarrassed, partly desperate to talk.

"A good kisser?"

"Mum!"

"What? You can tell me. It's very important. You don't want a washing machine, or some weird, dry, hollow kiss. Yuck."

"He's only kissed me on the lips. Very softly. He's a gentleman."

"Soft is good. Tongues are better."

"Mummy! Ssh!"

"Sorry. But it's true."

"Well, I'll let you know if it happens."

"When, Amber Kent. When."

The phone bleeped. She jumped. Excited.

"Don't stay up all night doing that."

She winked at me. Definitely when.

I closed the door behind me, leaving love's young dream in the grip of one another's illiterate thoughts. The image of Amber falling in love made me feel warm and happy. This wasn't it. But it would be. One day. It was such fun. In the beginning. I stopped myself. Now, now. Of course there were dangers. But this was not a time for worry. She was fourteen. It was a first crush. The boy played guitar. That's all. Her life was still dominated by girlfriends. They hadn't even kissed properly. This wasn't serious.

I looked back down the corridor. Was it? How had they met? Not through school, obviously. He wasn't the brother of a friend . . . I must remember to ask her in the morning.

I took myself and my tea to bed. It was just after eleven. I should sleep, but I couldn't get the image of Amber's illuminated smile out of my head. And so we enter the world of boys. I couldn't help it—I was a little . . . not jealous, but regretful, I guess, of that smile. Discovering another human being was such an adventure. Intimacy was a great secret. Long talks late into the night provided an invaluable learning curve, because you learned as much about yourself as you did about the person you were talking to. Mostly it was just fun. And I missed that.

I turned my light off. I had been trying for four years to train myself to sleep in the middle of my double bed, but I still curled up on the right-hand side so that Jimmy had enough room. I missed him. I missed a physical presence. I missed the good-night kiss, however cursory it had become. I missed the hand snaking over to my side, wanting to play. I missed it even though I had hated it. Why had I hated it so much? Wouldn't it have made it all better? I edged over to his side of the bed and laid my arm across it. He had tried. He really had. But I hadn't wanted him to make me feel better. I hadn't deserved to feel better.

"Oh, Jimmy," I mumbled into the pillow. I put my other hand down my pajamas and rested it between my legs. I pushed myself against it, egging it on, encouraging it out of its shyness. I groaned into the mattress. "Please," I begged an invisible force. "Please." What was I begging for? Intimacy, of course. To be touched. To be healed. To be filled again, made whole. My index finger found its way between the folds of skin, but no further. I was dry as unbuttered toast.

I HEARD NOTHING FROM JIMMY until he called the following Wednesday to say he couldn't make pickup—which was in twenty minutes' time—but could he come over later and see the girls, as he had something important to tell them?

Twenty minutes! I was trying to be amenable, but twenty minutes was taking the piss. Angrily, I switched off the exercise video and ran to the car. I made it just in time but had no snack and Amber took forever to come out. My presence was not gratefully received—as if I had made Jimmy disappear! I was getting a bit fed up with always playing the bad guy. When he finally showed up, he caused havoc and two of our three daughters were in tears.

"I've got an announcement to make." Jimmy smiled and spread his arms wide.

No preamble, no warning, no gently easing them into disappointment. Bam. Wedding's off.

"What?"

"Yup. Canceled." Why was he grinning like that. How could he? We had talked of nothing else since the girls had discovered it wasn't a vetoed subject. I had even rewritten a bit of Amber's song. She couldn't wait to perform it. Could not wait! The girls walked around carrying imaginary bouquets everywhere they went. Scattering imaginary petals from imaginary baskets. Normally, this would have turned me into a basket case—except, damn it, everyone was so happy. I was sober, the beasts had slunk back into the shadows, for good, I thought, and I was better off without them. And now he saunters in here, smiling casually, and drops a bomb.

"What happened?" I asked, staggered. I couldn't disguise the fury in my voice.

"You mean I can't do my speech?" asked Amber.

"What about being bridesmaids?" pleaded Lulu.

"Isn't Tessa going to be our stepmother anymore?" It was Maddy who asked the question. The only one not in tears. But her chin was wobbling. She's too good.

We all waited for the answer.

"Well, you know we watched the video of Mummy and me getting married?"

Where was this going? Don't you dare blame it on that! Amber will never forgive herself.

"Well, Tessa thought we should do something different." So now it was Amber and Tessa's fault. Well done, Jimmy. The girls reacted with stunned silence. Oh, Jimmy, they wanted that wedding again. They thought it was perfect. They thought it was how it was supposed to be. They didn't mind about the ending anymore. They just wanted the beginning again. What was there not to understand, Jimmy?

"So. We thought the beach."

More silence.

"Caribbean. In May."

"That's term time. You can't take them out of school in the middle of a term, Jimmy."

"I thought in exceptional circumstances you can. Family stuff."

"They mean bereavement, not a jolly. Amber has exams in June, Lulu is already— I mean, catching up is difficult, and Maddy has been picked for the football team."

"RGS has a football team?"

I ignored him. "Can't you do it in the Easter holidays?"

"It's too expensive to get everyone out there and rooms . . ."

Well, don't look at me. Mother isn't going to pay for your second wedding. Bad luck. "Think of all the money you'll be saving on fairy lights," I said.

Amber sniggered. Back in my camp. Then she remembered. "What about the band?"

"We've let them go."

"What? Dad! I've worked . . ." She ran her hand through her hair, trying to control her disappointment. It had been a surprise. The song had been a surprise. Even now she didn't want to ruin it for her father, although he was ruining it for her.

"Jimmy, we've talked nothing but weddings for days. You can understand why they're a little"—God, I could wrap a frying pan around his head—"upset."

"What about our dresses?"

"You won't need them on the beach. It'll be too hot. You can wear swimsuits."

Maddy and Lulu gazed at me with wide, sorrowful eyes, and I knew they were mentally replacing their beautiful fairy frocks with dark blue standard-issue Speedos. Make it better, Mummy. Make it better. Amber looked at me too. Make it better, Mummy. Make it better. Think, think, think.

"Okay. Well, you're still having the engagement party, right?"

Jimmy nodded.

"Well, can't the girls be bridesmaids at that?"

"With no bride?" asked Maddy.

"A minor detail, darling. She'll be there, the bride-to-be. You could be bride-to-be-maids."

They didn't go wild for it, but I wasn't thrown out of court either. "And I'm sure Tessa wouldn't object to some flower-throwing on the beach. You could get to do it twice!" I turned to Amber. "And I bet there'll be dancing and music at the party. There's never been a Kent party without live music, ever. Right, Jimmy?" I glared at him.

"Of course there'll be dancing."

"And live music?" I said pointedly.

He frowned, then nodded slowly. "And . . . live . . . music."

"See? Everything's fine."

"Yes, it is! Live music, didn't I tell you? A great band, a great band." All right, shut up now, just in case you can't find one at the last minute! The rebellion calmed. Jimmy and I walked through to the kitchen.

"What the hell was that about?" said Jimmy.

"I can't tell you, but you'd better get a band now. And you'd better tell Tessa—and fast."

"The engagement party was supposed to be just for mates, Bea."

"Tough shit. You don't build a bonfire in front of your children, then refuse to light it at Guy Fawkes. I know exactly what dress Amber wants to wear and it will cost you a small fortune, and the girls just want lots and lots of netting. Harrods, Sally, fourth floor. It'll be done in minutes."

"Oh, thank you, Bea."

"I'm not doing it, Jimmy. You have to."

He looked as if I'd slapped him. It was actually quite funny. But it didn't make me laugh. Then he hugged me. "I'm beginning to wonder if I'd be getting married at all if it wasn't for you."

Boy, do you know how to make a girl feel good!

"Thank you, Bea, again and again and again."

BETWEEN US, WE PULLED IT off. The engagement party became the wedding, and the wedding was relocated to a beach at some unspecified date in the future, depending on deals. Tessa found a band. Which didn't surprise me: working in the music business, she must have some uses. And I remained sober. Sometimes I felt worse than any hangover had made me feel. I was shaky. I sweated profusely and had a hacking cough. I went through a box of sugar-free Smints a day and a lot of V8. But I didn't drink.

Finally, the weekend of the big event arrived. I packed the girls into the car on Friday morning with their bags. I dropped them off at school, then drove on to Jimmy's to hand over the recently ironed dresses so they wouldn't get crumpled. He was suited and booted, devilishly handsome with his salt-and-pepper hair and blue eyes.

"I can't wait to see them all dressed up," he said, taking the dresses from me and throwing them over the banister. My heart sank, but I bit my lip. "Thanks, Bea."

"Amber's paraded around the house in hers every evening since you bought it. It's almost scary how good she looks in it." Don't nag. Don't nag. "You'll hang it up, won't you?"

"'Course, right now."

Part of me longed to ask if I could come to the party too. Just to see her. I was feeling so strong I thought I could cope.

"I'll make sure lots of photos are taken," said Jimmy, as if preempting me.

No. The ex-wife does not go to the ball. What was I thinking? "Have a wonderful time, Jimmy. Don't let Amber drink."

"She doesn't even like the taste."

I raised an eyebrow. "And she's never kissed a boy either."

Jimmy blocked his ears. "I don't want to know."

"Don't worry, he seems nice."

"I'm glad you like him."

"I do. Well, I'd better be off. Have a great time."

"You okay?"

I nodded. "Good. Off to meet a friend for breakfast, so better go."

He leaned forward and kissed me lightly on the cheek. "I'll drop them back on Sunday."

I waved a casual, whatever, hand and walked away.

FROM THERE IT ALL WENT steadily downhill. First I got a ticket. A knock like fifty quid hurts me. Then I ran out of petrol. I was furious—how stupid was that? Carmen, bless her, rescued me with a can of unleaded and a coffee and followed me to the petrol station, where my card was refused.

By the time we walked into the café, I felt as if I'd done an assault course, and eyed an almond croissant with lust.

"I'm so sorry," I said again, watching Carmen pay for the fruit salad and black coffee.

"Stop it. And if you need cash, I've got that too."

"It must be some mistake. I can't have reached my overdraft limit already. I haven't been out."

We carried the tray to a table in the window and I dug out the sticky plastic fork from the pot of fruit salad.

"So what are you going to do to keep yourself sane this weekend?" she asked.

"I was thinking lobotomy."

"Isn't that the carpool?"

"Twice around the park with *Anna Karenina* on the iPod, followed by the boxed set of *Six Feet Under*. Reflect my mood."

"Oh, my God, that sounds like bliss." Sounded suicidal to me. Carmen took a bite of her croissant. "What's this boyfriend like?" She waited for my response, but I was staring at the door. "Bea?"

"I don't believe it. I was just talking about her."

Carmen looked around. "Who?"

"See that woman? That's so weird . . . She was my maid of honor."

"So why are you hiding in my armpit?"

I pulled back. "I haven't seen her since Amber was born. We used to have such a laugh after work, but it got harder and I had to get home so Jimmy could go off to another bollocks meeting that wouldn't lead to anything. She gave up on me eventually."

"Go and say hello."

"I can't."

"For God's sake. Old friends are vital, Bea. I'd be a nutcase without mine."

I looked at her, embarrassed that to me she was an old friend. Was five years at the school gates my criterion now? "You're right," I said, feeling momentarily bullish. I stood up and walked over to Suzie's table. She looked exactly the same and I couldn't help smiling as I approached. "Suzie?"

She squinted against the glare of sunshine behind me. "Hi."

"It's been so long, I can't believe it. How are you?"

She glanced at her friend, then back at me. "Good, good, really good."

"Honestly, I was talking about you only a few days ago."

"To?"

"Jimmy. We were wondering what had happened to you."

"Um, well, um, got married, had two children, um . . . I still run our business."

"Wow, a business." I felt the judgment cut through me. Don't ask, please don't ask what I do. "What business?"

"What about you?"

We had both spoken at the same time. I refused to answer her question. "So you and your husband run a business?" I said, cutting her off a second time.

"Well, um . . ." Her friend touched her hand. "Actually, my husband, um . . . He died last year."

I crouched down, the last fifteen years forgotten, and took her hand in mine. "Oh, my God, Suzie, I'm so sorry—"

"Look, um, this is going to sound very rude, but I don't know who you are. I can't remember—were we at school together?"

I pulled my hand away. "It's Bea. Bea Frazier, Bea Kent . . . Jimmy and Bea."

Her jaw dropped two inches, and I saw the truth in that second before she had time to hide it.

"Bea, Jesus, I'm so sorry, I didn't recognize you . . . Your hair has . . . um, changed. You look great. It used to be a—"

"A black bob," I said, tucking my black bob behind my ear.

"It's been a long time," said Suzie, sounding defeated. "So, how's Jimmy? You had a son?"

"Three daughters."

"Wow. I'm so sorry I didn't recognize you, I'm not really myself yet."

I didn't want her to apologize. I was unrecognizable. I'd just forgotten it. "Anyway, I'll let you get back to your . . ." I tried to smile. "I'm so sorry about your husband."

"I'm glad you've still got Jimmy. He was always a great catch. Look, I'm sorry, Bea, really . . . Let's do this properly some time. Have you got a card?" I shook my head. Nondescript mothers don't have cards. "Take mine, call me. It would be lovely to catch up and see Jimmy again."

I walked back to Carmen. Actually, it felt more like a limp. The embossed stiff card bit into my palm.

"How was that?"

"Carmen, I'm so sorry—I'd completely forgotten. The bloody plumber's coming . . . He's outside the house. I've got to go." I picked up my bag and rushed out. "I'll call you later, sorry." Carmen held up my fork. "What about your breakfast?"

"No time," I replied, backing away.

"Look after yourself, Bea."

Look after myself? I spent my days looking after people. Looking after myself was just another chore. It's so much more *refreshing* to let it all go. Sometimes on my weekends alone I didn't get dressed, I didn't brush my teeth or wash. In fact, I didn't do anything but drink my calorific quota until I was sick, then delight in watching it come up again. Puking rendered me calorie-neutral and I loved it. That was looking after myself. For some reason, I could never make myself be sick when I'd binged on food, but white wine and vodka was a different matter. Liquid, it seemed, was fine. The freedom of total irresponsibility. The joy of stumbling chaos, that was how I liked to look after myself. My reward scheme. "I will," I said. "I promise."

* * *

THERE WAS NO PLUMBER. OBVIOUSLY. I'd just needed to get away. Then again, two of the three deliveries I had organized for that day didn't turn up either. My mother popped in to gloat. The Insinkerator ate a spoon. And the fuse box blew. I know these things aren't the end of the world, but everything takes time to organize, and it's dull and repetitive and then you have to go and do it all over again. Yesterday I might have coped better. But today something had happened that I couldn't ignore.

I had been kidding myself. A far greater distance existed between me and my old self than I had let myself believe. A single stone was nothing compared to how far I had to travel. I had seen myself in Suzie's eyes. I was a fat woman full of failed potential. It was all the excuse I needed. I was stronger than I had been a few weeks ago, but not that strong. The children were miles from harm. I wanted to fall into the abyss. Calorie-neutral, here I come.

I CAME AROUND IN THE kitchen at three minutes past four in the morning. The following day I felt too shocking to speak. Which was fine, since I had no one to speak to. I only went out to get some healthy food to redress the balance. Organic mush in a cardboard box and a smoothie called a detox from a nice café in Kentish Town. I walked there. To clear my head.

"Bea?"

I turned and peered through my dark glasses.

"I thought it was you."

I was being slow on the uptake.

"Nick. Caspar's dad."

"Oh, hi, sorry. Miles away."

"Hangover?" He was smiling.

"That obvious?"

"It's not sunny and the detox smoothie kind of gives it away."

"Hm" was all I managed.

"Very brave of you to do it twice in a row."

"Hm?" was all I managed again.

"The big shindig tonight. The Amber and Caspar show. Though I don't think James and Tessa know that yet."

He couldn't see that I was frowning, because my glasses were so big. But I was. He was a bit familiar, wasn't he? And since when was Caspar going to the engagement party?

"Fran's having her hair done and, of course, the girls wanted in on the act, so they've got dresses too. It was a brilliant idea of yours. Cora, our two, your two all in matching fairy dresses. Can't wait."

Fran? Cora? Who were all these bloody people?

"Her godchild on the guitar, her stepchild-to-be on the mic—it's going to be one hell of a party. I've never seen Tessa so happy. I'm so glad too. She deserves it."

"She does," I said. Why did I say that? I don't even know the bloody woman. Lady-child. She-thing. "Godchild?"

"Caspar. Best godmother in the world is Tessa King. She'll be a great stepmother too. Amber is so happy that you like her. Makes it all easier. Anyway, gotta go. I strongly suggest a sleep for you. And I'll see you later at the ball."

I made a thumbs-up sign, because I didn't dare speak. Caspar? Caspar was Tessa's godson? My daughter and her future step-godbrother, and everyone was okay with this! And Amber, pretending Tessa and I were bosom buddies so she could be with Caspar? There I'd been, thinking it was because she was trying to protect me. This wasn't about me. I was just a hindrance. A bore. Wouldn't it be so much easier if they could all dance into the sunset without having to deal with the ex. No one gave a shit about me. I was not only unrecognizable, I was replaceable. No, that wasn't even it. I'd already been replaced. Sleep, Nick, you drippy romantic bore? Sleep? I needed more than fucking sleep!

"One detox smoothie to go," called the boy behind the counter.

Too darn late.

Twelve

Young Love

"WHO'S GOT THE HAIR DRYER?"

"Can I borrow someone's mascara?"

"Shit, I've got a run in my stocking. Tessa! You got any spares?"

I stood up. Fran, my best friend from university and Caspar's mum, walked into our room wearing her underwear and a single thigh-high stocking. The other lay limply, like Peter Pan's shadow, across her palm. She stopped. "Bloody hell! You look phenomenal!"

Claudia followed her in, holding her head. "Help, my hair's gone frizzy! Shit, Tessa, you look like a film star."

Billie came out of the shower room. "Masca—" The word got lost in a long wolf-whistle.

I smiled.

"I've always wanted to be able to do that," said Fran.

"Give us a twirl," said Billie. I did. I had decided to go for a very bridal red. Scarlet, actually. The dress was pure silk and I was sure it wouldn't survive the night. But, hell, wedding dresses aren't supposed to. I knew this wasn't my actual wedding dress, since that was going to be a white cotton kaftan (don't be fooled, I wasn't talking a fifteen-pound job from Portobello market: it would be Heidi Klein's finest, with expert beading, sequins, and pearls, suggestively see-through with a matching white bikini), but somehow the red evening gown had begun to feel like that. Now that everyone was here, running around in a state of semi-undress, reminding me of a million nights in our youth, I was glad Bea had made us mark the event. We'd thought we were doing it for the girls, but here, with my friends, I knew it was as much for me and James.

"Is it just me or is it strange that I have James's ex-wife to thank for tonight?"

"Is she coming?" asked Billie.

"We didn't ask her," I said, pulling a face. "She and I haven't actually met. But I kind of wish we'd shown her the same magnanimity she's shown us and invited her."

"Nick's met her," said Fran. "Says she's great. Quite liberal, too. She let Amber stay over at ours."

"I didn't know that," I said.

"I think a mutually respectful distance is probably better than becoming bosom buddies. You don't want to find out too much," said Claudia.

I threw a pair of knickers at her. "There's nothing to find out."

"Gross! Are those yours?"

"Yes! I'm going commando. There isn't room for pants in this dress." It was strapless, cut low at the back and with a plunging sweetheart neckline that, courtesy of industrial scaffolding, kept the bosoms up. The bodice was cinched so tightly I could breathe only in gasps. The skirt fell to the floor, and a slit up the back let me move and, more important, hinted at long pins beneath. It was completely over the top. But if I couldn't be over the top tonight, when could I? And, anyway, you hadn't seen my future stepdaughter's dress. My hair had been coiffed forties'-style, my lips were scarlet, my skin pale, and my eyes lined with liquid black eyeliner. Ava Gardner was what I was going for, and, by the look on my friends' faces, it was working. We giggled. Maddy and Lulu were right. Dressing up was fun.

Talking of the girls . . . "Hey, you lot, how are you getting on?"

Cora, Maddy and Lulu, and Katie and Ella, Fran's daughters, had set up camp in their tiny room. Lulu was chief hairdresser, although Amber was supposed to be overseeing her. James had been banished to Faith and Luke's house in Acton, along with Caspar. James's flat in Hampstead had temporarily been designated a Red Tent, a sanctuary reserved for women. You couldn't see the floor for tulle. Fran, Billie, Claudia, and I crowded into the doorway to watch the girls pull up one another's zippers, brush their hair, and twirl around until we felt dizzy. We three women watched the five and shared a silent prayer of thanks for our luck, the love in our lives, and one another. I took Claudia's hand and squeezed it, knowing she was thinking of the daughter she'd lost. All happy events forever after, however sweet, would be tinged with sourness. There would always be someone missing from our party.

"This calls for a drink," I said. I heard no dissenting voices.

Down in the kitchen, I popped a cork and poured foam into four glasses. Then I poured a fifth. For Amber. She was a woman too now. Certainly a woman in the making.

"Amber! Champagne!" I called up the stairs.

"I'm so glad you're getting on better now," said Claudia.

"Oh, my God, the difference is amazing. She's been delightful these past few weeks." I looked at Fran. "I thank your son. My number-one fan."

"Not anymore, I'm afraid. That boy's bananas about her."

"Where is she?" asked Billie. "I can't wait to see her dress."

"Probably in the bathroom," I said, handing out drinks. I raised a glass. "To absent friends," I said.

"To Helen," said Billie.

We all drank.

"I'm not going to make a speech later," I said to Billie, Claudia, and Fran, "but there is something I'd like to say to you three. Thank you for all your support and advice over the years. Thank you for forgiving me when I didn't listen, and encouraging me when I did. Thank you for sharing your lives with me," I looked at Fran and Billie, "and your children. I want you to know that the only reason why I'm contemplating getting married is because I know I have you three watching my back. And I know that I can tell you anything, and I won't be judged. And I know if I start cocking it up, you'll tell me off, and if James is a pain in the arse, you'll back me up. There's no way I'd do this without you. It's too darn hard."

"Very sensible," said Fran, who knew a thing or two about marriage.

"Don't cry, Tessa. Your makeup will run." Billie handed me a piece of paper towel.

"To us!" said Claudia.

"To us!" we chorused.

A door slammed. Footsteps took the stairs two at a time. Another door slammed. We lowered our glasses. Everyone looked at me.

"Amber?" asked Fran.

"When did she go out?" I asked, worried. Losing James's precious jewel would set us back a bit.

"You'd better go up," said Fran, mother to all.

"Me?"

"Who else, sweetie?"

"Can't you do it?"

"You said things were better."

"They are," I whispered, "but I still feel like a fraud. Please go. She really likes you."

"No!"

"Stairs aren't easy in this dress—" She pointed to them. Okay, okay, I'll go. "Give me that glass," I said.

I knocked on Amber's door.

"Go away," came Amber's voice. "Please."

It was the "please" that struck me.

"You all right?"

She didn't answer.

"Amber?" I turned the handle. Suddenly it pushed back against me. "Go away! I said go away! What's wrong with you?"

"What's happened? Everything all right with Caspar?"

She didn't reply.

"What's he done?"

"Who?"

Oh, God, we were back to that. "I have a glass of champagne for you," I said. Trying another tack.

Silence.

"You don't want it?"

More silence.

"Okay. Well, we're leaving in about ten minutes." I turned to go, then turned back, trying to remember what big events had done to me at her age. "Listen, Amber, if you're worried about your dress, I want you to know that you look absolutely beautiful in it. Your dad will be so proud. We both will . . ." I waited for a reply. But all I got was a blast of music through the door. Angry guitar music. I guess I had Caspar to thank for that. Where were the Bonne Belles when you needed them? I walked back into the kitchen.

"What's going on?"

I shrugged.

"Where did she go?"

I threw up my hands. My friends looked at me, disappointed. "What? It's like getting blood out of a stone. She won't talk to me."

"Well, something's happened," said Claudia. "She was so excited earlier."

"I'll ring Caspar," said Fran. "Maybe they've had a fight over the song."

"Song?"

Fran raised an eyebrow. "Oops."

"What bloody song?"

"It's a secret," said Fran.

"Not anymore. Spill."

"Caspar and Amber have been working on a best-man song."

Talk about the missing pieces falling into place. "No wonder there was such a bloody fuss about the band. You've no idea how many favors I had to pull in to get decent live music at such short notice. Why didn't anyone tell me?"

"It was a surprise."

"For James. Not me." I shook my head. "Call Caspar. I can't deal with a bloody scene tonight. Prima bloody donnas." I poured myself another drink. "Maybe the lighting isn't right at the venue and Amber's decided not to go on."

"Oi, Tessa, put the broomstick down," said Claudia.

"You don't know what it's like," I pleaded.

"Nor do you," she replied, "to have some siren move in and cast a spell on your dad."

"*I'm* the siren here?" I lowered my voice. "Did you see that dress? It cost the same as mine!"

Fran came back into the kitchen. "Caspar says he hasn't seen her since this afternoon at the rehearsal and it went brilliantly. He's going to call her and call us back."

I rolled my eyes, Amber-style. "She's going to ruin it, I just know it."

"Something might have actually happened. Where's Bea? Are you sure she's okay with all of this?"

"It was her idea! She's not the problem. It's Amber. She's having one of her hissy fits. I'll tell you how this plays out. I'll have to get James, he'll spend half an hour with her, coaxing her out of her room, and when maximum damage has been caused, she'll put on a brave face, get over whatever imagined drama took place, put on that dress, and steal the bloody limelight. Just like the other night, when she stormed out, having demanded a taxi first. What happened to smacking them and sending them to their room?"

"They get bigger than you," said Fran.

"And they made it illegal," said Billie.

"Really? Pity. You know, once she's calmed down, James will be so proud that she managed to pull herself together and get over her nerves, or whatever this bollocks is. Oh, please don't look at me like that." I wagged a finger at them. "Just you wait," I said knowingly, "Amber Kent is tricksy."

"How old are you? Thirteen? Don't you remember what it was like?"

Oh, shut up, Claudia. I take back everything I just said about you.

"It's true, Tessa. You were very forgiving of Caspar and his hideous moods."

"Why is Amber so different?"

What I said about all of you—turncoats! I dug myself in. Because, because, because . . . she holds James's heart in the palm of her hand and only lends it to me when she returns to her mother's. "I was only asking for one night," I said petulantly.

"I thought you were doing this for the girls?" said Billie. "All of them."

"All right, all right, I'm a wicked witch," I growled at them. Which made them laugh. "But it's so hard sharing him."

"It could be worse. He could be like Christophe and not give a shit." Billie was right. Cora's dad had all but vanished.

"Okay, okay, I'll get James," I said, giving in. Everyone nodded.

WE ENDED UP GOING ON ahead with the tulle fairies in a vast people-carrier. I poured champagne onto the bile and hoped the acids would neutralize each other. By about the fifth glass, it was working.

There were so many friends at Century, the bar James had hired for the party, that I started to forget my fiancé was still at home with the mini-bride. Okay, it wasn't completely working, but I was having fun. Then Mum and Dad turned up, with Ben and Sasha, and my group was cemented. It was fun introducing my future family to my old friends. I liked Faith. Honor, I knew I could love. And Peter and Dad hit it off in an instant. Who knew fishing could be so funny? I could feel a new hobby coming on to add to the hundreds of others Dad had acquired since he'd retired a quarter of a century ago. I went up and hugged him. No girl could be more proud of her father than I was of Dad.

Mum looked great too. She had one of her walking sticks. One was good. Two was less good. The walking frame was bad. She only used her chair as a last resort. Lucy the hippie and Billie the Slavic gypsy seemed to be finding something utterly fascinating in each other, and later I saw them working the room like a couple of pros. I've always known there was something special about Billie, something mystical and unique, and my estimation of Lucy rose: she'd had the insight to see beyond the awkward exterior and plumb the depths.

Finally, I saw James. Drunk with love, I ran up to him and threw my arms around him. "I thought you were going to stand me up."

"Never," he said.

"Everything all right?"

"Well, we're here," he said.

Amber disappeared into the shadows. She wasn't wearing the blue dress. "What happened to her dress?"

A storm crossed James's face. "Don't ask."

"All that money—"

"Tessa?"

"Sorry."

"I need a drink."

He didn't have to say it twice.

THE DRINKS FLOWED AND THE noise level increased. I got so many compliments that I started to feel like Ava Gardner herself. Halfway through some defamatory story about an ex-boy-band member, which Matt, my assistant, was telling, there was a loud squawk through the speakers. We jumped.

Dad was on the mic. A stagehand moved him away from the amplifier and the noise died away. "Ladies and gentlemen, I'm sorry to interrupt the revelries, but I would like it very much if you would forgive an old man and allow him to say a few words about his daughter. The bride-to-be. As you all know, James and Tessa have decided to bugger off to the beach to get married and, for some inexplicable reason, have decided not to take us all along."

"You're invited, Dad!"

"Yes. But a father-of-the-bride speech isn't much good without an audience. So, ladies and gentlemen, without any further ado"—he looked at his notes—"I'd like to thank the vicar for— Oops, sorry, old version." He chuckled and put the paper away. People chuckled with him. Couldn't help it with my dad. It was something about the youth that came through his eyes and voice, even though his skin was old, and his bones were a little more bent than I'd have liked them to be. "Tessa was born very quickly. We never even made it to the hospital. Our daughter wouldn't wait and I think it's safe to say we've been trying to keep up with her ever since. Her curiosity was my gain. From the moment I caught her, and, I mean, literally *caught* her, to now, she has made me turn away from age and walk back to meet her, in her youth. The more she does, the more she grows, the more I gain. I honestly feel that the day she came to tell us she was marrying James was the day we finally met as true equals. Father and daughter. No longer parent and child. I'm so proud of you, Tessa." His voice choked a bit. A lump the size of a piece of coal came to my throat. "Proud of your friendships, which I know you hold so dear. Proud of your tenacity and refusal to give up. Proud of your mind, your wit, and your beauty, which you have never abused. And, of course, your excellent synchronized swimming."

There was a ripple of bemused laughter.

"James, I know you know you're a lucky man, and since she never stops talking about you, I feel confident in saying she feels the same. But, Tessa, I want you to know that luck is only one tiny part of marriage. Love, respect, humility, kindness, selflessness, and pure grit make up the rest. And then there is the final, secret ingredient that gives us the strength to jump the hurdles, cross the ravines, scramble up the slopes, and survive the desert. I used to think it was magic. But maybe it's hope. So, I would like to raise a glass to hope."

"Hope," echoed the smiling room.

"To James and Tessa."

"To James and Tessa," they called back.

"To the Kents and the Kings," people were shouting now.

"The Kents and the Kings!"

"I feel a great union coming on," said Dad, taking a sip. "And finally, but most important, to my beloved and brilliant wife Lizzie, who gave me two great gifts in this life. Her love and our daughter. I thank you for them both. Good night."

Well, what can I say? The crowd went wild and I ruined my makeup. I hugged Dad hard, he hugged me harder still. Over his shoulder I saw Amber. Watching us, watching James kiss me now, and I thought perhaps Claudia was right. If someone had come along and claimed my dad, how would I have felt? As isolated and miserable as she looked, probably. Excusing myself, I walked toward her, but people kept coming up and congratulating me, kissing me, complimenting me, and it was difficult to get away without seeming rude.

By the time I'd crossed the room, she'd gone. I made a mental note to find her, but the party took over time and space and, before I knew it, we were well into the early hours.

We hit the dance floor. My mother did a slow dance with Ben to a funky Beyoncé number. I danced with Luke. Then Mum. Then Ben.

Then James tapped me on the shoulder and I danced with him. It was more of a medley by then anyway. "Seen Amber anywhere?"

I shook my head and kissed him.

"I can't find her," he said, his eyes scanning across the bopping heads.

"I know Caspar was in search of her. Maybe they've escaped to a dark corner."

"I very much doubt it."

"Come on, James, she's nearly fifteen. She's allowed—"

"It's not that. They had a fight, if you must know, and he upset her a lot."

"Here at the party?"

"No, before. That's why she was . . . Anyway, I don't want to ruin our night."

"They didn't have a fight. We called. He said everything was great."

That stormy look passed over James's face. "What is it?" I asked, worried.

"Really, Tessa, I don't want to talk—"

"For God's sake, tell me!"

"He tore her dress. She wouldn't tell me exactly how but it doesn't take a genius and now I can't find her anywhere."

"No way, James."

"She showed it to me."

"That doesn't mean Caspar—"

"You're saying Amber's lying?"

There was that place between a rock and something harder I was getting so used to. "Of course not, but it must have been an accident or—"

James narrowed his eyes. "How do you rip a girl's dress by accident?"

I could see this escalating fast and furiously. I was sure that when Bea had proposed an engagement celebration, she hadn't wanted it to end with James and me at each other's throats. "You're right. Let's talk about it tomorrow."

Ben filled the gap between us. "I was expecting a groom's speech from you," said Ben jovially.

"Not very good at that sort of thing," James replied. "Sorry, Ben, please excuse me, but I've got to go and look for my daughter."

"Oops, did I say the wrong thing?"

I watched James go. "Is it just me or does the way he says 'my daughter' evoke thoughts of pure evil?"

"Actually even I got a whiff of the sanctimonious just then—what's up?"

"I'm thinking of getting myself a large, oval, gilded mirror."

"Ever thought of boarding school?" asked Ben.

"Frequently."

Ben pulled me toward him and gave me a hug. "Everything will settle down, don't you worry."

I leaned into him. "Can I tell you something?" Sensing the change in my tone, Ben immediately escorted me off the dance floor. Since I stuck out like a sore thumb in my flaming red dress, we snuck out onto the roof terrace to get away from the well-oiled well-wishers. It had been raining, and the teak boards glistened.

"What is it?" asked Ben, throwing his jacket over my shoulders to protect me from the cold.

"I watched their wedding video."

"Oh, Lord."

"It's been haunting me ever since. I don't know why I did it. And he isn't bad at that sort of thing, he's brilliant. His speech to Bea . . ." I could still hear the softly spoken words and see the love in his eyes. "It had me in tears and not just because it wasn't about me. I didn't want the same speech tonight. Actually, that's a lie, I do want the same speech, only different. Mine. Not hers. Instead he chickened out completely. I'm gutted."

Ben put his arm around me. "But, Tess, you can see from the way he looks at you that he loves you. You can't be in any doubt about that."

I stared at my feet. The leather straps were digging into the flesh. I only realized then my feet hurt. I wanted to sit down, but everything was wet.

"Saying anything to you publicly, in front of his children, is a slight to their mother. I'm sure he's just trying to preserve their feelings."

"What about mine?"

"Tess—"

"I know, I know. The girls come first. I'm the grown-up."

"Now you know why I've never wanted children. James is just doing what he has to do, and I take my hat off to him."

"But they're his children. It's easy for him."

"I'm not so sure about that, Tess. My colleagues with kids come into work on Monday morning and they look"—he scrolled through his extensive vocabulary—"beaten. One at a time, they admit to looking forward to coming back to work to get some breathing space. Biological ties or not, children sap the living daylights out of you."

"So I'm not the wicked stepmother?"

"No. And I bet even Super-Bea dreads the school holidays."

"Not the mistress of arts and crafts, the queen of the cupcakes—"

"Every woman I know who has children has been reduced to tears by their offspring. I make a point of asking them, so I can remind myself on those rare occasions I get drunk and broody."

"What do you mean rare? You get drunk all the time."

"I said drunk *and* broody."

I leaned my head on his shoulder. "I lie awake at night taunting myself with images of a fire starting in the kitchen and then, like a computer-game, test who James would save first."

"But, Tess, if Bea was lying next to him, he'd still run to save the girls first. That's the price you pay when you become a parent. It's a high price, I've no doubt." He shrugged, making my head bounce. "Isn't that why their marriage failed in the first place?"

I straightened up. I had no real answer to that question. It was my turn to shrug.

"Find out. If you understand it, you won't fear it so much, and that wedding video won't haunt you anymore."

"How can I, if James won't tell me anything?"

"He wouldn't. He's a decent man. And he loves you in all the right ways, which is the only reason I'm allowing you to marry him."

"Sasha must sleep well at night, knowing you'd carry her out of a burning building."

"Sasha?" Ben pulled a face. "No way. She'd be carrying me."

I heard a noise behind us and turned to see a cold, wet, miserable Caspar. "Caspar! What is it? What's happened?"

"There you are. I've been looking everywhere for you."

"You're soaking!"

"I need your help," he said. "It's Amber."

Wasn't I allowed to enjoy these warm, happy feelings a little while longer? "What happened between you two?"

He frowned. "Nothing."

"Nothing? Really? Then why isn't she wearing her dress and why aren't you doing your song?"

"She's not up to it."

"Why not?"

"She just isn't."

But why not? Because you got carried away. "If you think I can help, you're wrong. Amber doesn't really like me; I don't think I'm your best advocate here."

"I don't need an *advocate*. I need you to help me get her off the fire escape before she freezes to death and get her back to yours without Mr. Kent seeing her."

"Too late. He already knows."

"About what?"

"About the . . ." I looked at my godson. "Fight."

"We didn't have a fight. Oh, forget it, I'm getting Mum. I'm sorry I disturbed your tête-à-tête."

"It wasn't a tête-à-tête," I said.

"Where is she?" asked Ben.

Caspar hesitated.

"Where is she?"

He pointed to the corner of the roof terrace where a door was marked FIRE EXIT.

Ben set off at a run.

I'D THOUGHT HE WAS BEING a bit dramatic until I saw her. Huddled on the wrought-iron steps, Amber was wet, cold, and looked brittle enough to break. Her mascara was halfway down her face and her hair stuck to her thin arms and bony back. I temporarily forgot my fury.

"What's *she* doing here?" she spat.

"I couldn't find Mum," said Caspar apologetically. "She can help. She really can."

Amber put her head on her knees. Great. I wasn't even their first choice. There was an open champagne bottle on the step next to her.

"Is she drunk?" I whispered to Caspar.

"It's not that."

"Is she drunk? I'm getting a little fed up with all this teenage melodrama."

"Go easy, Tess," Ben whispered.

"Tessa, I'm telling you, it's not that—" I brushed Caspar aside, knelt down, and placed Ben's jacket over the girl's shoulders. "What happened, Amber?"

She buried her face in her knees.

"What happened to your dress?"

"Tessa, don't—"

I turned to Caspar. "She told her father you'd ripped it. That's a serious accusation. Did you?"

He looked as if I'd thrown a javelin through his heart. Of course he hadn't. Amber started shaking. I thought for a moment she was laughing. I pulled her around to face me. She wasn't laughing. It scared me. "Do you want me to get James?"

She shook her head vehemently.

"Oh, my God, Amber, you're not preg—"

"Jesus, Tessa, she's fourteen!"

I looked at Caspar. "Hey, I saw you in the hydrangea. You're just as bad, so don't fourteen-year-old me."

"Tessa, that was just a joke to wind you up. We knew you were spying on us from the kitchen. What do you take me for? We'd only just met!"

"Please," I said incredulously.

"Amber said that's what you'd expect of her. I didn't believe her, but she was right."

"Amber the slut. You going to rip my dress too?"

Ben and I were momentarily too startled to talk. We both stared at Amber, who promptly put her head back between her knees and hugged her legs. Her body heaved and I thought she was going to throw up. I stepped back. I'd had a teenager fill my shoes before with vomit and didn't want to repeat the experience. But she sobbed instead.

"Amber, I wasn't calling you a slut—"

Caspar reached down and grabbed her arm. "Let's get out of here," he said. She looked at him with such gratitude that I was suddenly uncertain. He lifted her into his arms, like a hero in the movies. He knocked over the champagne bottle in the process. It was empty. So she was drunk.

"I'm sorry, Caspar," she said into his ear. "I couldn't, I just couldn't . . ."

"It's all right. I understand," he replied gently.

Couldn't what? Go through with it? Lose her virginity? Tell her father the truth? I could see alcohol and exhaustion steal the last of Amber's fight. She buried her head in Caspar's neck and closed her eyes. He carried her up the steps and through the fire-exit door.

I knew one thing: I couldn't let Caspar take Amber anywhere in that state without risking the end of my short engagement. "I'll take them home," said Ben, reading my thoughts.

"I'll come with you."

"You're not going anywhere."

"But—"

"But nothing. Stay here, enjoy your party. Dance with your fabulous fiancé. We'll get her home to yours, don't worry."

But I was worried, and my feet were hurting, and I wasn't sure I had another dance in me. "Can't I just come home with you?" I said quietly.

Ben kissed my forehead. "Not in this lifetime, my friend."

BEN AND I MADE SURE the coast was clear, and got Caspar and his now-sleeping prize down to the street, hidden under my coat. Ben belted Amber into the back of the cab. I grabbed Caspar's arm. "You promise me you didn't get a bit carried away and tear the dress—I would understand. Sometimes things can happen more quickly than you want them to—"

"I'd swear on my life, Tessa, but I don't know if that would make a difference right now."

"Of course it would. But if it wasn't you, then who did rip her dress?"

"And call her a slut," said Caspar, with pained bemusement.

"Who would do that, Caspar?" I waited.

"You swear you won't tell?"

"Caspar!"

He took a deep breath. "I think it was Mrs. Kent."

"What? You *think*?"

"I know it sounds far-fetched—"

"It's ridiculous. Amber didn't even see Bea this evening. She was at . . ." My voice trailed off.

"She went home to get the words for the song. She didn't tell you because it was a surprise. I'm telling you, something happened between Amber and her mother."

"No, Caspar. Sorry. She's spinning you a line."

Caspar grabbed my arm and pulled me out of the way of a weaving gaggle of girls.

"She hasn't told me anything. She wouldn't. She loves her mother too much."

"So what gives you the idea that—"

Caspar interrupted me. "The other day when she left your flat after the video thing, she came to my house and stayed the night. A friend of hers rang up and pretended to be Bea. Mum believed us."

"I don't want to know—"

"She told me her mother was out, and she didn't want to be alone. I believed her. She obviously didn't feel very welcome at yours."

I ignored his pointed comment.

"The next day I was at her house and heard Amber tell her mother she'd come home the previous evening, but because Mrs. Kent was asleep on the sofa, Amber just went to bed. Well, obviously I knew that wasn't true. She'd been at *our* house. Mrs. Kent was in all along."

"So we know Amber doesn't have a problem telling a lie."

"That's not the point."

"It should be," I said, getting angry.

"Hello, lovely," leered some paralytic imbecile in a suit. "Wanna drink?"

"No, thanks," I replied. He looked as though he was going to be a pest, but Caspar put his arm around me.

"Tessa, think about it. Mrs. Kent didn't know whether Amber had come home or not."

The drunk sidestepped away.

"That's just not possible."

"Unless?"

I put my hands on my hips. "What are you saying?"

"She was too drunk to remember."

Ben put his head out of the taxi. "Come on, stop gassing! They're missing me on the dance floor. By the way, what's the babysitter called?"

Continuing to watch Caspar for signs of deceit, I replied, "Magda. The girls went home ages ago. I'll phone and let her know you're coming."

"I can stay with Amber," said Caspar.

"No."

"I'll drop him home and come back," said Ben.

Caspar looked at me. "You still think I did it?"

I didn't know what to think. "James wouldn't like it. I'm trying to protect you." He opened his mouth to protest. "Listen to me, Amber told him you did it, so go with me on this one."

He nodded forlornly.

I watched him pull the door behind him and carefully place Amber's head on his shoulder. I was baffled. Was this just a pubescent drunken drama or something I really had to worry about? I mean, Bea drunk was one thing, she was entitled on her night off, but ripping Amber's dress, calling her a slut, not knowing if she was home? No way. Not the Bea I'd been told about. That was as unlikely as, well, Caspar forcing himself on Amber.

Ben leaned out of the window as the taxi pulled off. "Ah, young love . . . Remember that?"

They did a U-turn and were gone. "Like it was yesterday," I replied, and walked back into my engagement party.

I FOUND JAMES AND TOLD him Ben had taken Amber home. Before he could start quizzing me, we were joined by my parents.

"Darling, there you are. We're off, I think. I'm all danced out," said Dad.

"What a swell party it was, Tessa," sang my mother. "Dad and Peter are going fishing together. In Scotland!"

"What? Dad?"

"You know my motto—never too late to try something new," he said. A motto he lived by. I can't remember if it was two or three degrees he'd acquired since retiring. You rarely saw him without a book in his hand. At eighty-four, he was going to take up fishing. He was an inspiration.

I smiled, comforted by the familiarity of my family. "You amaze me," I said. "When are you going?"

"Couple of weeks' time, for five days on the Isle of Skye. Never been."

I immediately looked at my mother. "I'll be fine," she said sternly. "Do you go, Honor, on this fishing malarkey?" Honor had approached our gathering.

"Lord, no. I'm going on a retreat, actually."

"Right, let me get you a taxi," said James.

Honor turned back to my mother. "I go to a naturist reserve and get back to basics."

"How wonderful. I love camping," said Dad, who was a little hard of hearing.

I clamped my jaw shut. Naturist? My God, is no one what they seem?

"Any animals?" asked my father.

My mother smiled at Honor. "Plenty, I should imagine."

"They're pretty tame and tend to keep to themselves."

"Sounds lovely," said my mother.

"Well, you could always join me. Good for the soul to try something new."

"That's what I say," observed Dad happily.

"Let me sleep on it. I'll call you."

My God, they'd exchanged numbers. Our four parents, still together after an aggregate of nearly a hundred years of marriage, left together. It gave me hope. Dad was right. Hope was what we all needed. James and I went down in the lift with them to the street and waved them off.

"You didn't tell me your mother likes to dance around naked."

"I'm told it's more sedate than that."

"Anything else you're not telling me?" I asked, watching him.

"Like?"

"I don't know . . . That your ex-wife likes a drink?"

"Bea!" He laughed. "A drinker!" He laughed again. "She was a party girl in her time but now retired. Ever tried looking after children on a hangover?"

I shook my head.

"Impossible."

But what if you didn't have to look after the children all the time? What if you had Every Other Weekend off? What if you came out of retirement, then found it hard to go back? No. I dismissed the thoughts. Something else was going on. Something I couldn't see. We were back at the entrance to the club. James put out his hand to open the door. Suddenly, I grabbed it.

"Can we go?" I said urgently.

"You sure?"

"Very."

"Home it is, then," said James.

But I didn't want to go home. I wanted to be alone with James. "I was thinking maybe that all-night kebab shop we found."

"That's what I like—a girl with brains and a good appetite."

"You don't by any chance have some sneakers on you?"

He patted his pockets. "Feet hurting?" I nodded. "I think I can sort something out, Ms. King." Then, with no warning, he lifted me off the ground, like a hero in the movies, and swept me up into his arms. "Let's not say good-bye to anyone."

"No," I replied, resting my head on his chest. "Let's not."

Thirteen

Sophie Guest

By the time I was awake, James had taken the girls back to Bea's, picked up breakfast, and returned home. There was no point in bringing up the subject of the blue dress—if I did, I risked boxing myself into the corner I'd been pushed into the night before. To ease my moral dilemma, I had given my word to Caspar that I wouldn't say anything, but I knew I was using that oath as a shield. Asking James to believe Caspar's side of the story was asking him to admit his daughter had lied and his ex-wife drank. That a sex-crazed teenager had tried to have his way with his daughter and was heroically defeated, was easier to accept. But the sex-crazed teenager was Caspar, and I didn't think him capable of it. Then again, who knew what a rampant male virgin was capable of? But if Caspar had done what Amber had told James he had, she wouldn't have allowed herself to be swept up in his arms— would she? Then again . . . It was no good. I was going around and around in circles and was none the wiser.

I understood why I hadn't mentioned it, but what I was less clear about was why he hadn't brought it up with me. Was each of us hiding something from the other? Was that how it all began? Did protecting the individual mean damaging the couple? If only, I thought for the hundredth time, I could pick up the phone and call Bea, we could sort it out in moments. But that wasn't going to happen.

MARCH CREPT ON TOWARD EASTER, and I saw the girls only a couple of times. Amber started attending an after-school drama club on Wednesdays, so I saw even less of her. I felt she was avoiding me, but I kept my suspicions to myself. I heard from Fran that Amber was a regular visitor to her house, but no one mentioned Caspar's name, so I didn't either. I missed one weekend with them all, because I went to stay with my godsons in Norwich. It was their second birthday. Their mother was my friend Helen, who had died when they were very small, so I had to go.

When I did see the girls, it was all very polite and well mannered, which made me more nervous. Amber was perfectly nice but strangely absent. Every time I tried to get close, I was politely rebuffed. Even the younger two seemed quieter, and I worried we were losing them, but when I brought up the subject, James dismissed it with the assurance that everything was simply getting back to mundane normality. But that felt too remote for my liking. I wanted to find a way through the polite barrier that had been erected. Then Fate showed me one.

I KNOCKED ON LINDA'S DOOR and opened it. She was barking into her headpiece but summoned me in with a clawed hand. She pointed to the coffee machine, then her mug. Linda drank way too much strong black coffee. She had so much caffeine in her system she hummed. Her foot tapped out a tattoo under the table. I poured some, sat down, and waited.

Linda leaned forward, plopped two fat saccharine tablets into the tar, and stirred it with her pen. "Look, you got yourself into this situation, you solve it. I need an answer by four." She pressed a button and flicked back the microphone, like an airline pilot. "Fucking Americans," she said. "What can I do for you, my precious? Need a good lawyer yet?"

"Ha-ha."

"You will."

"No, actually, I need a favor."

"Christ, I hate those. I don't have any sway with that boarding school anymore, if that's it."

"No, that's not it."

"Trust me, you'll come around to the boarding-school idea. So what have you gone and promised the little brat this time?"

"Nothing. I want it to be a surprise. Are we still keeping the studio free next week for the Belles to sort out their differences?"

"Yeah. But I'm expecting them back sooner rather than later," said Linda, with a glint in her eye.

"Do you think I could take Amber down there? I've got the girls for a weekend on my own—"

"Christ!"

"James is going to L.A. for a work junket, and it's the perfect opportunity for me to earn Amber's trust—"

"Buy her trust, you mean."

"No, earn it. I'm looking for an honorable draw, not an underhanded victory."

"Fool. Look, I'd help you if I could but it's a closed set, sweetie. You know perfectly well they can't sing."

"Oh, I don't want them to *be* there. I want Amber to sing."

"I'm not fucking reading you."

"Amber has written this song for her father and I'd like to record it for a wedding present from the girls to their dad."

"Still getting married, then?"

I didn't answer.

"You're not going to try and get me to sign her, are you?"

"No way. I'm trying to kill the beast, not create another."

"What?"

"Never mind. Can I? We'll be paying for the day anyway."

"If it's okay with Ca—"

"He said if it's okay with you, then fine."

"Well, fine, then. But just for the record, I think you're fucking nuts."

I laughed and walked to the door. She dismissed me with a wave and picked up the phone, ready to break someone else.

* * *

THE FOLLOWING SUNDAY, JAMES AND his brother went to play in a charity football match. Faith called me up and asked me to have lunch with her, since Charlie was spending the day with his cousins. I nearly refused, having envisaged a hot bath and a good couple of hours with my foot-scraper, but now I was becoming part of a family, foot fetishes had to be put aside for the greater good. My instinct had been to like Faith, but I knew she and Bea were close, so it was with apprehension that I walked into the pub on Hammersmith Grove.

Faith was at a table, reading.

"Lucy is coming to join us. I hope you don't mind." Faith folded the paper.

I immediately relaxed. I liked Lucy a lot. She was one of the few in James's family who didn't seem wedded to Bea. "Not at all," I said.

"I hear you're having the girls to stay while Jimmy's away."

"You think I'm mad?"

"Brave," she replied.

"Hi!" said a voice behind me. It was Lucy. She leaned over and gave me a kiss. I appreciated the familiarity.

"When did Jimmy last play football? Is he going to have a heart attack?"

"He's pretty fit," I said.

"We've heard," said Lucy, cackling.

"Ignore her," said Faith.

I shifted my chair to make room for Lucy. These two women were to become my sisters-in-law. I'd never had sisters before. I was suddenly quite moved. I wanted to like them. I really wanted them to like me.

The waiter came over and asked for our orders. Faith, who knew the place well, went for a Cobb salad. Lucy and I copied her.

"Chips with that, ladies?"

I nodded and shrugged simultaneously.

"Just to soak up the wine," said Faith. "Bottle of house white, please."

"And a jug of tap water," said Lucy. She leaned forward on her elbows. "So, how's everything with Amber? Given you an apple-pie bed yet? Spat in your coffee?"

"Probably."

"Come on, Lucy, she's not that bad," said Faith, tearing into a baguette.

"I adore her, just wouldn't necessarily want to become her stepmother. She's always had Jimmy wrapped around her little finger."

Faith looked at me. "You're no worse off with Amber than my other friends who've become stepparents. Everyone finds it hard."

"Yeah, but Amber's had sole charge of Jimmy for the last four years and the first four he had sole charge of her. This is more than your average father-daughter thing. It drives Bea mad—"

"Lucy."

"What?"

A small, uncomfortable silence followed.

I broke it. "James told me how he worked around Amber when she was a baby. It's very sweet."

The waiter arrived with our drinks, and Faith and Lucy busied themselves pouring out wine and water, an operation they seemed more intent on than the job required.

"What did I say? You don't think it was sweet?"

Faith couldn't quite look me in the eye. "He didn't really work around her . . ." Her voice trailed off.

I frowned. "You mean Amber was dragged from pillar to post?"

"Oh, no, he was very disciplined about her routine, obsessively so, almost. No, he just didn't work."

"That's not true Faith. He always had things in—"

"Development," interrupted Faith. "Come on! That's what drove Bea mad." She looked compromised. Again. "Obviously he got a job eventually. When Maddy was born."

"Only because his snob of a mother-in-law shamed him into it. Poor Jimmy, it sucked out his soul. Something Bea never understood."

"She'd carried that family for seven years, Lucy, had three kids. She was entitled to a break. If Jimmy had got off his arse sooner, she wouldn't have been too shattered to take the *Financial Times* job."

"She didn't want it. She wanted to play house."

"Lucy, you're so sure about what you do that you don't understand some people oscillate between choices. I know I do. When work's slow

I feel really guilty about not being at home with Charlie, and when it's frantic and exciting I feel stretched and guilty about not staying late with the rest of the team. Can't win. Bea wanted some time at home, but once you're home it's different. Bloody hard work for a start and no one says thank-you. I bet part of her misses the cut-and-thrust of the editorial room. She was brilliant at her job and now she spends her life cutting up carrot sticks." Suddenly, Faith looked at me. "Sorry, I'm sure you don't want to talk about this."

Are you kidding? I was on the edge of my seat. I had momentarily forgotten we were talking about my Salt-and-pepper Man and his first wife. Instead we were talking about a couple called Jimmy and Bea, and, frankly, they sounded fascinating. I can happily sit in a pub with a friend and dissect the life of a person I've never met and be absolutely gripped. Not only gripped, but comment, too. We do it every day, Brad and Ange, Madge and Guy. I wanted more on Jimmy and Bea.

"The party was great," said Faith, unsubtly changing the subject. "I thought what your dad said was so sweet. I can't believe he delivered you. You're obviously very close."

"At least that makes it easier to understand Jimmy and Amber, I suppose," said Lucy.

"It hasn't," I said honestly. "She was quite stroppy in the beginning, but now she just doesn't seem herself."

"I know what I said about her, but she's all right. Puberty isn't fun, is it?" Lucy grimaced.

"Do you think it's that?" I asked.

"She's fourteen—it must be," said Lucy. "It's not you. She loves her dad in a good way—she wants him to be happy. You make him happy. She's a good kid, really."

"They all are. Bea's done a great job with them."

"Faith! Jimmy's done it too, you know, not just Bea."

"With Amber, maybe, but the other two ... He was completely absent. You're like Amber, you've never been able to see his faults."

"And you're so discerning about Luke," said Lucy, loaded with sarcasm. "He's a lazy bastard. You do everything for him, then thank him for it. It's crazy."

Faith turned to me again. "Sorry. Families. You're probably not used to this."

I was saved from answering. "They're a nightmare," said Lucy.

"I suppose there are some advantages to being a one and only," I laughed.

"We love each other, really," she said.

"Of course you do. I didn't mean—"

"Don't be daft, I know you didn't," Lucy retorted.

"Can I ask you a personal question?" Faith was looking at me carefully.

"I don't promise to answer it truthfully," I replied. I was trying to be funny. I couldn't work out whether this was going well or not. How personal was she going to get?

"Did you miss not having siblings?"

"Oh, so you don't want to know how many people I've slept with?"

"Lots, I hope."

I tapped my nose. She turned serious again. "It's just Charlie . . ."

"No. I didn't. Friends fill the space. Plus Charlie has something I never had. Cousins who adore him. The girls talk about him like he's their brother."

"That's what Bea says." I adopted my benign, we're-talking-about-Bea-again silence and smiled. Faith stood up. "I need a pee." She disappeared around the bar.

"That was nice of you," said Lucy. "Faith tried so hard for a second. She likes to be reassured it was okay to give up. She had a horrible time. Both of them did."

"Both of them?"

"Bea and Faith," clarified Lucy. "That's one of the reasons they're so close."

"Getting pregnant was a problem for Bea?" I was confused. Unless I was imagining things, I was looking at a trio of stepdaughters.

"For Faith it was. Bea's problem was keeping them."

"Between Amber and Lulu, you mean?"

Lucy scrunched up her face. "Poor thing had five miscarriages. Jimmy begged her to stop, Amber was enough, but she wanted a big family. Safety in numbers, I've always thought. Protect her from her mother . . ."

I swallowed some wine. I felt bad for Bea. I knew what a miscarriage looked like. I'd seen one. "Poor Bea."

"Lulu was born at last and it was all worth it, and less than a year later out popped Maddy. God knows where she came from."

I knew Lulu and Maddy were close in age. I'd done the math. Lulu would have been only a couple of weeks old when Maddy was conceived. Obviously, I found that hard to swallow since it meant James and Bea were back at it bloody quickly, which didn't tally with my preconceived ideas about marriage failure, inhospitable deserts, and poor, neglected James. My mind had always got stuck on the image of a lithe, nubile, hormonally flushed Bea and proud-father James gleefully jumping back into bed without even waiting for the six-week checkup. I wasn't thinking about the consequences. I was thinking about where I fitted in.

"I guess that would put a huge strain on any marriage."

"A strain, maybe. Not an end."

"Why did it end?" I asked. Lucy looked at me sharply. "Sorry," I replied quickly, then thought better of it. "Bea did end it, though, didn't she?"

"Yes," said Lucy.

I saw Faith emerge from the side door marked TOILETS. It was now or never. "Do you think she's ever regretted it?"

Lucy opened her mouth. Then closed it. Then opened it again. "I don't know."

A waiter appeared at our table with a loaded tray.

"Great," said Faith, coming up behind him. "I'm starving."

"Another bottle?" said Lucy, looking away from me.

"Why not?" I said. The more we drank, the more I might glean, and maybe, somehow, in the absence of straight answers, I could fill in the blanks. But, after that, the conversation stayed off Jimmy and Bea. Purposely, I thought.

EARLY THE FOLLOWING FRIDAY MORNING I drove James to the airport. Of course I was nervous about a weekend alone with the girls, but I was excited too. Well, I was trying to be. Trouble was, James kept scattering seeds of doubt in my mind.

"Now, are you sure you don't want me to call Bea and reorganize the weekend?" It wasn't the first time he'd suggested it. "She won't mind, you know."

"I'm sure she could do with a few days off before the holidays start."

"She won't mind," he said again.

"No. It's all planned."

"Well, I think you're mad."

"They're your children."

"Exactly," he said, laughing.

"We'll be fine. Anyway, I have a little something up my sleeve."

"What?"

"I can't tell you. It's a surprise."

"Do we need Bea's permission?" he asked. My anger spiked. "It's not parachuting," I said.

"My advice. Keep it as low-key as possible. Park, maybe, if it isn't raining. Other than that, videos, puzzles, and drawing. Make it as easy as possible on yourself."

I'd noticed that was his way of doing things. "What about cabin fever?" I asked. "They'll get bored. So would I."

He shook his head despairingly. "Ignore me at your peril but, whatever you do, don't take them to a museum. They're packed on weekends and it's a nightmare. Or the aquarium or—"

"Anything fun. I've got it."

"That's not fair."

"It's okay. We'll play Guess Who? for forty-eight hours. It'll be great."

"I don't play Guess Who? for hours."

Yes, I'd noticed that too. "Stop fretting. We are going to have a fun girly weekend. Don't you worry."

"Nail polish isn't allowed—"

I whacked him hard on the thigh.

"Ow." He looked at me. "Do that again."

"Pervert."

"God, I don't want to go," he said, stroking my cheek. "I hate being away from you."

I leaned into his hand, which was a bit dangerous, since I was driving, and kissed it. He groaned. "Come with me."

"Then who'd look after your children?"

"Bea wouldn't mind."

"It's about time we stopped asking Bea to pick up all the slack."

James took his hand away.

"What?" I asked.

"It's our exit," he said, pointing.

"Oh."

I signaled and pulled into the left-hand lane. "James, I wasn't saying you're slack, I was just saying—"

"I know. What do you want me to bring you from L.A.?"

A ring would be nice? "Um . . . Robert Downey Jr.—no, make that an Owen Wilson to go."

"I'll see what I can do," said James.

We fell into silence. I negotiated my way off the motorway. A week holed up in L.A. at the infamous hotel Château Marmont didn't sound that bad, actually. Things were always better between us when we were on our own. That was the easy part of being a couple. It was all the rest that made it difficult. I glanced across at him. But it was worth it. "All I really want is for you to come home safely."

"I will," said James.

"And no sampling the local wares."

"Not my style."

So you say, but how would I know? Stop it. Linda was polluting my mind. "James?"

"Yes?"

"Why did you and Bea split up?"

"That's a mighty curious question. Most people ask, 'What terminal?' at about this point."

"What terminal?"

"Three."

"Okay. Good. So, why did you and Bea split up?"

James frowned. "Why do you keep asking me that?"

"I want to make sure someone explained it to Amber."

"She was ten, Tessa."

"I know, but shouldn't she—"

"The reasons are not important as long as the children know it wasn't their fault."

What scary book did you read that in? "How do they know that if you don't give them a reason?"

James fussed with the volume button on the radio. Impatiently, I switched it off. "Please, James. I really want to know. Why?"

"What did Faith say to you?" he asked suspiciously.

"Nothing. This has nothing to do with Faith."

"Well, something must have prompted this rubbernecking curiosity."

I felt as if he'd slapped me. I wasn't fishing for gossip here. I was agreeing to marry a man whose previous marriage had failed. Bea wasn't some evil, neurotic cow. Everyone liked her. I couldn't blame it all on her. Something had happened. Unless I understood, I would never know where I stood. With Amber. With any of them.

"Let's not argue before I go away," said James, putting his hand on my leg. Rather than soothing, it felt heavy. Guilty.

"We're not arguing. I'm trying to ask you a question about something that affects our future. I don't know why you can't talk about this."

"Divorce isn't fun."

"Of course it isn't. I don't dispute that. But I really think it might help things between Amber and me if I—"

"Things with Amber are fine."

"James, they aren't really. You must know that. She's cold, aloof—"

"Well, it was hard on her."

"Exactly, so tell me."

James retrieved his hand and shoved it under his opposite armpit. "We did our best for the girls, in the circumstances. If you had children you'd understand."

I was trying to be sympathetic, but that made me angry. "Don't pull that one on me. That's not fair."

"Pull what? Come on, Tessa, let's start again. I'm sorry."

"You're just saying that because you don't like where this is going."

"Christ, a man can't win."

I scowled for half a mile. James stared out of the window.

"Why can't we have a normal conversation about this? All I did was ask you a simple question—"

"No, you asked me an impossible question."

"You don't know why you and Bea split up?"

James didn't reply. Instead he shook his head despairingly and looked out of the window again. Blood. Out. Of. Stone. Just like Amber. I counted to ten and started again, determined, if anything, to reverse this escalation. "James, I know this is difficult for you, and I know and love that you just want everyone to be happy, but I think something is going on with Amber—"

"You should speak to that godson of yours. She was fine until he came along. Now she barely speaks."

"So you *have* noticed it?"

"Of course I've noticed it."

"So why didn't you talk to me about it?"

"Well, you're quite blinkered when it comes to Caspar—"

"*I'm* blinkered!"

"Tessa, he's seventeen, Amber's fourteen. She's the one who needs protecting. Bea and I just ..." James patted his jacket pocket and checked his passport. "Could you pick up my—"

"Bea and you just what?"

James chewed the inside of his lip. "Thought it better if ... She's very young and ... Look at your face! No wonder I haven't spoken to you about this."

"You and Bea what?"

James took a deep breath. "Decided it would be better if they didn't see each other."

I was furious. I clenched my fists around the steering wheel and locked my jaw.

"That's why I didn't say anything, I didn't want to upset you."

"Well, you failed."

James placed his hand on my leg and spoke in a placatory voice: "I'm sure you're right and it was just an accident, but Amber was very shaken. She barely spoke to Bea and she won't say anything to me—"

I couldn't take any more. "Why do you think I'm upset?"

"Admitting that Caspar is capable—"

"No, James. I would be happy to sit and discuss what happened that night. With you, with him, with Amber, with Bea too. If Caspar got carried away, I personally would prefer to know, so that we can make sure it never happens again, with Amber or anyone else. If Caspar doesn't know his own strength, or doesn't hear 'No,' Jesus, James, I want to know that! But, no, you and Bea decided between yourselves not to talk to me. Worse than that, you haven't even tried to get to the bottom of this, and I tell you, not only does that make me feel like shit"—I could feel the tears and was damned if I was going to let them out—"it makes me mistrust you both."

"I'm sorry. Please let's not fight about the children again."

"Don't fool yourself, James. We're not fighting about the children."

"Amber and I would never—"

I lost it and shouted so loudly I shocked myself: "I'm not talking about you and Amber!"

I stopped the car at the barrier of the short-term parking lot. I took the ticket that the Dalek spat at me and watched the metal arm lift. I would have preferred to throw him out at Departures without slowing down, but I had been told by someone never to go to sleep on an argument. Boarding a plane was worse. James was going away for a week, and I didn't want this knot of anger to turn malignant.

The air darkened as I aimed the car up the narrow corkscrew hollow and we drove up in silence, past floors packed with row upon row of boxy cars, until we reached the roof. For a fraction of a second, I had a terrible urge to put my foot to the floor and *Thelma and Louise* it over the edge. The impact of something concrete would feel like a relief after all this uncertainty. I slipped the car into an empty space and turned off the engine. Counting to ten wasn't working. I felt panic rip through me. Panic that I was losing James. I brushed away the tear and forced myself to look at him.

"What aren't you telling me?" I asked.

He shook his head.

"James, please . . . How can I understand anything if I don't know what's going on? People fear what they don't understand. It makes them suspicious, nervous, insecure. If you hide things from me, this isn't going to work."

James clamped his hands together. "I feel incredibly disloyal having this conversation."

"I'm supposedly going to be your wife. Don't I deserve a little loyalty too?"

He looked at me seriously, then nodded reluctantly. "She had an abortion."

"What? Caspar—"

"Not Amber! She's a child, for heaven's sake. Bea."

"You mean Bea had an abortion?"

"Yes. Now you know."

I waited for the penny to drop. It didn't. "Sorry, James, I don't understand. Why did Bea have an abortion? When?"

"I can't believe you thought it was Amber."

"We were talking about her."

"I thought you wanted to know why we split up? What was going on between us? Well, now you do. I talk to Bea about the girls because she is their mother. I'm sorry that makes you feel left out, but you can't let it. Though that isn't up to me, it's up to you. I've told you a million times how I feel about you, but it's not enough, is it?"

"Blind faith is hard when you feel like you're being kept in the dark," I said, and I still was. Women have abortions all the time. "Why was that the end of your marriage?"

"Nothing I tell you will undo the fact that I was married and had three children. Don't you see that?" James sounded cross.

"I don't want to undo that fact, I want to understand. I need to be able to."

James was quiet for a moment or two. Finally, focused somewhere I couldn't see, he started to speak. "A couple of years after Maddy was born. It was quite late in the . . . um . . . pregnancy." He was visibly uncomfortable. Oh no, poor James. Poor Bea.

"Was there something wrong with the baby?" I probed gently. Did James make Bea have an abortion against her will? Was that the thing he didn't want to tell me? He'd bullied her into it—

"No," he replied quietly. "It was a perfect, healthy little boy."

Oh no, worse. A mistake. A bad scan. Incorrect findings—

"Except that it wasn't mine."

"What?"

"The baby wasn't mine," he said again.

I was stunned. Of all the permutations, of all the possibilities, Bea's fidelity to James I had never questioned. Why not? Because I couldn't imagine being unfaithful to this man. I couldn't imagine needing to. Bea had an affair. The perfect ex-wife had slept around and got pregnant. Poor, poor James. I reached out to him. I watched a range of emotions cross his face. Shock, disbelief, anger, then shock all over again. "How did you find out?"

"It was one of those extraordinary things. I shouldn't know to this day. I wish I didn't. But Bea was away with the girls over half-term. I was at home. We had a flood, a leak—can't even remember now. It was the middle of the night and I had no idea who we were insured with. Bea did all of that. You probably think that's pathetic—"

"Pretty usual, I imagine."

"I had to go searching through her desk. I couldn't find it but, as Bea always told me, I can't find most things that are in front of my nose. It was the name I noticed. Sophie Guest. I don't even know why I looked at it. It was a medical report, a fetal autopsy, if you like. It told me in bold print that the eighteen-week fetus that had been removed was a normal specimen, male. I've had three children. I've seen them, their perfectly formed selves, on a screen at twelve weeks. Fingernails, toes, eyelashes, fully formed babies. At twelve weeks, Tessa, they are perfect."

I knew that. Claudia's baby had floated happily in her mother's amniotic fluid, sucking her thumb, at twelve weeks. On a black-and-white lunar photo, I'd felt a presence I could not ignore. A couple of weeks later, I saw that same perfect form, still. Lifeless. The minuscule heart had inexplicably stopped beating.

"Sophie is Bea's middle name," said James, running his hands through his hair. "Guest is her mother's maiden name. But that wasn't what made me click. I assumed it was a wrong address and Bea was planning to post it back to the sender, some discreet address in Islington. I thought how very sad for poor Sophie Guest, blood type O. Then I saw the date of birth and literally froze. Sophie Guest was not Sophie Guest, she was my wife, and the boy that had been 'removed' was my son. Or so I thought that night."

"What did you do?"

He sighed. "Tried to forgive her." He was staring into his lap. "I think I was in shock, actually. I wanted it to be someone else's."

I understood that.

"But she swore she hadn't been with anyone else. I didn't know what was worse. Either way, the trust was broken. I couldn't believe she'd got rid of our child without talking to me. It was awful. We stopped speaking, we stopped . . . well, everything died between us. It was always there in the room. The awful . . . truth."

"What happened?"

James straightened up. "Eventually she put me out of my misery and confessed that the child had not been mine. Shortly afterward, she left. She never told me whose child I'd been mourning."

I didn't know what to say. Responses formed in my head. Questions. Accusations. Recriminations. I sprang from shock to disbelief to anger and back to shock again. But words? Well, they failed me. What do you say to that? All I could do was take James's hand in mine and squeeze it.

"Meadowlands," he said, shaking his head from side to side. He looked at me finally, utterly dejected. "The clinic. It was called Meadowlands. It sounded so nice."

I leaned over and kissed him softly on the lips. Then again, harder, feeding him love, filling him up again. Trying to make it all better. I clicked out of my seat belt and leaned into him, over him, kept on kissing. I wanted him to wrap himself up in the memory of it when he was in L.A. I wanted him to think about our future, not about the son he had lost and then lost again.

Fourteen

Pink Water

WE PULLED UP OUTSIDE THE NONDESCRIPT BUILDING ON THE OUTSKIRTS of Epsom and I turned to the passenger seat. The poker face Amber had kept up since she'd got into the front of my Mini matched her father's. But it didn't bother me so much. In fact, I was beginning to see through it. The poker face itself was a tell. So I acknowledged it and moved on. "I know that was quite a long journey and I'm sorry, but you'll soon see it was worth it. Come on, the surprise is inside. Now, remember, not a word to Daddy when he rings. This is a surprise for him too."

The girls climbed out of the back. I could tell that Maddy and Lulu were excited, because they kept looking about, half-expecting the Seven Dwarfs to jump out from behind a bush. I rang the buzzer and a girl with an impressive array of alloys through her ears and nose let us in. Maddy and Lulu stared, agog. Amber pretended not to notice.

"You must be Tessa. Carlos is expecting you. Down the corridor, third door on the left." She turned to the girls and flashed them a metallic smile. "Can I get you ladies some drinks? Juice, Coke, Fanta—we've got those Innocent smoothies in cartons. That's what the Belles drink."

"The Bonne Belles?" asked Amber.

The receptionist nodded. "We've had them here all week." It was Innocent smoothies all around.

I watched the mask fall from Amber's face.

"So you're the one with the voice," said the She-Jaws.

Amber glanced at me for confirmation.

"Yes," I said. "But we've got a couple of backup singers here too."

Maddy and Lulu looked at Amber and they all laughed nervously.

"What are you called?"

"Lulu," said Lulu.

"I think that name's taken," said the girl.

Lulu frowned.

"I mean your band's name, one lead singer and two backup singers, like the Supremes."

More frowns. "The Three Degrees."

"A little before their time," I said.

"Eternal, then?"

They were laughing now, mostly at the metal woman, because they had no idea what she was talking about.

"Come on, let's get you down there and all will be revealed," I said.

Their curiosity piqued, they set off at a run. I tapped on the door and pushed it open. Carlos leaned back in his chair, feet on the mixing desk, an unlit cigar in his mouth. "Tessa, come in, come in."

But I couldn't. Three girls stood on the studio threshold and stared. A bank of tiny buttons and slides swung wide in front of them, a crescent moon of magic technology. Beyond that there was a glass wall and a room that looked like an instrument shop. Guitars were propped up, a huge synthesizer, a piano, saxophones, three drum kits . . .

"Sorry about the mess. We haven't had time to clear up from yesterday. But we're all set."

In the middle stood a solitary mic. Amber turned, wide-eyed, to me.

"I thought," I said, steering her and the other two into the room, "that you could record your best-man song and we could have a few CDs made for the rest of your family. What do you think?"

The smile said "I'd love to," but a line of hesitation was etched between her eyebrows. "I haven't got the words or the music."

"Don't worry. That's taken care of. It's the music to 'Can't Help Loving That Man of Mine,' right?"

She nodded.

"Well, a good friend of mine provided me with your brilliant words." I thought for a second it was going to backfire and she would storm off, so I took her hand to keep her with me. "Your dad would so love it and I thought the girls could be backup singers."

Immediately, they were jumping up and down, and Carlos, a big softy, gave them enormous handheld microphones. Amber still hesitated.

"So, how about it, Amber? Do you want to make a record?" asked Carlos.

"It was supposed to be a surprise," she said. Maddy and Lulu looked nervous all of a sudden.

"It will be," I insisted.

"How do you know about it?"

"Fran told me. She says it's brilliant. She told me how hard you and Caspar worked on it."

Amber leaned against the wall. "He should be here."

"Would you like him to be?" I asked gently.

Her face creased. "I've been so mean to him."

"He didn't say anything to me," I said.

"You mean it? He doesn't hate me?"

"No, Amber, far from it."

"Really?"

I was fairly sure of this, since he was hiding in the next room, waiting for my all-clear, desperate to be a legitimate part of her life again. I nodded.

She looked again, longingly, at the mic. "We shouldn't do it without him."

"Pleeeeeeeease, Amber, can we?" begged Lulu.

"I'd love to, really I would, but it isn't right. He did all the hard work."

I smiled. "What if I told you he was here?" I opened the door to the corridor. "Caspar!"

Amber yelped with stunned excitement, then clamped her hand over her mouth.

"What is it?" I asked. Something was scaring her. Had I got this wrong?

"What about Mum and Dad?"

"They're not here."

"Oh, Tessa, I . . ." She swallowed.

"Don't you want to see him?"

"I do, it's just . . . I told a terrible lie. I blamed him for something he didn't do."

"The dress," I said, as quietly as possible. Amber's eyes darted over her sisters' heads. She gave a brief nod. That was all I needed to see and hear. I pulled her close and lowered my voice further. "You're a great girl, Amber, a *great* girl. I think we've all put too much pressure on you recently and I'm sorry for that. I also happen to know that Caspar is a very special person. We'll work everything else out. Don't worry. I know we can't talk here, and you don't have to tell me anything if you don't want to, but I'm here for you if you need me."

She blinked.

"So? Are we going to do this?" I asked, straightening up.

Maddy and Lulu, as ever, looked to their older sister. Suddenly, Amber threw off her jacket and grinned. "You bet." The other two immediately followed suit.

Relieved, I called Caspar's name again.

"Darlin'," said Carlos. "You're going to have to yell louder than that. All the rooms are soundproofed."

"Why don't you go and get him, Amber?" I suggested. "He's in studio eight."

Amber looked fit to burst.

"Go on. He's longing to see you."

She bit her lip, then suddenly propelled herself out of the room.

"Young love," said Carlos. "Bloody liability."

Maddy pointed her microphone at him. "That's a rude word and you're not allowed to say it. Twenty p, please."

Carlos pulled his boots off the desk. "I'm sorry. You're absolutely right."

I grinned. Carlos was known for reducing starlets to tears in order to get a decent note out of them, not handing over coins for an eight-year-old's swear box.

When Amber and Caspar rejoined us, I noticed with pleasure that her chin was a little redder than when she'd left. Now, Caspar wasn't the hirsute type, but neither was he lacking in a bit of facial growth these days. Oh, the joys of snogging and nothing more.

He and the girls went behind the glass, he took up position with his guitar, and I sneaked a photo on my mobile to send to Fran and Nick, my coconspirators. He looked divine, sitting there tuning up. Amber was watching him with the awe I reserved for Eric Clapton.

I knew that Carlos was humoring me, until Amber stepped up to the microphone and sang a scale for him. She had an extraordinarily throaty sound for someone so young. The brief look he flashed me halfway through was enough. The girl could sing. It was as simple as that. Now Carlos wanted to know what he could get out of her. Occasionally, I heard a buzz from Amber's jacket pocket. I told her she had some messages and a few missed calls. She came out of the studio and checked her phone.

"Everything all right?" I asked, when she listened worriedly to a particularly long one.

"My friend's just been dumped," she said.

I grimaced.

The phone wouldn't stop buzzing. Eventually, Amber switched it off.

WE HAD A FABULOUS TIME. First there were a couple of versions of Caspar and Amber's song for James, with the girls on percussion and chorus duties. Then, bitten by the bug, we sat down with sandwiches and made a list of James's favorite songs and, within seconds, Carlos had summoned the words and music from his computer for Amber to do a grand karaoke. The little ones did a version of "Do Re Mi," which was hilarious. They lacked their sister's sound, but their giggles, chatter, and interruptions made something I knew James would treasure forever. Even Carlos, who lived his life with one eye on the clock, forgot the time.

It was Maddy's watery-eyed yawn that made me glance at my watch. Somehow it was nearly six.

Carlos got kisses from all of the girls and a manly handshake from Caspar.

I took my troupe outside. As ever, the younger two chatted excitedly about moments in the day that had set firm in their memory, but for once Amber joined in: "Do you remember, Tessa, when Carlos ..."

"And, Tessa, what about when ..."

"Tessa, wasn't Caspar brilliant?"

Tessa this, Tessa that ... I absolutely loved it. But, more than anything, I loved it when we reached the car and Amber pushed the front seat forward for her sisters to climb in, then straightened. "Thank you, Tessa. That was one of the most brilliant things I've ever done."

I noticed a thin streak of jet fuel cross the indigo sky high above us and thought of James, still thirty-five thousand feet above sea level. Down here on earth things were changing, and he hadn't even arrived in Los Angeles.

"My pleasure," I said. "Right, you lot, budge up. We've got to drop Caspar at the station."

"Can't he come with us?" asked Amber.

"No room. Sorry."

She and Caspar tried to hide their disappointment. I tossed an idea around my head. "You could get the train back together as long as you come straight home from the station."

They promised. It was only forty minutes on the train from Epsom station. They would probably be home before we were. "If you get there first, put the pasta on. I made a Bolognese sauce earlier. It's in the fridge and just needs heating up."

"You sound like Mum," said Caspar.

I smiled. "I'll take that as a compliment."

Actually, they weren't home before us, but the water had only just started to boil when I heard their voices outside the front door. I knew James was due to land pretty soon and would want to talk to his daughters as soon as he was off the airplane. Maddy, Lulu, and I had spent most of the journey concocting a plausible alternative story for our day, which meant that Caspar had been effortlessly edited from the proceedings.

We listened to the unpolished cut of our wedding CD. Carlos was planning to work a little of his magic on it, but I didn't want the girls to sound like the Bonne Belles or any of the other manufactured bands out there: I wanted them to sound like three kids having fun in a recording studio. And they did.

We were sitting down in the kitchen for spag Bol when the phone rang. Amber picked it up. "Hello?" She smiled. "It's Daddy! Hi! How was your flight? Is it hot? Have you seen any famous people? . . . Oh." She held the phone away from her face. "He's just getting off the plane." She switched to loudspeaker and placed the phone in the middle of the table.

"Hi, everyone," said James.

"Hi, Daddy," the girls chorused.

"Hi, Tessa."

"Hello, my love. I'm so glad you've arrived safely."

"I miss you *all* horribly."

"Us too," I said. Meaning me. I miss you. Come home.

"So, what have you girls been doing?"

"Zoo."

"Playground."

"Cinema."

They spoke simultaneously then burst out laughing.

"Wow, busy day," said James.

"Not all at the same time," said Maddy.

"I should think not. You all right, Tessa? The minxes haven't worn you out?"

"I'm not quite ready for the knacker's yard yet, thanks. Actually we've had a great day."

The girls agreed loudly. I knew James would be excited to hear their happy voices.

"Tessa, can I have a word with you off speakerphone?" asked James.

Amber looked worried. I kept it light, though my heart was suddenly beating louder. That was not the reaction I'd been expecting. "Sure," I said brightly. I picked up the phone and stood up.

"Had a few calls from Bea," said James.

Man, he hadn't even got off the plane! "Oh—everything okay?"

"I don't know. She said she hadn't heard from anyone all day."

I paused, treading carefully, not wanting to alert Amber to any danger. "I didn't realize that was necessary."

"Well, the girls usually put in a call at some point."

"Ah, well," I said, forcing a smile. "We haven't stopped all day."

"She tried Amber's phone and got no answer. She sounded very worried." I remembered the constant buzzing from Amber's pocket, the long messages, the texts. Clearly, Bea didn't trust me to look after her children. Well, if we needed to clock in, I should have been told. "Don't know who made more noise in the zoo, the monkeys or the girls. We couldn't hear a thing. It was such a busy day. We're all knackered."

"What are you talking about? Could you just call her?"

"Why don't you?" I said, feeling as though I was stating the obvious.

"It's very expensive. Can't you just—"

I ignored his last comment and interrupted: "I know it's a bit late, the girls are off to bed in a minute. Amber and I are going to stay up and watch a movie."

"What? Oh, damn it, I've got to get off the phone. I'm at Customs."

"Okay," I said. I held up the phone. "Say good-bye to Daddy." They did. I didn't. I returned to the table and finished my spaghetti. Suddenly, I felt an insatiable need for a large glass of red wine, but knew better than to relax before lights-out.

"Zoo, playground, cinema," I said. "Honestly, you lot are terrible at fibbing. I can't believe your dad fell for it." While I handed yogurts around, I picked up the phone again. "Do you want to call Mummy and say good night?" I asked, as if the thought had just occurred to me. The younger ones nodded, then glanced at Amber. Something silent passed between them, but, not knowing the secret way of sisters, I couldn't decipher the code. "She'll probably have gone out by now," said Amber.

"Oh. Okay." Where? I wondered. And with whom?

"Yeah, she usually goes out with friends when we're not there." Amber peeled back the lid of her yogurt.

"What about leaving a message? Or, if you want, you could call her on her mobile? She might like to hear from you."

Amber stirred her yogurt intently. "We don't usually call," she said. I knew Amber was lying. So did the girls. They became as intent on their plates as their sister. I could see the tension in Amber's body. I thought I understood why. Fibbing to Daddy was probably easier than lying to her mother about not seeing Caspar. I realized I had put her in a difficult position.

"I'll sort it out, Amber. Okay?"

She didn't respond.

"I promise."

Caspar was watching Amber as closely as I was. She didn't take her eyes off the yogurt, but I could have sworn the tension I saw in her shoulders took on a furious form. Afraid it would ricochet back on me, I changed the subject.

I gave Maddy and Lulu a quick bath. They called home, but Amber was right: Bea had gone out. They left a sweet good-night message, which I tried not to listen to, be moved by, or jealous of. I failed on all three counts. But at least I was aware I was failing and told myself I was being foolish. Understanding the failure of James and Bea's marriage meant I no longer feared it. It wasn't very nice of me, but now that the perfect Bea Frazier had slipped off her pedestal, we were on a more equal footing.

By the time I came downstairs, Amber and Caspar had waded through the ads, previews, and warnings on the DVD and were waiting to start the film. I poured myself a glass of wine and sat in the armchair, leaving them sitting close together on the sofa. I had little interest in the film they had chosen on their way back from the tube station, and would happily have got into a bath with my wine and a book, but I wasn't going to leave the two unattended. I had to be able to look James in the eye and tell him nothing had happened on my watch.

About twenty minutes into the film, Amber offered to make peppermint tea. Caspar paused the film, and while she was out of the room, we stuck to the safe topic of his family. When we found ourselves on the subject of his sister's latest method of disruption, holding her breath until she went purple, I knew we'd been chatting for a while, because it's a subject he prefers to avoid. We thought the same thing at the same time. Now what?

"I'll go," said Caspar.

"No. I will."

Amber wasn't in the kitchen and the kettle had long boiled. I looked in the downstairs loo. She wasn't there. It's a tiny cubicle under the stairs, and I was about to close the door behind me when something stopped me. A memory. A smell. Something. It was too brief to catch, but I looked around the room again, trying to locate it again. Caspar was on the threshold, watching me. I waved him back to the living room. Her bedroom was empty, so I tried the bathroom. It was locked. I knocked.

"Coming," said Amber quickly.

"You okay?"

"Mum called. Sorry. Start the film without me."

I would have, except I knew that Amber's phone was recharging next to the kettle in the kitchen, because I'd just seen it. And if she had been chatting to her mother, we'd have heard her. The loo flushed and the tap ran. I waited. A few moments later I heard the loo flush again. Still Amber didn't come out. I went back downstairs, and as I passed the loo, I looked in again. It wasn't the smell that had triggered the memory. The water was pink. I knew what pink water meant. Any girl of a certain age does. It means blood.

"Hey, Caspar, make tea, would you? Bea called." I shouted.

His forehead creased. "Oh, God, Amber okay?"

"Just catching up on the day."

I could see he didn't believe me, but I didn't pursue it. I went up to my room. I had made one shelf of the shower-room cabinet my own. I opened it and looked through my belongings. Nothing suitable for a fourteen-year-old girl. I returned to the corridor and knocked again. "Can I come in?" I asked.

Amber emerged, closing the door behind her quickly. She'd changed. "Fancied getting into something more comfortable," she said.

"Listen," I whispered, "I know I'm the last person in the world you probably want to talk to about this, but I can help."

She frowned.

"Have you got your period?"

She looked painfully embarrassed but she didn't deny it.

"Look, I spent months trying to put those bloody Lil-lets in when I first had periods and I couldn't do it. It used to make me cry, trying to follow those hideous diagrams. Feet up on the loo, pants around my ankles. I fell over once and nearly knocked myself out."

I put my arm around her shoulders and led her to her room. "The small Tampax are much easier in the beginning, because the applicator does the work for you. Or good old-fashioned sanitary pads will do the job."

I could see her swallow her shame and try to be the big girl she wanted to be. "But the boxes are so big," she said.

That was true. There was no hiding a bag of pads. "So what have you been using?"

Amber gazed at the floor. "Loo paper."

"Oh, sweetie. How long for?"

She gulped. "This is my second. I didn't know when it was coming. I didn't know what to do. I tried to buy them, but there was such a big choice and there were boys in the drugstore . . ."

"Couldn't your mum get them for you?" I asked. Now she looked like she was about to cry. I rushed on. "You know what? Stupid as it is, I still feel awkward buying them. Especially since I don't buy the smallest ones anymore. There's always a man on the counter when I go, guaranteed. Thank God for online shopping, frankly. Do you want me to wash some stuff? Those are your favorite jeans."

The change of direction caught her off-guard and she nodded. Poor thing. Accidents like that are horrid.

"Is it on the sofa? Is that how you know?" she asked.

"God, no. I know because I know, and when it happens to Lulu, you'll know immediately too. That's the sisterhood, my friend. We look out for one another."

Amber brushed away an imagined tear. "Thanks, Tessa."

"You go downstairs. Caspar's making tea. I'm going to the corner shop to get some biscuits for us all."

"We've got some."

"I know that, but Caspar doesn't and he needn't know why I'm doing a bit of late-night shopping."

"Oh."

"Don't you worry, I'll find something. Start watching the film."

"What about you?" asked Amber.

"Don't worry about that."

"I'll tell you what happens."

Caspar didn't even notice that Amber had changed, which made me smile to myself. He did, however, have a fairly hefty order for my shop run—drinks, sweets, chocolate. Honestly, I'd no idea where that boy put it.

I forgot my keys intentionally so Amber had to let me in. I passed her a bag. A few minutes later, she was back on the sofa, the goodies on a tray, tucking into some Maltesers. She gave me a surreptitious wink, which I held to my heart and hugged.

Feeling confident that I could now leave her and Caspar alone, I put on a wash, put away the washing-up, and laid breakfast for the morning, as I had seen Fran do. I booked a cab to take Caspar home at ten-thirty and took myself upstairs to bed. I kissed him good-night, as I usually do, then hesitated.

Amber took the difficulty out of the situation and stood up. "Thanks for a great day," she said, kissing my cheek. "And everything."

It was the first time she'd kissed me, and I was startled by how happy it made me feel. I wanted to hug her and tell her that everything would be fine, but instead I said good night and went upstairs. I forced my eyes to stay open until I heard her close and lock the front door, take herself upstairs, clean her teeth, and go to her room. If she stayed up all night texting Caspar, fine. As far as I was concerned, my charges were at home, safe. I closed my eyes and slept.

THE RINGING WAS A DISTANT bell calling me to church. I was late and the hem of my wedding dress was caught in the jaws of a digger. I yanked it free but found I couldn't run. "Coming," I wanted to call, but I couldn't speak, either. The ringing continued.

I woke up enough to realize I couldn't run or speak because I was asleep. Then I reached the lid of sleep and discovered I was in bed and it was the phone ringing, not the bells of St. Clement's.

I picked it up. "James?"

"Tessa, darling, it's Mum."

I squinted at my watch but couldn't see the time. It was dark in the room except for the orange glow that crept in at either side of the curtain. "What time is it?"

"I don't know, late, early." I heard my mother take a deep breath. "It's the middle of the night."

I burst through the surface, finally awake. "What's wrong?"

"I'm so sorry to—"

"Mum, what's wrong? Where's Dad? Is he all right?"

"He's fishing."

Of course. He was on the Isle of Skye with Peter, bonding over maggots. "What's happened?"

"Well, the thing is . . ." She paused. "I fell asleep in front of the telly—"

"Mummy, what's happened?"

"I woke up and—oh, hell, Tessa, don't panic but—"

"Mum!"

"I can't see."

I swore silently. "Where are you?"

"Well, I tried to get to bed . . ."

I held my breath.

"I'm so sorry, darling, I'm— I've knocked all the vases off the table."

"What vases? Are you all right? Are you cut?"

"No, no, no—well, only slightly. You see, I was cleaning them and, well, there's broken glass everywhere and now I'm stuck."

"Let me call an ambulance."

"No. This isn't life-threatening."

"You're surrounded by shards of glass and you can't see."

"Please, sweet Tessa, you have a key. It won't take you long. They'll have to knock down the door otherwise."

My mother would rather chew off her own leg than end up in a hospital before time. Though what "time" was, I no longer knew. But she was my mother, and her system worked for her. Who was I to take that away? "I'm leaving now," I said.

I SHOOK AMBER AWAKE. SHE stared at me from behind a dream.

"I'm so sorry, I've got to get you home," I said.

"Huh?"

"My mother isn't well. I've got to go and help her."

"My mother?"

"No, mine." I switched on the bedside light. She squinted at me. "I have to go to Oxford. Now. Can you help me get the girls into the car?"

"I'll get dressed," said Amber, awake—oh, to be young.

I started James's car and turned the heaters on. I chose his because it had four doors and it was easier to get the sleeping girls into and out of. I ran upstairs, picked Maddy up, and, without waking her, had her in the car, belted and under a blanket. Lulu woke, but I took her pillow and rabbit with her, and she was asleep again by the time I'd locked the front door.

Amber and I got in. We were on our way within ten minutes of my mother's call. I handed Amber my phone. "Can you call your mother?" I said. "You'd better warn her."

"Why?"

"She might have bolted the door."

"You can't take us home," said Amber.

"I can't leave you here to cope on your own. I know you could, but Daddy—"

"Can't we come with you? Mum will be asleep."

"That's why you have to call. To wake her up. I can't take you, because I'll have to get my mother to a hospital."

"What's wrong with her?"

"Please, Amber, call Bea."

I heard the ringing tone in Amber's ear. "Try the mobile," I said.

"I told you," said Amber. "She went out."

I glanced at the dashboard. It was nearly three. "Does she often stay out this late?"

"I don't know. We're not there."

Fair enough.

"Do you know where she goes?"

Amber shook her head.

"Do you know who she goes with?"

Amber just looked at me.

"Well, let's go and see. She might just be asleep. Keep trying."

I heard the mobile ring. At least that meant it was on. I drove to Kentish Town. It took seven minutes. I pulled up outside Bea's house. The lights were on and I was relieved until I saw Amber's expression.

"Let me go first," she said, retrieving the key from her denim-jacket pocket. I was too worried about my own mother to hear the concern she was trying to disguise about hers. She got out of the car and walked, not ran, to the front door. She appeared to puff herself up before she put the key in the lock, glanced back at me, then disappeared through the door.

I saw her silhouette walk into the sitting room through the net curtain that hung in the small bay window. I saw her leave. I saw her figure through the glass diamonds in the front door shrink from view. I drummed my fingers on the steering wheel, then looked at my watch for the umpteenth time.

Come on, come on. My mother was lying surrounded by shards of glass—

I hadn't even realized she'd come out again, and I jumped. Amber stood in front of the bonnet of the car, glowing in the headlights, staring wild-eyed at me through the windscreen. I got out of the car and hurried to her. There was something unnerving about the way she was holding herself.

"What is it, Amber?"

"Mummy's dead," she said.

Fifteen

Just One

I OPENED MY EYES AND A SHARD OF PURE WHITE LIGHT RIPPED THROUGH my retinas. I closed them again. Pain etched my head. It felt as if someone had embedded an ax in my skull. Everything around me was very soft. I was being swallowed whole by a bed of sponge. I couldn't smell anything familiar. I forced an eye open.

Wild roses slowly came into focus, clambering all over the walls. A small dormer window had its magnifying glass trained on the sun. I closed my eye again, shifted out of its sight line, and was left with meteors of orange blazing across the blackout blind of my eyelid. Where the hell was I?

I eased myself up off the squishy mattress and looked around. A quaint and dainty bedroom that I had never seen before emerged slowly through my blurred vision. I peeled off the covers. A sheet, an old-fashioned blanket, and a pink satin eiderdown. I had woken in the 1950s. I looked down at my glutinous body. No. My bra and knickers were still very much The Gap, circa 1998. The only other thing I recognized was the tang in my mouth. There's no mistaking the aftertaste of stomach acid.

I padded across the thick wool carpet and drew the curtains. Green rolled away from me as far as the eye could see. It was not countryside I knew. There was a pair of loose flannel pajamas on an antique button-back nursing chair, and a threadbare ribbed dressing gown hanging on the back of a white wood-paneled door. Since there was no sign of my own clothes, I put them on and ventured out of the room.

The smell of toast wafted up the stairs to me. A B&B? A hotel? A home?

Slowly, I took the thickly carpeted stairs one by one. The walls were covered with photos in cheap frames, of people I didn't recognize. I was beginning to get angry. Clearly, I had been taken somewhere against my will, since I had no idea where I was or why I was there. Three doors led off the hall. One was slightly open, and I could see worn hexagonal terra-cotta tiles on the floor. The smell of toast was coming from there. The kitchen.

I pushed the door farther open. A woman sat with her back to me at the table. Her hair was in a bun. I cleared my throat. Suddenly, my footing didn't seem so robust and I found I couldn't muster the energy to be indignant. The woman turned. "Hi, Mum," she said. She looked so old. So tired.

"Amber? What are you doing here?"

It was obviously not the right question to ask: she turned away from me.

"I mean, um, I didn't think you'd be here."

"You have no idea where we are, so please, stop it."

"I don't think that's any way—"

She stood up. Her chin was wobbling. "I mean it, Mummy. Stop it."

I couldn't bear to see my children cry. It had hurt since they were toddlers and split their little lips learning how to walk. Knowing, as my soul knew now, that physical pain was not the cause of the tears Amber was fighting wounded me to the core. What did I do? Should I get down on bended knee and beg forgiveness? No.

I felt a fresh wave of anger flood through me. Anger that wanted to find something to blame. My eye was drawn to a glass-fronted cupboard. A bottle of Teacher's. A little leveler wouldn't go amiss.

"I could do with a cup of coffee," I said, buying time. Amber turned away from me and put the kettle on. She seemed weirdly at home. I glanced at the cupboard again. Now I needed a moment alone. "Do you know where my clothes are?"

"Drying. They're not ready yet."

Damn it. "So, where are we?" I asked.

"Mr. and Mrs. King's house. It's outside Oxford."

King? Was that a school friend? I frowned but it hurt my head.

"Tessa's mother and father."

I looked at Amber.

"Yes, that's right. Daddy's Tessa."

My God. The venom in my daughter's voice made me sit down. It wasn't directed at Tessa. It was directed at me. Incredible how I still tried to hold on to some sort of high ground. When you're drowning, you'll cling to anything, even if it means bringing your saving grace down with you.

"You don't remember. Do you? Mummy?"

"You'd better take that tone out of your voice, young lady—" I was interrupted by the noise of tires on gravel. Amber glanced out of the window, then ran from the room.

I stood up to see what had made her move so swiftly. My daughters were belted into the back of a dark blue car. A silver-haired woman was in the front seat. She was wearing movie-star shades. The driver got out. My anger evaporated. The last person in the world I wanted to see now was Tessa King. I wanted to run, but my hands would not unclasp the side of the sink.

My gorgeous little girls were out of the car. I could see Maddy's mouth moving ten to the dozen as usual, and smiled. It hurt to smile. The ax was grinding. Tessa was supposed to have sole charge of my children for the weekend, so what was I doing here?

Lulu opened the door for the silver-haired film star, and I saw Tessa go to the boot. Maddy emerged with a plastic bag; Amber joined Tessa and collected two more shopping bags. They looked good together. I gripped the sink even harder.

Tessa went around to help the woman out. Maddy had still not stopped talking. She held on to the woman's hand and guided her up the path. The woman suddenly appeared to have a walking stick in her hand. She was leaning on it quite heavily. She didn't look old enough to have a stick, and where had it come from? Tessa walked behind them, holding another walking stick. I could see her over Maddy's chattering head. She was keeping an eagle eye on the woman I presumed to be Mrs. King, and then, as if sensing me, she looked through the kitchen window and straight at me. Our eyes locked.

I had imagined our eventual meeting a thousand times. The dry one-liners, the children flocking to my side, me thin and funny, of course, Jimmy standing close by with a torn look on his face . . . It was not to be. Here she was. In the flesh. My nemesis. The glimpse I had caught of her emerging from the car all those weeks ago had not done her justice. She was prettier than I remembered, and taller, as I had feared. Athletic-looking and leggy, too, damn her. Bloody blonde. If you wanted to find the perfect opposite of me, you couldn't do better than Tessa King. Jimmy had made himself clear. The man wanted nothing to do with me.

I pushed myself away from the sink and fled. I couldn't meet her like this. Not her, of all people. I was back among the wild roses by the time I heard them come through the door, but I was not alone.

There was a knock on the door.

"Come in," I said, as confidently as I could, given the circumstances. I sat up in bed, like an ailing aunt. Tessa walked in with a tray. I took a quick look. There, in front of me, I was pleased to see, she looked older than I'd thought. Tired. I stared at the eiderdown, listening to my heart pounding in my chest, and prayed I wouldn't have another panic attack.

"I've brought you some tea," she said. I noticed she had some for herself, but I was not so deluded as to think this would be a cozy chat. She handed me a mug, then sat on the nursing chair and stared out of the window.

Well, I wasn't going to be the one who broke the silence. Silence suited me just fine. Finally, she looked at me. She had the same bone structure as her mother. I had to admit, she was a handsome girl.

"I didn't think we'd be meeting like this," she said.

I forced the tea down my throat and, with it, any contrition I might have felt.

"You're probably wondering what you're doing here," she said.

"I would have left, but you've taken my clothes." Go in hard and go in fast. Jab, jab, jab, bring them down. I saw Tessa wobble. But there was an inner steel I hadn't anticipated.

"You were lying in a pile of your own vomit, Bea. I thought it best to wash them before you saw the girls. They'll be dry soon."

I raised my chin. "I went out with friends to an Indian last night and had a prawn curry. I thought it tasted funny."

Tessa regarded me steadily for a moment. Then she leaned forward and peered right through me. It did not feel nice. "Your daughter thought you were dead, and my mother lost her eyesight last night. I haven't slept. Do you think we could cut the crap?"

"I'm very sorry about your mother, but you really have no reason to talk to me like that. I ate some bad food."

"You tend to be conscious when you vomit from food poisoning."

"I was tired," I insisted. "I must have fallen asleep."

"On the kitchen floor?" Her voice was rising. Her cheeks were flushed.

"No. Obviously . . ." inspiration came to me, "at the kitchen table. I was reading, I—" was getting myself into a terrible mess. What could I tell this woman? Not the truth. I couldn't remember it, even if I wanted to. Which I didn't. Of all people, why did it have to be her? God, the humiliation. If she'd just leave the room, I could have a quick drink, sort my head out, get my story straight. Plausible, at least.

Tessa clutched her head with the hand that wasn't holding the tea. "Okay. It was bad prawns, and we have nothing to talk about." She stood up, and I wondered why I didn't feel a victorious sense of relief. Ha! Got away with it again! But even I, under that pink eiderdown, in my polluted state, knew I hadn't. You can't kid a kidder, until the kidder's drunk, that is, and I wasn't drunk enough.

Tessa turned at the door and I saw the steel again. It flashed in her eyes. It was then that I remembered she was a lawyer at a record company, not some ditzy assistant who liked the idea of free CDs, as I had preferred to think. "What had you eaten when you ripped Amber's blue dress off her and called her a slut? More bad shellfish?"

"Excuse me?"

"What exotic food made you pass out so Amber had to carry you upstairs to bed, undress you, clean you up, tuck you in?"

"How dare you put ideas like that in her head? Are you trying to turn my child against me?"

"You're doing a pretty good job of that all by yourself."

"I think you'd better go."

"Who's been getting Lulu and Maddy up for school every morning?"

"I have no idea what you're talking about."

"No. You wouldn't. You'd passed out. Lucky old Amber gets those memories all for herself." She pulled the door behind her with a defiant click.

She thought she was so smart, leaving me with a cliff-hanger like that, but she'd miscalculated. I didn't need to remember what had happened to know that it had. Clarity provided the excuse I needed. I pulled the bottle of Teacher's from under the eiderdown, this was the company I was keeping these days, unscrewed the top, and, with cherished defiance and self-pity, finished it off.

WHEN I WOKE, MY TEA had gone cold and the day was a long way nearer dusk than dawn. Everything felt fuzzy, and I wasn't sure what had happened, what I had dreamed or perhaps hallucinated. Had I really called my daughter a slut? I loved her. I wouldn't have done that. The house was quiet. My clothes were folded on the nursing chair. Unsteadily, I crossed the room and put them on. My skin smelled acrid. My lower lip had cracked. I had to go home, sort myself out.

"Hello?"

The voice was responding to a creak on the staircase. I wondered where my children were. Damn it, I'd hoped I was alone. My plan was to call a cab and have it waiting when the prison warden returned with the girls. Once they had run into my arms, we would be on our way.

"Bea? Come on in. Tessa's taken the children to see a film."

I walked toward the voice. Mrs. King was sitting in an armchair in front of a fire. It was unlit. She had a blanket over her knees. I wondered why, if she was cold, it wasn't burning. Despite the dark glasses, I doubted she was blind.

"Tessa wouldn't leave me with a lighted fire. Told me it was dangerous if I couldn't see the sparks."

I was taken aback by her perceptiveness. How did she know what I'd been thinking? I responded by attacking her. I was feeling mean.

"And you're supposed to be babysitting me?"

"Tessa thought the Teacher's would keep you down longer than it did."

I had to do a double take. The owl-like black glasses were fixed on me. "I don't know what you're talking about."

"She said you'd say that."

"She's a know-it-all."

Tessa's all-seeing mother laughed. "Actually, you're right about that. I put it down to her being an only child." She motioned to the sofa. "Why don't you sit down? Better still, you could make yourself useful and get us a drink."

I looked up hopefully.

"Not that kind of drink. Amber and Tessa poured it all away."

I examined her again, but she was looking in the direction of the far wall. So, the Kings didn't mince their words. Like mother, like daughter. Well, two could play at that game. "How can you lose your eyesight overnight?" I asked.

I didn't enjoy the silence that followed. I wanted desperately to apologize, but the words stuck like thorns in my throat. I didn't know where the meanness was coming from.

"Multiple sclerosis." The woman straightened her blanket. "I've had a relapse. First in a long time." I felt small and cowardly. "There's quite a severe lesion in my brain. The inflammation surrounding it is affecting my optic nerve. If I'm lucky, and we got to it quickly enough, the steroids they injected me with this morning will reduce the swelling and the damage won't be permanent. If not . . ." She pulled the glasses off her face and folded them neatly in her lap. Her eyeballs roamed furiously, randomly, in their sockets, searching for all that unseen light. "My name's Liz, by the way."

"Bea," I said pointlessly.

"Sit down, Bea," said Liz and, for some reason, I did. Liz put the dark glasses back on.

We didn't talk. The clock on the mantelpiece ticked loudly. Occasionally, a gust of wind found its way down the chimney and whipped around my ankles. The silence between us didn't feel uncomfortable. In fact, it felt necessary. The sky darkened. So did the room. Behind her large shades, my hostess was none the wiser. But I saw her shudder.

"Do you think *I* might be trusted with the fire?" I asked.

"Are you cold too?"

"Shivering slightly," I replied. Though I was aware that wasn't the same thing.

"A fire is a good idea. I love the sound of it."

I left my chair and walked on aching legs to the hearth.

"Everything should be in the basket." I knelt down. "My husband's a very good fire captain," said Liz.

"Where is he?"

"Fishing in Scotland. Isle of Skye."

"That's where my father-in-law goes."

"Yes," said Liz. "They're together, on their way back now. I tried to tell them to stay until the end of the weekend, but they wouldn't hear of it."

I closed my eyes. Peter, who had always been so nice to me, was fishing with Tessa's dad now and leaving his beloved river to come to *her* mother's aid.

"The circles are overlapping," said Liz, above me. "It would be nice if you were part of the cross-hatching."

I scrunched up some old pages of the *Independent* and tucked them between the iron bars in the grate. I didn't want to just be part of the cross-hatching. I wanted to be part of the whole. Like I'd been before Tessa King showed up and stole my family. I'd screwed the paper into a tight ball. My hands were smeared with black ink. I wiped them on my trousers, but the stain stayed. Out, out, damn spot.

"Anything I can help with?" asked Mrs. King. The blanket over her knees looked so inviting. I wanted to put my head on her lap and be told it would all be all right. I felt drained.

"My daughter is very angry with me," I said, surrendering to the exhaustion.

"And my daughter's furious with you too."

"Why on earth is Tessa cross with me? I would have thought she'd be dancing on my grave."

"Becoming a stepmother is hard enough without this," she said simply. "Amber has been putting her through hell. Why do you think that is?"

"Amber and James have always been very close," I said, breaking off a fire lighter.

"That's not it, though, is it?" I busied myself with kindling. "Amber's a very bright girl, sensitive too, aware. Something's happened to make her believe that your newfound *un*happiness is directly attributable to Tessa's newfound happiness. I'm sure she's a little jealous too, she's only human, and I'm sure she doesn't like the idea of Tessa sweeping her daddy off his feet, and I'm sure she's worried about where that leaves her. That's normal. This isn't. Let's stop pretending it is."

I chose the logs meticulously. Not so small that they wouldn't create a good base heat, not so big that they'd take too long to burn and fill the room with smoke. My rural beginnings came back to me. I struck a match, lit the corners of the fire lighters, and watched with delight as the blue flames raced around the kindling. The edge of some paper caught alight, and heat flared across my face. I felt a strong urge to bury my head in the fire. Liz was right. This was not normal. It had to stop.

"Not newfound," I said.

"Excuse me?"

"My unhappiness. It's not newfound. The drinking is recent. I can stop that. It's been barely weeks."

"Are you sure about that?"

"I only wanted to lose a bit of weight." The kindling was cracking and spitting now. I laid on a few more pieces, then set the logs to burn.

"Isn't drink the most fattening of all?"

"Not when it's drunk in place of food." I stoked the fire absently. "A couple of glasses of wine and I didn't want supper. Then I discovered that with a few more than a couple I could be sick. I'd never been able to be sick before, though I'd tried. Once I nearly drank bleach to get the damned food out of my belly."

Liz reached out her hand. It hovered in midair. I stared at it, afraid of human contact. "You're bulimic?"

"Worse," I said. Why was I telling her all of this? But now that I'd started I couldn't stop. "A failed bulimic. I'd eat. Stick my fingers down my throat until it ached, retch, but nothing ever came up."

Liz's hand was still held out to me.

My own fingers were swollen. There was a graze I couldn't account for on three knuckles. My wedding ring was not there, but the indentation at the base of my finger still marked the place it had encircled for sixteen years. My nails were cracked and flaky. Too much cleaning without gloves. Half-moons frowned their disappointment at me. I held up my hand until it touched Liz's. I half-crawled, half-shuffled across the rug to her feet and laid my head on her lap.

"I think you've been taking care of everyone for a very long time, Bea. You've forgotten how to care for yourself."

I closed my eyes against the jaunty pattern of Liz's rug. I had killed a baby. I didn't deserve looking after. When would the pain go away? When would this hole be filled? The first fat tear fell into the nook between the corner of my eye and the bridge of my nose. Liz didn't say a word. She stroked my hair, gently, soothingly, and I cried.

Later, worn out, I ventured into the garden and picked fresh mint, which I brewed into strong tea. We were drinking it when I heard the car. My heart burst to life. My children. I couldn't face them.

"You don't have to see them now," said Liz. "I can tell them you went to bed. The little ones don't know anything anyway."

"What about the fire?" I said. "No. I have to face them eventually. Better now, don't you think?"

"I do, as it happens. But I'd understand if you weren't ready."

"It's not fair on them."

"Bea, a long time ago I learned to my detriment that putting your family first, putting others first, regardless of the pain you are in, was not always the healthiest thing to do."

I didn't understand. I could hear their voices now. Doors slamming. Laughter.

"You need time to heal properly. Patch-up jobs won't do."

"Heal?"

"From whatever it is that's causing all this."

"Are you a witch?" I asked.

Liz smiled. "No. A woman. Who needs a wand when we have intuition? And Bea, please try and remember that very little of this is Tessa's fault."

"A mother protecting her child?" I said ruefully.

"Isn't that what we're supposed to do?"

I returned to the sofa and picked up a book. The words bounced around on the page. I was too nervous to go to greet them.

When Maddy and Lulu saw us in the sitting room, they ran straight in. Amber stood in the doorway. Tessa glanced at us, then at the embers in the fireplace, and went into the kitchen.

"Mummy!"

I stood up and hugged them.

"Are you better?"

"Has your headache gone?"

"Tummyache," said Lulu. "She was sick. Like I was after Dan's party and I ate all of Bob's head."

"Bob the Builder cake," I explained to Liz. "That was years ago, Lulu. How do you remember these things?"

"I remember everything," she said, which frightened me slightly.

"Hello, Lizzie," said Maddy. "Can I sit on your knee?"

"Of course you can," said Liz.

"How are your eyeballs?"

"Maddy!" I exclaimed.

Liz held up a hand. "Still misbehaving," she said.

"Can I see?"

"Maddy!" I said, again.

"It's okay, Bea. Maddy tells me I look just like the funny pirate in *Pirates of the Caribbean.*"

My eight-year-old turned to me. "He has a wooden eyeball that pops out all the time. We're going to play it tomorrow. I'm Elizabeth," said Maddy, taking Liz's cheeks in her two small hands and peering under the glasses.

"*I* want to be Elizabeth Swan," said Lulu.

Maddy's head moved as she tried to follow one of Liz's wandering eyes. I found it quite disturbing, but Maddy was giggling, which made Liz smile. I couldn't watch.

"What about you, Amber?" I asked. "You'd make a fine Captain Jack Sparrow."

She didn't reply. I looked back at the doorway. Amber had gone.

I MANAGED TO PUT TOGETHER some supper for the children. Tessa went upstairs with her mother while we ate in the kitchen. On the way up to give the girls a bath, I saw her come out of a room. She caught sight of me, then retreated into it until we'd passed.

I wondered whether Jimmy was coming back. If she had told him. I wondered many things as I tucked the girls into bed.

Tessa wasn't the only one avoiding me. Amber seemed to have disappeared too. From the bathroom window I saw her on a seat in the garden, talking into her phone. I wondered, too, if I was the cause célèbre of her gossip. Fourteen-year-olds love a drama. But that was unkind. If what Tessa had said was true about Amber thinking I was dead, I mean really dead, not just getting off on the attention, she wouldn't shout that from the rafters.

A while later, when the younger two were asleep, I found her stoking the fire. I handed her a log and some extra kindling to get the flames going again. I was desperate for a drink, just to steady my nerves, but there was none in the house and, short of stealing a car, no way of getting any. Which was just as well. The temptation to obliterate the thoughts that spun in my head was enormous. I'd even opened the fridge a few times, looking for something else to cram inside me, but managed to close it each time empty-handed. I didn't know how long my resilience would last.

The fire burning steadily now, I poured more mint tea and handed Amber a cup. "I owe you an apology," I said.

Amber sat with her back to me, still prodding the fire. She looked over her shoulder, her wide hazel eyes sizing me up, taking me in. I had apologized before. Until now, however, I hadn't known exactly what I was apologizing for. About a month ago, I had come downstairs and found Amber cleaning red wine off the kitchen walls. I had no idea how it had got there but knew that Amber was not responsible. I told her I'd slipped and been too tired to tidy it up. Since I had no memory of the truth, I told myself it wasn't exactly a lie. I had apologized for leaving the mess, not creating it. She had given me a quiet smile, which I had chosen to take as acceptance. Didn't I know what rot was caused by things left unsaid? I'd spent my entire life having conversations with my mother. But only ever in my head.

"A real one," I said. "I'm sorry you found me in that state. I'm sorry about all the times before that too. I've said things to you that I didn't mean."

Poke, poke, poke. Amber would have wanted to make this easier for me, but she didn't know how. There wasn't an easy way out of this.

"I've put a lot of responsibility on your shoulders. I'm going to try very hard not to do that anymore."

Amber put the poker back on its hook. She turned her back to the fire and brought her knees up to her chest.

"What do the girls know?" I asked.

"I told them you had a bug."

"Anything else?"

She put her cheek on her knees. "I told them not to talk about the wedding and Tessa because it upset you."

"It must have seemed that way."

"Wasn't it that?"

"Yes and no, I suppose. Daddy and I split up because he was very busy with work and I felt like I was doing everything on my own. We weren't a team. To manage, I started living, thinking, acting as if I was on my own and I guess that wasn't very good either. He's different now. He's brilliant with you three, and you see him all the time. He's very caring and loves us all. I guess, oh, I don't know, Amber, it's tricky . . ."

"I don't get it, Mum."

And why should she, she was only fourteen. "I guess I wished he'd been a bit more like that before. For me."

Amber didn't speak for a while. Then she said, "Keira's dad died falling down the stairs. He hit his head on a radiator and never woke up."

God, I'd forgotten about that. It had happened some time ago. He was a real alcoholic. A drinker for years. You could smell the booze on him at drop-off.

"I thought that's what—" Amber's voice choked.

I pushed myself off the sofa and got down on the floor. "I'm so sorry, Amber. It won't ever, ever happen again. I'll get help if I have to." I held her and she cried. She'd been brave for a long time.

When the fire had burned down, we went into the kitchen and reheated some soup Tessa had left out for me. Amber told me about the recording studio and I did my best to squash the bile that rose in my stomach. And she told me she'd started her periods, which made me cry. I'd spent all these years striving to be the sort of mother a child could talk to, then fallen at the last. Instead, Amber had told Tessa. It hurt like hell, and made me hate Tessa more.

"There's something else I need to tell you, Mum," said Amber.

"Anything."

"I told Daddy that Caspar ripped my dress. I don't know why. I was scared and—"

"It's okay."

"Now Daddy hates him. So I've been sneaking over to Caspar's house. I was only trying to—"

"Protect me, I know. I'm sorry. Amber, I can't remember what happened. Can you tell me?"

Amber shook her head.

"Please?"

"I came home to get the words to the best-man song. I didn't tell anyone, because it was a surprise. You were"—she closed her eyes—"you were leaning on the kitchen table. I think you'd been crying. I tried to give you a hug and . . ." Her chin wobbled.

"I ripped your dress."

She nodded.

"Why?"

She shrugged.

"What did you do?"

"I ran away. I didn't do my song. I hid on the fire escape and drank a bottle of champagne and then I felt really, really ill. Caspar put his fingers down my throat to make me sick so I didn't get alcohol poisoning. I was horrible to him, Mummy."

I pulled her to me. "I'll get help. Whatever it takes. It's not you, none of this is your fault."

She swallowed. "Is it Tessa's?"

I kissed her head. "No, my love. It's mine. And I'll sort it out."

It was only nine o'clock, but Amber was exhausted. So was I. We washed up the bowls and went upstairs. We didn't talk about tomorrow. It was enough just to get through today. I discovered that Amber was sleeping in Tessa's room, but Tessa was still nowhere to be seen. I brushed my teeth and got back into the squishy bed, eyes burning with salt and exhaustion. I prayed for sleep, but sleep didn't come. A drink would have helped. Just one.

Sixteen

Cease-fire

OBVIOUSLY, NO ONE WAS GOING TO POUR A HOUSEHOLD'S WORTH OF alcohol down the sink. Surely Mr. K liked a glass of something occasionally, even if Mrs. K was off the sauce. Moderation, that was the key. Just a glass to stop the shakes.

I opened the door a fraction and listened. The house creaked under the weight of sleep. Emboldened by need, I hurried down the stairs, keeping to the edge, and slipped into the kitchen. The cupboard I'd taken the Teacher's from was bare. Sticky circles marked the places where the bottles had recently been. One was the color of Night Nurse. They hadn't had to hide the crème de menthe from me. I wasn't that bad.

My quick search of the cupboards revealed nothing. But there was a pantry I had yet to explore. A single forty-watt lightbulb hung from the slanting roof. I pulled its cord.

Homemade jams and chutneys displayed their chests proudly from the top shelf. Damson '05. Blackberry '06. Plum '06. Greengage '05. Apple and Cider Chutney '06. I picked up a pot of blackberry jam and turned its cool glass between my hot, sweaty hands. I could make out the plump berries, lovingly picked, stewed, and bottled, waiting to be scooped out onto warm bread and butter. I pressed the jar to my forehead. I wanted this sweet, preserved life, firesides and tea, not one where I snuck around at night searching for hidden bottles, afraid of where one drink would take me but too weak not to start.

Go to bed, Bea, I told myself. Go. To. Bed. Don't begin tomorrow. Begin now. I was reaching up for the switch when I saw it between some rolls of loo paper. I reached over and picked it up. Amontillado.

I was unscrewing the cap when I heard Tessa's voice in the hallway. I pulled the light cord, closed the door behind me, and sank to the floor, clutching my prize.

". . . Hang on. I don't want to wake anyone." I heard the kitchen door close and a beam of light shot through the gap at the bottom of the door. "Where the hell have you been?"

While the person I presumed to be Jimmy replied, I heard Tessa open the fridge door. From the glutinous splodge sound that came next, I imagined she had heaved out the heavy two-liter milk container and dumped it on the kitchen counter.

"Well, I called the bloody hotel and told them to . . . Yes. This was a real emergency . . . It was early evening your time—where were you? . . . What do you mean, 'out'?" Then Tessa, who had obviously been keeping it together, burst into tears. "Oh, James, Mum's eyes have gone. The doctor took me to one side and said I shouldn't get my hopes up too high."

I nearly gave myself away by lamenting out loud at hearing this, but Tessa was beside herself and probably wouldn't have noticed. "Even Dad and Peter got my message and they're in the middle of fucking nowhere! . . ." I heard the perforations on a paper towels tearing. "They're here . . . Yes, all three . . . Well, I didn't have much choice . . ." She blew her nose. "Yes. Lying facedown on the kitchen floor in puke . . . She's lucky she didn't choke . . . Didn't you listen to my messages? . . . Pissed, you mean! Great. Fucking pair of you! . . . I don't want to know . . ."

I heard Tessa slosh some milk into a saucepan and the hiss of gas. "Whatever, it doesn't matter. What plane can you get on?"

A couple of cupboards opened and closed. I started praying, trying desperately to remember if I had seen chocolate powder on the shelves above me. "What do you mean 'can't'?" The cupboard door slammed. "James, your ex-wife is an alcoholic. Amber has been covering for her for weeks. She's at her wit's end. Bea obviously needs help. I need to look after Mum. I haven't even thought about work. James, I can't do this . . . I need you here. No. It's the Easter holidays, remember . . . No. I am not sending them back with her . . . No! James, you're not listening to me. This was not a one-off . . . I know because Amber has told me. Oh James, I didn't want to tell you this until you got home. I'm so sorry but the night of our engagement party Amber went home and found Bea drunk. Please, James, you have to hear me out. She was aggressively drunk. She told Amber only a slut would dress up for her daddy like that and tried to rip her dress off her. Amber lied to you about Caspar because she didn't want Bea to—"

The pantry door opened. Tessa jumped. "Shit!" She dropped the phone. I stared up at her and put up my hands in surrender. She looked at the jam and the sherry, then bent down to retrieve her phone.

"I'll call you back," she said, then frowned. "No, James. I'm not going to tell you what the right thing to do is. Work that out for yourself for once." She lowered the phone. For a second, I thought she might club me over the head with it. But instead, her eyes glistening with unshed tears, she held out her hand. I passed her the jam. A tiny laugh escaped her throat but she took it and put it on the side. I didn't move. For a while, nor did she. I watched her brush away the tears she didn't want me to see and turn back. She stretched out her hand again. Reluctantly, I passed her the sherry. Then, to my surprise, she held out her hand a third time. For me. It was shaking slightly. "You'll get piles sitting on that floor," she said.

"Already got them," I replied. Her hand was the same as her mother's. I took it. She gripped my forearm with the other and pulled me up. I saw the tin of chocolate powder as I rose. I took it off the shelf. "Is this what you were looking for?" I offered.

"Might be better than sherry," she said.

"It's marginal," I said.

"I know," she agreed.

The one nice thing about being caught red-handed is that you don't have to exhaust yourself with lies. I stepped out of the pantry. The kitchen was Gestapo-bright.

Tessa went back to the stove. She poured more milk into the pan. It was a battered old metal thing with a warped wooden handle. I looked at the clock on the wall. It was past two but I was wide-awake.

"Is that true, what you said? Or were you just trying to get Jimmy back?"

She glanced over her shoulder. "I would never have said those—"

"But is it true?" I interrupted. "I called her a slut?"

"Yes it is. I'm sorry. You shouldn't have to hear this from me."

I pulled out a wooden chair and sat down on it heavily. "She didn't tell me," I said, mostly to myself. Tessa didn't reply. Not an easy thing to say to your mother. Of course she didn't tell me. I knew what it was like to have a mother you couldn't trust. I was never sure what would come out of my mother's mouth. Not because she was drunk. And it was never hurtful. Just bloodcurdlingly embarrassing. What I had done to Amber was far worse.

For a while the only noise was the gas, the slow scrape of a wooden spoon on aluminum, the ticking clock, and an occasional hoot of an owl on the hunt. I watched Tessa; the hem of her nightie was trembling. Was she cold or afraid? I heard Lizzie King's voice in my head. Was any of this really Tessa's fault?

"Won't James come back?" I asked.

"The fact I even had to ask him," said Tessa. She remained standing with her back to me. "He can't just . . ." She stopped herself. I was not her natural confidante. But then again, who better than me? She must have a million questions she wanted to ask. I would. I did.

"Abdicate responsibility?" I ventured.

She turned. "It's a bit weird talking to you about these things."

"There's no one better, if you think about it."

"Dad and Peter packed up their worms the moment the message got through to them," she said. "Dad I understand, but Peter? He could have stayed, but he wouldn't hear of it. You and the girls are too important to him. James, on the other hand, their *father* . . ." Tessa rubbed her eyes. This was her second night without sleep, and I could tell the adrenaline was waning. She turned away before I could see the tears again.

"Sit down," I said. "I'll make the chocolate." I could tell she didn't want to. I wanted to think it was because she liked lording it over me, the disgusting drinker, the weak worm, but it wasn't that. This was awkward; she was as uncomfortable as I was. But it was strangely enticing, too. I pulled out a chair. Her legs betrayed her and she slumped into it. I spooned the sweet brown powder into mugs and watched the milk fizz beneath its skin. I could hear Tessa's brain whirring, so I decided to put her out of her misery. "I was only going to have one," I said. "I couldn't sleep." She looked at me for a long time. I suppose we had reached a major crossroads. Honesty versus fantasy. I'm glad we chose honesty. Or that Tessa did, anyway.

"I don't think that's true. It's what you tell yourself, but it's not true."

I stirred the hot chocolate. "It's not as bad as it looks."

"It sounds terrible. Trouble is, you can't remember those bits. Or choose not to. I can't decide."

Selective amnesia, perhaps? Now that I'd been told about the night of the engagement party, emotional flashcards appeared in my brain. I couldn't recall exactly what I had said, but there was an echo that was just loud enough to shame me. I could still taste the irrational anger. Trouble is, it hadn't felt irrational at the time. It had felt justified and justifiable. But it is not justifiable to scare your children like that. Ever. Guilt snaked around my gut like a girdle. Suddenly I understood the meaning of "vicious circle." Guilt and shame made me thirsty.

"I'm not an alcoholic," I said defiantly.

"It doesn't sound like recreational drinking to me."

"Come on, alcoholics sleep in parks, drink strong lager at eight in the morning, and piss themselves," I said, forcing a laugh.

Tessa was not in a laughing mood, and again I saw she was doing her best to hold back the tears. "I'm not James. Don't expect complicity from me."

Fair enough.

"I've been on the Internet," she said. "It's not about having a drink. It's about not being able to stop. And you can't stop. There are a million testimonials from drinkers who thought that because they lived in a nice house, kept down a job, they weren't actually alcoholics. But it's bollocks. Functioning alcoholic, the biggest oxymoron of them all."

"I am functioning."

"You might be, but the rest of us aren't doing so well."

"You think your problems with Amber are all my fault?"

"You've hardly been making it easy for her."

"Jimmy and Amber have always been thick as thieves. You would have had a tough time with or without . . ." Me drinking? Am I really a drinker? It had been only a matter of weeks. Maybe months now. Since . . . I put a mug of hot chocolate in front of Tessa. Since . . . along came a spider.

"I was only trying to lose weight," I said, and sat down beside her.

Tessa blew a small storm across the top of her cup. "Strange weight-loss program."

"Admitted, but I've lost twenty-one pounds, so something's working."

"Not your liver," she said. "And I'm sure your children would prefer you overweight and conscious."

"Does it matter what I would prefer?"

Tessa studied me carefully before answering. "I don't know. You have children. So probably not. Jesus, no one's saying it's easy. But neither is being single and approaching forty with no kids. You think this is my romantic ideal? Sitting alongside my fiancé's ex-wife in the middle of the night having cocoa?"

"It's good chocolate at least," I said, taking a sip.

"Small mercies."

We smiled fleetingly at each other, then sat quietly. I relished the thick, sweet taste. The clock struck three. "In the First World War the frontline troops called a mini-armistice on Christmas Day and emerged from their respective trenches to play a Germans versus British football match."

"Who won?" asked Tessa.

"I don't know. Neither, I guess. By Boxing Day they were killing each other again."

She looked at me for what felt like a long time, then returned to her drink.

A minute or two later, she went to a bowl on the side, picked out two apples, fetched a knife and chopping board, and sliced them. She sat down opposite and offered me a piece. "Thank you," I said, taking it.

"Can I ask you a question?"

I imagined a heavy, muddy ball in her hands. I nodded, and the whistle blew.

"Why did you have an affair?"

The ball sailed past me. "What?"

"James told me."

Jimmy told you what he thought he knew, but that was not the same thing.

"I didn't have an affair," I said.

Tessa arched a single eyebrow. I held her gaze. I may be many things, but I'm not a liar. Well, not about that, anyway.

"I did not have an affair," I stated, once more, for the record.

Something must have rung true in my voice, because she hesitated. I wondered what Jimmy had told her, how much.

"Why would he tell me that?"

"It's complicated," I replied.

"I know." She paused again, and I knew that she knew my dark secret. "James told me about Sophie Guest," she said.

I bit down hard on my lip. Sophie Guest. What a sweet way of saying "abortion." Why hadn't I written "Minnie Mouse," like everyone else who'd snuck in to do away with unwanted business? Sophie Guest was real. She was me. The other me. The one who'd go through a procedure like that and damn the consequences. And then, a few weeks later, leave me to live with those consequences alone. Always alone.

"Did he tell you why?"

"You got pregnant. It wasn't his."

There was the King directness I was so enjoying. Many responses flooded my head. I could not articulate a single one.

"I take it you've never had an abortion?"

Tessa shook her head.

"Well, lucky you, but be careful to judge too harshly before you know what you're judging."

Tessa seemed to accept this remonstration well. "Sorry," she said.

I exhaled loudly. "It's hard talking about this," I said. "Hard" wasn't the word. "Torture" was better. I'd rather swallow seven Battenburg cakes whole than put into words what I did.

"A stupid one-night stand?" asked Tessa, as gently as she could.

"I wish," I said, before I could stop myself.

Tessa's body language took a dramatic turn. She reared back in her chair. "Christ, Bea, you weren't"—she swallowed—"raped?"

"No. Though I wish I'd thought of that. He might have been able to forgive me then."

"Who?"

"Jimmy."

"Forgive you for what?"

"Killing his unborn son."

Tessa's eyes widened.

There. I'd said it. "The baby was his. Of course it was. I've never been with anyone else." I paused. "Ever."

"I don't understand," she said. "James told me—"

"He wouldn't listen to me. He does that when you're trying to tell him something he doesn't want to hear." She nodded. "It was easier for him to think I had slept with someone and got rid of it than to accept the truth. He didn't believe I could have done what I did. He insisted I was covering up some infidelity, so in the end it was easier to tell him what he wanted to hear. And keep the truth to myself."

Tessa waited. Her lower lip hovered expectantly. The truth was what she was after. The bloody truth.

"If this made sense to me, I would tell you how it happened. But it doesn't. So bear with me. I haven't talked about this for a long time." I stared into my empty mug. "What am I saying? I've never talked about it . . ."

I WAS PREGNANT WITH MADDY within weeks of Lulu being born. We were so happy that Lulu had made it, after all the ones we'd lost, and the birth was nothing like the carnage it had been with Amber. Our love knew no bounds. Leaking breasts, floppy stomach, filthy hair, the last remnants of afterbirth staining my pants, all of this was nothing to my husband. He loved me; it didn't matter what sort of dilapidated state I was in, and he was going to show it.

It wasn't the best sex we'd ever had, but in a strange way it meant the most. My periods never returned, but, then, I wasn't expecting them to. I was breast-feeding. I wasn't supposed to get pregnant. That particular old wives' tale is a load of shit. I was too exhausted to be tired. Too fat to put on weight. Too in love to care. Piles, varicose veins, and a hernia swiftly followed. I had trembles of panic about the state I was getting into, but everyone reassured me. You're having a third baby. Don't worry. What do you expect?

Amber started big school, Lulu learned to crawl, and I ate to survive the days and nights. The pounds piled on. By the twelfth week of my pregnancy, I had already put twenty-eight pounds on top of the weight I'd never lost after Lulu was born. Despite his initial claims of triumph, Jimmy faded from view. I was bloated, uncomfortable, and overweight, and I literally shuffled through the last trimester. I begged to be induced at thirty-eight weeks, but the doctors wouldn't do it. The only complication at Maddy's birth was the look of disappointment on Jimmy's face when they announced she was a girl. He'd denied it, but I'd seen it. When he was at home, his attention belonged to Amber. She demanded it, and since I wasn't prepared to stamp my feet and scream, she won. Lulu wasn't even walking when Maddy was born, and the long, broken nights started before they'd ever finished. But it wasn't so much Maddy keeping me up as Amber.

Adjusting to big school took longer than I had bargained for. Her nights were fretful, anxious, and dream-filled. She was now six, but Jimmy let her into our bed when I had fallen asleep feeding in Maddy's room. When I was in bed and she appeared, I took her back to her own. She would scream for Daddy, but Daddy was away more and more often, a whipping boy to some devilish talent agent. In the middle of the night, Amber hated me and I hated her right back. She didn't think much of her new sisters, either, and sometimes I had to agree with her. Maddy made barely a sound, but she was a sucky baby and needed a lot of food. I didn't get more than a couple of hours' sleep at a time for about a year. Maddy was feeding, Lulu was teething, and Amber, it felt, enjoyed kicking me when I was down. Why is any of this important? Because when I look back, I realize that I was planting the seeds of madness that lay dormant until mother hormones woke them up again with a fourth pregnancy.

Maddy was one when I realized I wasn't returning to form. I'd gone back to my old self after Amber, but I hadn't had a chance to get into shape after Lulu. When Maddy arrived, I was sixty pounds over my normal weight. My clothes didn't fit, and everywhere I looked mothers were skipping around in tight jeans and short skirts with babies in slings. I was a frump.

I did everything. The cabbage diet, the grape diet, the grapefruit diet, the Atkins diet, the other one that isn't Atkins, with a long name, that cost a fortune. I managed for a few days, four, five at the most, then something would happen. Amber had a tantrum, Maddy was sick, or Lulu was back in urgent care with another hard-to-explain bump. And Jimmy would have to go away again, just when we were beginning to find each other, and I would reach for food. I didn't realize it was comfort eating, because I always had an excuse. Children's leftovers were my downfall. And so began a long year of yo-yoing.

As a last resort, I joined WeightWatchers secretly. Maddy started nursery, and I had time to go to the gym. I cannot tell you what it took to shift that weight, but finally I was on to something permanent. I felt a flicker of recognition when I looked at myself in the mirror. It wasn't just the weight; it was me. I was on my way back. I had always liked myself. It was good to see myself again.

Jimmy said he'd have a vasectomy. Then he bailed out. I was furious. After everything I'd been through, the miscarriages, the endless pregnancies, single parenthood in every way but on paper, he wouldn't do that one simple thing for me. To me, it crystallized everything that was wrong with our relationship. I'd done everything to provide him with his precious family, while he did as he liked. I longed for him to come home, but when he was there, it was more fraught than ever. Everyone wanted him. The time he spent with the little ones was cursory, which made them uncharacteristically fractious. He would look at me and ask, "What's wrong with them?" It would have hurt me less if I'd caught him banging our next-door neighbor on the kitchen table. As usual,

Amber got his best, but even that wasn't a patch on what she was used to, so she took it out on me. I got the dog ends from him, and he got nothing in return from me.

I didn't notice I'd skipped a period, because life was hectic and time was flying by. Then I started to feel ill. I thought I had the flu and took DayQuil to survive. Finally, I worked out why the medicine wasn't working. I was horrified; it took me another three weeks to pluck up courage to do the test. Every time I went to the loo, I checked my pants, waiting for the miscarriage, but, of course, Murphy's Law, now that I wouldn't have minded Mother Nature taking her curious course, she left me be. Jimmy was away more than ever—Cannes TV festival, Edinburgh festival—having a terrible time, poor thing. I felt sicker than I ever had and cried every day. I told no one. Not even Jimmy. The solution, when it came to me, seemed perfect. We couldn't afford a fourth child, anyway. As it was, my mother was paying for the first three. She still is. One weekend I told Honor and Peter my mother was going into a hospital, left the kids with them, checked into Meadowlands, and had it taken out.

I STARED AT THE GRAIN of the wooden table. I had to stop talking to control my breathing. I might have sounded matter-of-fact as I continued my monologue to a silent, wide-eyed Tessa, but my heart was pounding. These were feelings I'd never put into cogent thoughts, and thoughts I'd never put into words. "I thought I was doing the best thing," I said eventually. "It turned out to be the worst. As soon as the pregnancy hormones leached out of my system, I woke up to what I had done. And then that letter arrived. In my state, I'd checked a box about being informed, donating the fetus to medical research, I don't know, I still can't remember doing it. I had killed our perfect, healthy son. I was eighteen weeks pregnant. I had no idea I was as far along as that. Trouble was, you couldn't tell bump from bulge since my weight had fluctuated. A hole opened up . . ."

I'd thought that another child would kill me. But not having one was a slow death by guilt and self-loathing. The soul of that child sat heavily on my shoulders and accompanied me wherever I went. The eating that I had finally brought under control spiraled rapidly out of control again. Within six months, I had put on what had taken two and a half years to lose. I know now I should have tried harder, but at the time, the words had lodged in my throat, creating a dam, and though I could hear my own silent screech, like a hideous tinnitus, Jimmy heard nothing. The loneliness ate me up, but I wouldn't let Jimmy touch me. I repulsed myself and hated him. How could I make love to him knowing what I knew? How could I make love to him and risk another child? I wouldn't have had another abortion, ever, ever, ever, but how could I explain that to the ghost of the child I had killed? Jimmy was adamant. He didn't want a vasectomy, and in the end, it wasn't necessary. We had stopped touching each other, and slowly our marriage turned to dust.

"When Jimmy confessed he'd seen the letter, it was easy to let him believe the baby was the product of a foolish, drunken one-night stand."

"And he believed you?" asked Tessa incredulously.

"It was easier for him to think I'd slept with someone else than aborted an eighteen-week-old fetus for no reason."

"But you're not the type to have an affair," she said. "You're devoted to your family."

"Anyone is the type, Tessa. In the right circumstances."

"Didn't he want to know who, when, where?"

"No. Jimmy's not like that."

I watched Tessa struggle with the implausibility of my story. How could I have let my husband believe I'd slept with another man, when I could have told him the truth? Because the truth was not acceptable for the modern woman. I couldn't cope. I had failed. At the time, I wasn't able to admit that to myself. So I left.

I put my head into my hands. I was exhausted.

It was Tessa who broke the silence. "Why did you keep the letter?"

Interesting question. "I don't know."

"Did you want to be caught?"

"Maybe. If Jimmy punished me, maybe I wouldn't have to go on punishing myself."

"*Punish.* Listen to yourself. You didn't need to be punished. What you went through was horrific." Tessa reached across the table and placed her hand on mine. I don't know what I was expecting—the superior smile of the victor, a disapproving snarl, a blank, unforgiving stare? Instead, she squeezed my hand. "It's not your fault."

We looked at each other, her hand on mine. The clock went on ticking. I couldn't speak.

"James has to take some responsibility."

I pulled my hand away. "James . . . I don't think I'll ever get used to that."

Tessa didn't say anything.

"He doesn't know. Tessa, imagine what it would do to him. Do you have any idea how often the abortion debate comes up? Premature babies surviving younger and younger. Some only days older than—" my voice faltered. "No, he'd hate me."

"He could never hate you, Bea."

"I killed his son."

"Because he'd deserted you, left you alone with three kids. No wonder you couldn't cope."

"Why couldn't I cope? It's pathetic."

"Because it's fucking tough."

"Whose side are you on?" I asked.

She paused. "I don't know. Your children's, I suppose."

"Thank you."

She looked as if my answer had amazed her. It had certainly amazed me. "And that's why I'm going to say something now that I don't think you want to hear."

I braced myself.

"Bea, you *have* to stop drinking. And I mean completely."

"Oh, God . . ." I moaned. "I don't want to go back to eating again."

"But alcohol is such a depressant, not to say personality-altering."

"So is being fat."

"Get help, then. I know it's easy for me to say stop. I can have one drink and go to bed. I can also get pissed and have a laugh, then not drink for a few days. I can open a packet of Minstrels, have four, and leave the rest. I don't have that addictive thing. God knows, I have others—"

"I thought you were perfect." I smiled at her.

"I thought *you* were," she replied. "The impossible act to follow."

"I wouldn't try to do that."

"There's always smack," she said.

"Leave that for the grand finale. I suggest prescription drugs to start with."

"Good thinking," laughed Tessa. "I tell you, there have been moments in the last few weeks when we've had the girls where I've longed to get my hands on some Valium."

"So you're not perfect."

"No. Deeply flawed. Like everyone."

"You look perfect."

"Bea, no one thinks they look perfect. I've got a huge nose."

"Actually, I'd noticed that."

"Thanks!"

Weird. Here I was, giggling with the woman I assumed I'd hate. But why would I hate her? Unless Jimmy had had a major personality alteration, he was not the silly, vain, bimbo type. I wasn't like that. And he'd loved me.

"Seriously," I asked, "what are your flaws?"

Tessa thought about this. "I cling to people and make their lives my own."

"I guess I'd have to agree with that, since you're about to marry my husband and live with my children."

The mood changed suddenly. It was my fault. But that's honesty for you. It isn't always hard to swallow, but she'd been dishing it out for a wee while now.

"Ex-husband," said Tessa slowly. "My understanding was that you'd given him up."

I looked at her for a long time. Now for the moment of truth. "I want him back." Briefly, I felt the most extraordinary affinity for the woman sitting opposite me. Why wouldn't she want my life? It had been a great one until things had conspired against me. Jimmy was a good man. My daughters were good kids. Okay, so it wasn't the perfect Prince Charming setup, and the baggage was heftier than she had probably envisaged, but it was a good package and she knew it. And that was why this time her response came as no surprise to me.

Tessa shook her head. "You can't," she said. "It's too late."

"Is it?"

Tessa bit her lip, but didn't reply.

I stood up. "We'll be out of your hair first thing."

The whistle blew and we returned to our trenches. I couldn't tell you the score, but I think it was evening out. In my favor.

IN FACT, TESSA LEFT FIRST. I was up early so she must have gone at dawn. When I came down, a woman from the village was restocking the kitchen. She'd made a breakfast tray for Liz. Out of politeness, I offered to take it up. A quick farewell, then my family and I would be on our way. I eased the door open with a foot, placed the tray on Liz's knees, and went to open the curtains.

It was a beautiful day. Spring seemed to have leapfrogged summer, and I found myself staring out at what looked like mid-August blue sky. I turned back and watched Liz as she felt around the plate for a slice of peach. She was making a valiant effort, but I could tell she needed help.

"Careful," I said, sitting down next to her and taking the tray. "The tea's hot." I prodded a piece of fruit with a fork and handed it to her.

"Thank you."

"When are Hugh and Peter back?"

"They've been delayed. Problem with the ferry."

"Oh, no."

"Don't worry. Tessa's organized a rota of people to come in and check on—"

"We can stay until they get here."

"I'll be fine."

"Liz, please, let me help."

"Did Tessa put you up to this?" she asked impatiently.

"Did your daughter ask her fiancé's ex-wife to look after her beloved mother? Let me think about that." I laughed. "No. I don't think we're quite there yet."

"Maybe one day." She stabbed about for a bit of fruit. I didn't say anything. "Look, I'm getting the hang of this already," she said, holding up a piece of peach victoriously.

There was a knock on the door. Amber and Maddy came in.

"Lulu says we're going to Granny's," said Amber indignantly. "Is that true?"

"Good morning, Mummy, good morning, Liz," I reminded them.

They mumbled a vague greeting.

"We always go and see my mother during the holidays," I explained to Liz.

"Do we have to? It's so boring there. I want to go home," said Amber.

"I wonder why," I said.

"It's not that," retaliated Amber.

"Maybe Caspar could visit us at Granny's," I said.

"Granny wouldn't like him. He's not posh enough."

"She didn't like your father for the same reason. Silly old trout." Amber giggled. A beautiful sound. I pointed at Maddy. "Don't you dare tell her I said that."

"I'm sorry you're going. It's been lovely having you all."

"Can we come back?" asked Maddy.

"You'll always be welcome," said Liz. She wasn't looking at me, but I knew who she was talking to. She had no idea how this was going to pan out, either. For me or her daughter.

"Will you teach me how to make jam in the summer?" asked Maddy.

"Of course. You can be my eyes."

"Don't be silly. Your eyes will have stopped rolling by then," said Maddy.

"You think?"

"Yes. They're moving slower than yesterday."

Liz and I smiled at each other, though only one of us could see it.

"Thank you, Dr. Maddy. Now, where is Lulu? She said she'd read to me before you left."

I was staggered. "She did?"

"Yes," said Liz. "The whole of the *Little Red Hen* series."

"Lulu!" Maddy shrieked.

I winced.

Lulu appeared at the bedroom door with her books.

"Are you really going to read to Liz?" I asked.

She nodded shyly.

"That's great, Lulu."

Lulu shrugged. "Well, she doesn't interrupt me when I'm trying to finish the words, because she can't see them."

I didn't know whether to laugh or cry.

"Every cloud . . ." said Liz.

Lulu climbed onto the bed, then looked at me imperiously.

"You can go now," she said.

Funny. Now that I could, I didn't want to.

Seventeen

Hold Fast

"CHRIST, YOU LOOK LIKE FUCKING SHIT."

Ah, the dulcet tones of Linda first thing on a Monday morning. I forced a smile. "So would you if you'd had my weekend," I said.

"I told you the recording studio was a sodding bad idea."

The recording studio? Was that only two days ago? It felt like months. "That was the one good thing, actually."

"Yeah? I spoke to Carlos. He said your little step-minx was quite a find. I think he might have ideas for her."

"No way. You said it yourself."

"Looks like Lily Cole and a voice like Billie Holiday. Her curled-up naked in a big piece of amber, locked inside the *angst* of puberty, singing about how to make yourself an individual when all around are automata. Pushy mums will love it, horny dads will love it, and the kids'll eat it up. I can see it. Huge."

"No, no, no, no. No. No."

"Well, think about it."

"Linda, no."

"Has she got an agent? Bounce some figures around."

"Christ, Linda, anyone ever tell you you're a rottweiler?"

She smiled proudly. "Why thank you, Ms. King."

"You are not getting your manipulative paws on James's daughter. If she still wants to sing at eighteen, you can talk to her, but not a day before. I've seen what you do to the young ones and it ain't pretty."

"Nice, stable family. She'd be all right."

Yeah, right. Mother a drinker. Father an ostrich. And future stepmother the archetypal witch. "Do you tell yourself these things so you can sleep at night?"

"No. My very accommodating pharmacist helps me with that." She opened a drawer. "You want a couple?"

"No, thank you," I said archly while making a mental note. Second drawer on the right.

"You will."

"What I do need, however, is to take some time off."

"Darlin', you've only just joined the company."

"I know. But my mother's ill."

"Yeah, and the kids have a school play, a dentist appointment, and someone has to take the old dear to chemo. It's the sad time we're in, Tessa. Parents as demanding as the bloody children. And so cranks on the effing conveyor belt of life."

I assumed she was joking. "Two days, max. Until the medicine starts to work."

"Tessa, Janet's mother's in a hospice, Tony's dad has Alzheimer's and his mother had a car accident a few years ago and never fully recovered. Val's son has Asperger's and her mother has just had a stroke . . . I could empty the office like that," she clicked her fingers, "if everyone took a couple of days just to see if the meds were working."

I should have explained the gravity of the situation from the start. "Actually, it's a bit more complicated. Mum needs to go to a hospital and my father's been held up. There's no one—"

"We have McCloud and Tanner this afternoon. You can't go."

"But—"

"No, Tessa. This meeting's important. Someone else will have to take her." My expression gave me away. Linda narrowed her eyes at me, picking up a scent. "And don't think about doing anything dramatic like quitting, because your résumé isn't looking as consistent these days, and you wouldn't want another contretemps with a boss, would you?"

"What's happened?"

"What do you mean?"

"To you."

"Nothing."

"Why are you being so . . ."

She raised an eyebrow. "Mean? Tessa, we're not in the frigging playground anymore. I've always been like this. It's just you've never had the pleasure of witnessing it firsthand. No time off. Sorry."

"I'm quite well versed in employment law and I know that after—"

"I wouldn't pull that one, darlin'. It might sour our relationship."

"It just soured." I walked to the door and left.

Outside, in the corridor, I started to shake. I walked straight past Matt and just managed to close my office door on his inquiring face before I burst into tears. Surely this wasn't happening. Surely I'd just picked a bad moment. Surely she'd realize how unreasonable she was being and put it right. Surely we'd progressed further than this. I sat down angrily, in shock, but after a while came to the sorry conclusion that Linda had been deadly serious. I didn't know what that crap was about not being in the playground, because right then it felt as though we'd never left.

I THOUGHT LONG AND HARD before I called Bea, but in the end I decided she was my only choice. There were sweet people in the village who'd do it, but I needed someone to be my eyes, ears, and voice. And right at that moment, it felt as if I had more in common with Bea than with anyone else in the world. So I asked her a favor I had no right to ask and was filled with gratitude when she said yes.

"I'm so fucking cross. I don't know when Dad and Peter will be able to get a boat—" I was still reeling from my encounter with Linda.

"It's okay. I'll do it," said Bea calmly.

"I'm so sorry to ask you."

"Tessa, you took care of my kids when I couldn't. I owe you."

She sounded so kind and understanding, I only just managed to thank her before welling up again.

"The benefits of having no life," said Bea, and laughed a dry laugh. "Anyway, the girls like it here."

"I could quit."

"Don't do that," said Bea sternly. "Finding a new job is harder from the outside. I was going to go back to work after Maddy started school . . . Sorry, what am I talking about? Tell me what needs doing."

"When you get to the hospital, talk to a man called Mr. Evans. Please check that they're administering the interferon—"

"Hang on, let me get a pen."

When Bea came back on the line, I gave her a list of questions that I had been in too much of a daze to ask the day before. Exactly which nerves had short-circuited this time? What was the expected recovery time and when would we know if we were dealing with a permanent problem? Would she heal or would she be left with optic neuritis? Would we have to change her medicine from weekly to every two or three days? What was the long-term burden going to be on Dad? Had she suddenly jumped to second stage?

"Shit, I should be there."

"It's okay, Tessa. I can cope. I'll talk to them and call you straight away. I've got it. I understand the basics of this disease now."

She was a quick learner.

"You're wasted on the carpool," I said.

"You think?"

"I'm so sorry about—"

"Stop apologizing. To be completely honest, a stay with my mother was guaranteed to set me galloping into a bottle of gin." Bea paused. "What news of Jimmy?"

"He says he can't come back," I replied. "It's not possible now but he'll leave early. He'll miss the final party, which I thought was big of him."

Bea was intelligent enough not to defend him, but I could tell she wanted to. I wondered in that moment whether she loved him more than I did. But I had other things to think about, so I put that alarming idea to one side with all the others, like my eighty-four-year-old father looking after my blind mother. And how far she'd bounce back this time. Could they afford full-time care? No. Could I? Not without a bloody good job. I had no choice . . . I'd have to commute. Bea could fill the gap, but not permanently.

The meeting dragged on, as legal meetings do when lawyers are being paid by the hour. I managed a quick call to Bea during a break, but she was at the hospital and her phone was off. I thought I'd go mad when they ordered in the sandwiches. I had the most horrible sense that Linda was enjoying my discomfort. She kept asking me probing but irrelevant questions.

Finally, at ten to nine that evening, the meeting was called to a close. Someone suggested drinks. I legged it, dialing home as I ran.

"Hello?"

"Mum, it's me. I'm just running to the station now. I'm so sorry—"

"Don't be silly. Go home."

"No, I want to—"

"Darling, we'll all be asleep by the time you get here and still be asleep when you leave tomorrow morning."

"But—"

"Honestly, Tessa. Go home. Get some rest."

I stopped running. Home. A bath. Sleep. What I wouldn't give . . . No. How could I not be there?

"Tessa, darling, please. I'm feeling much better. Bea's been amazing. This is just a relapse, okay?"

"I worry—"

"I know. I would too. But I've been good for a long time. In three weeks I'll be better. The treatment works. I want you to remember it's a bitch of a disease but it leaves ninety-five percent of us living. I haven't suddenly jumped to second stage or anything like that, so please, don't exhaust yourself schlepping up and down here every day imagining the worst, because it isn't going to happen."

My throat tightened. Where did all my words go when I needed them most?

"Dad wants a word."

"Dad! How did he get back?"

"Don't ask." My mother chuckled. "Beware, he has the whiff of the evangelical about him. Fish! I mean, honestly."

"Where's Bea?"

"Watching TV with Peter and Amber. They'll leave tomorrow. I wouldn't hear of them going tonight. It's been very nice to have them here."

I felt awkward, redundant, and strangely homesick, standing motionless on the busy London pavement.

"I love you, Tessa," said my mother.

I felt an overwhelming urge to sit down right there. My energy had left me. "I love you too. Thank you for always being the most brilliant mother."

Normally, she would have said something jokey, sarcastic, probably along the lines of how I'd buried all the bad memories, but not tonight. "You made it easy," she replied.

I don't know why tears kept welling in my eyes. Tiredness, I suppose. "No, Mum, you did."

I started walking again while I waited for my father to come on the line.

"Hello, precious."

"Hi, Dad. How did you get back?"

"Peter has some fishermen friends."

"I thought it was too stormy to cross."

"This was an old schooner, well versed on the high seas. It was exhilarating."

"I'm glad I didn't know."

"That's why I didn't tell you."

"Is Mum really okay?"

"She will be," said my father.

I watched as one foot followed the other down to the towpath that would take me home. It was dark already, but I felt too tired to be afraid.

"Dad, James didn't come home."

"He's working, Tessa. Lizzie isn't his mother."

"No, she's mine, and that's not why I was asking him to come home. His daughters needed a bit of TLC."

"Peter and Honor will take over now. Bea's changed her plans. She's taking the girls to stay with them for Easter."

"They shouldn't have to pick up the pieces. It makes me so cross."

"Why?"

"Because he doesn't realize we need him."

"Darling, what the hell do you think he's doing out there if it isn't about what you need? He's going to have to support two families now."

"He doesn't even support one, Dad. His ex-mother-in-law does that, and, as you know, I look after myself."

"And you think he likes that? You think it's fun that his ex-mother-in-law pays for his children? No wonder he works so hard, Tessa. He needs to make a gigantic leap. And, my sweetheart, such leaps take effort."

"But it hasn't happened," I said disloyally.

"So you'd rather he was the type of man to give up? Come on, Tessa, don't give him a hard time for trying to do the right thing. That's not fair. He's a good man."

There was that feeling again. My legs had turned to stone. I brushed away an empty crisp packet and sat down on a well-worn bench, then felt guilty and bent down to pick it up. I walked over to a bin and threw it in. "I'm afraid," I said.

"What of?"

"That the same thing that happened to Bea and James will happen to me and James. He has this way of cutting himself off when things aren't going so well. He did it to Bea, he's done it to me over the Amber thing, and he's doing it again over this. That's why he hasn't come back. He doesn't want to face up to what's going on. He can't take responsibility."

"He doesn't need to right now. You're here doing it for him."

"They're not my kids!" There. I'd said it. The truth. It was not my problem. My mother was my problem. My aged father. Work. But not some drunken woman whose own sense of regret was wreaking havoc on three young lives. That was not my problem.

"Darling, marriage is all about being a team. He couldn't be here, so you had to carry the baton alone for a while. You did that. Amber and Bea are okay. When he's home, he can take over, see with his own eyes what's going on, and together you can work out what you're going to do about your respective families. You have backup for the first time in your life. Use it."

"I tried. He wouldn't come."

"Tessa, do you really think that sitting on a plane for eleven hours is the best use of his time? Another thing. If you'd been in L.A. and your mother had needed help, do you think he'd roll over and go back to sleep because she wasn't his mother?"

I didn't have to answer that. "I know you're right. Why, then, do I still feel like this?"

"Like what?"

"Alone."

"Have you told him that?"

"No."

"Darling, men are many things but they aren't mind readers. When I'm being dim, your mother writes me notes. It's very helpful. Spell it out."

"What if there are things I don't understand myself?"

"Like what?"

I looked out over the river to the deluxe flats opposite. "Like feeling insanely jealous of a fourteen-year-old girl?"

"Tell him."

"And feeling like a second-choice bride?"

"He'd be horrified. Tessa, he couldn't love you more."

"I worry he won't be as interested in our children as he is in his first ones?"

"Have you talked about children?"

"I've been too afraid to. I say it's because I don't mind, but really I'm terrified about what he'll say. He's had three, could he do it all over again?"

"Wouldn't you rather know than live in fear of an imagined outcome?"

"I suppose so."

"Stop giving him a hard time over things he doesn't deserve a hard time over because you don't have the courage to tell him what's bothering you."

"You are way too smart for an old man," I laughed.

"Your fault for introducing me to Open University. Everyone's so worried about keeping their hearts healthy. I've been more afraid of losing my marbles."

"No chance of that, Dad. You're my career adviser, bank manager, accountant, and therapist all rolled into one."

"All for the price of a pint," he chuckled. "Go home and call him. Mum's right, there's no need to come rushing back here."

Dad was right too. On all counts. The aging process is a bastard, but wisdom comes no other way. "Dad," I said, standing up, "will you talk to me for a bit longer? Just while I get off this scary towpath and find myself a cab?"

"It would be my pleasure, my beautiful girl. I'm simply longing to talk to you about fish . . ."

It was ten-thirty when I let myself into the Hampstead flat. Although mine was closer to the office, I wanted to go home and this was my home now. Where James was. Or wasn't. But where he'd come back to. Our team headquarters. I threw off my work clothes and dumped them on the chair in our bedroom, cleaned my teeth, and climbed into bed. I left a message on James's phone, asking him to call me when he was through with his meetings. Whatever time that was. I left all accusations and recriminations out of my voice. I just wanted to hear his.

Despite my ruminations, I was soon deeply asleep, but reared up like a stallion when I heard the phone. "James?"

"Everything all right?"

"I miss you. Come home."

"Oh, Tessa—"

"It's okay. I know you can't, but I just wanted to tell you that I wish, wish, wish you were here."

"You know I would be if I could."

"I do." I wrapped myself up in the duvet. "I'm sorry I got cross before."

"Totally understandable."

"Really? I don't understand it."

"They're my children. You have enough on your plate without having to deal with them and Bea."

"You do understand," I said, slightly taken aback. How did he manage to simplify everything?

"I'm not stupid, Tessa."

I clung to the phone. Actually, I would have liked to crawl into it and magic myself down the line, across the mid-Atlantic ridge, down Route 66, into room 1238 at the Château Marmont. "James, can I say something?"

"Anything."

"Really? Because sometimes there are things I feel I can't say."

"Like?"

"Anything to do with the girls."

"Come on."

Okay, I thought, here goes. "Too much attention goes Amber's way to the detriment of the other two," I said. "Lulu needs serious help with her reading and writing. But she's not getting it. You never sit and read with her."

"There isn't time."

"James, you're doing it again."

"What?"

"Slamming me down. You do that whenever I try to talk to you about anything that's a bit difficult."

"That's not true."

"It is. I told you there was a problem between Amber and me, but you didn't want to talk about it. You wanted to think Bea's drinking was a one-off. You wouldn't even entertain the idea that someone other than Caspar ripped that dress—"

"But Amber told—"

"And so did I. But you believed her! Can't you see that puts me in an impossible position? You make me feel like a second-class citizen when you put Amber first all the time. I get jealous and that makes me feel insecure, and insecurity can turn even the most level-headed woman into a fruitcake. A dangerous one at that. It's easy to see why stepmothers can become so evil. Our husbands have a love interest who is half our age and twice as beautiful."

"Please, Tessa, tell me you're not jealous of Amber?"

I closed my eyes. This was harder than I'd thought it was going to be. "I'm sorry, but if I lie to you now I'll regret it in the future." God, I could be Bea talking. "I am jealous. Less so now that I understand her animosity, but I worry that I'll always feel threatened by the relationship you two have."

"Trust me," he said sexily. "I love you in a completely different way."

I managed a laugh but it was short, small, and shallow. Humor is a great elixir, but it isn't a miracle cure. "Whatever way you love us, there are still two of us and only one of you. And that's not to mention the other two."

"Who?"

"Maddy and Lulu!"

"Tessa, I was joking!"

"This isn't a time for jokes."

"Sorry. I didn't realize humor was banned."

"Don't do that, James. Don't make me out to be the grouch. I don't want to be Bea."

"Nor do I."

"Are you sure?"

"Tessa, I was just trying to lighten the tone."

"You're not listening to me. I don't want you to lighten the tone. I want you to realize how important this is to me."

"Okay. I'm sorry." I could hear him breathing down the phone. There was a knock on his door. "Hang on."

I was tiring from the fight, heaviness creeping up my limbs. I closed my eyes. Then I heard a woman's voice and the tiredness evaporated.

"Jimbo, come on. It's drinks time."

"Down in a minute. Just got to finish a call."

The door closed and James came back to the phone.

"Who was that?" I asked, though I'd sworn I wouldn't.

"Agent from the L.A. office."

"Drinks? Jimbo?"

"I'll miss them," said James. "This is more important."

I pulled the duvet tighter around me. "Is what I'm saying honestly making no sense to you?"

"I suppose Lucy and Faith have made the odd comment—"

"And Bea."

James sighed.

"It's okay. You can say her name. It's when you don't that I get nervous."

"Yes, and Bea. So everyone's telling me I'm making her into a princess. Like that's a bad thing. Isn't that what all little girls want to be?"

"Yes and no. It's complicated."

"I've got three daughters. You'd better explain it."

"Pretty dresses and being worshipped and adored is all well and good, but we've also got to be able to hike up the hem, climb down the tower, and slay the dragon for ourselves."

"I wouldn't fancy the dragon's chances against Amber," James said.

"No. You and Bea were a good balance. But you may have noticed Bea isn't around much when I am, so I'm left pretty unsupported, and Amber ends up being overindulged. I don't have the right to do what Bea does. And I don't want it. I'm not her mother. You've got to be stricter. Or at least fair."

He sighed again. "You think I let her get away with too much."

"It's for her own good, James. Being a daddy's girl is fine at four, but it's not such a good look at forty."

"I know too much attention goes her way, it's always been like that. I was working when the other two came along but, to be honest, I used that as an excuse not to be so involved. God, this is hard to admit . . . It does get a bit boring by the third. Who cared if it was pear, banana, or squash? It was all mush to me. There was nothing exciting about changing another stinking nappy. I didn't spend as much time with Lulu, even less with Maddy, and then I felt guilty. I tell you, with kids you get out what you put in and they didn't welcome me home every evening with open arms like Amber did." He cleared his throat. "So, naturally . . ." His voice faltered.

"And Bea tried to tell you?"

"I used work as an excuse to hide. I'd manage to come up with some inescapable meeting and skip the little ones' bath and bedtime altogether."

"I don't think you're alone in that."

"We ended up resenting each other."

"Easily happens," I said.

"I don't want that to happen to us, Tessa. I love you too much."

"And I love you. That's why I need to say all these things. It's too important to fuck up."

"I'm sorry, my love, I really am. I should have listened to you. I just want us all to be happy. We have so much to be grateful for."

I wished so much he was lying next to me. I needed to feel his skin. But perhaps we had had to be separated by a continent for this conversation to take place.

"I'll deal with Amber," he said.

"She needs you now more than ever."

"We'll deal with Amber, then."

I sighed. "I like the sound of that."

"I'll do anything I have to. Anything. Give me a chance to change. I know how costly it is not to. We do this together. We're a team, right? I do not want to lose you, Tessa King. You. Not Bea."

The low groan escaped my lips before I could stop it.

"God, I wish I was there in bed with you," he said.

"Not as much I do."

"I'd watch you drift off to sleep, and just as the wave caught you, I'd slowly undo the buttons on my old pajamas."

"How do you know I'm wearing them?"

"You always do when I'm away."

"How do you know?"

"You never put them back."

"Busted."

"Ssh, I'm telling you what I'd do to you if I were there." I sshed. "I'd slip my hand under the material and trace my fingers all over your body. First your breasts, your stomach, then your hips, and, finally, I'd ease open your legs."

I groaned.

"You'd groan just like that. But you'd still be nestling on the edge of sleep."

I put my hand down between my legs and imagined it was James. For a few short moments, it almost was.

THE FOLLOWING AFTERNOON I WAS in my office, stifling a yawn, when Linda walked in. Without knocking.

"Number fucking one," she said.

Whoop-whoop. I forced a smile. "Congratulations."

"We're going to the pub to celebrate. You coming?"

"No. I'm going to finish off here and get a train to Oxford."

"Oxford?"

"My parents."

"How is she?" asked Linda.

"My mother?" I said coldly. "Well, her eyesight hasn't returned, but she seems okay. Thanks."

"Fucking awful disease, MS. My nan had it."

I nodded in a noncommittal yet sympathetic way. She wasn't going to get me to roll over that easily. She walked over to my desk and picked up a piece of paper that had nothing to do with her. Then she put it down. "Well, if we're all out, seems daft you sitting here all conscientious on your fucking tod. May as well go." Then she left my office. That was as much of an apology as I was going to get. I wasn't proud, I'd take it. I closed down my computer, took my files with me, and left.

DAD WAS WAITING FOR ME in the doorway when the taxi pulled up. He came down the path to greet me. He looked wonderful. I glanced at my reflection in the side mirror. My hair was filthy, my skin looked gray, my clothes were crumpled, and I smelled of other people's paninis. But it didn't matter, because Dad helped me out of the car, enveloped me in his arms, and hugged me for a long time.

"Good news," he said. "Mum has got a bit of peripheral vision back. Incredible woman."

"That's great!" I burst into tears. "Sorry," I said, wiping my eyes and laughing. "I don't know what's wrong with me at the moment."

"You're tired," said my father wisely. I was teetering on the edge after four broken nights. No wonder new mothers went mad.

"Come and have a cup of tea. Mum's wrapped up and sitting in the garden. Did you speak to James?"

I put my arm through his. "Yes. For hours."

"You were supposed to stay in London for a good night's sleep."

"Just doing what my daddy told me."

"Everything okay?"

"Better than okay. Thanks to you."

"Don't thank me. I can only make suggestions. The rest is down to you. Go out to the garden. I'll bring you tea."

"You sure you're not getting tired, Dad?"

"Me? I feel on top of the world."

MY MOTHER WAS LYING ON the recliner normally reserved for summer. Her head was tilted back, her eyes were closed, and she'd been tucked tightly under a blanket. She looked so peaceful that I didn't want to disturb her. I took a seat at the other end of the terrace and watched her. That was what my parents were to me: a blanket, tucking me in against the elements. I closed my eyes and listened to the wood pigeons' guttural song. Someone was mowing a lawn in the village. I could hear the sound of the radio drift through the open kitchen window. These were moments to cherish. I heard Dad's footsteps on the flagstones, and a cup of tea floated into view. He looked at my mother.

"I think she's dozed off," I said.

"The pace of life is so much more frenetic than it used to be. It's become a privilege just to stop and think occasionally," he said, sitting down next to me.

"That's exactly what I was thinking."

"It's why I loved the fishing. Me and nature. I thought at first I'd get bored, but my mind soon steadied and my soul opened up. I watched a water boatman skate across the water and was mesmerized." I didn't speak.

"I came to a realization there that ultimately we're all responsible for one another. It was incredibly powerful, but peaceful too. I learned an important lesson. At eighty-four, that's not bad. If we take care of our world, our world will take care of our souls. That's happiness. That's what we're all searching for. Comes down to care."

"And hope," I said.

My father took my hand. He smiled, nodding. "I feel boundless," he said.

"That's what it feels like to lie spread out like a starfish, naked in the grass, and stare at the sky." My mother's face was pointing our way now, but her eyes were still closed.

"Hi, Mum," I said.

"How long have you been listening?" asked Dad.

"Since the beginning of time," said my mother in a faux-spiritual voice.

"I think she's taking the piss," said Dad. He stood up and went over to her. He made her budge up, then sat down next to her, took her hands and rubbed them. "You warm enough?" he asked. She nodded.

They appeared to be gazing at each other intently, though Mum kept her eyes closed. If I watched carefully, I could see the perpetual movement under the lids, but it didn't worry me so much now.

"Bea has called a couple of times," said my mother.

"Sober?"

"Darling," said my mother, reprimanding me in one word, "the woman has been through a lot. Did you know she had five failed pregnancies between Amber and Lulu?"

"Yes. But that's not why she drinks."

My parents waited for me to expand. But I couldn't.

"Don't be so sure. Nothing in life happens in isolation. The scales are always moving. Sometimes the good and the bad balance each other out. Sometimes you reach tipping point," my mother said.

"It was very hard on us," said my father.

"What was?" I asked, sitting up a little straighter.

"Hugh," said my mother softly.

He patted her hand. "I've been thinking," he said. "Perfection is a very hard thing to live up to. Your mother and I have had a great marriage, but it's not been without difficulties."

"Well, obviously ups and downs—"

"No, Tessa, I'm talking bottom of the crevasse. Like everyone else." I was going to interrupt, but Dad quieted me. "A few years after you were born we decided to have another child."

"You told me you'd only ever wanted one."

My mother placed her shades back over her eyes and sat up. "Hugh?"

"Liz darling, Tessa needs a little of the sheen to be rubbed off. As a wedding gift."

My mother didn't say anything, but she didn't stop him again.

"If we'd told you the truth you would have felt you weren't enough, and we didn't want you to feel like that, because you were and are. But we still tried and we kept failing."

I watched my parents share a thousand painful memories in the space of a second. "It was hardest on you, Liz darling," said Dad. "I didn't want to go on putting you through it."

"You weren't putting me through it," said my mother.

"That was how it felt to me."

"It's hard for a man to understand what a woman goes through in successful pregnancies, let alone the ones that fail," said Mum.

"But I only seemed to make things worse. It was easier to bugger off to the pub."

"Like James," I said quietly. "He pulled away from Bea."

"It was my fault," said Mum. "I locked you out. I was the one who felt a failure."

"You were never that. You were always so brave."

"I made you feel surplus to requirements."

Dad nodded. "Maybe. That's no excuse, though."

My mother reached up to stroke his thin hair. "What made you stay?"

"Stay?" I said, unable to stop myself interrupting.

Dad shifted.

"You were going to leave us?" I asked, stunned.

"I thought about it, yes." I was reeling. Dad had been going to leave us? "How did you know?" he asked Mum.

"Well, you could have gone and had lots of children with anyone else. It didn't take a genius to figure that out."

"Liz, you daft thing, it was never about that. I only thought about leaving because I'd lost *you*."

My mother lowered her hand. "The hardest thing to do when you're angry is reach out. We both retreated. I'm sorry."

"My darling, you've nothing to be sorry for."

"Why didn't you leave?" I asked, still sitting forward. I noticed my mother sit a little straighter too.

"Nothing dramatic. Mum had gone to pick you up from school—you must have been seven. You and she were walking up the garden path. You were talking nonstop as usual and pulling your mother's arm out of its socket." I couldn't help smiling. I could almost taste the memory. "I realized this was where I belonged. Maybe not right at that moment, but time moves on, things change and settle and change again, and I knew that I would belong again." He turned to me. "Not rocket science."

It felt pretty profound to me.

"I thank the gods every day for that moment of clarity. When doubts resurfaced, I clung to that moment and it got me through."

"You had more doubts?" I asked.

"It's a long journey, Tessa. Everyone has times when they wonder, 'Is this it?'" said my mother, coming to my father's defense. "You need to know that. Dad's right. The perfect union doesn't exist. Sure there are relationships that check most of the boxes most of the time, but not all and not always."

"So I'm learning. But isn't it good to aim high?"

"High, yes. But not unreachable," said Dad.

"James is a wonderful man, Tessa," said Mum. "But be under no illusion. Marrying him will be the toughest thing you ever do."

Dad took my mother's hands again. "And the most rewarding."

She smiled, and in that smile I saw the girl she'd been and the woman she'd become. It was all and nothing to do with me. My father leaned over and gave her a kiss.

"I've got to make a work call," I said, standing up.

"Don't worry, we're not going to start getting jiggy with it," said Dad.

"'Jiggy with it'?" I asked, laughing. "Where did you pick up that lingo?"

"Fisherman-speak," he replied.

He was right, I didn't have to call anyone but I wanted to leave them alone. Perfect unions may not exist but perfect moments do. This was one of those, and they were entitled to have it without me. I felt strangely elated, despite their dire warnings of difficulties ahead. If perfection didn't exist, then life was what you made it and with whom. I found that empowering, not daunting. Daunting was when your fate was in the hands of others. Was James the only person in the world for me? No. He'd just happened to turn up at a time when I was open to the idea of finding a pod partner. Not very romantic, but realistic. It was up to us to find the romance in it, James and me. From the window seat in the sitting room I watched my parents talking and thanked them silently for finding their way back to each other. I realized now how easy it was to get lost.

MY FATHER DIED THE FOLLOWING morning. The most shocking thing about it was that it came as no shock at all. I had gone into their room with their morning tea on a tray. They were just stirring. I put it on the dressing table and went to my mother's side of the bed to give her a cup. Daddy turned back his covers and, in his worn blue pajamas, stood up and stretched. We discussed how well we had slept, and I agreed that Mum's eyes were now roaming idly rather than searching frantically. She said she could see sunlight coming through the curtain.

Dad needed no more encouragement. He went to the window and threw open the curtains with gusto. "Good heavens," he said. "What a perfectly beautiful day. Liz darling, the daffodils are coming up." He turned and smiled at us, then looked back. "Just when the winter months start taking their toll, Mother Nature sends us bright yellow flowers to remind us to hold fast, summer's coming, all will be well."

I was just standing up to join him when he took two quick steps backward. He didn't make a sound, simply sat on the bed, one hand steadying himself against the old mattress, the other held over his heart. I caught a flash of something in his eyes, and then he dropped backward. His eyelids fluttered and closed.

The doctor told me the "flash" I had seen was his pupils dilating rapidly, common in sudden massive heart attacks such as this had been, but I knew differently. His soul was returning to the universe, to the water boatman skating on the skin of a river, but on the way it had passed through me. I like to think a little of it remained there.

My mother was exceptionally calm. She said his name once. He didn't answer, so she didn't ask again. From the dent in the mattress she found his head, resting a few inches from her left thigh, and put her hand on his forehead. There it stayed, occasionally stroking, while I sat on the other side and held his hand. How or why we knew not to run screaming to the phone, pummel his chest, breathe frantically into his mouth, I can't imagine, but we did none of those things. Later, the doctor told us that nothing would have brought him back after that attack. We knew that too. I had seen him go and my mother had felt it.

After a while I picked up Dad's legs and swiveled him around on the bed. Mum placed his head on his pillow. It was easy. He had died as he had lived, with his womenfolk's well-being in his heart. All I had to do was straighten the sheets and blankets. Only then did we speak.

"We need some breakfast," said my mother. "It's going to be a long day." She turned down my offer to help her dress, which I took as a silent request to leave them alone. I went downstairs and cooked a breakfast the English would be proud to call their own.

Outside, those early daffodils nodded gently at me.

I nodded back. Hold fast, Tessa. All will be well.

Eighteen

For Better for Worse

AFTER BREAKFAST, I WENT INTO AN ORGANIZATIONAL OVERDRIVE. I called the doctor, the vicar, the publican. It was the perfect pyramid scheme. Within half an hour, ladies with casseroles and bunches of wildflowers began to ring the doorbell. I texted my few good friends who had particularly loved my father. Ben's flowers had arrived first, just as the tide of death-related bureaucracy had threatened to engulf me. Early-spring daffodils. Hold fast, and all will be well. Their color and sweet scent had got me through the rest of the morning. I held fast. There was a note attached: *I can be there in an hour if you want me to be.*

I tried James several times, but his phone was switched off. He was fast asleep in L.A. What good would it do to wake him? I wished he was there, though.

I went back upstairs with a cup of tea for my mother. I knocked on the door to my parents' bedroom and went in. My mother sat in the armchair under the window, facing the bed. Dad was still lying there, unchanged, but I checked. My mother had drawn the curtains across the south-facing windows. The breeze made them flutter. It felt cool in the darkened room. My more macabre side might have called it refrigerated, but I was doing my utmost to keep that voice quiet. There was an open photo album in Mum's lap. "Luckily, I know them by heart," she said. "I was going over a few favorites."

I put a mug of chamomile tea beside her to cool. "Not an easy question this, but the vicar wants to know whether Dad is to be buried or cremated."

"Cremated," said Mum immediately. "I'll keep him in a jam jar."

Perhaps she wasn't dealing with this as well as I thought.

"Don't look at me like that, darling. We made the decision together. Obviously, he didn't specify the receptacle, but he loved my jam, so I think a jam jar's apt, don't you?" I hoped a reply wasn't necessary. It wasn't. Mum went on: "It's to be kept until I go. Then, and I am sorry to ask this of you, we'd quite like to be sprinkled somewhere together. Or planted with some new fruit trees." No way. I was not going to make jam out of my parents. "I didn't think you'd like the thought of that, but we do love our fruit trees."

I leaned closer to her. "Can you see me?"

"No."

"Then you're weird," I said.

She smiled. "My dear girl, I've always known what you were thinking. I used to be able to tell by the type of silence in the house whether you were being conscientious or up to no good."

I heard a car pull up outside and wondered absently who had sent flowers now. Incredible how word got out.

"Are you all right, Tessa?" asked Mum.

"I don't think I really believe this is happening." I knew my father's lifeless body lay a few feet from where I stood, but I had such a strong sense of him that the word "death" could not be put into the same sentence as his name. "I called Human Resources at work, to tell them I wouldn't be in, but I couldn't bring myself to tell them why."

"It'll take a while to sink in," said my mother.

"I don't want it to sink in."

"I know."

There was a loud knock on the front door. "Are you up for more visitors?" I asked. People had been turning up all morning. I'd not known my parents had so many friends in the area.

"Actually, I might rest now."

"Good idea. The vicar will be over later to talk about the funeral."

I ran down the stairs, expecting another lady from the village with a hot pot. It wasn't until I saw James standing on the flagstone next to the boot scraper that I knew for sure my father was dead. He dropped his bag on the ground, opened his arms, and I fell into his chest. "Daddy's dead," I mumbled.

"I know," whispered James into my hair. He kissed the top of my head. "I know."

I rested there for a while, listening to his heart, feeling his strong arms around me. "I don't understand, I thought you were going to stay in L.A. till the end," I said.

"The moment I put the phone down after speaking to you I changed my mind. I don't need to play golf to prove I'm good at my job. A very strong voice in my head was telling me to get on a plane. I have a pretty good idea whose it was now."

"I'm so glad you did. I tried to call you but the phone was switched off. I thought you were asleep."

"I was in the air," he said. "I got the last flight out by a whisper."

"You must be exhausted. Oh, James, I'm so glad you're here."

"I'm sorry it took me this long to get back."

"How did you know about Dad?"

"Bea told me."

I waited for the monster to growl and noticed, as I took James's hand and led him inside, that it didn't. Bea had called to see how my mother was doing and I'd picked up the phone. She hadn't expected me to be there, so I told her why I was. "Amber rang me in tears," I said. "At first I thought something had happened again with Bea, but she was beside herself at the thought that I no longer had a daddy. It's really freaked her out. James, you mean the world to her."

James pulled me toward him. "We still have a lot to talk about but right now my main concern is you."

I tried to speak, but he put his finger to my lips. "All I could think about on the plane home was you. I want you to know that I'm here for you. I'll make tea, run you a bath, leave you be, hold you tight. I love you, Tessa. I don't want to lose you."

I shivered.

"Come here, beautiful. You're freezing. It's probably shock."

"He was eighty-four," I said. It was not shock.

"I know, but he seemed so robust, so dependable," said James.

"I'd started to notice things, small things. His hand trembled, he was tired, he'd shrunk a bit. I know this will sound cold, but in a small way I'm happy for him. Is that weird?"

He shook his head, but I wasn't sure.

"No incontinence, no senility, never having to watch Mum . . ."

He hugged me again. "Ssh," he said. I didn't really want to ssh. I wanted to talk about all the thoughts that had flooded my head since Dad had collapsed onto the bed, but it was hard to when I was pressed against a suit jacket.

"Where's Liz?"

I pulled away. "Upstairs with Dad."

James watched me closely.

I knew the expression. I had looked at my mother in the same way. "He's staying at home until tomorrow. Mum's orders. He looks very peaceful."

"I'm so glad I'm here," said James, hugging me again. "I'll never let you go."

Standing on tiptoe in my socked feet, I found his lips, placed mine on them, and stayed there, breathing in his smell. I had lost one major ally but—and this was the bit I had yet to understand—I felt stronger than ever before.

MUM, JAMES, AND I HAD a very late ploughman's lunch at the kitchen table. Surely grief wasn't supposed to make you ravenous. We drank a soft red wine and sawed chunks of cheddar off the block they always bought from a nearby dairy. I toasted Dad, then popped a pickled onion into my mouth.

"I'd like to thank your father," said Mum to James. "That fishing trip couldn't have come at a better time."

"I . . . You are incredibly kind to say so, but—"

"But nothing. Honestly, that trip seemed to give him time to put his life's learnings in order. It was quite something."

"I thought you'd had a relapse because he wasn't here with you. Tessa was worried from the start."

"Tessa worries too much," she said. "Our biggest challenge now is going to be managing Tessa's worry about me home alone."

"Right," said James. He looked relieved he wouldn't be shouldering the blame for his father taking Dad away from Mum days before his death, thereby robbing them of their last few moments together.

"Wrong," I said, "because that isn't going to happen."

"Really?" said my mother. You could hear the steel in her voice.

"The commute isn't that bad. It focuses the mind when you know you've got a train to catch."

Mum chewed a bit of cucumber I had sliced for her.

"Surely they've given you time off," said James.

"Not indefinitely," I replied.

"I have very good friends in the village," said Mum to James. Well, in James's direction. I knew who she was talking to. Me. And I knew what she meant. Back off, Tessa, I don't need a nursemaid. "Now I feel a little tired, so I'm going upstairs for a lie-down. Will you wake me when the vicar gets here?"

"Of course."

"Should I take something up for Dad?" said my mother, then put her hand on James's shoulder and laughed. "Only kidding."

I shook my head.

"Stop shaking your head, Tessa."

"How do you know I am?"

"I told you, I know how you think."

"Ditto. And you're not getting rid of me that easily. How are you going to do all the things Dad used to do for you?"

"God, you are stubborn," said Mum, wagging a finger at me.

"Can't imagine where I get it from," I replied.

"Have a nice nap," said James merrily.

I waited until Mum had left, then, annoyed, turned to James. "You're going to have to back me up on this," I said.

"Of course I'll back you up. On what?"

Spell it out, said Dad. I pushed my plate to one side and stood up. "Fancy a walk?"

"That would be nice. I haven't walked anywhere, except inside an airport terminal, for days."

I took his arm. "Come on. We'll clear up when we get back. There's a place I want to show you."

AT THE END OF THE village, a bridle path rose up along a ridge. Another path sank low into a rocky ravine—largely ignored by the locals, since the route down was quite treacherous. I took James's hand and we navigated the tangled roots and brambles until we were on the streambed. It was like a grotto down there: the air felt different; sunshine pierced the canopy of interlocking branches overhead and danced on the wet pebbles. You could walk for hours in the water—or until your feet started to freeze.

"Perfect time of year for down here," I said. "The nettles shut the place off in the summer and you can't get through. Best thing Mum and Dad ever did was get out of London. I'm sure Mum's long stay of execution has been down to this bucolic life. At first I thought they'd go stir-crazy, but it's amazing how busy the country keeps you."

"Were you serious about commuting?" asked James.

"She can't live alone in her condition."

He shrugged. "How long do you think her eyes will stay like that?"

"They say three weeks, but an event like this could delay any improvement. I don't care what the doctors say, stress is a major player."

"She seems incredibly calm," said James.

I stopped walking. "Worrying, isn't it?"

"I don't know. You said yourself it didn't come as a shock."

"No, but I've had an old father for a long time. I haven't just lost my life partner. Mum has been with Dad since her early twenties. Her whole life was wrapped up in him. I think there's a difference."

James came back to where I stood. The icy water pressed against my boots as it flowed around my ankles. "Of course there is. And of course you have to keep an eye—sorry, bad choice of words—look after her until her sight improves."

He still wasn't reading me. I carried on walking. "But then what, James? She has MS permanently. It just hides itself. Stress is bad, so is doing too much. She may think she can go on by herself, but Dad carried a lot of the everyday burden of life. She did the sedentary things, he did everything else. Getting down on her knees to light a fire won't be easy. My worry is that she'll realize all this and then go rapidly downhill."

"She said you'd worry too much."

"Not too much." *Spell it out.* "James, I'm telling you, I can't leave her on her own."

I knew his brain was interpreting my words. It left two options. I move to Oxfordshire. She moves to London to live with . . . Hang on, we only have three bedrooms. I have three children who stay regularly, so we'll have to move to a bigger place, preferably one with a granny flat. Well, that sort of property doesn't come cheap, which means moving away from the area, the school, the girls . . . He looked at me. I waited.

"Liz should be allowed to decide what she wants to do," said James.

"Every time there's a relapse, you don't bounce back quite so high. It's gradual, so the casual observer would probably miss it. It happened with her legs, so now she needs a stick all the time, and it will happen with her eyes. My point is, I'm not sure if she's allowed to decide."

"She's a very independent woman."

"I didn't say it was going to be easy." I laid a hand on his cheek. What I had taken for a wonderfully positive nature was actually a refusal to see the ugly side of life. It was admirable, in the right circumstances, but sometimes life got ugly, and turning a blind eye wasn't just unimpressive, it was complicit. And that was exactly what he'd done when Bea had started to put on weight.

"You think I'm just saying this because your mother's illness is an inconvenience to me?"

"No." Yes. Wasn't that *exactly* what you were thinking?

"Yes, you do."

It was my turn to duck. "What worries me is that we're perfect in a bubble, James, absolutely perfect, but look what happens when it bursts. We fight. It's terrible. My mother is as important to me as your children are to you. We need to find room for everyone. Me included. I'm not like Bea. I'm not going to disappear to the bottom of the list and be grateful when you remember my birthday."

"It wasn't like that. Everything I did was for her." James was stricken. "Sorry."

"No. It's okay. But if that's true why didn't it work out?"

He ran his hands through his hair. "The one thing she wanted was to get out of her mother's financial grip. The only thing that has ever upset Bea is her mother's snobbery. I worked like a dog to give Bea her freedom, then got blamed for being away."

"You said you stayed away."

"I don't think a man can be blamed for not rushing home for the babies' bath time every night after another god-awful day in the office," he said crossly. "We're not saints. We need a moment, too, you know. And when all you get is a frosty reception, it's even harder. I'm not saying these things about your mother because it doesn't suit me that she's ill. If it was my parents, we'd be having the same conversation. I'm thinking about *her*. She *is* an independent woman. And the last thing in the world she'd want is you giving up your life to nanny her. Don't patronize her. Ask her what she wants to do."

"But—"

"But nothing. Just because I don't automatically agree with you, it doesn't mean I'm some selfish, dumb wanker who just wants an easy life."

"I'm sorry." I stood on tiptoes and kissed him.

He opened his mouth.

"No, you're right," I said, before he could speak. "I'm sorry. Mum needs our support, not me riding roughshod over her."

"Look, Tessa, I realize now that I've sometimes been too quick to abdicate responsibility, but sometimes you're too slow to. Bringing up children is easier on everyone if you don't worry about all the little details. I'd never notice if my daughters went to school wearing mismatching socks. I don't mean color. I mean pattern. And if that evokes a patronizing laugh from you, then you're right, we're probably heading to a bad place. I'm sorry, but those details go over my head."

I put my hand to my heart. "I promise not to care about mismatched socks too."

"Thank you." He pulled me toward him. "There's something else you have to do for me."

I thought he was going to suggest something smutty, since my loins were already waking to the look in his eye. But he surprised me. "You have to want to be happy," he said.

Sometimes "I love you" isn't enough. I pulled James to me and kissed his mouth. It opened and his tongue felt hot against my cold lips. I wanted more. More heat. More softness. More hardness. Leaves lay where they'd fallen the previous winter, preserved in the still, cool air under the trees. The recent sun had dried the upper layers, and when I lay down, the ground was soft under my back. James lay on top of me. I could hear the leaves crackling and breaking under my weight. I combed my fingers through his gorgeous salt-and-pepper hair and pressed his face harder to mine.

I opened my eyes and looked at the bright sky through the black silhouette of a thousand branches. Heaven, I thought. It was too cold to lie like a starfish naked on the ground, but I was pretty sure I knew another way to feel boundless. I reached down and unbuckled James's belt without taking my mouth away from his. By the feel of him, the cold wasn't going to put him off. I lifted my hips and we pulled down my jeans and pants. Not far, but far enough. We barely moved as he pushed inside me. Couldn't. The clothes stopped any large gestures. I groaned as I filled up with him, love, lust. I arched and rocked against him, slow, slight movements. We rubbed away the sadness and got lost in the incredible power you feel when you stare into the eyes of someone you love who loves you back.

My parents' relationship had begun on the bank of a river. Now so would ours. But this time it would be a real one. With ups and downs, crevasses and peaks, and somehow we would find the equipment we needed to climb out of the lows and come down safely from the highs. My whole body shuddered and I cried out. We lay there, panting, among the fallen leaves. James stroked my hair and continued to stare at me and I thought how lucky I was to know how this felt. How very lucky. And it made me cry. James brushed away the rogue tears.

"Your dad had a wonderful life," he said, smiling down at me. I put my hand to his cheek. I wasn't crying about my father. "And we'll work something out with your mum." I wasn't crying about her either. "I love you," he said. I had a sudden, terrible moment of clarity. The secret that had destroyed James's first marriage could destroy his second, since in these moments of near-bliss I would always have to ask myself, would we be here if he knew? James helped me up and with our arms wrapped around each other we made our way home. I couldn't speak. James, I am sure, believed he knew why I kept my own counsel, but, of course, he didn't. Only I knew, and that was no way to walk into marriage.

I stood for a long time on the threshold of the slightly moldy guest bathroom, catching the odd word between my mother and the vicar downstairs and listening to James slosh water over himself. Twice I walked to the top of the staircase, but stopped. Going downstairs wasn't going to make this go away, so, with a gentle knock, I turned the handle of the bathroom door and went in.

"Hey gorgeous," he said. James's knees stuck out through the bubbles, as did his chest. He was too big for the bath.

"Hey," I closed the door behind me.

"No tea?"

"The vicar's drunk it all." He smiled at me. "James, I need to talk to you."

He pointed to the loo. "Take a seat."

I pressed the heels of my hands into my eye sockets.

"What is it? What's wrong?" he asked, sitting up. I could preamble for hours, I could lay cushions all around him, but nothing would lessen the blow.

"Bea didn't have an affair."

James cocked his head to one side. "Why are we talking about her again?"

"She was never unfaithful to you, James. She didn't fall out of love with you and run off with someone else. She always loved you. She just got very, very confused for a while. I'm fairly sure it was some long-term postnatal depression, but who knows?"

He squinted at me. "Affair, one-night stand, what's the difference? I lost her long before she had the abortion . . ." He closed his eyes for a second and rubbed his forehead.

Women are not alone in thinking up scenarios that have never happened or are unlikely ever to happen. James must have tortured himself with images of his wife with another man, but he had never considered the possibility that the child had been his.

"No. I mean she never slept with another man. Ever. There was only you." My words floated over the bathroom and settled around him.

He sat in them. Motionless, for a moment. Then he looked at me again, to check that it was me, to check the words, to try to understand their meaning. He saw in my face the confirmation he wanted to shy away from. "No," he said.

"I'm sorry," I whispered. "It's been killing her ever since."

"How do you know this?"

"Women talk."

"Faith? She knew and didn't—"

"No, James. Bea told me. Here. The night I caught her trying to steal the sherry."

"What?"

I hadn't got around to telling him that bit. So much had happened. "You've always told me your wife left you because she didn't love you anymore. I don't think that's true. But you need to hear it from her."

"Why are you telling me this now?"

I looked at him sitting in the bath, hugging his knees, his hair swept back off his high forehead. "Because I love you." His face creased, and I stood up. "I'll give you a moment," I said, and closed the door behind me.

JAMES WAS DRESSED, CLEAN-SHAVEN, AND smelling of limes when he walked into the sitting room. I put down the book I was pretending to read.

"Thank you," he said. "That couldn't have been easy."

I smiled at him. "It's not supposed to be easy."

He brushed an imaginary bit of fluff off his nose. "Amazing how one piece of information can make sense of so much chaos."

"You need to see her," I said.

"What about you?"

"You can't do anything here."

"But Tessa—"

I didn't want him to beg me to let him stay, because I'd give in too easily. Today I felt I had my father's support. Tomorrow I might not. I was really trying to do the right thing here. But it wasn't easy.

"You think the eating and drinking hinge on her mother," I said. "I'm not so sure. She needs to get better for everybody's sake, and she can't do that without your forgiveness."

He swallowed. Maybe it was too soon to ask him to forgive. I reached up and took his hand. I could see the muscle in his jaw and squeezed hard.

"Was I such a bad husband?"

I didn't try to answer. "I know you want to stay here for me, but I think you should go." There was a lump in my throat.

"Your dad taught you how to slay the dragon, didn't he?"

"Yes he did," I answered. "I was very lucky."

"Tessa King, you're an amazing woman."

"Am I?"

"Yes."

"Then come back to me."

"I will."

I walked him to the front door. We kissed good-bye and I felt sadness well up inside me.

He held me hard, his chin resting on my head. "One day we'll laugh about all of this," he said.

"I sure hope so."

"We will."

"Go, before I start crying."

"Too late," he said, wiping away a tear. He held my face in his hands and kissed me again. "I love you so much," he said.

"I know," I said sadly. I knew, too, that James had always loved Bea. Back in another time. But I had thrown open the doorway to the past, and now that time was here again. Loving me might not be enough.

My mother joined me as I waved him off. "I know it's a cliché but sometimes you have to love people enough to let them go."

I put my head on her shoulder. "And hope they love you enough to come back?"

"Yes."

"High risk," I said.

"Most things worth fighting for are."

It was then that the tears came. Tears for my father, for my mother, for James and Bea and the son they might have had, and for myself. And when I had finished, I sat down to wait.

Nineteen

Reentry

I DROVE PAST THE BAR THREE TIMES BEFORE I PLUCKED UP THE COURage to park. I sat quietly behind the steering wheel and counted to ten. My grand total is a hundred and seventy. But it never seems so desperate in factors of ten.

My heart ceased its war cry and settled into an even flutter. I slipped two pound coins into the meter. I couldn't envisage staying for more than an hour. My heels clicked on the paving slabs. It had only been a few weeks, but I had traveled so far since I had met them last. I wondered if they would see it. Did I want them to? I looked down at my feet. The heels said a lot. I was wearing them, but it would take a discerning eye to notice I was not as steady on them as I seemed.

"Bea! Over here." Carmen rose from her chair. "What do you want?"

"I'll go to the bar. Anybody want anything?"

She hugged me. "My God, you've shrunk."

"Wow, Bea," said Angie. "You've lost masses of weight."

"Have I?"

"Come, you, you must know," said our resident fitness queen, Lee.

In all the commotion of these last days, I had forgotten to weigh myself. "I threw away the scales. They were driving me mad." Stick close to the truth and you may get away with the lie.

"Well, you look fabulous. Congratulations," said Carmen. "Sit down, Bea, it's my round. What do you want?"

I looked nervously around the table. Lee had a glass of red wine. Angie had vodka and tonic. Holly, too. Carmen was on champagne. I took a deep breath. "Lime and soda, please."

"With a chaser on the side?" asked Carmen, smiling.

"I'm driving," I said.

"One won't hurt," she said.

I didn't reply.

"I'll have another. I've been looking forward to this all day," said Angie.

"Whoever made this plan is brilliant. We miss supper and bath time and you get to sneak out of work early," said Holly. "Everybody gains."

"You sure you don't want a proper drink?" asked Carmen, backing toward the bar.

"Sure," I said.

"No wonder you've lost so much weight. That's the trouble with my diet. I can't survive without a drink at the end of the day," said Angie. "Honestly, I'd rather skip supper."

"Me too," said Holly. "I envy your willpower."

I smiled politely. "So, how's everyone been?"

"Great," said Lee. "It's lovely having the kids at home."

"Yeah, really good," said Holly.

"I find the holidays a bit hard," said Angie, "but they're all so social now, they don't seem to mind me going to work as much as they did when they were younger. We're off to Sardinia for the last week of the holidays, so they're not too fed up with me. What about you, Bea?"

"Jimmy's parents have the girls at the moment. I needed a bit of time to sort a few things out."

"Like?"

"Oh, you know, the house ..." I scraped the barrel and came up empty. The women nodded sympathetically, but I wasn't sure what they thought they were nodding about. It was a non sequitur. So I filled the gap. "Jimmy's getting married."

"What?"

"Shit! Carmen get back here," hollered Angie. "Jimmy's getting married."

Carmen came over with a tray of drinks. "I don't believe it. Since when?"

"How old is she?"

"How long has he known her?"

I held up my hands. Carmen sat down and passed around the drinks. "Are you okay?"

I nodded.

They exchanged a look.

"Is she pregnant?"

I laughed, remembering my own reaction to Jimmy's news. The same assumptions. The same prejudices. Do all second wives walk into such a lion's den? "Actually, she's a pretty spectacular girl," I said. Truthfully.

My words were misinterpreted. I hadn't thought I'd sounded sarcastic.

"All tits and arse and tight—"

"Carmen!" Lee hit her.

"Sorry."

"No, I mean it. She's a bright, nice-looking, insightful, generous person."

"Well, Jimmy always had good taste in women," said Angie, touching my shoulder. "I just never thought he was over you."

"He follows you around like a puppy," said Holly, agreeing.

"We've always thought it a little unfair that your ex-husband paid you more attention than our husbands paid us," said Lee.

"Speak for yourself! My husband pays me plenty," said Carmen.

We pretended to block our ears. Carmen was prone to going into detail.

"'Least we understand the diet now. To be honest, we were getting a little worried about you," said Angie.

"You were?"

"Well, you haven't been yourself recently."

"Yourself" meaning the silent suffering mistress of school scrunchies or the "yourself" that predated that? The fun, happy, sexy woman I was before child rearing ate me alive? The former, of course. They'd never known the latter. I was the woman who'd scoop up their children at a moment's notice when they couldn't get out of work or their nannies were held up. I was the woman who ferried their children to and from parties, because I had nothing better to do. I was the woman who could be called upon to organize outings, fairs, shows, picnics, sports days . . . Maybe it was no bad thing not to be that "yourself" anymore.

"Hey, Bea, what's wrong?" Carmen leaned forward and took my hand.

It was only then that I realized my cheeks were wet. "Sorry," I said.

"What on earth are you apologizing for?"

I brushed the next tear away, but I'd sprung a leak. I laughed stupidly. A self-deprecating titter wasn't going to nullify the fact that I was sitting in a bar with tears streaming down my face at five-thirty in the afternoon.

"Let me get you a proper drink," said Angie.

"No!" I yelled. They froze. "Oh, to hell with it! I'm sorry, I seem to be in the grip of a nervous breakdown." It was meant to sound funny, but it didn't. I brushed aside another fast-rolling tear. "And, yes, I'd love a drink. I'd love one more than Carmen would love the latest Balenciaga bag. But I can't. Because when I do, I can't stop."

I watched the women I had called my friends take the audio equivalent of a double take. Yes. You heard right. I have a problem with drink. I had thought they were my lifeline. In fact, they were just a bunch of women with children the same age at the same school. They didn't know me at all. It wasn't their fault. What had I given them to go on? Nothing but an overriding need to bend over backward. Yes, I had been taken advantage of, but only because I'd let them. *If I help you enough, maybe you'll ask me to stay.*

Lee was the first to move. She leaned over the table and took my hand. "Oh, Bea, you poor thing."

"Brilliant diet . . . black coffee and booze."

She stared at my hand, rubbing it gently with her thumb.

"Fucking stupid, eh?"

"No more stupid than ruining your insides with laxative abuse," she said.

I blinked, not understanding. "You? But you're so healthy and fit."

"On the outside. But if I go near an egg, it's home-enema time for me. I've completely buggered my intestines. That's why I'm so conscious about what I eat. Trust me, I understand black coffee and booze. I was in college in the States at the time and had no money. Laxatives were cheaper."

"So, what are you going to do? Cut down?" asked Angie.

I shook my head. "Cut it out completely. It's not just a couple too many and I pass out. I become angry and mean, and poor Amber gets the brunt of it. I can't risk it. She's been through enough."

"Oh, sweetie," said Carmen, "why didn't you tell us?"

"Not an easy thing to tell, right?" said Lee, answering for me.

"When did it all start?" asked Angie.

"Good question," I said. "A long time ago, except it wasn't drink in the beginning."

Four faces frowned at me.

"It was food. I used to binge. Nothing like a refined-sugar high to get you through another lonely night."

Holly shook her head. "And there was I, always thinking how incredibly sorted you were."

"Sorry to disappoint."

"You kidding? It's a relief."

"Yeah. Superwoman makes everyone else feel like shit," said Angie.

"Me—Superwoman? You're the one who holds down an amazing job, brings up three kids, is still married, and somehow manages to make school concerts."

"I have a secret twin," said Angie. "She's called Chronic Exhaustion. My husband calls her Stroppy Bitch for short."

"It's weird," said Holly. "I've sometimes envied you your situation, time off every other weekend. Free to bring up children without interference."

"Or support," I pointed out.

"Take off the rose-tinted spectacles, sweetie. We all do it single-handedly," said Carmen. "Sure, the men swan in for a kiss and a story, if you're lucky, but the hard graft is down to us."

"It's true," said Angie. "Rob and I both work, but when I get home, I do supper, homework, bath, and bed. Rob opens a beer and puts on the telly. I organize the shopping, the holidays, the weekends, our evenings out . . . Everything. Drives me mad."

"And then they start coming home late . . ." said Carmen, and picked up her glass. "And you wonder, did it all count for nothing?"

There was a lengthy pause.

"But your husband's amazing," said Lee. "You guys are always so happy."

I watched disbelief pass across Carmen's face. "That's what I thought." She was silent for a time. "Oh, shit, there's a young woman at his work . . . I don't know but I don't think anything's happened yet. I've no proof he even likes her." She stuck her fingers into her solar plexus. "Except in here. I feel sick. He's pulling away from me and nothing I do seems to stop it."

"Oh, Carmen, it'll be okay. You've just got to hang on in there," said Holly. "We all go through tough times. Alex and I went for counseling after our third was born, because I was so resentful."

"And?"

"We're still together."

"Talk to him," I said.

"I feel so stupid, though. I hate feeling so insecure."

"Tough. Make him realize what he's jeopardizing," I said. "Make him understand that you need him. I'm not the only Superwoman at this table. We all do it—pretend we can take everything on the chin. Bring it on—what else can you throw at me? We all say men need to be needed, as if it's something pathetic, but you know what? Why aren't we allowed to need a man? What's so wrong with that? Isn't that what a partnership is? My advice, go on holiday. Immediately. Just the two of you. He loves you. If his head's been turned, turn it back."

"Sorry, Bea, I didn't mean to commandeer the conversation."

"Angie's right," said Lee, "it's a relief to hear your perfect marriage is just like everyone else's."

"Well, fuck it," said Holly. "While we're on the subject, my eldest daughter and I haven't managed a civil word to one another since the beginning of the year. She hates me."

"But you said you were having a great holiday," I said, perplexed.

"I lied," she replied unapologetically. "It's been hell."

I STAYED LONGER THAN AN hour, forgot about the meter, and got a ticket. But it didn't matter, because for the cheap price of fifty pounds I had discovered something priceless. Those women were great, and I was lucky to call them friends. I offered to drive Lee and Carmen home. It was out of my way but they both accepted. They were using me, and that was okay. A little weakness went a long way. It made us each feel stronger, and a strong team was what you needed around you when you were shaky and unsure. We discussed Holly's daughter, Carmen's husband's crush, imagined or otherwise, and, to lighten the atmosphere, we dissected Lee's sluggish bowels. We shared our insecurities and felt more secure for it.

I dropped Lee home first. She got out, then tapped on the window. I opened it. "Joking aside," she said, "it took me a long time to stop taking laxatives. I tried and failed many times before I succeeded . . . You'll probably think this is too American, but therapy helped." She reached through the open window and took my arm. "I'm just saying, you fall off the wagon, you darn well tell us, Bea."

"And if you go anywhere near a laxative?"

"I'll tell you."

"Deal," I said. Carmen and I waved and I pulled out into the traffic.

"I feel better after two hours' chatting to you lot than I have in ages," said Carmen.

"Ditto."

"I've been driving myself mad about that woman in the office."

"Easy to do," I said.

"Why don't you come to mine? I think I've got some virgin piña-colada mix. We can pretend, and if you want, you can tell me why you started binge-eating in the first place."

"It's quite a story."

"Don't worry, sweetie," she smiled, "it's enlightened self-interest. I've got one for you."

I glanced briefly at Carmen, then peered through the windshield. For the first time in ages I could see the road ahead. It was then that it dawned on me that a spiral goes both ways.

WHEN I GOT HOME, I called Honor and arranged to collect my children the following day. Amber was visiting Caspar, but I expected her home soon. I could do soup and sobriety in the pleasure of my own company, but it wasn't my life. It wasn't real. I had to battle with Lulu over reading, then stay sober . . . That was the test. I had to hear about bridesmaids' dresses and not sink my teeth into a Bakewell tart. I had to see a baby boy in the park and not want to swallow a razor blade. It helped to know I had friends I could call, but maybe Lee was right. Maybe professional help would be better. I thought about looking up Alcoholics Anonymous in the Yellow Pages, then decided to put on a load of washing first.

I had just gathered up the contents of the laundry box when I heard a knock at the front door. "Use your key!" I yelled. I came downstairs with an assortment of dirty clothes, peered through the glass, then yanked open the door. "Jimmy! What are you doing here?"

"Hi, Bea."

"The girls aren't in."

"Actually, I came to see you," he said. "Can I help you with that?" He reached out to take some of the clothes, but the disturbance upset the critical mass and they tumbled about my feet.

"Sorry. Made more work for you, as usual."

We both crouched down. My knee touched his. He was very close. I gathered up the tank tops, socks, shirts, and pants, suddenly nervous.

"I'm afraid I haven't got much to offer you except herbal tea."

"Herbal tea is perfect."

We walked through to the kitchen, me in the lead, Jimmy following, as we had done countless times before. On his territory, he always let me go first too, and I wondered why I hadn't let myself see that all he had ever done was try to put me first.

I racked my brain to work out why he was here. "I thought you'd be with Tessa at Liz's," I said, stuffing the dirty laundry into the machine, irrespective of color or creed.

"I was," he said, pulling out a pine chair.

"Oh." I filled the kettle with London's finest. "How are they coping?"

"A bit too soon to say. Tessa's main concern is where Liz is going to live now. She wants to be with her mother."

"In the country?" I turned off the tap.

Jimmy shrugged.

"Are you moving to the country, Jimmy? Is that why you're here?" I could feel my voice rising in panic. I didn't want to be any more of a single parent than I already was. He let me down often and, yes, he did make more work for me, but the girls knew he was around the corner if they needed him. Jimmy was closer to his children than many of the other fathers I knew. He was a regular in their lives, not a visitor. I didn't want him to become one. "Because that does concern us."

"I know, Bea. I don't know where to start. Could you sit down, please?" I realized I was waving a full kettle in the air. I plugged it in and switched it on. Then I sat down. "What is it? What's going on?"

Jimmy reached out and took my hand. He held it gently, his thumb resting between the knuckles of my fore and index fingers. He closed his eyes.

Please don't tell me you're dying. Please. Please, God, don't tell me that. Don't.

"Tessa told me about the baby."

I snatched my hand away, repelled by the soft human contact. He took it again, firmer, and held it. "It's okay," he said. "You did nothing wrong."

I snorted. "No. There's nothing wrong in murdering a perfectly healthy child because you couldn't face a few more fucking pounds. Well, the pounds came anyway, so he died for nothing."

I wouldn't have been surprised if he'd slapped me. I had spat the words out with the sneering anger I'd heard in Amber's voice many times, and hated its ugliness. I tried to pull away but he held on to my hand. I was shocked. I thought I was feeling better, but the poisonous anger hadn't gone very far.

"I didn't mean it like that. I meant you did nothing wrong in the circumstances. Bea, I'm not surprised that the thought of another baby sent you over the edge. You were right, it was too much, we couldn't afford another, and if I'd had an eye on you we would probably have come to that conclusion together. I was in the wrong, Bea. Not you."

"You wouldn't have recommended we get rid of it," I said. Jimmy was too soft for that. "Not in a million years."

"You're wrong, Bea. Another child meant being even more beholden to your damn mother, which I have always resented," he said. "Somehow I think I blamed you for that."

"Me? I'm the one who hated it."

"I know. But you had the heart to put your pride and ego aside and do what was best for our children, knowing you'd be made to pay over and over again." He stood up and went to the cupboard above the kettle.

I had forgotten about my offer of herbal tea. I let him take over.

"I took my injured pride and decided to act all self-important and convince myself that my job was bigger, harder, and more of a self-sacrifice than yours," said Jimmy, throwing tea bags into mugs. "If I was half the person you are, I would have suggested I stay at home and you go back to work. At least we'd have had a chance then. Remember the offer from the *FT*?"

I tried not to.

"I knew I was doing it, too. I drove you to this." He put the kettle down without pouring the water. When he turned to look at me, there were tears in his eyes. "If there's blood on anyone's hands, it's mine."

I stood up and went to him. "No, Jimmy," I said, putting my arms around him. "No."

He leaned into my embrace, but he wouldn't be swayed. "You've always protected me, haven't you? But this *was* my fault, not yours." I could hear his heartbeat. It matched my own. He brushed a hand over my hair. "No wonder you hated me," he whispered.

"I never hated you."

"Yes, you did." He searched my face. "You couldn't even look at me. And I understand why. I'm just so sorry I pushed you into that lonely place."

"But I was determined to stay there. However much you loved me, I wouldn't let it be enough. I didn't deserve anyone's love after what I'd done."

"That's your mother talking, and it isn't true. You are loved, by everyone who knows you. The only sad thing is you don't realize it."

I wanted to stay there and listen to the reassuring thump of his heart forever. Perhaps it could beat for both of us. Because mine was broken.

"They say that the fetus might be able to feel pain—" My voice was strangled. I started to cry.

"Oh, my darling, no one knows that."

"But I read—"

"It wouldn't be allowed if that was the case."

"They're trying to change it."

"Who? The *Daily Mail*? Religious fanatics? We didn't want four children. My regret isn't that we didn't have the child, it's that we didn't make the decision instantly and save you from all this unnecessary pain. The guilt is mine now. You did nothing wrong."

"I'm sorry I didn't tell you."

"I'm devastated I didn't let you. There are so many things I'd change if I could."

"Me too," I replied. We stood holding each other against the cheap kitchen cabinets for a long time, my cheek resting against his chest, his arms encircling me. I felt safe. "I didn't know it was a boy until afterward," I said.

"What difference would it have made, Bea?"

"You always wanted one."

"I haven't wanted a boy since the second the doctor handed Maddy to me. I'm ecstatic with what I've got. Our girls are perfect dragon-slayers in the making, which is mostly thanks to you, since my input has been negligible."

"Dragon-slayers?"

"I'll explain another time."

"Your input is vital, Jimmy. Jesus, why do you think I feel so guilty about walking out on you? On top of everything else, you're the first and most important relationship our girls will have with a man. I'll happily do all the ironing if you hold Lulu's hand and tell her she's brilliant and study Maddy's drawings as closely as you would a van Gogh. And I'll cook a million fish fingers if you promise to spend time with them that doesn't equate to that strange combination of spoiling them and neglecting them."

He held me away from him. "I'm not going to do that anymore."

"I'm not saying it's easy to be a part-time father. In fact, it must be one of the hardest things in the world. Of course you want to spoil them when you haven't seen them for days, but I know for a fact that the girls would rather you do join-the-dots with them than take them somewhere exciting."

"Tessa said much the same thing."

Tessa. The bubble popped and I withdrew my arms from around my former husband. I poured water onto the waiting tea bags and sat down again at the kitchen table. "I did wonder about the clean uniforms that came back those Sundays."

"All Tessa."

"Does she know you're here?" I asked. I wasn't shit-stirring. I genuinely didn't want to think Jimmy was sneaking off behind her back after everything she'd done for me. I wanted to win, but I wanted it to be a clean fight. Jimmy looked at me. Isn't it funny how sometimes you can scream silently in your head at your partner and they don't sense even a tremble, yet at other times the tiniest murmur of a thought and a ticker tape appears across their forehead, sending you a "receiving loud and clear" message?

"I see," I said. This had been Tessa's idea. "She didn't throw you out, did she?"

"No, it was all very gently done. She asked me to work it out, once and for all. I have fallen in love with her, Bea, but she made me realize that if I don't change, she and I are heading down the same path. I couldn't have been more in love with you, yet it went wrong, and that scares the shit out of me. I thought about everything she said, putting my head in the sand, switching off, taking criticism as a personal attack, refusing to see that I'm biased toward Amber, and, frankly, doing the bare minimum with the younger two and expecting applause every time." He looked out over the garden. "We went on a long walk and talked it through." He closed his eyes briefly, remembering something I wasn't part of. "I swore to her I'd change. And I will. As of today."

I was grateful he was looking away, afraid he'd see the hurt in my face. He hadn't been able to make these changes for me. Yet it was all I'd ever asked for. I had to be very brave now. And brave for a long time afterward.

"I know that Tessa is concerned because of how she and I deal with our children. It's the only thing we've ever argued about."

I swallowed hard. This was the bit I feared most. "What about Tessa having some of her own? Does she want kids?"

"I'm fairly sure she does."

"You haven't talked about it?" I asked, surprised.

Jimmy faced me. Then he shook his head. "It probably won't come as a surprise to you that I've sort of ducked the subject."

"Do *you* want more?" I asked. I waited for his reply. It took a minute.

"Can't say I'm longing for them, no."

"Have you told her?"

"I think she's afraid to ask."

"Jimmy!"

"I know." He ran his hands through his hair. "I like where we're at with our girls. Let's be honest, the baby years weren't a barrel of laughs, were they? Do I want to go back there, now, at my age?"

"You loved it when Amber was a baby," I insisted, coming to our children's defense, Tessa's defense.

Jimmy nodded. "But then I had no idea what lay ahead. We were young, I wasn't working, and, of course, I knew her so well."

"You have to know them all."

"I physically wasn't able to."

"You don't have to be physically there, Jimmy. You have to be mentally there. That's what I'm telling you. You have to *want* to be there, or she's right, it will happen again. Jimmy, you have to tell her or you've lost her anyway."

"How can I say, 'It's okay for me to have kids but, sorry, do you mind if you don't?'"

I placed my hands on the table, wanting to make my point. "Maybe she doesn't want them. Maybe you're assuming too much."

"What woman in her late thirties doesn't want kids?"

"I don't know. By the end of your thirties you might have seen enough to know it's not all gurgles and talcum powder. She has quite enough kids in her life as it is, what with Cora and Caspar and whatever the rest are called. Either way, you have to tell her."

"It was tough, wasn't it, having them so close?" he said.

"My perineum has never been the same," I replied.

Jimmy laughed, but seconds later he was serious again. "It's funny talking to you two. You both keep defending the other when I expect the opposite to happen."

"What do you mean?"

"Tessa told me that if I could change for her, shouldn't I be prepared to change for the mother of my children? The truth is, I'm here because of her, Bea." He reached over and took my hand. "But I'm glad I am."

I blinked at him, unable to gauge the fathoms below me. Had she told him I wanted him back? Or did I have to do that for myself? It was possible he was just clearing the air so that he could go back and tell her, "Job done." Or maybe he was finished with the lot of us, and a bachelor life was what he sought. Women were complicated, there was no denying it, and he had quite a few in his life. "What are you saying?" I asked. The time for second-guessing was over.

Jimmy rubbed his face. "I don't want to get this wrong again, Bea. I don't want to mess up your life, Tessa's life, or, God forbid, the girls' lives, and I don't want to fuck up mine either. I don't want to regret doing or not doing something. I don't want to fix something that should have been left alone and I don't want to leave something alone that should have been fixed. None of this is Tessa's or the girls' fault. The responsibility is ours and we need to sort it out."

I sensed a waver. Could it be he still loved me? If I could use the children, our history, as bait, and reel him in. But what about the person who'd returned him to my table? What did I owe her?

"You know she loves you very much, don't you?" I blurted out before I changed my mind.

"Yes, I do. It hurt leaving her, Bea. It hurt watching her try to do the right thing. This is a fucking nightmare, but I've always told Tessa I loved you and you left me and that broke my heart." He flattened his hand on his chest. "I can't look her in the eye now and tell her I never loved you."

I waited for him to put me back in the past. But he didn't. He just stood there, his hand on his heart, searching my face. My throat tightened. I could feel the tears coming again. Were there still more? "I'm so sorry I left you, Jimmy. I'm so sorry I took the kids away from you."

"Don't cry, Bea, please." He came and knelt at my feet. "In a weird way it might have been for the best."

I wiped away the tears with my palms.

"Our divorce gave me our children back. Because you weren't there doing everything, I had to focus on them. I do know them now and, I tell you, every other weekend isn't fucking close to being enough. I hate having to get to know them all over again every two weeks. Tessa may think I do the bare minimum with the little ones, but we have fun together. We make each other laugh. But, God, their lives move quickly. I spend a weekend talking to Maddy about one girl, and two weeks later it's a completely different name. I think Tessa might be right about Lulu. She might need to see a specialist about her letters and numbers."

I wiped my nose on my sleeve. "Actually, I think I might have worked that out. It was something she said to Liz. Lulu is a lot slower than the other two. Particularly Amber. Because I'm always on my own with them, she has to hurry up all the time. It's not like you can make supper while I do reading. She makes mistakes because she's trying to work at my pace rather than me letting her work at hers. And it's not just work. It's walking, biking, playing . . . She moves in a slower orbit, with her head in the clouds. I need to find more time for her or at least let her continue at her own pace."

"No more 'I,' please. We're in this together. They are our children, our responsibility, whether we live with one another or not."

Live with one another. Or not.

Jimmy took my hands again. "I forced myself to get over you. I told myself my wife had died. I learned to live with the woman who looked and sounded like her but wasn't her, because she didn't love me anymore."

I wanted to tell him I'd never stopped loving him. But that wasn't true. I hadn't loved him. For a long time, I hadn't even liked him. I had fallen out of love with him. Then fallen back. Harder. But the damage had been done by then. I bit my lip. I wanted to hurt myself as much as I'd hurt him. I tasted blood. But it didn't come close.

"So, I suppose what I'm asking is, are you really back from the dead, Bea?"

I stared at his hands, then looked into his eyes. "If I were, would you come home?"

Jimmy chewed the inside of his cheek.

I heard the key in the lock and withdrew my hand. "Amber!" I exclaimed. Jimmy stood up. Shit. I peered down the hall and saw our daughter dump her coat on the floor at the bottom of the stairs.

"Hi, Mum!"

"Someone's here to see you," I said, feeling as if I'd been caught doing something naughty.

She frowned.

"Daddy."

"Daddy!" she yelled, and ran down the hallway. She flew into his arms and was immediately firing questions at him, ten to the dozen. "When did you get back? Did you find that Juicy Fruit lip gloss? Have you seen Tessa? Is Liz okay?" Without waiting for him to answer, she kissed his cheek. "I've got so much to tell you. First"—she blushed—"I've got a boyfriend."

Jimmy pretended to be surprised.

"You knew?"

"Well, a little bird told me."

Amber smiled, then glanced at me and rolled her eyes. "Tessa. She's such a gossip." She cackled happily. Suddenly, she stopped and looked seriously at her father. "We're going to have to look after her and Liz now. Tessa likes to pretend she's brave all the time, but she isn't. No one is. Isn't that right, Mum?"

Jimmy and I caught each other's eye. The divorce had given Jimmy his children back, but I owed that most precious gift to Tessa. Like Jimmy, I didn't want to get this wrong. Can you really come back from the dead? Or was a little exorcism required? Was reentry as dangerous as the flight out had been? How many times could you ask children to adapt? Was I prepared to make someone else pay for my mistakes? Could we live with that? But if we could, I knew we'd be happier than we'd ever been. Well, I would. Amber yawned. "Mummy, can you put me to bed?"

I was taken aback. Amber, so keen to be a grown-up, was asking to be put to bed, like a child. Perhaps she'd seen a little too much of the adult world recently and had decided she liked it where she was, for the time being.

"Of course, darling," I said, and took her hand. She kissed her father good night and pulled me out of the room.

"I've got something to tell you," she whispered, then grinned.

I smiled back. She didn't have to tell me anything. My daughter had been kissed. Properly. That was why she wanted me to put her to bed: so she could tell me. Not Jimmy. Not Tessa. Tonight she wanted me. Her mum. These occasions would become more rare. She was growing up fast. I wrapped my arm around her and squeezed. She giggled. I had to pay attention. I had to know when it was my turn and not miss it, because childhood doesn't come twice. I turned back to Jimmy. He was watching us. Then again, neither does life. But love? Husbands? Chances? We had a lot still to talk about.

"Will you stay?" I mouthed.

"I'd like that."

Twenty

Boundless

"You did the right thing," said my mother, stroking my hair as she had been doing for the last twenty minutes.

"Then why do I feel so terrible?"

"You get the payoff later."

"When?"

"When Saint Peter lets you into heaven," said my mother.

I opened my eyes, checked she was smiling, and closed them again. "You have a warped sense of humor."

"Your father is still upstairs in our bed. I must have."

"So when do I get this payoff? I'm nearly forty . . . You know the statistics. More likely to be killed by a terrorist and all that jazz."

"It's rubbish, a male conspiracy to make sure we conform and remain ever-grateful. You don't want to keep a man from his children just to overturn statistics. And ill-gotten goods are light in the hand. You'd find a way to ruin it even if you didn't realize you were."

"What do you think he'll do?" I asked my wise witch of a mother.

"The right thing."

"Which is?"

"I don't know."

I finally sat up. "*Now* your third eye lets you down?"

My mother didn't say anything for a while. "Do you know what's possible?"

"Go on."

"It's possible that all you're doing is deflecting your grief over your father's death onto James. It's easier to be sad about a man who might come back than a man who never will. I think you did the right thing, because knowing about the abortion when James didn't was too much baggage to carry. Still, telling him is one thing, pushing him away is another. You're allowed to love him too, you know. It's not like you broke them up. They did that to one another and when you met him he was single. You're allowed to stake your claim."

"But we don't have children, and children need their parents. Isn't that what we're told every day on the news?"

"In a perfect world, maybe, yes, children need two parents, but not necessarily at the same time. Amber, Lulu, and Maddy might get lucky. If Bea sorts herself out, they might get more than two parents. They might get two families, each one providing something that the other doesn't. One with a little more space, one with the safety of boundaries, one with a little more independence, one with a little more unity. Best of both worlds. As long as no one falls between the two stools, as it were, I think it's a pretty good model. Divorce can be the best thing for a child. And I, for one, am very proud of how you've dealt with your part in this. Just think, you might get to be that very rare thing." My mother paused. "A good stepmother."

Right then, I didn't think I'd get that chance. "I don't think he's coming back, Mum," I said. If I was brutally honest with myself, I'd have to admit I was still a little shocked that he'd left. I'd thought he would stick to his long-held watertight argument that the past was the past and the future was ours. But it seemed that the bucket had been leaking all along, and now, when I held it up to the light, I could see the hairline cracks I'd allowed myself to believe weren't there.

It was when I'd sneaked downstairs in the middle of the night at James's flat and made myself watch their wedding video that I'd first noticed I was standing in a puddle. There are weddings and then there are weddings. In some you know that the couple have the secret ingredient that gives them the chance of making it, and others feel empty from the start. I would have liked to be at Jimmy and Bea's wedding. I could tell it had been a good one. I would have got very pissed and danced with gusto to "Come On, Eileen" and ended up snogging one of the ushers. The only strange thing about the video was how few people I recognized in it. Apart from family, I hadn't met any of their friends.

"Whatever happens, Tessa, you've already proved that you'd be a good stepmother and they'd be lucky to have you, all of them, Bea almost more so than the children."

A mother talking. I thanked her silently for her unrelenting support but was fairly sure that if anyone was going to fight my corner in my absence, it wasn't going to be Bea. Bea wanted Jimmy back, not only for herself but for her children, and wasn't it plain to me how forceful a mother's love was? Hadn't I benefited from it all my life? I think Bea had come grudgingly to like me, but that didn't mean she was going to throw the game.

I sighed and got off the sofa. "How are you feeling?" I asked.

"Pretty good, considering."

I understood that.

"But, then, I'm not quite sure he's left us yet," said my mother.

I understood that, too.

I WAS MAKING COFFEE THE following morning in a bid to wake up after another sleepless night when I heard a car horn honk outside. My heart leaped into my throat. But it wasn't James. It was my old friend Ben and his wife, Sasha. I put down the tools and went outside.

Ben wrapped his arms around me. "Thought you might like some decent pastries," he said. Sasha held up a bag from Paul, the French patisserie.

"City snob," I said.

He mock-shuddered at the rural air polluting his lungs. Sasha came up and took my arm. "How are you?"

"Much, much better for seeing you two."

"And your mum?"

"Come and see her. She's being amazing. As ever."

"How's her eyesight?" asked Ben.

"Hard to tell, but perhaps improving slowly. The eyeballs roam slightly—don't be put off. She's still in bed but she'd love to see you. Dad's there too."

"Huh?"

"Mum said she wasn't ready for a night alone."

Sasha and Ben glanced at each other. "He obviously didn't snore," said Sasha, who clearly loved nothing better than a night without her husband farting and snoring next to her. I had shared many a bed, though not in that way, with Ben, and I was aware that he could elevate duvets. Heavy-togged ones at that.

"Well, not now, certainly." Graveyard humor, I know, but we laughed. "Don't worry about Dad. You get used to it pretty quickly."

"How long's she keeping him here?"

"The undertakers are coming any minute. It's okay, my strongest sense of him isn't up there anyway. It's in the sitting room, just in front of the fire."

"He was always prodding that thing," said Ben, who knew my parents better than his own. "Do you think she'll mind if I go up?"

"I don't think she'd mind if you went and talked to her in the bath." I squeezed his arm. "I'll bring up some coffee."

"Let me help you," said Sasha.

Ben went upstairs, knocked gently on the door, and opened it.

"Hi, Lizzie," I heard him say.

"Ben!" my mother exclaimed. "You absolute angel! Thank you for coming."

I smiled at Sasha. Mum didn't have to see Ben: she would have known his voice anywhere. Our "family" were coming to her side, and I knew then that we would be all right. There was safety in numbers, whether it was blood or water or something in between.

BEN AND SASHA STAYED THE night. It was a godsend for me to have them there, because it kept my mother and me from slipping into long, gloomy discussions about the future. Instead we buried ourselves in memories of the past, which Sasha, bless her, pretended to be interested in. The time when Dad had decided to build a chicken house . . . The time when Dad and I had gone backpacking . . . The time when Dad had taken me to school in his scout's outfit . . . etc., etc. I even forgot to listen for the phone. Briefly, anyway.

Leaving Mum to have an afternoon nap, we went out for a walk along the bridle path. I took the high road; I didn't want to see the light dancing on the water. I left it alone along with the memory of what had happened between James and me. I must love him, I thought, if I had it in me to risk losing him. Of course I told Ben and Sasha everything that had happened. For the large part they remained silent while I spoke about the breakdown of James's first marriage, Bea's collapse after the abortion, and the false pretenses under which they had divorced.

"No one tells you how hard it's going to be," said Sasha.

"My dad did, before he died. He wanted me to know exactly how hard it is."

"But if everyone knew, no one would ever get married," said Ben. "Maybe he scared you too much."

"I was always scared," I said. I had been given a generous insight into life on the other side of the fence by my friends, and I knew that to reach a rose you had to bypass thorns.

"It's a bit like democracy," said Ben. "It's not perfect, by any stretch of the imagination, but it's better than the alternatives. And until someone comes up with something else—"

"I could happily live in a women's commune," said Sasha.

"I've always rather fancied the idea of you in a habit," said Ben.

"I didn't mean abstinence. Men would have visiting rights," said Sasha, "but when their work was done, they'd be sent away again and we could all get a good night's sleep."

Ben didn't seem remotely put out by the idea of being sent away. In fact, he started whistling "Climb Ev'ry Mountain." Sasha pushed him. He grabbed her hand and kissed it. It was nice to see. Made me feel happy and sad at the same time. I had come so close, but it had somehow slipped away from me. Well, I thought stoically, it would make it that much easier to take care of my mother if I didn't have to justify it to another half, who would, despite his best intentions, come to resent the burden.

And if three's a crowd, what does that make six? Seven, including the ex. I thought about Amber, Lulu, and Maddy, and realized I missed them. It was an awful lot of baggage, but now that I risked losing it, I felt empty without it. I wondered how Bea was bearing up and was sorry I couldn't call to see how she was. I missed James with an ache I couldn't describe. There was a hole—more than a hole, because it spread beyond the boundaries of me and seemed to swallow everything else. I missed Dad, too, but it wasn't the same. Mum was wrong about that, because, no matter what, I knew my father was mine. Alive or otherwise, he loved me. I couldn't say the same for James. I knew what he had thought he'd felt, but the landscape had changed. I'd changed it.

AT SOME TIME IN THE middle of the night—I didn't look at my watch, because I didn't want to know how little sleep I was getting again—I went down to the kitchen and made myself a drink. As I sipped the scalding chamomile tea, I heard footsteps on the stairs. The door opened, and Ben stood on the threshold. He looked ruffled, sleepy, and about nine years old. "Thought you might be awake," he said.

"I feel numb in the daytime, then my brain goes into overdrive the moment I lie down. I'd resort to whisky, but we poured it all down the bloody sink when Bea was here, and I haven't had a chance to restock. I found some Night Nurse, but it's seven years out of date."

Ben poured milk into a glass and sat down opposite me. He drank it, leaving a white mustache on his upper lip. Now he looked six.

"You and Sasha seem well," I said.

"We are," he said. "At the moment."

"The path of true love and all that," I said.

"The path of any love." I thought he was going to elaborate, and eventually he did. "Sasha wants to adopt a child. Two, actually. They're brother and sister."

"Wow," I said. Sasha and Ben had always seemed committed to life as a child-free couple.

"She'd been looking into it for a while, then found a little girl who made an impact. She comes with a baby brother, so it looks like a job lot."

"You don't sound convinced," I said.

"I'm terrified, for all the reasons I didn't want to have my own. What do I know about parenting?"

"What does anyone know?"

"At least you had a good model."

I couldn't deny it.

"That might be why you told James about Bea. You have an image of the perfect family unit locked in your head and think that anything less is a compromise."

"That's exactly what my father said. I'm seeking perfection, but perfection doesn't exist."

"No, it doesn't. And, for the record, you would have been a great stepmother."

"Thanks." We sat in silence for a while. "Fancy a midnight feast?" I asked.

"Always."

I got up and rummaged in the fridge. I found ham and cheese, a jar of cornichons, and white pickled onions. I took a packet of crackers out of the pantry, briefly recalling Bea on the stone floor with the sherry bottle in her hand, and placed them in front of Ben. I heard footsteps on the stairs.

"Sasha?" I said.

"She usually sleeps like the dead," said Ben. "Sorry."

I held up my hand. The kitchen door opened and I was surprised to see my mother. "Mum, you okay?"

"Hungry," she said.

"Well, you're just in time for a midnight feast." I pulled out a chair and quickly found myself cutting up bite-sized pieces of cheese and ham to make little cracker sandwiches so she could feed herself.

"What are you two plotting down here?" she asked.

"I was telling Tess we're thinking of adopting two children."

"Excellent idea," said Mum.

"What about Sasha's work?" I asked, maintaining caution.

"She'll stretch herself like any other working mother, and I'll be forced to stop thinking about myself, which, frankly, is beginning to tire even me."

"Not possible," said a voice from the doorway. Sasha stood there in one of Ben's T-shirts and a pair of his socks. She looked bloody sexy. Ben pulled her onto his knee and fed her a cracker.

"Exciting times," I said to Sasha.

"You're a terrible keeper of secrets," she said, elbowing him.

"Come on, Sasha, this is Liz and Tess we're talking about. They're family. And, anyway, it concerns them."

"It does?" asked Tessa.

"Well, who else would be godmother? And since my mother's barking, I'd expect Liz to step up to the plate and be granny."

"My pleasure," said Liz.

"And mine," I agreed.

"Is there such a thing as a godgranny?" asked my mother.

"There should be," said Ben. "You'd be perfect."

The four of us sat in the kitchen, eating and chatting, until light crept through the window and summoned us back to bed. I slept well into Sunday and woke feeling better. The first thing I did was check my phone, but James hadn't called. He had a lot to sort out with Bea, but I would have appreciated a heads-up.

I got out of bed and opened the curtains. I was lying to myself, of course. Did I want to know where I stood on the Bea/Tessa swing-o-meter? Absolutely not, since I now suspected it had always pointed in her favor.

Strangely, I felt no bitterness, because I knew in my heart of hearts that James had had no idea either. He had done what he'd said he'd done. He'd forced himself to get over her, he'd tried his best, but how do you get over the love of your life? How do you ever completely get over anyone you've ever loved? I wasn't sure you did. I think that if you'd loved them at all, then you'd always love them a bit. I got dressed and went downstairs. After all, wouldn't I always love Ben a fraction more than I ought? As the day ticked past, I felt a growing emptiness in the house. It wasn't that Dad had gone altogether, but I was aware of his presence fading. He was leaving us gently. I stared at the daffodils through the kitchen window as the kettle boiled for more tea and thanked him for the strength he'd somehow left behind.

THE MORNING OF DAD'S CREMATION was gloriously warm. We should have been dressing for a perfect English summer wedding. I stopped the car outside the single-story red-brick crematorium that crouched in a landscaped garden planted with a variety of primulas. My mother got out of the passenger seat, pushed the Gucci sunglasses Sasha had lent her up the bridge of her nose, and took my arm. Then we walked toward the building.

People had already arrived. Fran and Caspar had come, which was way beyond the call of duty. There were faces from the village I recognized. Then the coffee-morning women stood up one by one and told my mother who they were, in case she didn't recognize their voices. There were the guys from the pub, old friends who'd driven miles to be with us, and a couple of Dad's former colleagues.

Seeing them all made me proud of him. I knew I'd got lucky. Friends had lost fathers in their sixties to strokes and heart attacks. Dad had outlived many of his own friends by more than a decade, so it was not with a heavy heart that I took my seat. Mostly, I felt blessed.

And then I saw Peter, Honor, and the three girls. My heart stopped for a second, then punched a hole through my ribs.

"What is it?" asked my mother, sensing me tense. I didn't have time to answer, because Maddy broke free of Honor, ran down the middle aisle, and threw her arms around me. That was when the lump arrived in my throat.

"You've been crying," she said.

"Only a little," I replied.

"Hello, Maddy," said my mother.

"Can I sit on your knee?" she asked.

"I don't think—"

"That would be lovely," said Mum, and sat down to accommodate the sprightly eight-year-old. She clambered on, lifted Mum's glasses, lowered them with a nod, and kissed her cheek. Damn that lump.

Honor came to retrieve her granddaughter, but I held up my hand to tell her all was well, Maddy could stay, so she went back to her seat. I was grateful. I didn't want to talk to her and discover here, now, what I already knew. That James wasn't coming. That was that. Amber blew me a kiss, then went to sit with Caspar and Fran. I stared at Dad's coffin. Stay with me, Dad, I pleaded, for just a moment longer.

The vicar said nice things; I read an excerpt from *Moby-Dick*, and felt strangely removed from the proceedings. What else would they have done? Bea couldn't have brought the girls alone. It would have meant too much. If James had come, I would have read too much into it, and then he would have had to let me down from a greater height. They couldn't possibly have come together, but they had clearly wanted to be represented. My mother and father had made an impact that they had wanted to acknowledge. That was why they had sent Honor, Peter, and the children. It was what I would have done in the circumstances.

DAD LEFT THIS WORLD THROUGH an electronic trapdoor. For such a long life, it was a short exit. I knew it was perfunctory, but Mum and I had decided that a happy memorial service when her eyesight was better was what Dad would have preferred. *The Pearl Fishers* was piped through the surround-sound system, presumably so you couldn't hear the flames boost to the exact temperature needed to reduce my father to a jam jar of ash. I watched him go—or the coffin, anyway—and knew that the man he'd been was not inside it.

After that, we were ushered out pretty quickly, and I noticed people emerge from the subtle side doors to gather up our flowers and replace them with the next lot. Morbid fascination made me hang back a fraction longer than I should have, and as the silent flower-bearers finished laying out a carnation creation that spelled GRANDMA, hey presto, another coffin emerged from the hold. It wasn't exactly the same as Dad's but it wasn't very different. The door through which I had entered opened as the door through which I was leaving closed. What had Linda said? "The effing conveyor belt of life." There it was, in a single-story nutshell. Rather than feeling disappointed by the lack of pageantry, I felt comforted by the commonplace efficiency of the production line. Henry Ford would have been proud. More than that, Dad liked efficiency.

I WALKED INTO THE "ROSE GARDEN," whose name conjured up White House grandeur but failed to deliver, and was surrounded by Dad's friends. I couldn't get near Mum, and was worried about her getting tired, but so many people wanted to talk to her it would have felt churlish dragging her away. Occasionally, I caught a flash of the girls as they ran around the garden. And then I saw him. James was here. My heart punched another hole in my rib cage. I'd done such a good job of convincing myself it was over that I would have been less surprised to see Dad. He'd chosen me, and I was overjoyed. I wanted to run to him, jump into his arms, wrap my legs around his middle, and hold on forever, but there were a lot of people about who might have thought such behavior inappropriate at a funeral. Besides, he was on the opposite side, looking out over the countryside, and hadn't seen me.

I felt two small hands slip into mine. Lulu and Maddy were at either side of me. "You're still here. I am so happy to see you," I said, which made them smile.

"Good," said Maddy. "Because we want you to be happy."

"Maddy! You just made her cry," said Lulu.

Maddy looked devastated.

"No, sweet pea," I said hastily, "it's only because I'm so pleased you all came."

"See?" said Maddy.

"When did your dad get here?" I asked.

"He's not here. He's at home with Mummy," said Lulu.

I held back my frown. Lulu often got things wrong—all the time, in fact. She said things she didn't understand or hadn't grasped. I glanced to where James was standing, waiting for me to jump into his arms. But he was gone. I scanned the thinning crowd—there was only so much looking at wreaths people could take before the brew beckoned—but couldn't find him anywhere. Then, walking away with an elderly woman, I saw a tall man with salt-and-pepper hair.

My world collapsed. Of course it hadn't been James staring out over the countryside. He would never stand apart from his daughters, no matter what the occasion. I realized only at that moment how much I had been holding out for him to come back to me, how my calm acceptance of the situation was not courage but denial.

I looked down at the little hands in mine and felt my eyeballs burn. I mustn't cry, I mustn't cry, I must, must, must not—

"You okay?" asked Ben, suddenly at my side.

I couldn't speak, but shook my head.

"Come with me," he said, then smiled reassuringly at the girls. "See you back at the house for cake."

I didn't dare look down.

"Perfect timing," said Ben. He pointed out the vicar. He was walking toward us with a—I squinted. It wasn't . . . it couldn't be . . . There really was a fucking jam jar in his hand. If my heart hadn't been breaking, I might have laughed.

"We'll take that," said Ben. He grabbed Dad's ashes and led me away from the spectators into the garden. He thrust the jar into my hand. It was warm. "You can cry now," he said.

And I did.

It felt as though someone had wrenched open my jaw, stretched my gullet, thrust their fist down my throat, and pulled out my soul. I hugged my father and Ben hugged me. Occasionally, there would be a break in the tears and I would stare out over the shrubs and rosebushes and, beyond them, the road that brought in the dead.

"Your dad was a lucky man, you know, Tess. Not many people get to leave life as painlessly as that, after such a full life as that, with the people who loved him most by his side."

"I'm not crying about him," I confessed, feeling worse because it was true, even though his remains were placed neatly on my lap. "It's James. He's not coming back."

"You were pretty sure of that on Saturday."

"I was pretending," I said. "I don't know what real love is, if it even exists, but I felt . . . I felt in my core that this was something . . . oh, I don't know . . ."

"Go on, Tess."

"This is hard to say to you."

"Why?"

It took a long time to answer. Ben waited patiently.

"I suppose because I thought you were it, and it turned out I was wrong about that, so what the hell do I know? I'm a fantasist. I cling to whatever's on offer around me and make it fit my ideals."

"I don't think that's true, Tess."

"You give me too much credit. I threw myself at you and nearly made you wreck your marriage, which, as marriages go, is a pretty good one."

Ben prized my fingers off the glass jar and held them in his. "I'm not sure it can ever be either/or. I don't even know if it should. I think you can love more than one person, just not in the same way exactly. Everything I said to you I meant and still mean. In many respects we're so right for one another but no one's perfect, and I don't want you getting up close and personal with my imperfections. Sasha and I can bash it out. Our relationship gets better for the beating, because we end up with a deeper understanding of one another. It's a lifetime's work and it's not always fun, but it's good, it's rewarding, and I do love her. You and I, we already have a lifetime in the bag. I'd rather keep it safe and occasionally think about where I would take it if a parallel universe were ever to open up."

I sniffed loudly. "You always make me feel better," I said.

"Not if I was your husband."

He was right, of course.

"So tell me about what you feel for James."

I sat back on the bench and felt a copper plaque, which commemorated a previously departed soul, cool my shoulder blade. "I wanted to be a better person for him. I wanted to make him proud. I wanted to love his children. I wanted to bring out the best in him. He made me want to raise my game. He made me want to grow up. I feel steady with him, even-keeled. I feel like it just fits, you know, everything. Got to be honest, the kissing wasn't bad."

"That's better," said Ben.

"What?"

"You're smiling."

"It wasn't perfect—how can it be when there's such a lot of baggage to deal with—but I was looking forward to rising to the challenge. For both of us." I put my head on Ben's shoulder. He kissed my forehead. "And now he's back with Bea, which part of me knows is the right place for him, but there's a larger part of me that's just devastated we weren't given a chance to find out how good *we* could be." I rolled the jam jar in my hands. "Because I think we would have been pretty darn good and I feel absolutely fucking shit about it."

Ben squeezed my shoulders.

"We had potential," I said, in a mock U.S.-agent accent.

"You still do."

"Not with James, though."

"But you still do, Tess. Bundles of it. Don't forget that."

Didn't feel like that right then. It felt like I was back on the slag heap with all the other discarded goods that had "faulty" stamped on them. No one wanted me. Or no one wanted me enough. Which amounted to the same thing. I had been beaten by an overweight alcoholic ex-wife, even taking into account how much I had come to like her. That said it all, really. I had come so far and yet I was back at the beginning. I was old enough to know that I could cope on my own, I wouldn't fall to pieces, I'd be all right in the end, but there was no doubt about it: life was a fraction easier when you had someone else on-side. It brought complications of its own, of course, but, still, the pod felt better with two.

"I'd like to take Dad to the pub for a final pint before we head home. Would you join me?"

"It'll be my pleasure."

We stood up. "You know what, Ben? You should adopt those children. You'd never ask them to be the perfect kids you might have had, because you never wanted them and therefore they can never let you down. You'd be a wonderful father."

"Well," said Ben, taking Dad out of my hands, "I know who I'd model myself on."

MY MOTHER SEEMED COMPLETELY UNFAZED that I had absconded with Dad, simply hugged me on my return and then we were separated again. I never made it out of the kitchen. People came and went, some I knew, some I didn't, to tell me in a variety of ways what a grand man my dad had been. Maddy and Lulu were playing Scrabble. New rules. When it was Maddy's turn, Lulu got out her replacement letters; when it was Lulu's turn, Maddy went back to reading her book. Amber was outside with Caspar. Every time I looked out of the window, they had their tongues thrust down each other's throats. It made me smile. An old man might have died, but there was kissing to do. Fran was miraculous and took over, with Honor, as hostess, leaving Mum and me to concentrate on snippets of a life we still didn't know everything about.

Four cups of tea and a lot of chat later, I was exhausted. Our low-key, under-the-wire funeral service had not been as we'd imagined. People from the village kept dropping in with sandwiches, bottles of wine, flowers, and kind words, but now I just wanted to be alone. With my core family, which, weirdly, seemed to include Peter, Honor, Amber, Lulu, and Maddy.

Ben and Sasha left shortly after the last well-wisher. Funny how they knew when to arrive and when to leave me be. Mum took herself upstairs to lie on her bed alone. Fran took Caspar and the girls back to London. She was used to carting children around and didn't want Peter and Honor having to make the extra journey when she could easily drop the three of them off en route. There were no complaints from Amber and Caspar.

The girls kissed me good-bye and Amber gave me an audio book that Bea had especially wanted Mum to have. There was a card with Mum's name on it in her handwriting. It felt strange to hold it, and I wondered when I'd see her daughters again. I had got so close to them recently, but now had lost all rights to them. I found it nearly unbearable to wave good-bye. I was watching my future, with all its complications, drive away. I would have been a good stepmother. I'd never felt childless before, but I did right then. Peter and Honor, who had said nothing about James and Bea to me, asked if they could go upstairs to Mum's room and give her the audio book.

I found myself alone in the sitting room. For the first time since waking, I glanced at my watch. It was only four in the afternoon but it felt like midnight. Exhausted, I slumped into Dad's chair. I don't know how long I'd been sitting there when I heard a tap on the windowpane. It filtered through my semi-meditative state. I wanted to ignore it. We had no more room for flowers and I was all talked out. The tap came again. I forced myself to stand up and turned.

"James?"

He smiled through the glass.

I got up and went to open the front door. Another trick of my mind?

"Hello, Tessa," he said.

"What are you doing here?"

"I need to talk to you."

I rested my head on the door frame. "Not now, James. It's been quite a day."

"Please," he held out his hand, "just for a moment."

I stepped outside. The afternoon sun was still warm. I breathed in the clean air and felt a little revived. "You just missed the girls," I said.

"I know. I wanted to talk to you alone."

"Your parents are still here. It was nice of them to come."

"I'm sorry I didn't."

So am I. More than you will ever know. "It would have been difficult."

We walked away from the house, down the lane, and left the village behind.

"I need to tell you what's happened."

Wild daffodils sprang up along the verge. I hoped they'd give me courage. "Couldn't it have waited?"

"No," said James.

We reached the stile that led to the bridle path. On automatic pilot, I climbed over it and jumped down into the field. The solid earth beneath my feet brought me back to my senses. I didn't want to walk the bridle path, high or low. It was too painful. James climbed over after me and started to walk. Then, realizing I was still leaning against the post, he came back. "I'm sorry I didn't make it to the funeral. I should have been there."

"Where were you?" I asked, against my better judgment.

"With Bea."

I wasn't sure how I was supposed to respond to that. It was too soon to be pleased for them. I wasn't superhuman.

"We had a lot to talk about."

"Pity you couldn't have done that when you were married." Then you wouldn't have been free to break my heart.

"You're right."

Little joy in being right. Hadn't I been good enough? I'd sent him back to Bea, now I just wanted to be left alone.

"The drinking is only the latest manifestation of Bea's problems," James said.

No shit, I thought. The extra sixty pounds didn't alert you to that?

"Booze replaced food, food replaced work . . ."

I was getting angry and, more than anything, upset. Hadn't I told him all this? Now was not the time to talk about Bea. I'd just cremated my father! I let you go. Don't ask me to make you feel better about which choice you've made. Not today, of all days.

"We shouldn't have let all our friends slip away. You need your mates when things get tough."

Yes. And right now I needed mine. "I'm sorry, James, I need to go home." I turned to climb back over the stile. James held my wrist.

"Wait."

"No."

"Please, Tessa. I'm not finished." He ran his hand down my arm. I shuddered. I didn't want to hear what he had to say. I didn't want to know that he and Bea had a lot of ground to make up, that they had a marriage to reclaim and a family to put back together. I wanted to throw him onto the ground and make him mine again. Damn my treacherous libido. Damn my heart. I was good, but not that good. He held on to my hand. I looked at his strong fingers around mine and felt pain shoot through me.

"I love Bea—"

I pulled my hand away. "Please—" I begged, clambering up the stile. "I'm not as brave as you think. I mean, I am. But I'm not, too. God, I'm not making sense. I need to go before I do something I won't be proud of. I can't just switch this off—"

"I don't want you to switch anything off," he said. "Let me finish."

"But you love her."

"Yes I do, but I'm not in love with her anymore."

I stepped back onto the grass. "You're not?"

"No. I was. Deeply. And it took me a long time to get over her, but I managed it. I never ever want to go through that again."

He was staring very intently at me. For a second there, I thought he might suggest a weird three-way thing between us all, but it was worse than that.

"Oh God, don't tell me, you need to be alone. You bloody wanker, fucking men, I don't know why I ever—"

"Tessa, be quiet." He put his hand over my mouth. "I don't want to be alone and I don't want to remarry Bea. I'm in love with you. I'm sure we'll make a thousand of our own mistakes, but I promise you, if you'll have me, I won't make the same mistakes again. Whether we have children or not."

I pulled his hand away. "You want more children?"

"Only with you. And this time I'd get my hands very dirty."

"Oh James—" I threw myself at him, but he held me away from him.

"Hang on." James crouched down and put his knee on a highly potent spring stinging nettle. "Ow," he said.

I laughed, very nervously. Actually, it was more like a choked croak. He reached inside his jacket pocket and brought out a red Cartier box. I swallowed a pocket of air. "You've been busy."

"Didn't want to get this wrong again." He held it up and looked into my face. "Tessa King, I absolutely, completely, with every inch of me, love you. Will you please, please, please, marry me? For life?"

This time there was no pause. He didn't even get to open the box.

"Ow," I said, as I landed on the same nettle. Luckily, James knew exactly how to kiss it better.

"Is that a yes?"

I kissed him back, then smiled. "Damn right it's a yes."

I RAN UPSTAIRS TO TELL my mother the news and show off my beautiful, perfect eternity ring. Eternity, not engagement. I liked that. I wasn't engaged. I was committed. For life. I burst through the door without knocking, but my mother wasn't there.

"Down here," called James.

I ran back down, threw myself around James, kissed him, and went into the kitchen. I had to steady myself for a second. Peter was sitting at the table, the paper open in front of him and a glass of red wine in his hand. Just like Dad. I blinked.

"Sorry," he said. "Couldn't take any more tea. It was open."

"It wasn't that. You just reminded me of Dad."

"I'm sorry."

"No," I said. "It was nice." I recovered quickly. "Sod the tea. Let's open champagne."

"Champagne?" asked Peter.

I thrust out my left hand at him. Peter knocked the chair backward in his rush to congratulate us. "Couldn't be happier," he said. "I mean it. Couldn't be happier." I watched father and son embrace, and was glad that Dad had known Peter. And vice versa. It would make it easier for Peter to understand me. There was no champagne in our Bea-proof house, so James and Peter offered to go to the liquor store. A celebration was due, today of all days.

"Should we get the girls back?" I asked.

"No. We'll tell them tomorrow. Tonight it's just you and me."

I nodded. "Where are Mum and Honor?"

"Decided to take some air before we headed home," said Peter. "Come on, son. Let's go before the screeching starts."

"Oi, I don't screech," I said, longing to screech.

James walked over and put his hand over my heart. "I think your dad would have been pleased," he said.

"He is."

"I love you, Tessa King."

"And I love you, James Kent."

"Honestly," said Peter. "We're only going around the corner."

We laughed stupidly, then laughed more stupidly because of our stupid laughing. Eventually, I pushed him out.

I expected to find Mum and Honor sitting on the terrace, catching the last afternoon sun. But they weren't there.

"Mum! Hello!" I wandered out into the garden where Dad had whiled away so many hours. I bowed to the daffodils. They bowed back. "Mum!" I shouted, a little louder. They couldn't have got far.

"Over here," came a voice.

"Where?"

"The other side of the orchard."

Beyond the garden there was a patch of wild meadow. Well, it was called wild, but it had been carefully trained. My parents had sown wildflower seeds and worked hard at keeping weeds at bay. It was a beautiful boundary between their garden and the rest of the countryside. No privet hedge for Mum and Dad.

"Where?"

"Here."

"I can't see you."

Suddenly, a hand appeared above the long grass and waved at me.

"Mum! You okay?" I panicked. Had she fallen? Where was Honor? Was that sobbing? I ran, ducking through the trees, into the grass, and nearly put my foot through my future mother-in-law's naked sternum. "Bloody hell!" I exclaimed.

"Hello, darling," said Mum, as if it were perfectly normal to strip off and lie in the grass with her arms and legs spread out. They were giggling.

"What are you doing?"

"Saying good-bye," said Mum, "and it feels wonderful."

"Aren't you cold?"

"The adrenaline's kicked in," said Mum. "I feel invincible."

"Why don't you join us?" asked Honor.

I glanced back at the house.

"Oh, don't worry, no one can see."

They did look rather wonderful, lying there, arms and legs outstretched, naked as the day they were born. Without allowing myself another thought, I threw off my funereal clothes and hurled my black boots into the undergrowth. Mum was right. I felt a rush of adrenaline surge through me. With Honor on my right and my mother on my left, I made up the circle. On instinct, I stretched out my fingers and we all held hands.

"Nice ring," said Honor, lifting her head off the grass.

I smiled, staring up at the deep pink clouds. They were right. It did feel wonderful.

"Does it sparkle?" asked my mother.

"I'll say," replied Honor, turning my hand in hers. I was smiling too much to talk. They squeezed my hands.

"We heard the car," said Mum.

"Welcome to the family," said Honor.

"Ditto," I replied.

Our circle fell silent and, just as my father had described it, I felt my pulse slow, my mind steady, and my soul open up to the universe.

"So, my darling, how do you feel?" asked my mother.

The ground was soft beneath my body, the air blew gentle kisses over my skin, the sky reached up to my father and back again. I closed my eyes. "Boundless," I replied.

Epilogue

I WAS SURROUNDED BY LAUGHTER BUT DIDN'T PRETEND TO JOIN IN. I wanted to place one of my stepdaughters on my lap and hug her tight, but I had taught myself not to do that. At nine, even the youngest considered herself too old for such public displays of affection. On our own, at home, was fine, but that wasn't when I needed her validation. I felt a hand land on my shoulder, a smile forming automatically as I turned.

"Thank you so much for everything you did for the concert," said the woman looking down at me.

"I'm happy to help," I replied.

"It was amazingly generous of your company."

Maddy beamed. If her headmistress said I was amazing, I must be doing something right. I saw the woman glance at the empty seat next to Maddy.

"She'll be here," I said.

The headmistress smiled warmly and took her seat. I turned to James. "Cutting it a bit fine, isn't she?" I whispered. "Should I call?"

"She'll be here. She wouldn't miss this for the world," said James.

The lights dimmed and an awed murmur rose up from the assorted parents, siblings, and add-ons, and dissolved into hush. Maddy and I turned to look at the back.

"Mummy!" she squeaked, and leaped off her seat. I watched Bea make her way along the narrow aisle with ease. It had taken another year, but the final, stubborn pounds had left her. She looked terrific. I budged up one place so she could sit next to Maddy, but Maddy came too, so she'd be between us.

Bea stopped to chat with a friend.

"Sit down!" exclaimed James in a tense whisper. "It's about to start."

She blew me a kiss as she passed and took her seat. "Sorry," she said. "Meeting went on."

James put a finger to his lips and pointed toward the stage. The thick green velvet curtains were drawn back to reveal a single spotlight on stage, and there, in the middle of that glowing puddle, stood Lulu. I glanced down at the program. Lulu Kent to read a poem of her own composition. Without a quiver in her voice, without a mumble or a pause, she began to recite the verses she'd written for the school's annual poetry competition. The winner opened the junior school's show. And there she was. The opening number.

I could see Maddy, Bea, Jimmy, and, beyond him, Amber silently match each word in perfect synchronization, and felt warm inside.

At the interval, Amber and Maddy ran off to find their star of a sister, but parents weren't allowed backstage, so we ambled through the crowd toward the bar. I listened while Bea and James were complimented on Lulu's progress.

"Who would have thought her capable?" said one woman.

Bea caught me listening and winked.

"A brilliant poem. Did she really write it all by herself?" asked another.

I rolled my eyes at her. Bea laughed.

"Every word," said James. "We didn't even know she was entering it until she won."

The woman pursed her lips, clearly not convinced.

"Let's get to the bar," said Bea.

"Who's checking for poison this time?" asked James.

"It's all poison," I said. "Some demi-sec stuff. I made a note when I came in."

"Don't worry," said Bea. "I have friends in high places." We walked toward the trestle table at the side of the room. There was Carmen, her magnificent cleavage on show, pouring drinks with a flourish. She saw us coming, reached below the counter, and brought out a bottle of fizzy elderflower.

"The others probably need something a little stronger," said Bea.

"Don't worry," she said, reaching under the sheet again. "I stashed a nice pinot noir." She poured generously into two white plastic cups and handed them to James and me.

"You look good behind a bar," said James.

"Just call me Daisy and slap my arse," said Carmen, laughing. "Tell you what, if the alimony doesn't come through I might be doing this full-time."

"He's not going to shaft you out of the money," said Bea.

"That little cow doesn't come cheap. She's walking around with a new Mulberry bag." Carmen waved a hand dismissively. "Whatever."

Carmen was nice to me, but I got the sense she held back full acceptance of my presence as a gesture of solidarity to the First Wives' Club. I understood why and was just grateful for her civility. I suspected Bea had insisted.

I'd had much less welcoming receptions from some of the other mothers at the school gates on the few occasions when Bea had been caught up at work and we'd put our tag team into operation. She and I had both become part-time working mothers in the year since my father's death. Bea had got back in touch with her maid of honor, Suzie. Suzie had started a successful business with her husband, but when he died, everything collapsed. Bea and Suzie were rebuilding it together. As partners. She did twenty hours a week while the girls were at school; I did twenty hours a week being a stepmother. The rest of the time I was a lawyer and a wife. Though not in that order.

"Had the usual 'compliments'?" Carmen asked Bea.

"A woman I thought liked me practically accused Lulu of plagiarism."

"Darling, you've lost half your body weight. No one likes you anymore, and I mean no one. Including me." Carmen opened some cheap-looking long-life orange juice. "I've got to say, the change in Lulu is remarkable, though," she said.

"Well, it was Tessa who called it," said Bea. "Dyslexia had never crossed my mind."

"Rubbish. It was you and Mum," I said.

"No, it wasn't, it was you."

Carmen raised her glass to me. "Well, whatever, it's a delight to see."

"Mrs. Kent!" called a voice from the crowd. I turned. So did Bea.

A woman I didn't recognize was waving in our direction.

"Yours," I said.

"I'll give you fifty if you take it," said Bea.

"What's she after?" I asked suspiciously.

"School scrunchies," said Bea.

"No way," said Carmen, slamming down a bottle. "Your scrunchy days are over."

"You don't have to tell me."

James intercepted. "Miss Peterson," he said. "How are you?" Miss Peterson, I noticed, flattened down her unruly hair before taking his hand. "I wanted to talk to you about an idea I've had to get fathers more involved in the school. The gates can be a daunting place for us dads."

"Surely not for you, Mr. Kent." Bea and I took a surreptitious step backward.

"A father-and-daughter away-day. We all take a day off work, no exceptions."

Miss Peterson clasped her hands in delight. "Oh, Mr. Kent, you are marvelous." I couldn't look at Bea, because I knew she was giggling into her plastic cup.

"Come on," said Bea, grabbing my arm. "I think we're wanted." Three red heads were poking through the gap in the curtain and waving frantically. I fell into step behind her and walked toward my stepdaughters. I smiled happily to myself. Bea was right. We were wanted. Both of us.

Acknowledgments

There are a great many people I would like to thank for this book, and a few special ones without whom I would not have been able to write it at all. However, since I think it better not to name names, these acknowledgments may look a little thin. That doesn't mean you are not in my thoughts. You are. I think marriage is one of the few remaining taboo subjects, and talking about it isn't easy. So, to those people who were brave or drunk enough to share their inner fears, suspicions, annoyances, joys, dependencies, infidelities, frustrations, and fantasies, I thank you. Most of you know who you are; others, whom I accosted in coffee shops, bars, buses, and ladies' rooms, never will, but I thank you all the same.

There are a few, however, I can name. Gaby, I don't think I would have survived the year without you. You gave me the keys to your house twice and a place to work. You feed my children, order my shopping, and keep me laughing when I feel like screaming. Your mother would be so bloody proud of you. I am. Priya, I wish you didn't live so far away, I wish you weren't my expert on MS, I wish I could work out how to use Skype. Your advice has been invaluable. And Cath, for a thousand little things, on top of which you scooped me up when I was on my knees and whisked me off to France again. Open the rosé, I feel a song coming on ... To my sisters, as always, for their inherent understanding; frankly, I wish you'd both come home. To my parents; we named our daughter Ruby to salute your fortieth wedding anniversary, it is a joy to see you both so content. You are a great incentive to hold on to the mast. Thank you for being such incredible grandparents. To

Electra, again, for strong hands and wise words. To Marion, for the magic.

On the other side of the pond Dorian Karchmar at the William Morris Agency, NYC, took me on—the book did the talking and we became instant friends. I feel so fortunate to have her wisdom and wiles on my side—I raise a glass of Greco di Tufo to you in thanks. Jeanette Perez at HarperCollins also took me on—editing a book with a lactating, hormonal head-case must have been a challenge. You met it, then supassed it. The book is better because of you. Thank you. Back on home turf, I'd like to thank Eugenie Furniss—can't believe I didn't manage to put you off! To Merla, for practically everything else. I feel privileged to have such impressive women on my side.

Thanks to everyone who works at Chez Christophe. What would I have done without your coffee, cakes, and wi-fi? This book only got finished because you gave me a place to hide.

I owe a debt of gratitude to TG Teoh and the amazing team at St. Mary's who got me out of a tight spot. Thank you. Especially the registrar, Chrissie, whom I forgot to thank the first time. I thank you all for your calmness; I knew I was in the best possible hands.

Lastly, forever, to Adam. It passed! Bloody hell, it's hard, but it's worth it. Sometimes I don't know how we'll manage to get to the end of the day, other times I know in my soul we'll make it, and what scares me then is that the rest of our lives will be nowhere near long enough.